Windrush: Crimea

Windrush: Crimea

Jack Windrush Series – Book II

Malcolm Archibald

Copyright (C) 2016 Malcolm Archibald
Layout design and Copyright (C) 2016 Creativia
Published 2016 by Creativia (www.creativia.org)
Cover art by http://www.thecovercollection.com/
Edited by D.S. Williams
This book is a work of fiction. Names, characters, places, and incidents are the product of the author's imagination or are used fictitiously. Any resemblance to actual events, locales, or persons, living or dead, is purely coincidental.
All rights reserved. No part of this book may be reproduced or transmitted in any form or by any means, electronic or mechanical, including photocopying, recording, or by any information storage and retrieval system, without the author's permission.

For Cathy

Prologue

Inkerman Ridge: November 5th, 1854

Captain Dearden was dead; his mouth open in a soundless scream to protest at the agony of the Russian bayonet which protruded obscenely from his belly. Corporal O'Hara lay across Dearden's body, writhing as he stared at the gaping holes in his chest and the blood that pumped from the ragged stump of his left arm. Beside him, Aitken crouched, choking on the blood that filled his mouth and ran in dark rivulets down his chin and chest. Half a score Russian infantrymen lay among them, shot or bayoneted, unheeded in death as the world had neglected them in life.

'Get the bodies,' Jack ordered. 'Pile them up into the breastwork.'

The men stared at him. Their eyes were dazed, their mouths slack with shock, but they did as he ordered, adding the corpses of friends and enemies to the low barricade of sandbags which was their only protection against the dropping musket balls and murderous round shot.

'Here they come again.' Coleman gripped the blood-sticky stock of his Minié rifle and staggered to his feet. The once-proud scarlet of his tunic was torn and shredded, his face powder stained, gaunt and unshaven. Blood congealed on the ragged hole in his trousers just above the left knee.

'Hot as hell and thick as thieves.' Thorpe spat blood on his hands and ran a grimy thumb over the length of his bayonet. 'Just listen to them.'

Jack peered through the shredded mist and rain. Across the ridge, the Russians were not yet visible, but they were vocal enough, chanting that same, deep-throated battle hymn with which they had advanced so often before. Was it three times or four? It might even be five; he couldn't be sure, but he knew that each time they recoiled they left the small detachment of British weaker and fewer in numbers.

'Ammunition? Has anybody got any spare ammunition?'

Jack already knew the answer. They had used up all their own in repelling the Russian attacks and had robbed their dead comrades of what they had. He checked the ammunition pouch he'd lifted from the dead body of Brodie. 'I have three balls left.'

Thorpe spat again. 'That's one more than any man needs.'

There was no response to the attempted humour. Coleman poked his head beyond the breastwork and shuddered. 'Jesus, there's still thousands of them.'

Jack joined him. Coleman was right. A chance slant of wind blew a gap in the mist, revealing the full strength of the Russians. They seemed to stretch right across the ridge, an unbroken wall of flapping grey coats and wickedly long bayonets advancing slowly and steadily through the stunted, tangled oak trees of the Inkerman Ridge.

'I thought somebody said the Russians could never face British bayonets.' Logan curled disproportionately large hands around the stock of his Minié.

'Aye, but nobody told them that.' Thorpe tilted the barrel of his rifle, looked down the fouled bore and dropped in his last bullet. Once that was fired, he had only his bayonet and as much courage as remained after the long, long day of horror and death.

'Are we so important?' Raeburn raised his voice. 'Are we so important that they must throw the entire Russian army at us?' He looked around; his eyes red-rimmed with fatigue and wide with fear. 'There's only a few of us left!' At that moment he looked all of his seventeen years, a boy in a man's world, a child near to the brink of tears.

'It's not us that's important,' Jack told him. 'It's the position. If they take this redoubt and the battery, they have the lynchpin of the whole British line. We must hold.'

'Listen to him!' Thorpe mocked. 'If they take this redoubt! There's not even a gun left in the bloody thing! And who do you think you are, anyway? Bloody Wellington? Not Lord Raglan anyway: you haven't the stupidity!'

'I'm your officer!' Jack reminded. But he knew that hardly mattered just now. They were about to die beneath a torrent of Russian bayonets. He was the only surviving officer within this company of malcontents, an interloper in a closed society of men who had been fighting merely to exist since the day the world had cursed them with birth. He no more belonged here than he belonged anywhere else, but now it seemed that he would die beside these hard-faced, bitter-eyed men whom he would have despised in another place, another world.

The singing increased, accompanied by the rhythmic drumbeat of boots on the ground and the sinister swishing of the long grey coats.

'Up we go men!'

There was a weary sigh, a long drawn out curse and the half-hidden sound of somebody praying, but the red-coated soldiers rose from the slight sanctuary of their corpse-and-sandbag barricade and looked outward toward the advancing enemy.

The Russians were close enough so that Jack could make out details of their flat, expressionless faces as they marched forward. They had advanced before, and the company had sent them reeling back – as the tangled bodies on the ground proved – but this time there were many more of them and correspondingly fewer of the regiment to fight. He looked around the thinned ranks. They had started with nearly five hundred men, but now there were less than thirty fit to fight. They had probably a hundred rounds in total, and there must be two thousand Russians closing on them.

'They're brave men.' The Bishop gave a calm opinion. He sighted along the barrel of his rifle. 'Thank God for the grace of the Minié though. These beauties can kill two or three men at once.'

'When God granted us that, I would have liked him to grant us another thousand men as well. We're the 113th, the worst regiment in the British Army. A regimental disgrace, that's what we are.' Thorpe gave a twisted grin.

'So why fight for that?' Coleman jerked a stubby thumb toward the flag that drooped from its staff.

Jack looked over his shoulder. He'd nearly forgotten than Colonel Maxwell had thrust in the flagpole a few hours and a lifetime before, but now it was there, flapping above them with the multi-crossed flag of Union, the symbol of British pride and fortitude and hope in the canton with that alien number embroidered in black across the buff field.

'If we're such a bloody disgrace, why fight for that regimental flag?'

'Drag the bloody thing down!' Logan agreed. 'It's nothing to do with us anyway!'

'What?' Jack stared as his youthful ideas of honour and patriotism surfaced once more. 'It's got the British flag on it!'

'The British flag!' Riley mocked. 'Would that be the same Britain that rejected you and me?'

Fletcher leaned against the sandbags and said nothing. He had no education, but he was as sharp and perceptive as any university-trained solicitor. His deep eyes switched from Jack to Riley and back.

'Yes. Take the flag down boys!'

Jack reached for the flap of his holster, remembered his revolver was empty and raised his voice. 'We will not surrender; the Russians are coming!'

The bayonet was cold against his throat as he stared into the slum-bitter eyes of Logan and heard that harsh gutter voice grate in his ear.

'You keep your neb out of this, Lieutenant. That's not our flag, and we're not fighting for it.' Logan's grin was entirely without humour or mercy as the ragged privates lowered the flag. Jack heard the roar of triumph from the advancing Russians and despair chilled him. Major Snodgrass had been correct all along. The 113th did not have the stomach for a fight; when things got tough, they ran or surrendered. Now the Russians would take the centre of the British line and roll up both flanks. His weakness had lost the battle.

Chapter One

**Malta
March 1854**

They stood on the parade ground of Fort Saint Manoel with the darkness of pre-dawn slowly fading and an unnatural hush over the assembled men. Jack tried to ignore the sweat which already beaded on his eyebrows and hung irritatingly on the tip of his nose. He gripped the Gothic hilt of the 1845 pattern Wilkinson's sword that hung at his waist and blew away a fly that hovered over his face, wishing he were anywhere but within this star-shaped fort on Manoel Island. If Jack swivelled his eyes slightly to the left he could peer through the dark to the entrance to Marsamxett Harbour and the anchorage of Sliema Creek, busy with a score of vessels, their Mediterranean rigs now familiar and their hulls sleek on the placid blue water. If he looked right and ignored the harsh limestone of the walls, he could nearly see the towers and churches of Valetta, capital of this sun-tortured island.

It didn't matter in which direction he looked, just so long as he didn't face his front and see the terrible spectacle that was about to occur. All his life he had dreamed of joining the army and performing deeds of valour; he'd grown up with tales of bravery and heroism and had accepted that death and hardship were part of a soldier's life. He had seen something of the reality in the humid forests and broad rivers of Burma, and today he was about to see another military casualty. Rather than a splendid death leading a heroic charge against an enemy position, Private Scattergood of the 113th Foot was to be publicly executed, hanged by the neck until he was dead, for stabbing a sergeant in the back.

Fifteen yards to his right, Major General Sir John Reading sat erect on his brown horse, seemingly unaffected by the spectacle he had ordered. The tail of the horse twitched in a vain attempt to relieve the animal of the tormenting flies.

Jack tried to take his mind elsewhere; anywhere apart from standing here watching the execution of a private soldier. He drifted back to his home in England and relived again the terrible moment when he learned which regiment he was to join. He was Jack Windrush, once of Wychwood Manor in Herefordshire, now a lieutenant in the 113th – the Baby Butchers – the least considered regiment in the entire army. Even after three years, he found it hard to believe his fortunes had sunk so low. He had left his home with the ill-will of his step family following close behind and marched quickly to an inn. It was the work of a second to find a seat, break the simple seal and unfold the parchment.

At sixteen inches by ten inches, the document was much smaller than he'd expected, and when he read the contents, he felt the sick slide of despair. Skipping over the leading paragraph that stated that the Commander in Chief of the Army reposed special trust and confidence in his loyalty, he came to the 'do by these presents constitute and appoint you John Windrush to take rank and post as ensign in the 113th Regiment of Foot.'

He had stared at the fateful number and swore quietly to himself.

113th Foot. Oh, good God in heaven.

The 113th Foot was the regiment nobody wanted to join. There had been other regiments which bore the same number, but they had been excellent, honourable units; this latest incarnation was certainly not. Born in the civil disobedience after Waterloo, its infancy had been marred by disgrace when it quelled a riot by musket butt, boot and the bayonet, with women and children being among the victims. Since then, no commander had wanted the 113th under his command, and only the dregs of the recruits slouched into the ranks.

Sick to the core, yet with no other option, Jack clutched his commission and some of the gold sovereigns his stepmother had reluctantly deposited in his bank and sailed to join the regiment in the East.

Jack thought of his first and so far, only campaign. He'd been present with the Army at the conquest of Rangoon, where more men died through disease than from Burmese bullets, but after that, the real war had started. He remembered the heat and humidity of the jungle, the whine of the mosquitoes and the sun burning off the early morning mist of the river. He remembered the wiry, brave

Burmese infantry and their ability to melt into the green foliage of the forest. Most of all he remembered the smiling face of Myat, the Burmese woman and the manner in which his small band of men had transformed from a disparate rabble to veteran soldiers.

Now he stood in the square, waiting for the execution of a private soldier driven half-crazy by heat and boredom. There were no birds in the bright bowl of the sky, nothing but the unrelenting sun and a host of mosquitoes attracted by the sweat of hundreds of scarlet-coated men. Every regiment that waited impatiently for embarkation orders for the East had been ordered to supply a quota of men to witness the execution of a murderer and the further degradation of the 113th Foot.

Somebody coughed behind him, the sound harsh in the hush, but a vicious whisper from a sergeant reprimanded the man into quiet. As the dawn rose, blood red and shockingly swift, the execution party of the 113th marched slowly forward, bearing Private Scattergood between them. There was no drumbeat, no music, nothing to announce the end of a young man's life, save the curious stares of his assembled comrades and the solitary scream of a circling gull. A priest followed, the expression on his face showing his disapproval.

Major General Reading gave a small, nearly imperceptible signal and the Provost Sergeant stepped slowly forward. Scattergood, stripped to shirt and trousers and with his hands pinioned behind his back was close behind him, face sweating, eyes darting from side to side as he sought hope or mercy. There was none.

As he came to terms with his imminent death, Scattergood raised his head and marched forward, staring at nothing as stony-faced guards led him up the steps to a recently-made platform. The scaffold stretched above them with the noose hanging down at neck level, its sun-borne shadow a straight bar intersecting at right angles to that of the upright, making a mocking image of the Christian cross of forgiveness. Scattergood's eyes were now haunted, bereft of hope as they scanned the watching men. With only a few more moments of life before he embraced the most ignominious of deaths, he knew he was friendless and alone. Nobody cared how he felt; they only wanted this damnable business over with so they could get out of the baking heat and carry on with their lives.

A nervous young lieutenant mounted the stairs to the platform, with the sound of his boots on the wooden steps echoing hollowly around the square. The priest followed next, with the Provost Sergeant keeping one hand firm on

Scattergood's left arm. There was a moment's pause as they stood on the platform; Jack thought that a man with a blunt knife could slice the tension from the air, and then the priest murmured some phrases and Scattergood responded in halting Latin.

'I never knew Scatterhead was a bloody Papist,' Thorpe said.

'Silence in the ranks!' Jack ordered. It was enough to watch an execution that morning; he had no desire to witness a flogging as well.

Scattergood stepped onto the trap, closed his mouth firmly and glared at General Reading. As the Provost Sergeant slipped the hood over his head, Scattergood began to speak. 'You'll die slow, Reading,' he said, and then the hood muffled any further words.

'Step clear, gentlemen, if you please,' the Provost Sergeant said, his quiet words audible across the packed square. His nod was nearly imperceptible, yet it was enough to end Scattergood's life as an unseen hand threw the lever that opened the trap door beneath the private's feet. There was a collective gasp as Scattergood fell, with the noose tightening around his neck. He kicked and writhed for long minutes as the soldiers watched; some in horror, some in fascination. One young redcoat folded in a dead faint as Scattergood choked to an agonising death.

'Bastard,' an anonymous voice sounded. 'Murdering bloody bastards.'

'Take that man's name, sergeant,' Major Snodgrass ordered without moving from his place in front of Jack's company.

Major General Reading opened his watch, glanced at the time and snapped shut the cover. Turning his horse without a word, he ambled from the parade ground. It was five thirty in a beautiful morning, and Queen Victoria ruled over her empire in peace and tranquillity.

'Windrush.' Captain Haverdale was in his early forties with a drawn face discoloured by service in the tropics and eyes from which hope had long since departed. 'I'll take the men on a ten-mile route march and then return them to barracks. I want you to find me some wine.'

'Yes, sir.' Windrush nodded toward the slowly swinging body of Scattergood. 'I think we'll all need some after witnessing that.'

Haverdale's eyes darkened. 'That was justice, Windrush. If you can't watch a simple execution, I would suggest you find another career.'

Or another regiment. Haverdale's remark stayed with him as he left the fort and crossed into Valetta to search for a wine shop. The quickly rising sun contained sufficient heat to make any exertion difficult as he struggled through the straight narrow streets of the city with their exotic gallarijas and scores of tiny shops. It wasn't hard to find what he sought and with half a dozen bottles of Sicilian wine held in a basket, Jack began to make his way back to his regiment when he heard loud, braying laughter.

'Here's fun, Walter!'

On a ledge overlooking the harbour, two red-coated captains stood beside a small brazier. The taller held a pair of tongs into the glowing heat as his companion watched.

'That'll do, Walter. Throw it!'

Smiling, the taller captain withdrew the tongs, blew on a now-heated copper penny and tossed it over the wall, where a gaggle of raggedy urchins clustered. When the coin descended like manna from heaven, they ran toward it, with the most active leaping above his fellows. When the tiny, grubby hand closed on the coin the boy's scream rose high and shrill.

'You scoundrels!' Jack hadn't seen the suntanned man in the old-fashioned cloak and broad-brimmed hat until he approached the two officers. 'That was an unmanly act!'

'What the devil does it have to do with you?' The smaller officer stepped toward the suntanned man.

'You wear the uniform of British officers and gentlemen.' The man was about fifty, with the brightest blue eyes Jack had ever seen. He grabbed at the tongs in the tall officer's hand and threw them over the wall. 'You are a disgrace.'

'And you, sir, are an interfering fool.'

The smaller officer noticed Jack watching. 'And who are you? Some sneaking puppy of the 113th, I see?' His mouth twisted into a sneer. 'Did you enjoy the show this morning?'

With the bottles clinking in their basket, Jack faced the captain. 'Not any more than I enjoyed watching British officers sully their honour in this manner.'

'Good God!' The smaller man stepped backwards. 'You preach, sir. You, a creature of the blackguard 113th, preach to me!'

The frustration and disgust of the day chased any vestige of control from Jack's tongue. 'What do you mean sir, by insulting my regiment?'

'What do I mean, sir? I mean this, sir!' Without hesitation, the captain slapped Jack backhanded across the face.

'That's the way, Bradley! Show him!'

The shock sent Jack staggering backwards, but instinct made him bring up his fists and land a left jab on Bradley's chin before he recollected his duty. He had just witnessed the result of a man striking a superior, and now he had committed the same offence. Dropping his fists, he awaited the inevitable retribution.

'Go on Bradley!'

Shaking his head, Bradley advanced, landing two stinging lefts to Jack's face before ducking low and punching wickedly into his groin.

The sudden agony forced Jack double, but the sound of Bradley's loud laugh spurred him on. Fighting the pain, he rose again, blocked Bradley's next roundhouse right and threw a straight left that smacked hard against the captain's nose. Blood came in an immediate scarlet flow as Bradley yelped and stepped back.

'Oh, well done, sir!' The suntanned gentleman roared. 'Now go on and finish him off!'

'Nobody will go on. You will both return where you belong.' There was no mistaking the authority in the order, and Jack looked up. Major General Reading stared down at him. 'I witnessed you strike a superior officer. Either you send in your papers or resign, or I shall have you cashiered.'

'Excuse me, sir,' the civilian stepped forward, removed his hat and bowed. 'I observed everything that happened here.'

'And you are, sir?'

'My name is Joseph Bulloch. I saw these gentlemen throw heated coins to the local boys, and this officer,' Bulloch indicated Jack, 'remonstrated with them. That one, Bradley, I believe, insulted his regiment and struck him; he quite naturally retaliated and then dropped his hands, whereupon you happened along.'

General Reading grunted. 'Striking a superior officer is a grave offence, Mr. Bulloch, as this lieutenant well knows.' He turned an imperious eye on Jack. 'What is your name, sir?'

'I am Lieutenant Jack Windrush, sir; of the 113th Foot.'

'And you two?'

'Captain Bradley and Captain Walter, of the 118th Foot.'

Reading hauled at the reins of his horse. 'Windrush, I want you to report to my headquarters at noon tomorrow.' Kicking in his spurs, he pushed on, leaving Jack to the jeers of Bradley and the torment of his thoughts.

A host of tiny birds played around the tall trees that grew in the courtyard, and the scarlet uniformed men snapped to attention the instant Jack stepped through the door. The atmosphere of opulence and confidence only increased when he moved through the splendid palace, and the grandest of all was the room in which Sir John Reading greeted him.

'Ah, Windrush.' Behind a desk whose size and splendour would have graced any royal court, Reading looked up from a pile of paperwork. 'You could make it on time, I see.' He indicated the gold-faced clock on the wall. The hands were just touching twelve.

'Yes, sir.'

'You and your regiment have recently arrived on this island, Windrush, yet you have already brought yourself to my notice.' Reading was obviously a man who came straight to the heart of the matter. 'You were at the execution yesterday morning and saw fit to brawl and strike a superior officer the same day. That is hardly an auspicious start to your career.'

The clock had not finished striking twelve, and already Jack could feel that career sliding away.

'Indeed, Windrush, I am contemplating discharging you from your regiment. If you are a typical example of an officer of the 113th, then the British Army is better off without you, or the 113th.'

The clock sounded its final chord and whirred into near silence. 'The captain struck me first, Sir. I do not know if I am typical or not.'

Reading grunted. 'Your regiment is known as the Baby Butchers, as their only actions so far have been to shoot into a mob of near-starving mill workers and run away from a load of Indians.' Reading's eyes were sharp as any bayonet.

'We saw some action in Burma, sir,' Jack reminded. *Best not to delve into the 113th behaviour in the Sikh War.*

Reading snorted. 'A dozen of the 113th chased a handful of dacoits through the jungle while the rest sat around catching fever. The 113th are poor material with poor officers and I am ashamed to have them under my command.'

'They are British soldiers, sir, and they will act as such when the time comes.'

'Don't bandy words with me, Lieutenant!' Reading leaned back in his seat. After a minute's contemplation during which the soft ticking of the clock dominated the room, he spoke again. 'So, in your vast experience, Lieutenant, you think a taste of battle will cure all their ills?'

'I know they will do their best, sir.' Jack said. 'They came up to scratch in Burma when it mattered.'

Grunting, Reading tapped his fingers on the desk. 'You are Jack Windrush, late of Wychwood Manor. Your mother was a kitchen maid and your father was Major General William Windrush; you believed you were destined for the Royals, so being posted into the 113th must have been a shock...' He held up his hand when Jack began to speak. 'Don't interrupt me, boy. You are the son of an honourable man, but as a by-blow, you can never be a real gentleman.'

Jack kept silent, listening to the sound of birds in the courtyard and feeling the warmth of the sun through the tall windows. He couldn't object; Reading spoke only the truth. Being unable to join the Royals had been a sickening blow, but if Reading relieved him of his commission, Jack's life would be bleak indeed. He had no skills and no talents; his life was geared around his commission, and if that was withdrawn, his annual allowance would also end. He might have to re-enlist as a private soldier, and he knew he would never fit in with the hard men of the ranks.

The loner hand of the clock jerked into motion, marking the passage of another minute before Reading spoke again.

'However, Windrush, although you can never be a gentleman, there may still be a way in which you can retain your *honourable* position as an officer in His Majesty's forces.'

Hope glimmered at the edge of a corridor of utter despair, but Jack kept quiet. *I will not beg.*

'Indeed,' Reading said, 'I can't think of anybody better suited to the task I have in mind.' He rang a small brass bell that sat on his desk, and a very well-presented lieutenant entered the room as if he had been waiting outside the door.

'Fetch Mr. Bulloch.'

Jack looked up as Bulloch entered the room, doffing his hat. 'Good afternoon gentlemen. Is this the man you have chosen, General Reading?'

'This is he,' Reading confirmed. 'He is an officer of bad blood from a regiment of scoundrels.'

Bulloch raised both eyebrows but didn't say a word. 'Shall I tell him, General? Or do you wish to do the evil deed?'

'It is my duty, Bulloch.' Reading came straight to the point. 'Windrush; we have a Swedish diplomat presently in Valetta. His name is Stevensen, and we don't trust him.'

That was blunt. 'Yes, sir. How does that concern me?'

'I want you to find out all about him, in any way you can.' Reading leaned back in his chair as if the interview was at an end.

'Sir,' Jack stared at the general. 'I don't understand. How am I meant to do that?'

'You said yourself that you're a British Army officer, Windrush. If you wish to retain that station, I expect you to use your initiative.'

Jack's heartbeat increased at the blatant threat. 'I'm not sure what you mean, Sir.'

'I mean, Windrush, you are to take any possible method to find out about this man.'

'General Reading is giving you *carte blanche*,' Bulloch interposed. 'You may use any method including direct observation or personal intrusion into this fellow's home.'

Jack opened his mouth to protest that he was an officer and not a spy, until he saw Bulloch give a quick shake of his head.

'Thank you, General, for permitting me to use the services of this officer,' Bulloch said quickly. 'I don't know much about you, Windrush, but I do know that you are a man of principle, courage and spirit. I saw that yesterday. You have been on campaign already I believe?'

Jack nodded. 'Yes, sir. I was in Burma, at the capture of Rangoon and the siege of Pegu.'

'That will do for me.' Bulloch replaced his hat. 'May I take him away now sir, and inform him of the details?'

'What?' Reading nodded. 'Yes, yes, take him away, Bulloch and do what you will with him. Now I want results, Windrush. Find out about this man, and we can put this unpleasant situation behind us.'

'I am no spy!' Windrush said as soon as Bulloch closed the general's door.

'No?' Bulloch raised his eyebrows again. 'Is that such a bad thing to be?'

'It's dishonourable,' Jack said. 'It is not the sort of thing a gentleman would do.'

'Even if it may save thousands of lives?' Bulloch grin made him look like a schoolboy, except for the deep grooves which ran from the sides of his mouth to his nose. 'I am a spy,' he said, 'so according to your lights I cannot be a gentleman, yet my family has held lands in Hampshire since the Domesday Book and probably for a century or two before.' He laughed at the confusion on Jack's face. 'But enough on that subject I think, Windrush. We have important matters to discuss.'

Bulloch had a small room at the top of the building, with a window that overlooked Piazza Tesoreria, the city's main square with its busy traffic and raucous people. 'Have a seat, Windrush,' he invited cheerfully, 'and I'll tell you what you need to know.' He slid into a heavily carved chair behind the desk, poured two glasses of red wine and passed one across to Jack.

Unsure what to expect, Jack took the glass and sat opposite Bulloch. 'Thank you, sir. If I may make so bold, who exactly are you?'

'I am Joseph Bulloch, and I represent the British Government out here in Malta.' Bulloch grinned again. 'And that is all you need to know, Lieutenant Windrush.'

Jack nodded. 'All secret is it? Well enough Mr. Bulloch. So who is this Swedish fellow then, and why is he being investigated by the government?'

Bulloch shrugged. 'We don't know, Windrush and that's the truth of it. He appeared unannounced in Valetta and took up a very respectable residence, and then some people in whom we are very interested, visited with him.'

'I don't understand,' Jack said. 'What sort of people?'

'You may be just old enough to remember the Chartist troubles of '48, when there was near insurrection in Britain and half the kings of Europe lost their crowns?'

'Vaguely, sir,' Jack said. 'I was at school at the time, worrying about irregular Latin verbs.'

'Fascinating things, irregular Latin verbs; we'll have to talk about them sometime.' Bulloch sounded genuinely enthusiastic. 'Well, Malta was not immune from the political disturbances. Out here there was a movement to get rid of the British and gain independence. It came to nothing, as most of these things do, but we keep an eye on the old members of the group.'

'Is that so, sir?'

'It is so, sir, and two of these scoundrels have come to see this Mr. Stevensen,' Bulloch said. 'We have enough trouble with this Russian affair without Malta blowing up in our faces, Windrush, so I want to find out what Stevensen is all about.'

'Don't you have any agents of your own, sir?'

'Not that I can spare. The best I have is out East in Bulgaria; this Russian nonsense is soaking them all up. The Russians know what they are about and are trying to stir up trouble all over the Empire.'

Windrush sighed. 'Why me?'

'I believe General Reading already answered that. You were born on the wrong side of the blanket and are an officer in a blackguard regiment,' Bulloch said candidly. 'Therefore, you are desperate to be accepted and can be manipulated into performing unsavoury acts that a true gentleman would never accept.' Bulloch's wide grin did not remove the shrewdness from his eyes. 'In short, Windrush, you are buggered. You can either comply with our demands and retain your position as an officer or refuse and wave goodbye to that splendid scarlet uniform. Oh, and spend the rest of your life trying to explain why you lost your commission.'

'I see.' Jack took a deep breath, recognising the truth. 'So what am I expected to do?'

'It's quite simple,' Bulloch said happily. 'You are expected to break into Stevensen's house and see what incriminating evidence you can find. Oh, and don't get caught. If a British officer should be caught doing such a thing Horse Guards would cashier him for sure, and the local police would throw him into some medieval dungeon to rot forever.'

Jack's mouth gaped open. 'How the devil do you expect me to break into a house? I'm a gentleman, not a housebreaker.'

'You are an officer in the British army, Windrush.' Bulloch's smile never faltered. 'There is nothing to which you can't turn your hand. And when you succeed, I will put in a good word with General Reading to have you sent east, if you are certain that is what you wish.'

'Of course I'm certain,' Jack said.

Bulloch sighed. 'I'm sure I don't know why you young men are so eager to go and get killed.' Reaching down, he opened the middle drawer of his desk and produced a small leather case. 'This may come in handy,' he said. 'It's a lock-pickers wallet, made in Birmingham, like all the best cracksman's tools.'

'Thank you,' Jack held the case awkwardly, unsure what to do with it. Eventually, he opened it and glanced inside. There was a collection of thin metal objects, each one the length of a small pen and with an intricately-shaped head. 'What am I meant to do with these?'

'Use them,' Bulloch said. 'Now I don't even have a description of this Stevensen fellow, so I can't help you there, I'm afraid!'

'I see, sir,' Jack said.

'Thank you for your time, Windrush. I hope to hear about your success very shortly.'

It was a blatant dismissal. Jack nodded. 'Yes sir.' He lifted his hat and left the room.

The men slouched outside their quarters, red tunics undone and boot laces untied. Jack glanced around; according to the regimental records, there were thirty men based here at Ta Bubaqra, deep in the south of the island and far away from the rest of the army. Not one looked up when Jack walked up. Some sat in a circle exchanging banter and curses as they played with dog-eared cards; others sat and scratched at insect bites as they sought shade in the lee of the stone-walled houses. Two men just stared into space through dull, hopeless eyes while another pored intently over a small, leather-bound book. Jack spared him a few seconds – many ordinary soldiers could not read a word; a man who chose to spend time with a book was a rarity and could become a barrack-room lawyer – major trouble.

A corporal and a private soldier passed a water bottle back and forward, swaying as they sipped at the contents. Whatever it contained, Jack realised, was undoubtedly more interesting than water. He stopped beside the drinking men.

'How are things, O'Neill?'

The corporal started, looked up and stood to attention. 'Sorry sir, I didn't see you there.'

'Pass over the bottle,' Jack ordered, 'I'm as hot as you are.' He took a quick swig. 'Local wine is it? I had to buy imported swill from Sicily. Trust you to find the good stuff.'

'Yes, sir.'

'Sit down man.' Jack sunk to the ground at his side. 'We fought together in Burma, for God's sake.'

'I was there too sir,' the second man said.

'I remember, Thorpe.' Jack handed back the bottle. 'How could I ever forget you?' He acknowledged Thorpe's grin with a lift of his finger. 'Now listen, you two. We all know what sort of men we have in the 113th. I need a housebreaker.'

'Have they kicked you out, sir?' Thorpe asked. 'Are you looking for a new career?'

'Mind your tongue!' O'Neill belatedly remembered that he was a corporal and next in the chain of command.

'I did not hear that Thorpe,' Jack said quietly. 'You men know the regiment as well as anybody else. Do you know of anybody who could help?'

O'Neill screwed up his face. 'There's a lot of blackguards in the 113th, sir.' He hesitated. 'I don't know of any cracksmen though. That's a bit too skilled for this regiment.'

Jack looked around at the slum-haggard faces of the privates. Recruited from the dregs of the gutters and the sweepings of the countryside, they were drunkards and brawlers, petty thieves and poachers. He recognised a pickpocket who had changed his name to hide from the law; one was a gentleman ranker soaked in gin, another a bigamist on the run from both his wives and the surly fellow was a policeman kicked out for brutality – welcome to the 113th Foot.

A weary-looking private slouched over, flapping a hand irritably at the mosquitoes that clouded around his head. Taking the bottle from Thorpe, he took a deep draught. 'God that's foul. If it's a cracksman you want, Riley's your man, sir.'

'Shut up Coleman, you—' Thorpe nodded warningly at Jack.

'Riley; where is he?' Jack glanced around. He focussed on the man with the book. Cracksmen were reputed to be more intelligent than the average criminal. They may even be able to read and write.

'He's not here sir.' Coleman glanced at the furthest of the houses and gave a greasy grin that almost proved the lie.

'Thank you, Coleman. I'll find him myself.' It was apparent that Coleman was hiding something.

'You bloody fool, Coley!' O'Neill hissed as Jack strode toward the house Coleman had glanced toward, cracked open the door and stepped into a dark room.

'Riley!'

'What the hell do you want?' The voice came from the interior. 'Can't you see I'm busy?'

Jack pushed the door wider to allow in daylight. The speaker lay on a rough mattress in the corner of the room, with a blonde-haired woman at his side. 'Get rid of the woman, Riley; we have things to discuss.'

'I'm not to be got rid of on your say-so!' The woman slid sideways off the bed, holding a single blanket around her.

'It's best, Charlotte.' Riley sounded more educated than the majority of the 113th; that was hopeful.

The woman tossed her hair, still holding the blanket. She looked at Jack through suddenly narrow eyes. 'Who's this?'

'I am Lieutenant Jack Windrush,' Jack said softly.

'Sorry, sir.' Riley sprang to his feet, standing to attention with the tails of his shirt flapping around naked thighs. 'We're not used to officers coming here, sir.' He looked sideways at the woman and flicked his head very slightly toward the door.

'Wait,' Jack worked out what that simple motion meant. 'Mrs. Riley can stay if she wishes.'

'Thank you, sir,' the woman gave a sudden smile.

Jack saw the expression of dismay cross Riley's face.

'You know, sir?'

'I guessed,' Jack said.

There was a minute's silence as both men mentally reviewed the regimental standing orders that were pinned prominently in half a dozen places around the island:

> *Regimental standing orders 1848*
>
> *Section XV: Marriage*
>
> *No woman is to be allowed to reside in Barracks who objects to make herself useful in Cooking etc. it cannot be too often repeated to the men that they are on no account to marry without leave. A man marrying, without having obtained leave from the commanding officer of the regiment, will never be permitted to receive any of the indulgences bestowed on such as marry by consent. It is impossible to point out the inconveniences which arise and the evils which follow a regiment encumbered by women; poverty and misery are the inevitable consequences. Officers therefore cannot do too much to deter their men from marrying and there are few men, however hard they think it at the moment, that after a short period, will not be much obliged to thank them for having done so.*

'You have had no permission to marry,' Jack said softly.

'No, sir,' Riley was equally quiet.

'You do realise that Colonel Murphy has ordered that even if the marriage is permitted, there are only two wives per company in this campaign?' Jack said. 'And your name was not on the list.' He took a deep breath, aware it was his duty as an officer to report this offence. 'You are now liable to serious charges that could have you flogged and would have Mrs. Riley removed from camp.'

'Officers are permitted to take their wives,' Charlotte sounded bitter. 'Anyway, how do you know I am his wife?'

'Blondes are rare in Malta,' Jack told her, 'and all your husband's colleagues were very protective of him.'

'What are you going to do, sir?' A bead of sweat trickled down Riley's face, lingered on the tip of his chin and dripped to the stone-flagged floor.

'That depends on you, Riley.' Jack knew that he was about to venture onto hazardous ground, an area that could ruin his career. He fought a sardonic smile. Career? He had none unless he succeeded in this dirty venture. 'You had better get dressed, Mrs. Riley and wait outside.'

Once again Charlotte looked to Riley, who gave a brief nod. Jack turned his back as she dressed, ignored her final desperate glance to Riley and waited until she left.

'All right Riley, you and I both know that you're already in trouble and if I ignore that, then I will be too.'

'Yes, sir.' Riley remained at attention. Jack let him stay like that; he wanted him unsettled.

'Colonel Murphy may only give you fifty,' Jack increased Riley's discomfort, 'or he may give fifty for each offence.' He allowed the prospect of the flogging triangle to press further down on Riley's already depressed face. Jack knew by his accent that he was from a different background to most of the men; to Riley, the cat would be even more degrading.

Jack's two steps took him to the far end of the cottage. He took a deep breath as if he was thinking deeply. 'There may be a way I could overlook that Mrs. Riley is with you.'

'Yes, sir.' Riley didn't allow any emotion to reach his face.

'You were a cracksman, I believe?' Jack kept his voice casual.

'Yes, sir,' Riley replied automatically, and then looked at Jack with a start.

'Good; then we have a job to do, you and me,' Jack said, 'unless you wish me to inform the colonel about your lady wife?'

Chapter Two

Malta
April 1854

The house known as Dar-il-Sliem – 'House of Tranquillity' – stood a bare hundred yards from the Grand Harbour. It overlooked the massed shipping of the Royal Navy and the associated merchant ships and transports, whose reflected lights danced across the dark water. Red shutters covered a score of windows that punctuated the baroque façade, with squat columns flanking the round-headed door.

'Gerolamo Cassar was the architect,' Riley spoke quietly, 'the same man who designed the Grand Master's palace.'

'Oh?' Jack had no interest in the architect.

'He laid the ground plan for Valetta as well,' Riley said. 'Europe's first ever planned city. He was a genius of course.'

'Was he indeed?' Jack said. 'I am delighted to see you did not waste your time in the Knight's old archives.' He didn't try to keep the sarcasm from his voice. 'You were meant to be studying the house to learn how to break in, not researching its history.'

'Cassar built this place, but a hundred and fifty years later it was altered for Vincente de Borg, a name which will mean nothing to you.' Riley's voice was neutral. 'He commanded a small fleet of ships that fought the Ottomans, and everybody else in the Mediterranean.'

'I don't know the name,' Jack said.

'The name is not so important, sir.' Riley lifted a small telescope and scanned the building. 'It was his reputation that counted against him. He was so successful that he made enemies, so on two occasions, people attempted to assassinate him. They may have been jealous husbands, for he had a reputation that way as well, or maybe rival captains who lacked his ability to make money from the enemy, or even men hired by the Turks, but he decided he needed an escape route if things got dangerous.'

'A secret passage?' Jack said.

'Their Achilles heel.' Riley adjusted the focus of his telescope and glanced sideways at Jack. 'That means their weakness—'

'I am familiar with the expression,' Jack said.

'Sorry sir,' Riley said quickly. 'I'm used to talking to... I am not used to talking to officers, sir.'

'Carry on Riley.'

'The escape route was a passage from a house by the waterfront, down by the harbour and into Dar-il-Sliem, Borg's house.'

'That will be our way in, then.' Jack said.

'No, sir. That will not, begging your pardon, sir; if I have found out about this passage, then so will Stevensen. That is where he will concentrate his security.' Riley's smile was unexpected. 'If we can arrange something there to divert Stevensen's attention, we can get in and out of the building before he draws breath.'

Jack nodded. 'That might work. Good thinking, Riley. There is a corporal in you, I think.'

'No, thank you,' Riley shook his head at once. 'I'd prefer to remain as I am, sir.'

'As you wish.' There was obviously far more to Riley than met the eye and potential for a higher rank than a corporal. 'Now, it would be useful if we knew where Stevensen's office was,' Jack said.

'Upper floor, end room,' Riley said at once. 'The plans were in the archives, both the original architect's design and after the eighteenth-century renovations. That room has been used as the office since the builders handed it over. I can't see Stevensen having time to change anything in the last month.'

'Show me.' Jack took the telescope. The shutters were open at the window that Riley indicated. He saw the shape of a man and studied the face by what light a lantern provided. About forty, handsome, with cropped blonde hair and a thick moustache, he looked every inch the Swedish gentleman. 'I'll arrange a diversion,' he said, 'if you can get us inside the building.'

'I work alone,' Riley said.

'Not this time,' Jack told him.

'You might make a noise, sir.'

'I'm coming with you; that's an order, Riley.' Jack put an edge in his voice.

There was a moment's silence before Riley spoke again. 'You were a public-school man, sir, so you may well make a good cracksman.'

'Thank you.' Jack ignored the slight, but pointed, bitterness in Riley's voice. The terminology 'public school man' indicated a similar background. Jack stored that information for future use.

At a quarter to three in the morning, a halo glowed around the sliver of moon. Riley adjusted the canvas satchel he wore across his back and looked skyward. 'The air is heavy. There's a storm coming in.'

'You could be right,' Jack said.

'That could be useful,' Riley sounded casual. 'You took my advice about clothing then.'

Jack glanced down at himself. Dressed in a mixture of black and grey, he wore soft-soled shoes and had pulled a dark forage cap over his head. 'I feel as if I should be at a masque ball or a theatre.'

Riley threw him an odd look, opened his mouth and closed it again. 'Yes, sir. You won't be easily recognised; you'll merge with the shadows and the soft shoes are quieter,' he said. 'Sir.'

'I've arranged for a slight diversion in fifteen minutes from now,' Jack said. 'Hopefully, that will give us time.' He glanced at Thorpe, who stood a yard behind them, chewing on a wad of tobacco. 'You keep a good look out, Thorpe. If you see or hear anything suspicious, give us a blast.'

Thorpe held up a hunting horn. 'Yes, sir.'

'Come on then, Riley,' Jack said.

'Wait for that cloud to hide the moon, sir.' Riley watched the sky until the moonlight faded. 'Right, here we go.' He tossed a grapnel hook onto the top of the wall that surrounded the house and swarmed up with Jack at his back. Riley reversed the rope so it dropped to the inside of the wall and they slid down, landing with a soft thump.

'Give it a moment in case somebody saw movement.' Riley's voice was as calm as if he was sitting in his wife's parlour. 'Right sir, keep behind me and move smoothly.' He ducked low and ran toward the house. Jack followed with his breathing nervously harsh as they slammed against the back wall beside the window they'd already selected. Riley tested the shutters. 'Closed and bolted,' he said. 'See where it holds? That's where the bolt is.'

'What now?' Jack asked.

'Watch and learn.' Riley flicked the canvas satchel from his back. 'Keep watch, sir.' Removing a well-swaddled bundle, he revealed a brace-and-bit and showed it to Jack. Fitting a large cutting edge, he placed the central point against the wood of the shutters close by the bolt and carved out a circular hole some six inches in diameter. The noise of metal on wood seemed to reverberate around the quiet garden.

'Can't you do that quietly?' Jack asked.

'No. Keep crow – watch – sir, if you please.' Thrusting his arm through the hole, Riley drew the internal bolt and pulled the shutters open. He tested the window, grunted when it refused to open and removed another bundle that contained a small stone. 'This is a glass cutter's stone.' It took him only a few seconds to cut through one of the panes and unhook the catch inside. Placing a piece of dark paper over the circular hole in the shutters, he dragged the window open and climbed inside the house, with Jack at his heels.

Stopping to close the shutters, Riley lit a small bull's eye lantern, adjusted the aperture so that only a pencil-thin sliver of light probed into the dark and moved confidently toward the door.

Jack followed, hoping that Riley had studied the internal plans of the house as thoroughly as he had the outside. The door led to a marble-floored corridor, with the lantern-light picking out the grim faces on a succession of portraits.

There were only a few steps to the door on the opposite side of the corridor. Riley turned the door handle and grunted when he found it locked.

'Can we force it?' Jack pulled his watch from his pocket; he had allowed fifteen minutes before the diversion; five had passed, and they were not yet within the room.

'I've got a betty.' Riley produced a wallet that contained a selection of picklocks, the mirror of the one Bulloch had handed to Jack. 'Hold this please, sir,' he handed over the lantern. 'Keep the beam on the lock.'

'This lantern's hot,' Windrush took the lantern.

'It gets hotter.' Riley knelt at the lock and fiddled with his pick-locks. After a remarkably short time, there was a slight click, and he pushed the door open and moved inside the room.

Jack followed and closed the door. The room was square, dark with the exterior shutters closed and surprisingly stuffy for its size. Riley remained just within the doorway as he probed with the thin beam of light. 'There's no safe,' he said, 'so anything important must be in the writing bureau.'

They moved toward it, feet silent on the thick carpet. A long-case clock ticked softly in one corner of the room, with the light of the lantern reflecting from a glass-fronted bookcase.

The writing bureau was heavily carved, with a column of locked drawers on either side of the sitting aperture. Riley unlocked each drawer in turn before opening them from the bottom up. He took out a folding ruler, measured the breadth and height, fiddled underneath and shook his head.

'There you are, sir. I've done my bit. There are no secret drawers in this bureau.' He stepped back as Jack sorted through the drawers. He had only a vague idea what Bulloch and Reading may want, so took every piece of paper he could find, sliding them into the black canvas bag he wore. There were some documents that looked official, several personal letters that he glanced at but discarded; a few maps and some forms that were partially filled in.

'There's somebody in the corridor, sir,' Riley's voice was urgent. He closed the shutter of his lantern. The sudden intense darkness was stifling.

Jack heard the soft tread outside and tried to make himself as small as possible beneath the bureau. He had not brought a weapon and knew that if the householder caught them here, the British Army would not support him. It was obvious that Riley was an expert cracksman so being in his company would be tantamount to guilt without the necessity of a trial.

There was the murmur of voices speaking in a language that Jack didn't recognise but guessed was Swedish. He could neither see nor hear Riley and wondered if he was still there – or had he somehow managed to ease away in the dark.? Jack flinched when somebody pushed open the door and walked in.

The flicker of a candle highlighted a strong chin, proud nose and high cheekbones, and then a second man pushed the door wide open. For a second Jack saw him clearly, a tall man with a weather-beaten face disfigured by a black patch over his left eye. A second man joined him, less tall but broad, with short hair so blonde it was nearly albino and a mouth like a man-trap.

'Is there anything amiss?' The tall man's words were in English with a soft, slow-speaking drawl that Jack could not place.

'No, sir, the door had not been locked.' The first man stepped inside the room and held the candle high. Jack remained still beneath the desk as the yellow glow pooled around him. He knew Riley would have the sense to keep silent, glanced at the open drawers and prepared to thump anybody who stepped too close. The man with the eye-patch would be a formidable opponent though; he looked as if he had survived about forty tough years of life.

The candlelight flickered and then steadied as the man looked around. 'Nothing amiss, sir,' he said, and both men left the room, closing the door. There was the scrape of a key turning in the lock, a soft click and then silence.

'Give them five minutes,' Riley's voice was soft in the dark, 'in case they linger outside.'

Jack nodded, aware of the thumping of his heart. Although he had organised the diversion, the sudden racket from the opposite side of the house still made him start. There was the sound of raised voices, a loud bang and a rattle as if somebody was rolling a steel drum over a cobbled road, which, Jack thought, was quite likely knowing O'Neill.

'Right, Riley, let's get out of this.'

Riley knelt at the door, picked the lock in seconds and slid into the corridor. Their retreat was much faster than their advance had been as Riley sped out the window, pushed the shutters closed and ran to the surrounding wall. The noise from O'Neill's diversion rose if anything, with loud voices, the blast of a whistle and a high-pitched barking.

'Dogs!' Riley groped for the rope he had left ready for their retreat. 'Get out of here, sir; blasted dogs!' There was genuine fear in his face as he looked along the line of the wall. For the first time that night, Riley hesitated. He stumbled and would have fallen had Jack not supported him and hoisted him upward.

The dogs erupted around the side of the house; three large mastiffs, all teeth and fury and slavering jaws. Jack leapt for the rope an instant too late and swung helplessly for a second. He felt the searing pain as the leading dog clamped its teeth on his ankle. Swearing, Jack kicked out, feeling his flesh rip as the mastiff worried at him. He tried to pull himself up the wall, but the weight of the dog held him back; he kicked again, once, twice, and swore as a second dog barged in to grab at his flailing leg.

'There's somebody there!' The call was in English, with that same drawling accent, and accompanied by a wide splay of light across the garden. One by one and then in twos and threes, lights came on in the house as unseen hands opened the curtains and threw back the shutters.

Jack turned his head away from the light so as not to be recognised just as a pistol cracked out two feet from his head. He flinched and blinked as the muzzle-flare temporarily blinded him. 'What the devil!'

There was a loud howl from beneath, and he felt the pressure on his leg relax. He jerked it free and scrambled up the rope, to see Riley lying prone on top of the wall, holding a short, double-barrelled pistol. 'I hate dogs,' he said. 'Up you come, sir.'

Chapter Three

Malta
Spring and Summer 1854

General Reading looked up as Jack limped across the room to his desk. 'I heard that there was a disturbance near the harbour last night. I hope nobody caught you.'

'No, sir.' Jack placed the pile of documents on Reading's desk. 'I took everything I could find, sir. These are the papers I thought looked most interesting.'

Reading shuffled through them quickly and rang his brass bell. The same young lieutenant appeared, looked down his aristocratic nose at Windrush and sprang to immediate attention. 'Sir?'

'Fetch Mr. Bulloch.'

A moment later Bulloch appeared. 'Morning General, morning Windrush.' He lifted the documents. 'You were successful I see.' He flicked through them. 'Did anybody see you?'

'Yes, sir; as we left,' Jack said, 'but I don't believe that they saw our faces. Private Riley did most of the work, sir.'

'Did he indeed?' Bulloch lifted an eyebrow. 'And where did he acquire the skill to break into a house?'

'I believe he was a burglar, sir,' Jack said.

'Not by that name, I wager.' Bulloch frowned as he looked at one of the sheets of paper. 'And I wonder about Stevensen's real name as well. None of these papers is in Swedish. They are in English, Maltese, Russian and French, yes, but not Swedish.' He placed them in the leather case he carried. 'Did you notice anything unusual about the house, Windrush?'

'Only that three men were patrolling, and they spoke English as well, sir.'

'English has been used as the lingua-franca in Malta ever since we occupied the island,' Bulloch said, 'so speaking English is not unusual.'

'They did not speak it like Maltese, sir,' Jack said. 'They spoke it like native speakers, I think.'

'Like Englishmen?' Reading asked.

'No,' Jack thought for a moment. 'Not quite. I didn't recognise the accent, sir. It may have been from one of the colonies; Canada perhaps or Van Diemen's Land.'

'A Demonian?' Bulloch sounded suddenly interested. 'It could be a ticket of leave man – or an escaped convict.' He took a deep breath. 'What was he like?'

'There were three that I saw. Two were mundane, men who you wouldn't notice in a crowd; the other was tall with an eyepatch. He spoke more.'

'He was tall with an eyepatch and a colonial accent.' Bulloch altered his voice and said, 'Did he speak with a drawl like this, unhurried and soft?'

'Yes, that's it,' Jack agreed.

'I will watch for them,' Bulloch said. 'You, of course, won't be here.' He looked at Reading. 'Now that Lieutenant Windrush has more than done what you ordered, general, I am sure you will soon keep your side of the agreement.'

Windrush almost felt the tension in the room as Reading stiffened in his chair. 'The 113th are bound east, and Lieutenant Windrush will be with them. I trust his regiment will not let us down if they are ever fortunate enough to see action. I am not sure that a regiment that includes murderers, blackguards and, it seems, a professional burglar, should be allowed to represent the British Army.'

'In that case,' Bulloch said, 'the French and Turks would have to fight alone.' His grin did nothing to take the sting from his words.

'Your beloved 113th will be part of the Army of the East, Windrush,' General Reading said, 'and God help the general who has you under his command.'

Jack controlled his rising anger. 'My boys proved themselves in Burma, sir.'

Reading fixed him with a cold glare. 'You have far too much to say for yourself, Windrush. You will find that chasing dacoits through the jungle and facing regular European soldiers, even Russians, are two different things. Dismissed.'

Jack felt Reading's eyes poisonous on his back as he left the room.

They stood in the lee of the wall at the Grand Harbour, watching the regiments embark and listened to the singing of the men.

Cheer Boys cheer,
For country mother country
Cheer boys cheer
For a willing strong right hand
Cheer boys cheer
There's hope for honest labour
Cheer boys cheer
For a new and happy land.

Coleman spat on the ground. 'New and happy land, my arse. They're going out East; don't they realise what the East is? A shit hole of flies and filth, with women riddled with disease and men who smile to your face and plan to cut your throat behind your back.'

'They're off to scuttle the Ruskies in Scutari,' Thorpe said as the red-coated men filed on board the steamship to the sound of the band. They marched past the paddle-boxes, boots clumping on the wooden deck, officers looking debonair and military, the men singing, cheering, happy to be sailing to war.

'When's it our turn, sir?' O'Neill asked for the tenth time. 'It's been weeks now since General Reading promised us we're heading out and the boys started going east.'

'I wish I knew, O'Neill.'

As time passed, the 113th grew restless, watching other regiments arrive on the island and leave days later, while they remained static in their scattered quarters. Petty offences increased, with the sergeants busy keeping the men under control and Colonel Murphy ordering men to double duties and various forms of field punishment. 'Any more trouble and it will be the cat!' Major Snodgrass threatened as they paraded before him in the baking heat. 'I haven't forgotten your behaviour in India, by God.'

'They treat us worse than cattle,' Coleman grumbled.

'Their time will come,' Thorpe's murmur was bitter with resentment.

'Silence in the ranks!' Major Snodgrass ordered. 'Take these men's names!'

The resulting silence was ugly. Jack ran his gaze across the men – although their faces were devoid of expression, their eyes were vicious. Any British regiment contained an element of the underclass. In the 113th the percentage was far higher. Their combined poisonous gaze followed Snodgrass as he blasted them. In the background, Colonel Murphy stood stiffly with the empty sleeve a reminder of the arm he had lost at the battle of Chillianwala.

'If we don't move soon, Captain Haverdale said quietly, 'there will be a mutiny. This rabble is getting restless.'

The harsh blare of a bugle roused them in the dark of a late July morning, with the air pressing languid upon them and the dust of the previous day still grating between their teeth.

'Ready, boys! We're shipping out!'

It was the call they had long been waiting for, yet the men were so used to disappointment that they responded with lethargy rather than enthusiasm.

'It's another mistake,' Coleman said. 'They'll get us ready and march us back down to Valetta and Mdina, or somewhere else thousands of miles from the Russians; then they'll march us back again.'

'The grand old Duke of York is alive, well and residing in Malta.' Riley's tones was distinct amidst the uneducated and illiterate murmurs of his fellows.

'Who the hell's the Duke of York and how come he's so grand?' The accent was uncompromisingly Scottish west coast; the speaker below average height with a gaunt, lined face. Jack marked him out as potential trouble and resolved to learn his name.

He called his men together and ushered them across country to where the regiment rallied at Kalkara, overlooking the Grand Harbour. They formed in rigid scarlet ranks, sweating, trembling with the effort of standing to attention under the mid-morning sun.

'Our ship is in, gentlemen,' Colonel Murphy announced, 'today we sail for the East.'

Jack had not expected the sudden outbreak of enthusiasm from the men. They cheered, threw their hats in the air, shook hands as if celebrating something significant or waved their Brown Bess muskets like madmen.

'For a regiment that is not supposed to be keen to fight,' Jack said, 'they seem very eager to go to war.'

Major Snodgrass grunted. 'Give them one week on campaign, and they'll be cheering just as loudly to run home.'

'My men won't run,' Jack said.

'I thought that before Chillianwala,' Snodgrass sounded bitter. 'And they ran like frightened rabbits.'

'My men behaved well in Burma.' Jack did not add 'most of the time' as he remembered the beginning of that campaign and the men he had left behind.

Snodgrass grunted. 'One cannot compare the Burmese with the Sikhs. Or with the Russians.' He stiffened as Colonel Murphy slid down from his horse and approached them.

'I trust your men are all ready to go, gentlemen?' Murphy faced them, slight and weathered, with his voice hoarse and his eyes deep-sunk in his face.

'All ready sir. Which ship are we on?' Snodgrass asked.

'*Poseidon*,' Murphy said, 'the name augers well. *Poseidon* was the Greek god of the sea.'

'Where is she?' Jack examined the ships in harbour. As well as three Royal Navy warships there were two steam paddle ships and a battered brig that limped under topsails only. He guessed the answer even before Murphy focussed his telescope.

'That sailing ship,' Murphy said, 'But only the devil knows how we are to fit the entire regiment in her.'

'It does not matter,' Snodgrass said. 'We're only the 113th; nobody cares a damn about us.'

'There will be no wives accompanying the regiment,' Murphy said. 'There is no space. They will follow by a later transport. I will make no exceptions: that rule includes officers as well as men.'

Jack raised his eyebrows. It was a rule that made perfect sense when the ship was so crowded, but it would be hard for the men. In his opinion a soldier's life was not right for a married man; it was too unstable, too precarious and added unnecessary worry to a soldier's lot. Soldiers should be married to their regiment and profession. If they wanted to use a woman, there were plenty of prostitutes drawn to every garrison town like bluebottles to a pile of dung. All the same, men such as Riley would feel the loss.

'We are the British Army,' Murphy coughed and turned aside, not quite quickly enough to hide the bright dribble of blood at the side of his mouth. 'We will cope.'

'Of course, we will, sir.' Snodgrass gave an impressive salute.

'It's like the bloody Ark,' Coleman said, 'filing on board two by two like bloody animals.'

'Except the animals had more space than we do.' Thorpe looked at their accommodation. 'If we all lie down at once we will be piled three deep on top of each other.'

'Stop grumbling you lot,' O'Neill shouted, 'it's only a short voyage across the Med, a week at most. Think yourselves lucky you're not sailing from England to New South Wales in this old tub. Now get settled!'

'Parade on deck in twenty minutes,' Snodgrass shouted. 'I intend to maintain military discipline on this ship so when the 113th arrives out East we will be fit to fight.' He lowered his voice. 'Or as fit as you blackguards can ever be.'

With all six hundred and forty officers and men of the 113th on parade, the deck of *Poseidon* was packed. Every square inch was occupied by a red-coated soldier, with the crew watching from aloft and openly cursing the loss of freedom on their vessel.

'Men!' Snodgrass stood on the slightly raised quarterdeck with the captains and lieutenants gathered around him. 'Colonel Murphy is indisposed at present so I, as senior major, am taking command.'

Jack felt, rather than saw, the shiver that ran through the ranks. He looked sideways, seeing the bitter lines on the face of Snodgrass and the tell-tale red-veins on his nose.

'Many of your men have come to us from other regiments,' Snodgrass said. 'You were not wanted there. You are the drunkards, the troublemakers, the insubordinate, and the slow.' He stopped then. Jack could see the expressions of the men; they were sullen, unresponsive. He waited for Snodgrass to say something to inspire them.

'We in the 113th have given you a second chance,' Snodgrass said. 'I will make sure you are up to scratch. However poor you may be, I intend to make soldiers out of you. Those that don't come up to the mark… Remember Private Scattergood.'

Jack was not the only one who winced. The reminder of their executed colleague passed like a black shadow across the men. Some faces fell into more profound gloom; some gave a momentary scowl or gave a deep intake of breath. Riley threw Snodgrass a look that should have curdled the blood in his veins. The little Scotsman at Riley's side gave no hint of any emotion except a slight twitch of his thin lips.

'That was hardly diplomatic.' Lieutenant Elliot had purchased into the 113th from the 50th Foot only a few days previously. Jack recognised the pride with which he touched the insignia that revealed his exalted rank. One week ago, he had been a lowly ensign; now he felt himself a leader of men.

'We'll see how the men react,' Jack murmured. He was aware of a seagull circling overhead, the bird's eyes bright as it surveyed the men below. *If we are the Lords of Creation, why is that creature free while we are under orders to sail to a slaughterhouse over which we have no control?*

'There are too many of you for everyone to parade together.' Despite the constant creaking of the old wooden ship, Snodgrass's voice carried to all parts of the deck. 'So we will do this navy fashion and divide you into three watches. That way there will be more space below.'

'And no rest period for the sergeants or crew,' Elliot said quietly.

'The strictest discipline will be maintained,' Snodgrass said. 'I depend on my officers and non-commissioned officers to keep you in order.'

Bored of watching the humans, the seagull winged away. Lacking the freedom of the bird, the men who filled the packed scarlet ranks on the deck below waited for orders. The 113th sailed to war.

With the men working eight hours out of every twenty-four, day and night, *Poseidon* was never quiet. Snodgrass had the men marching up, and down the limited space the deck allowed, had them aiming their Brown Bess muskets from kneeling and standing positions and had them wheeling around the main mast in a circular motion.

'Captain Neilson.' Snodgrass faced a saturnine officer with a face yellowed by years in the tropics. 'Take over here. Keep the men busy!' He paused and pointed to a prostrate figure beside the rail. 'Why is that man lying down?'

'He's seasick, sir,' a sergeant said.

'Get him up! That is only weakness!' Snodgrass's face darkened. 'Stand up sir! Get to your feet!'

The man tried to respond, lurched groggily and promptly vomited over the deck.

'You disgusting fellow! That's gross impertinence!'

Riley stepped out of the ranks. 'He couldn't help it, sir! He's sick!'

'Damn your impertinence! Put that man in irons, sergeant! We'll have him flogged tomorrow and see if he's so clever after that.'

Jack stepped forward. 'Sir, if I may, he meant nothing by it. He was speaking up for his colleague.' Jack saw Snodgrass stiffen and a beefy sergeant pushed back the small Scotsman and a soft-faced soldier who had shifted forward as if to intervene.

'Fifty for that man, sergeant. And you, Windrush, will be on duty for the next twenty-four hours. If I see you below decks before midnight tomorrow...' He let the implied threat hang in the air.

Jack met Riley's eye and gave a slight nod. He couldn't help; he could only let his erstwhile housebreaking companion know that he sympathised if nothing else. The thought of the quiet-spoken, intelligent Riley stripped and flogged was not something Jack wished to contemplate.

Jack had heard that the Mediterranean was a quiet sea, but the storm that blasted them the next day would not have disgraced any North Sea squall. Lumpy seas smashed into the creaking brig, straining her sideways, so her port yard arms nearly dipped into the waves, and her reluctant passengers yelled as they tumbled around the deck. The seasickness increased tenfold, and the ship's surgeon was overworked with minor bumps and cuts as well as a few more serious breaks. It was a full twelve hours before the weather moderated to a gale and then Snodgrass ordered the regiment assembled.

'This is a reprieve, not an ending.' Captain Evans, the commander of *Poseidon*, was short, dark and Welsh. He gestured to the angry clouds that swirled around. 'We've worse to come so don't fool around with your soldier games for long.'

'I assure you, Captain, that this is no game,' Snodgrass said grimly.

Jack took a deep breath as the Provost Sergeant brought Riley out from the black depths of the ship. Stripped to the waist, Riley held himself erect as his gaze fixed on a face in the ranks of the 113th and gave a brief nod, as if of reassurance.

Jack scanned his men; Riley had nodded to either that small-made Scotsman or the soft-faced man – boy even – who stood at his side. Perhaps both, although from the expression of mixed fury and anguish on the boy's face, Jack suspected it was him. He frowned; there was something wrong here, something on which he could not put his finger.

Riley walked firmly to the gratings that had been lashed upright beside the ladder that led from the main deck to the quarterdeck. Except for that single nod toward the men, he had looked only in front.

'That man's in the wrong regiment,' Elliot said. 'With his bearing, he should be in the guards, not the 113th.'

'His bearing will alter after fifty of the cat.' Jack swallowed hard, fighting his nausea.

'Have you seen a flogging before?' Elliot sounded nervous.

'Only at school,' Jack tried to sound nonchalant.

'Me too,' Elliot said. 'It was not quite the same though.'

'Not quite,' Jack agreed. He tore his horrified gaze from Riley to the watching men. The boy looked sick; his eyes were anguished and his hands curled around the fabric of his tunic as he stood at attention. Jack saw him lift a hand to his eyes as if to wipe away a tear, and hurriedly put it down as a sergeant barked at him.

There was quiet for a few moments as two corporals tied Riley to the gratings. Spread-eagled, the naked skin of his back looked very pale against the dark wood of the grating. Jack could nearly taste the tension as the assembled 113th watched, eyes narrow, hard, frustrated and contemptuous. He felt their rising hatred for Snodgrass in particular and officers in general; including him, no doubt. Thunder rumbled a mile away while lightning flickered a bright threat through ugly dark clouds, nature acting as a symbol of the tension on board Poseidon.

For a moment Jack remembered a past experience, knocking at the door of his headmaster before an appointment with the cane. He remembered the dread churning of his stomach and the sick fear; did Riley feel like that? He didn't look apprehensive; he looked relaxed.

A sudden gust of wind ruffled the surface of the sea, kicking the tops off the waves; was it the dying flick of the storm's tail or a portent of worse to come? Some of the men staggered; Jack saw the vicious-faced Scotsman steadying the boy. The ranks swayed, righted themselves and faced their front.

'Sergeants! Keep these men standing to attention, or there will be more feeling the cat!' Snodgrass removed his hat. 'Surgeon – pronounce that man fit to receive punishment.'

With a seaman supporting him Dr. Goss staggered to Riley, glanced at him and nodded to Snodgrass.

'Proceed,' Snodgrass leaned forward slightly as if to get a better view and the Provost Sergeant nodded to the burlier of the two corporals, who ran his fingers through the tails of the lash, stepped back for balance on the heaving deck and laid on with a grunt of effort.

Jack saw a shiver run through the ranks as the first stroke of the cat landed on Riley's back. Others followed in a merciless procession of pain. Soon a red streak extended from Riley's right shoulder to the left side of his back, deepening in colour as the flogging continued. After twenty strokes Riley writhed a little but made no sound. After twenty-five, the Provost Sergeant ordered the second corporal to take over. Jack took his gaze from the suffering Riley to examine the men. The veterans, those who had transferred, voluntarily or otherwise, from other regiments looked on without visible expression: they had probably seen worse before. What they were thinking, however, he could not tell; their thoughts and their souls were the only things in their regulated lives over which they had control. The recruits looked shocked, angry or sick; they had not yet learned to control their outward emotions. Three of the youngest fainted; Jack stopped himself from moving forward; the Johnny Raws would have to learn to accept unpleasant sights if they wanted to wear the uniform of Queen Victoria. He focussed on the boy who stood in the second rank from the rear, sandwiched between the Scotsman and Thorpe. He looked very young, very pale and very upset. Jack narrowed his eyes, trying to place him; there was something familiar about that man, and something not right. He was leaning against the Scotsman – was he holding his hand?

Dear God, he was! Jack felt a twist of disgust. He had heard of such behaviour among some of the boys at school although he had never personally encountered it. Jack took a step forward, hesitated and stopped.

The realisation came to him in a mixture of relief, shock and concern. Yes, the Scotsman was holding the boy's hand, but there was nothing improper, or at least nothing immoral about it. That boy was no boy; he was a woman in a man's uniform. That was Charlotte Riley. Dear God! No wonder she had looked upset, watching the ship's corporals flog her husband.

'Punishment complete, sir,' the Provost Sergeant reported.

'Very good; carry on Provost Sergeant. Captain Fleming, take over here. The usual drill.'

Snodgrass replaced his hat, turned on his heel and stomped across the deck, leaving a smell of stale brandy. Charlotte Riley straightened up, her eyes unreadable; only the hatred was evident. Jack wondered how she'd gotten on board and decided not to investigate. One flogging was one too many.

The Provost Sergeant ordered Riley cut down, threw a great coat over his back and escorted him below deck, with the surgeon taking a surreptitious sip from a silver flask. Charlotte Riley watched; behind the moisture, her eyes were like acid. The day's routine continued, with two-thirds of the men filing below decks and Fleming having the others practise musket drill on deck. Until the storm returned.

Jack had crossed the Mediterranean on his long journey to Burma and thought he understood the sea, but the ferocity of the storm took him by surprise. One moment the men were drilling on deck, the next the wind was screaming through the rigging. The brig heeled to port, nearly on her beam ends as waves smashed against the hull and sent hundreds of gallons of lukewarm seawater cascading among the staggering soldiers.

'Get these bloody lobsters out of the way!' Captain Evans pushed Fleming aside as he took his position on the quarterdeck and roared a string of orders that saw bare-footed seamen dodging reeling soldiers and leaping up the ratlines to haul in the straining sails.

'My orders were to drill the men,' Fleming looked even older when he was at sea; he was grey of hair and grey of skin, a man who had given up any hope of career advancement many years before and who followed orders and nothing else.

'You'll be drilling them in Davy Jones' locker then¡Evans shouted. 'If they get in the way of my lads I'll have then thrown overboard!'

Jack saw the confusion cross Fleming's face as he realised he would have to make a decision that ran counter to Major Snodgrass's orders.

'Shall I start getting the men in sir? Before we lose half of them over the side?' Jack thought it an idea to encourage Fleming's thought-making process.

'What?' Fleming stared at Jack, and then glanced at the hatch down which Snodgrass had disappeared.

'Colonel Murphy wouldn't like his men to be washed overboard,' Jack deliberately used rank as a lever.

'The colonel is incapacitated,' Fleming reminded. 'He's bad with consumption.'

'He will recover,' Jack said, 'he's tough.' He staggered as the wind strengthened and altered angle so *Poseidon* bucked madly and the men aloft had to hold grimly on as the masts spun and the yard-arms dipped toward the surging maelstrom of the sea. He saw an entire file of soldiers fall on their side and roll toward the rail. One man slipped over the side and hung on desperately, screaming for help as his feet and legs dangled in the lunging waves.

'Wilkinson!' A soldier stepped forward and then fell as the deck heeled to an impossible angle.

'Hold on!' Jack slid down the ladders and slithered across the heeling deck, grabbing hold of anything he could for support. Captain Evans roared orders that saw the seamen furl every scrap of canvas aloft and the helmsman struggle with the wheel, trying to turn the ship, so her bows faced into the wind.

By that time Jack had reached the man hanging from the rail. 'Hold on!'

'I'm going to fall!' Wilkinson screamed; his eyes were wide with terror, his mouth hanging open, showing rotten teeth.

Reaching forward, Jack grabbed hold of his arm, just as Wilkinson lost his grip and fell overboard.

'Get a rope!' Jack saw Wilkinson's face, mouth wide, saw one hand emerge from the sea in despair, and heard his long wail of anguish. A seaman joined Jack at the rail and tossed a line; he shouted something, his words whipped away by the wind.

'Hold the end of the line!' Jack yelled to the seaman. He poised on top of the rail, saw Wilkinson's head appear and disappear under the sea, and jumped. He landed with an untidy splash, felt momentary panic as he sunk beneath the surface and struck out in what he hoped was the right direction.

From down here the sea was even wilder, the waves higher, curling at the tips as if reaching to haul him down to his death. Jack saw Wilkinson's head bob on the surface of a rising wave, saw his arm lift in either hope or despair and then another wave rose between them, blocking his view. He had a momentary glimpse of the rope dancing on top of the sea, grabbed it and thrust into the sea. He opened his mouth to shout to the soldier, swallowed half a pint of salt water, gagged, tried to swear and coughed instead.

Dear God: am I to drown with nothing achieved?

He rose on the crest of a wave and looked around. *Poseidon* seemed a long way off, her masts spiralling to a ragged sky, her rail lined with white faces and scarlet uniforms. There was no sign of Wilkinson; nothing except the sea, with the wind whipping the surface into a haze of spindrift.

The wave sunk again and Jack shouted, hoping for a reply from the missing man. He heard nothing except the roar and hiss of the sea.

'He's gone, Windrush!' A speaking trumpet distorted Captain Evans' words into a metallic blare. 'Hold onto the rope and...' The wind stole the end of the sentence. Jack held the rope and felt somebody hauling him back to *Poseidon*.

He gasped as he submerged, closed his mouth too late to avoid swallowing seawater and cursed as he slammed against the rough hull with a flesh-ripping thump.

There was a single soldier among the seamen hauling on the rope. The others watched, stone-eyed as he crawled over the rail and collapsed on the deck in a gasping heap. When he looked up the soldier's lips were moving, and then he stepped back and became merely another anonymous face in the amorphous mass of redcoats. Jack recognised him as the private he'd seen reading a book.

'You're a bloody fool, Windrush!' Snodgrass had started his day's drinking. 'You could have drowned out there and for what?'

'To save a man's life, sir,' Jack said.

Snodgrass snorted. 'An officer's life is worth a hundred of a private soldier, especially the scoundrels in this infamous regiment. And you won't get any thanks from them; gratitude is an unknown quantity among the lower orders.'

They stood on the quarterdeck with the dying kick of the storm howling through the rigging and the seamen working aloft.

'They're our men, sir, our responsibility.'

'Did you save him?' Snodgrass asked suddenly.

'No, sir,' Jack said.

'In that case, Windrush, you put your life in danger and nearly cost the regiment an officer shortly before we go on campaign. That is a gross dereliction of duty. I would send you to the colonel if he were not indisposed. As I am acting for him, I will decide your fate; you are orderly officer until we reach Bulgaria or wherever it is we are bound.'

'Yes, sir.' Jack could say nothing else. Instead, he retched and vomited more sea water.

When he scrambled below deck, Jack didn't have to ask who the silent soldier was who stood beside Riley.

'It's all right, Mrs. Riley,' he said softly, 'I know who you are.'

Charlotte emerged from the shadows as Coleman, and the small Scotsman eased aside. 'I'm not doing any harm,' she thrust her chin out stubbornly.

'You are breaking regulations,' Jack said. 'How is your husband?'

'I'm all right sir.' Riley lay on his face on a wooden cot.

Jack looked at his back. The cat had created a livid purple bruise that ran diagonally across his back, with the skin broken in half a dozen places. 'What did the doctor say?'

'I'll be back on duty in two days,' Riley said.

'Only if you're fit,' Jack said. 'I am sorry that happened.' He added, *and damn the regulations*. Nodding to Charlotte, he rose to leave.

'I'll kill Snodgrass for that.' The words were low, uttered in a hiss far more menacing than any shout.

'We've seen one hanging in this regiment, Mrs. Riley,' Jack said, 'I don't want to see any more.' He held her eyes until she looked away.

That storm had sent *Poseidon* back a hundred miles, ripped the topsails to shreds and damaged the rigging. Jack swore in frustration as Captain Evans seemed to take as long as possible to make the necessary repairs and *Poseidon* wallowed in a greasy swell. When they did sail again, Evans realised that that salt water had contaminated the fresh water, so called at Piraeus, the port of Athens for more. There were days of negotiating the price, haggling between Evans and Snodgrass over who was liable to pay for the thousands of gallons and when they sailed again, they hit more bad weather.

'We're cursed,' Elliot said as *Poseidon* threaded her way through the Aegean, dodging squalls and islands. 'By the time we get to the war all the fighting will be over.' He nearly overbalanced as the vessel lurched to port, but the bulkhead of the cabin saved him.

'That's something to be grateful for,' Snodgrass said. He nodded forward. 'These men will run, again.'

Elliot straightened up, winced as one of the hanging lanterns swung against his head and sat back down again. 'Anything's better than this blasted ship! We must be weeks behind all the other regiments!'

Jack nodded. He shared Elliot's frustration. With no money behind him, he couldn't purchase promotion so only some desperate act in battle could help him advance. Ever since he was commissioned into the 113th Jack knew he had three options; gain promotion to a much higher rank; transfer from the regiment into a more distinguished unit – or try to raise the reputation of the most ill-regarded regiment in the British army. The first was virtually impossible; nearly every officer promotion in the British Army was by purchase, and he was dirt-poor. The alternative was to perform some ludicrous act of heroism in full view of higher ranked officers, which meant virtual suicide as British officers were expected to be recklessly brave. The other options were equally improbable; no other regiment would welcome an officer from the infamous 113th while raising the reputation of a regiment meant its participation with distinction in a series of hard-fought actions. Higher command did not trust this regiment to stand and fight so would not even allow it into battle.

With the storm abated and *Poseidon* battering through seas that were only choppy, Jack again slipped below.

'How is Riley?'

'He'll be fine,' O'Neill sounded guarded.

'I'll speak to him.' Jack rose and pushed his way through the crowd, coughing in the foul air. He saw Charlotte's face, and then she vanished behind a screen of soldiers. The small Scotsman stood in front of her, pugnacious, almost challenging him to interfere.

Riley greeted him with a wry smile. 'I'm all right, sir. I had worse at school.'

'At school? What sort of school did you attend?' Jack saw a veil replace the smile.

'Nothing special,' Riley's accent deliberately roughened as he spoke.

In Jack's experience, only two types of school would treat a boy in such a manner; the schooling ordered by a judge or the public schooling of Eton, Winchester or the like. Riley's accent and education argued for the latter. Gentlemen-rankers were not unknown in the Army, typically men fleeing from gambling debts or sexual scandals. Riley did not seem like a man foolish enough to gamble.

'You can tell me sometime,' he said. 'Look after Mrs. Riley, will you? Not many women would travel in a troopship.'

He didn't ask about matters of decency or privacy. That was not his concern. He only hoped they would reach Bulgaria or wherever they would fight the Russians. However, Jack's frustration grew further when *Poseidon* eventually did reach Varna. It was the fifth of September, and the army had already left. The roadstead was empty; the army had already gone.

'What the devil do we do now?' Jack asked.

Chapter Four

Black Sea
September 1854

'We ask for sailing orders,' Captain Evans said.

'Will we ever get to this blasted war?' Elliot asked.

'Once you do, Elliot,' Snodgrass said seriously, 'you will almost certainly wish that you had not.'

With the young officers openly bemoaning their bad luck, Captain Evans returned to *Poseidon* and sailed fifteen miles north to Balchik Bay. They arrived just as dawn was breaking from the sea to the east, sending shafts of rosy light onto the ships that rode at anchor.

'Painted ships upon a painted ocean,' Jack misquoted Coleridge as he stared overboard.

'Dear Lord in heaven; there's a sight for the eyes to behold,' Elliot said.

Even the prospect of incurring the wrath of Major Snodgrass could not prevent the officers from crowding into the bows. Warships and transports of all sizes and descriptions filled the bay. With paddles churning the sea into a creamy froth, merchant paddle-steamers attached tow ropes to the bulky Indiamen that held the troops and eased them into five distinct lines. Smoke lay in a greasy black pall above black-painted hulls, obscuring masts and clinging like mist to topsails and royals.

'I've never seen so many ships at the one time,' Elliot said.

'Not many people have.' Even Fleming sounded impressed. 'There must be hundreds here, three, maybe four hundred ships.'

'British maritime power,' Elliot sounded proud. 'And filled with the cream of the British Army, all sailing to somewhere to defeat the Russians.'

'I wonder where that somewhere is,' Haverdale said. 'We've been out of touch with anybody for so long the war could be over, and we might be sailing home.'

'Oh, don't say that!' Elliot nearly wailed.

Watching and protecting everybody were the grim guardians of the Royal Navy, silent and professional as they shepherded the merchant vessels and patrolled the edges of the fleet with their gunports closed, but crews agile and ready for instant action.

'I thought I had seen an army when we invaded Burma,' Jack said, 'but it was nothing compared to this.'

'Look at that.' Fleming pointed to something that floated in the water. Jack looked and shuddered. It was a man's head and upper torso, bobbing up and down in the wake left by the scores of paddle-steamers. As he watched he saw another, and then another; heads and bodies and body parts bouncing on the waves.

'What the devil…?' Jack wondered.

'Don't ask me,' Elliot said.

'There's something wrong here,' Jack said softly. 'Something has happened: maybe there was a battle with the Russians when we were swanning around the Med.' The frustration at being cut off from news for so long built up within him. 'What the devil is going on?'

'I think we're about to find out,' Elliot pointed to an eight-oared gig that approached them.

'*Poseidon* ahoy!' The hail came from a smartly-uniformed naval officer in the stern. 'You're a bit behind time are you not?'

'We had problems.' Captain Evans replied through the speaking trumpet. 'What's happening? Where are we headed?'

'We're going to bell the cat!' The naval officer balanced easily despite the crazy rocking of his gig. 'We're all off to the Crimea to destroy Sebastopol.'

'What happened? There are bodies all over the sea. Was there a battle?'

'Cholera!' the lieutenant said happily. 'It followed us from Varna; it's killing hundreds of the lobsters. We're much safer at sea!'

'Oh, sweet God in heaven – cholera!' Captain Fleming stepped back from the rail as if the disease would rise from the sea and board *Poseidon*.

'Where is our station?' Captain Evans asked.

'What's your cargo?'

'The 113th Foot.'

There was a pause as the lieutenant signalled the information in a flurry of flags.

'Here we go,' Fleming said, 'he'll order us back to Malta or even England.'

'Take station to the rear of the convoy,' the lieutenant eventually ordered. 'And wait for orders.' The gig turned in an impressive display of nautical skill and surged away with the lieutenant sitting in the stern sheets and the oars rising and falling in perfect unison.

'Take station in the rear,' Snodgrass said sourly. 'The only place that the 113th should be.'

Evans had not waited for Snodgrass to speak; the seamen were already altering the set of the sails.

For the remainder of that day, they remained in Balchik Bay, acutely aware of the periodic splashes as one ship or another added to the corpses in the water. Jack was thankful when night came, ending the sights of bobbing bodies. The memories of the dancing, grinning heads remained, yet at least he was soldiering, he was no longer acting the spy. He put that episode of his life in a compartment in his memory and firmly closed the lid.

As pink dawn tinged the eastern sky on the seventh of September, the fleet sailed in a flurry of canvas and the steady chunking of paddle-steamers. At the tail of the convoy, the men on *Poseidon* felt small and insignificant; they were a tiny cog in the machine of war. Jack and Elliot stood on deck watching the line of ships that stretched ahead, smeared with smoke from the steamers as the water was chopped and frothed by the wake of each vessel.

'What a sight,' Jack said.

'Six hundred ships, so I heard.' Elliot's face was animated.

A flurry of flags fluttered from the mastheads of the Royal Naval vessels that led each of the two lines of British ships, stretching a full five miles into the distance.

'Here we go,' Elliot said. 'Off to the Crimea, victory and glory.'

'Oh God I hope so,' Jack said. He saw Fleming's face pale.

They were both wrong. The very next day they rendezvoused with the French fleet off the mouth of the Danube, cast anchor and once again remained static while the army fretted and suffered through disease. Small boats passed to and fro, carrying splendidly attired officers on visits to neighbouring regiments. Nobody came to *Poseidon*.

'We are the pariahs of the army,' Fleming said sourly.

'That's not surprising.' Now even Elliot seemed depressed by the unexpected delay. The hours passed away, with Major Snodgrass becoming increasingly irate and the men more resentful under his authority.

'I'll check the men,' Jack said.

'That's the sergeant's job,' Fleming told him. 'Best not interfere.'

'They're my men,' Jack said as he slipped below, remembering the anger and bitter tension after Riley's flogging.

'Where's the colonel?' O'Neill's voice rose above the hubbub of the packed and stinking troop's accommodation. 'Where's Colonel Murphy?'

'He'll be back when he's fit,' Jack didn't know the answer.

'I'll swing for that Major Snodgrass,' Thorpe touched a hand to his bayonet.

'You'd be better to make sure your kit is clean,' Jack decided to ignore the threat. 'Major Snodgrass is holding an inspection in half an hour.'

'Another bloody inspection?' O'Neill opened his mouth to say more until Jack interfered before he got himself into trouble.

'And you'd better be ready for it; we don't want the French showing us up, yet alone the other regiments.' Jack looked around the deck; many of the men were staring at him. 'You men better prepare for the major's inspection too,' he said. More privates were pressing around him, flint-eyed soldiers with no reason to love an officer.

'Officers never come down here,' one sallow-faced man said.

'They know better.' The short Scotsman man pushed himself to the front. His colleagues gave him space.

'Officers stick to their own place,' another man spoke; he had a tanned face and a broken nose, with the herculean physique of a railway navigator.

Jack heard the implied threat in the harsh voices. For the first time, he felt insecure among British soldiers. He straightened himself as best he could under the low deck beams. 'There is nowhere on this ship that an officer cannot go.' He kept his voice mild as if he hadn't noticed the danger.

'No other officer would lower himself by mixing with us,' the bookish private joined them. 'And no other officer jumped into the sea to try and save a private soldier.'

'You were on the rope, hauling me back on board,' Jack spoke in the sudden uneasy silence.

'Trust the Bishop to try and rescue an officer.' The voice came from somewhere in the mass, with a ripple of humourless laughter following.

'I never had the opportunity to thank you.' Jack knew he could not shake the hand of a private soldier, much as he wanted to.

'I was doing my Christian duty,' the Bishop said.

Jack nodded. 'Thank you.' He raised his voice. 'You men make sure you are ready for the inspection. We will be landing in the Crimea soon, and we must all be at our best. Major Snodgrass has been trying to ensure we're fit to fight the Russians. You and I and everybody in the regiment must help the major to make us the finest regiment in the army.'

Jack had not expected rapturous applause for his speech, but he hoped for something better than total silence. 'I'll leave you in peace to prepare.'

As he stepped away, he thought it best to ignore the short, cynical laugh.

'Calamity Bay? Who the devil chose that as a place to land?' Elliot lifted his face to the sun. 'But what a glorious morning.'

'It's Calamita, not calamity,' Fleming said pedantically. 'Get your men ready; we are the last of the infantry to disembark of course; we spoil the look of the place.'

There was an eerie atmosphere as the British Army left the ships and rowed or sailed onto the beach. Although the armies of the Honourable East India Company had massive experience in campaigns all across that sub-continent and there had been wars in South Africa and China, it was the first time in forty years that British soldiers had fought a European war. Most of this army had never faced an enemy or tested themselves in battle; nobody knew how they would act.

'This is nothing like the Irrawaddy.' Thorpe displayed his military experience as he stood at *Poseidon*'s rail watching the army slowly fill the beach. 'We had to work in the tropical heat, not on a beautiful autumn day.'

'Look at the officers,' Jack recognised the harsh Scottish accent. 'What a pack of prancing peacocks!'

Jack couldn't fault the description. Dressed in full dress uniform including their swords, the groups of officers were conspicuous as they watched their men file ashore. 'No packs for the men either; they look terrible.' Gaunt and shaking, the infantry moved slowly, more like men convalescing from a prolonged hospital visit than soldiers at the very beginning of a campaign.

'That's what cholera does,' Snodgrass sounded more controlled than normal. 'We've been cursing the slowness of the voyage, but it saved us from being infected with cholera.'

'Well done the 113th,' Jack said softly.

'Maybe our luck is not all bad, then,' Elliot added.

'There's the Russians now.' Captain Evans pointed a long telescope to the cliffs, half a mile or so beyond the landing site. All at once half a dozen more telescopes focussed on the spot, with Snodgrass lifting a pair of field glasses.

'Cossacks,' he said. 'I think. Horsemen anyway; scruffy-looking scoundrels.'

It was a long five minutes before Jack could borrow a telescope. He saw an officer in a bottle-green uniform surrounded by a group of shaggy horsemen with long lances.

'They look a handy bunch,' he said. He mentally compared them with the Burmese cavalry he had met. 'If they had any artillery, they could sweep us off the beach before we get established.'

'Luckily they haven't,' Snodgrass said.

'I wish we were ashore,' Elliot said. 'We could take a company up the cliff and push these Ruskies off!'

Snodgrass snorted. 'Our blackguards would have one look at them and run away.'

The rain began in mid-afternoon, with water-parched men lifting open mouths to the skies and the troops ashore huddled in sodden misery without shelter. What started as heavy rain soon worsened to a storm that swept over the British Amy, adding discomfort to cholera-weakened men and multiplying the number who dropped in sickness and death onto the soil of the Crimea.

'Thank God for a nearly dry ship,' Coleman jerked a thumb toward the land. 'We've been lucky once again.'

'The gods of war are smiling on the good old 113th,' Riley said quietly. 'And only God can help us if they should ever frown.'

The good old 113th? Jack had never heard it called that before. Either Riley was developing sarcasm, or there was the beginning of some regimental pride among the men, whatever the officers thought. He looked over the privates yet again – there was more to them than some of the officers realised. With some nurturing and a couple of successes, they might develop into an adequate regiment.

It was not until the early morning of the 19th September that the commanders permitted the 113th to land, the last infantry unit of the fleet to set foot on Russian soil. What they walked into shocked Jack. From the sea, the army had looked sickly enough, but once on land, he realised that there were already hundreds of sick and dead as exposure, dysentery and cholera continued their ravages.

'What the devil has happened here?' Elliot stopped at a pile of stores that lay abandoned just above the beach.

'There's no transport to carry them,' a laconic artillery officer told him. 'Wellington would have a fit if he was here.'

'What turmoil,' Jack said, 'but at least we are here; the 113th is part of a major British army in a war with a European power.' He looked around, feeling a surge of unexpected pride.

'Are all wars like this?' Elliot looked in horror at a man thrashing in the final agonies of cholera.

'Probably,' Jack said. 'Maybe the 113th isn't the best regiment in the army, but Lord Raglan has undoubtedly made a complete shambles of this landing.'

Hard by the shore, the French were already waiting in formation, with bands playing and flags flying, while inland the green-uniformed men of the Rifles and hard-worked cavalry guarded the British flank.

'Where are we positioned, sir?' Jack asked as Murphy made his appearance among the men. Stick-thin, he looked as if he needed help to sit on his horse.

'With the Fourth Division.' Murphy sounded hoarse.

'Glad to have you back, sir,' Jack said.

Murphy nodded. 'I had a recurrence of fever. It's been in my bones since India.' He didn't mention his consumption. 'Major Snodgrass, take us to the rear of the army, please.'

'The rear sir? Are we the rearguard?' There was a hint of pleasure in Snodgrass's voice.

Murphy shook his head. 'No, Major. The Fourth Division is tidying the camp and taking care of the sick. We are burying the dead and following the army to collect the stragglers.'

Snodgrass took a deep breath. 'Yes sir; of course we are.'

When at last the allied army marched, the sun was halfway to its zenith, pummelling the men beneath. Jack watched them go, the red-coated men already staggering under six days rations of biscuits and four days of meat, with greatcoat and blanket, rucksack and water keg and heavy Minié rifle.

'God, I wish we were with them,' Elliot said.

'We must do as the general commands.' Fleming sounded so relieved that Jack wished to upset him.

'Maybe the Russians will attack us, as the weakest part of the army.' He tried to sound casual. 'There were Cossacks on the heights when we landed. Perhaps they are gathering now, waiting to sweep us back into the sea.' He stopped when he saw the look of fear that crossed Fleming's face.

'Lieutenant Preston, take a score of men and guard the flank.' Murphy looked around the confusion that the army had left behind. 'We better get this blasted mess cleaned up. I want the dead buried and the sick taken on board the ships to sail back to Scutari.' He swayed slightly and shook away Jack's steadying hand. 'I'm all right, damn it! Go and find some transport to carry these poor fellows.'

'Yes, sir.' The allied armies had managed to march about half a mile in half an hour, leaving a scattering of sick, British and French, lying behind them. Already some of the men were jettisoning their equipment, with packs, shakos and even a water bottle lying on the ground. The only wagons Jack saw were in the hands of the French. 'How many men do I have, sir?'

Murphy put a hand on Jack's shoulder as he swayed again. 'You can have thirty. I want you to bring in the dead and bury them. Once that's done find a wagon to collect all the equipment that the army is dropping all over the place.'

'Yes, sir.'

'Corporal O'Neill!' Jack shouted, 'I need a wagon.'

'Very good, sir.' O'Neill waited for a moment. 'Where do you suggest I get one, sir?'

'I'm sure you can find one, corporal.'

O'Neill looked around. 'Maybe it would be best after night, sir.'

Jack hid his sour grin. 'I think we understand each other, O'Neill. Now let's get these poor fellows buried.'

By dusk, they had dug over a hundred graves, carried over a hundred bodies and placed them as carefully as they could beneath the ground. Every so often, Jack borrowed a telescope and examined the countryside around, spending time studying the nearby French camp. 'They do things differently from us,' he said quietly, 'and so much better.'

'Are you ready, sir?' O'Neill headed a small group of privates. Jack recognised Coleman and the small Scotsman with his bitter-eyed companions. 'I've got some good lads here.'

'Names?' Jack asked.

'Logan,' the Glasgow man slurred and winced as O'Neill rammed a hard finger into his ribs.

'You say 'Sir' when speaking to an officer.'

'Logan, sir.'

'Ogden, sir,' the broken-nosed Hercules said at once.

'Hitchins, sir,' the sallow-faced man's accent rolled from the Shropshire hills.

'You men are under my direct command,' Jack said. 'If there are any questions asked about what we were doing, you say that you were following orders. Is that understood?'

They nodded, careless of authority.

'And if you let us down,' O'Neill said, 'I will personally rip your head from your body.'

'What are we doing, corporal?' Ogden asked.

'We are adding to the supply column of the British Army,' O'Neill told him grandly.

'This way, men.' Jack took a deep breath and headed inland, stepping through what only two days ago had been flower-bedecked plain but was now a rutted, stinking morass.

'Sir,' O'Neill spoke in a low whisper. 'Have you done this sort of thing before?'

Jack shook his head.

'It might be best if we took the lead, sir.' O'Neill looked over his shoulder at the privates who grumbled behind them. 'I chose these boys myself. They know what they're about.'

Jack nodded. 'On you go then, O'Neill. I don't want any slip-ups to ruin the operation, particularly not by me!' He stepped aside and allowed the privates to move forward.

'Where the hell are you going?' A sentry challenged them.

'That's where the hell are you going, sir,' O'Neill corrected. 'We have an officer with us.'

The sentries watched them hurry into the gathering gloom, with O'Neill leading and his eclectic collection following. For the first time in the campaign, Jack felt the tension he'd experienced in Burma when he was outside the security of the British lines. He felt the pull of the open spaces to his left, knowing that the whole Crimean Peninsula stretched beyond him, and then the appalling size of the Steppes. Only God and the Czar knew how many Russians were marching down on the disease- ravaged allied army. He shivered as he thought of the vast spaces of Russia and the armies that had failed to conquer it before. Now it was Britain with her tiny, mismanaged forces and over-dressed, gentlemanly but bumbling commanders, and France – her ally – who were invading this vast nation with her intense national pride and mysterious depths. The prospect was suddenly appalling.

'Sir.' O'Neill's soft voice disturbed Jack's reverie, and he came back to reality. He had been walking instinctively toward the bonfires that silhouetted the dim shapes of tents and the shuffle of moving men.

'Bloody Frogs,' Coleman grumbled. 'Trust them to have tents.'

'Coleman, you and Hitchins go left and make a noise.' O'Neill gave quick orders. 'You know what to do.'

Jack watched the two privates obey; within a minute there was the click of metal on stone and a soft grunt.

'*Qui va la?*' One of the French called.

There was a low moan, and two French soldiers moved forward. For one second, firelight glinted on wickedly long bayonets, and then the French vanished beyond the periphery of the light and into the dark.

'In we go, boys.' O'Neill led them into the French camp, keeping to the shadows and moving as confidently as if they belonged there.

'On the right side,' Jack murmured. He stopped as a group of Zouaves walked past, distinct in brilliant baggy silk pants below their tunics and rakish fezzes above. 'Here we are, men.'

Local to the Crimea, the *araba* wagons were heavy and cumbersome, but far better than nothing. Some had solid wheels; some were half covered like the prairie schooners of the American West. They were arranged in long, neat lines and watched over by a dozen lounging guards wearing long coats.

'Here, sir,' Coleman appeared from the dark. He passed over a Zouave tunic, scarlet trousers and fez. 'There's one for you too, corporal.'

'Well done, Coleman.' Jack slipped the tunic on. It was tight across his shoulders. 'Keep close men and keep quiet.' He removed his forage cap and donned the fez, finally slipping the baggy silk trousers over his own and barely sparing a thought for the unfortunate French soldiers who had to endure the chill of the night undressed and uncomfortable.

Feeling a lot less confident than he hoped he appeared, Jack stepped forward into the wagon park, nodded to the sentries, and threaded his way through to the far side, where a hundred or more horses were tethered nose to nose in two long lines.

'Any of you men know anything about horses?'

'I do, sir.' Hitchins sensibly kept his voice low. 'I was a ploughman.'

'And a poacher, eh, Hitchie?' Coleman added.

'Good man.' Jack ignored Coleman's contribution. 'You and I will select the best horses then. These are two-horse wagons, so I want eight horses; sufficient for two wagons plus spare horses.'

Hitchins nodded. 'Very good sir.' He hesitated. 'If you don't mind me saying, sir; these are two-horse wagons, but one horse can manage them, sir, when they are unladen.'

'Do you know about the arabas?' Jack tried to hide his surprise.

'I know nothing about Arabs, sir. I know about wagons though.'

About to explain that the wagons were called arabas, Jack closed his mouth. 'What are you suggesting, Hitchins?'

'We can take more horses than eight, sir, if you want them.'

'How many can you get?'

Hitchin shrugged. 'As many as you wish, sir.'

'Twenty?' Jack plucked a number from the air.

'All right, sir. Who is getting the wagons, sir?'

'Corporal O'Neill will do that.' Jack saw that O'Neill already had the men organised and was selecting the two most robust vehicles.

'Spoked wheels now,' O'Neill said, 'it gives a lighter ride, and for God's sake try and find wagons with some suspension. These things will be carrying wounded men.'

'Carry on, O'Neill.' Jack left him to it while he and Hitchins stepped to the horses' lines.

They moved among the animals, looking at teeth, coats and legs, with Hitchins sighing and cursing in turn. 'Some poor-quality rubbish here, sir.'

Hitchins didn't try to disguise his disapproval. 'Trust the Frenchies to steal everything first and have no idea about horseflesh.'

'Select the best, Hitchins and keep your voice down.'

'Do you know about horses, sir?'

'I've been riding since I could walk,' Jack said and closed his mouth. He had to keep distance between himself and the other ranks. He was their officer, not their friend.

'*Qui est ce?*' The challenge rang out loud across the restless horses.

'Ami!' Jack thought it best to answer at once. He didn't want a nervous sentry firing a shot and starting a battle. Stepping forward, he allowed the French to see his uniform. What was the penalty for an officer stealing from an ally? Probably cashiering at least, plus a hefty jail sentence.

'They're loose, sir.' Hitchins whispered in broad Shropshire. 'Eighteen of the best.'

'Wait until this Frenchy has gone.'

'The wagons are ready.' Logan kept back from the horses. 'If that thing kicks me, I'll do for it!'

'It's harmless, Logan,' Jack said, 'as long as you watch for the hooves and teeth. Keep your voice down! There's a Frenchman just over there.'

Logan glanced over. 'Do you want me to do for him, sir?'

'No, I want you to keep quiet!'

'*Qui est ce?*' The Frenchman repeated, louder. He shouted something else, and two more French soldiers joined him.

'Here's trouble.' Logan sounded happy at the prospect. His right hand strayed inside his tunic.

'Keep quiet and keep your heads down!' Jack hissed. *What was best to do? Keep still and hope the French walked away? Or try to bluff them?*

He realised that neither was possible as the French approached. There was a dozen of them in the long blue coats of line infantrymen, some fitting bayonets with ominous clicks and all talking, gesticulating and very dangerous.

'Come on, you bastards,' Logan muttered, pulling his bayonet from underneath his tunic.

They came from two sides, yelling loudly and probing with their bayonets. Hitchins was first to run, with Ogden close at his heels. 'Come on, sir.' O'Neill tapped Jack on the shoulder. 'There's no reasoning with men in that mood.'

'You too!' Jack hauled Logan back as he glowered at the French, muttering curses and threats.

'They're in front of us as well,' O'Neill shouted as another surge of Frenchmen cut them off from any retreat.

'Run!' Hitchins yelled, high-pitched.

'Which way?' Ogden asked.

Jack felt a flicker of something like panic. This situation was worse than facing the Burmese – then he had been a soldier doing his duty, and he could legally shoot his way out of trouble. Here he was breaking every law known to man, looting from an ally. If the French caught him, he could expect only disgrace; worse, he had led his men into a situation where they faced the cat. The best he could do was to give himself up and say his men were following his orders.

Jack stopped running and stood upright. 'Gather around me, men.'

'We'll fight the bastards,' Logan flourished his bayonet, apparently prepared to take on an unknown number of Frenchmen for whatever reason.

'No, we won't.' Jack pushed his hand down. 'Put that away, Logan. The French are not our enemies.'

The sudden clamour came from the northern fringe of the French lines, accompanied by one shot, then two, then an irregular crackle of musketry. A bugle called, and then another and the French soldiers turned away.

'The Russians have attacked,' O'Neill said. 'Saved by the Ruskies!'

For a moment Jack wondered if he should lead his men to help the French, but common sense told him that his handful, minus their muskets, would be more hindrance than help.

'Hitchins, get these horses back; hitch them onto the wagons. I want four wagons. O'Neill, Ogden, help him. Logan, you and I are the guards.'

The shooting intensified, coming closer as the unseen Russians pressed forward their attack. Jack flinched as a stray musket ball zipped past him to bury itself in the dirt a yard away, then he swore as one of the horses emitted a high pitched scream.

'The bastards are after the horses,' Hitchins raised his voice. 'Bloody Russian brutes!'

'Keep working,' Jack shouted, 'never mind the shine!'

More musket balls whined around them while the acrid reek of burned gunpowder tingled their nostrils. Unsettled by the noise and despite all Hitchins' efforts to calm them down, the horses were panicking.

'That's two wagons hitched, sir!' Hitchins shouted, 'I'm working on the third...'

The sudden surge of men took Jack by surprise. He looked up as a body of French infantry ran past him, with one or two throwing away their weapons in their urgency to escape. Behind them was a troop of Russian cavalry, dimly seen in the intermittent light of the camp-fires. Jack saw bearded men with shaggy hats, long lances or long straight swords, riding hard through the French lines.

'Hurry it up, men!' he shouted, 'The Russians have broken through.'

'That's three wagons ready,' Hitchins yelled. 'One to go!'

'Leave it,' Jack said. ''We'll settle for three. Get out of here!'

The Russian cavalrymen were slashing right and left, hacking at the running French, doing what cavalry were intended to do. Jack lifted a musket from the ground, hauled back the hammer and levelled it. If any of the cavalry threatened his men, he would fire. Otherwise, he would not draw Russian attention.

A movement amidst the cavalry caught his eye. Three men had stopped, with the light from a campfire flickering over them. Two were apparently officers, tall men shouting orders. The third wore a darker uniform, but Jack instantly recognised his face. He was broad in the shoulders with a neat blonde moustache.

'What the devil!' For a second Jack had him in the sights of his musket and pondered pulling the trigger. The last time he had seen that man had been in Dar-il-Sliem in Malta. What the deuce was Stevensen doing as part of a Russian cavalry unit in the Crimea?

'Sir!' O'Neill shouted.

Jack glanced over his shoulder. O'Neill was gesticulating to him. 'We're ready, sir!'

When Jack looked back at the Russians, the group of officers had moved, and he couldn't see Stevensen.

'Sir!' O'Neill sounded desperate.

A bugle sounded shrilly and a formation of French infantry moved forward, fired a volley and advanced against the cavalry. All around Jack's men the horses were panicking; the French fired again, the muzzle flares bright against the dark, the sound of their musketry loud and the clouds of powder smoke drifting in an acrid haze. For an instant, Jack saw Stevensen once more, his figure steady amongst the prancing horsemen, his sword raised. Slightly behind him rode the tall man with the eye-patch.

'The French have the situation well in hand,' Jack said, 'let's go, men!'

Chapter Five

Crimea
September 1854

'You say that there was a renegade Englishman with the Russians?' Colonel Murphy frowned across his desk. Unlike the men, he had set up a tent for himself, with the Colours in their cases behind him.

'He is distinctive sir; he's tall and wears an eye-patch. Not the sort of fellow you could lose in a crowd.'

'You tangled with a renegade Englishman in Burma if I recall, Windrush. It would be a bit of a coincidence if you met another here.'

'Yes, sir.' Jack hesitated. 'He might not be English, sir. He may be a colonial – Australian perhaps.'

Murphy pushed himself erect. 'I see; thank you Windrush. You brought back three wagons and seventeen horses I hear. I only expected one araba and a pair of horses.' He nodded. 'That was good work.'

'We were lucky sir. If the Russians hadn't raided, we would have been caught.'

'In the Army, Windrush, luck matters as much as bravery or skill. I'd prefer a lucky officer over an unlucky one.' Murphy nodded. 'The Russians were raiding for prisoners. They captured a French officer.'

'Would that be for information, sir?'

'I presume so, although there is no knowing the Russian mind. They are as much Oriental as Occidental.' Murphy turned aside to cough. 'I'll pass on your intelligence to General Cathcart. He commands the 4th Division, as you know.'

He wiped the back of his hand across his mouth. 'Now get your men ready; we are following the army today.'

'Are we going to Sebastopol, sir?'

'I hope so, Windrush, I certainly hope so.'

Jack looked through the open tent flap; discarded packs and equipment littered the path of the advancing Allies, with the occasional dead, sick or exhausted man lying supine. Inland, smoke soiled the brightness of the autumn morning.

Murphy nodded. 'Yes, Windrush. The Russians are burning all the farmhouses and destroying everything that could be useful to us. They're using the same scorched-earth tactics they employed against Bonaparte.'

'Yes, sir, but we won't be advancing as deeply into Russia as the French did.'

'Nor do we have as many men,' Murphy said quietly. He looked at the neat line of graves dug by the 113th. 'Pray for a short war, Windrush. I don't think we can stand a long one.'

Beyond the muddy river, the Heights rose before them, steep and smooth and deceptively lovely. It was twelve o'clock on the 20th September, with birdsong sweetening the bright morning air, audible even above the slither and thud of thousands of boots through the grass and sheaves of newly harvested wheat, the clatter and chink of cavalry harness and the martial sounds of military bands. From somewhere ahead came the barking of dogs. When the allied army crested a small ridge which looked down upon the valley of the Alma, they halted to eat while the commanders discussed their next move.

'Lunch?' Coleman's voice was distinct through the ranks.

'Of course, don't you know?' Riley affected an even more educated drawl than normal. 'The generals must all eat before sending the men to slaughter the enemy. Port and brandy and chicken for the officers, stale water and bone and gristle for the men, God help us.'

Jack stood on a small knoll and surveyed the valley. Gentle but heavily wooded slopes descended on both sides of the river, partially masking the recently-deserted villages of Almatomak on the right and Bourliouk in the centre. Jack ran the names around in his head; they sounded flat, ugly – without any character. Like everything else in this God-forsaken country. He scanned the slopes on the opposite side of the Alma; there were dark patches of some vegetation about half way up and no sign of a civilian population. The Russian scorched earth tactics were working. For a moment he wondered if a Russian officer was watching him right now, focussing the lens of his telescope on him and planning his imminent death.

'There must be thousands of them waiting for us!'

Jack had not noticed Captain Haverdale struggle up the knoll, panting for breath as he eased his protuberant belly before him. 'Can you see them, youngster?' Haverdale passed his telescope over and pointed, 'about halfway up the hill?'

Rather than vegetation as Jack had believed, the dark patches were Russian infantry, rank upon rank, thousands upon thousands of fighting men in solid phalanxes, with the powerful sunlight now reflecting from a myriad bayonets, buckles and badges.

'I can see them.' Jack's heartbeat quickened; this was nothing like hammering at stockades in Burma or chasing dacoits through the jungle. This was a real war, European style; the meeting of massed armies in open battle. Honest, honourable, bloody – the kind of warfare he had dreamed of as a boy.

'Can you see them?' Haverdale's voice was as tired as his face. He coughed, twice, and looked up. 'Now look in front of the infantry.'

Jack did so. At first, he saw nothing, until Haverdale murmured advice in his ear and he focussed his attention and saw the long snouts of cannon behind stout defensive walls.

'Jesus!' There were two earthwork redoubts a short distance apart and about halfway down the forward slope of the Heights. As he focussed the lens, he saw the barrels of a dozen cannon in the nearer redoubt, with infantry massed on either side. The slopes in front of each stronghold had been cleared of trees so that any infantry advancing to attack would be utterly exposed. While the Allies had been marching to lively music and dropping with cholera, the Russians had prepared to meet them with blood, iron and massed artillery.

'I hope Lord Raglan has something planned,' Jack said. 'That's a strong position the Russians have there.'

Haverdale's grunt was as cynical as anything Jack had ever heard. 'Don't expect anything clever from Raglan; or from any other British general.'

'The Duke of Wellington was a genius…' Jack began, but Haverdale interrupted.

'The Duke of Wellington is dead,' Haverdale said 'and we can't live in his shadow forever. Raglan is a fool. There he is, talking to the Froggy general; what was his name?'

'St. Arnaud,' Jack said.

'If you say so; don't know why they are bothering to talk. Raglan will just go for a frontal attack and trust to the bayonet and the bravery of the soldiers. Damned fool.'

'He'll need the 113th then,' Jack said. 'When will he call for us?'

'You know better than that.' Haverdale's tone hardened. 'They don't want us there. They don't trust us and who can blame them after Chillianwala.' He shrugged, 'Anyway, let somebody else take the casualties.'

Elliot broke in. 'But we need the glory to get the regiment's reputation back...'

'There's no glory, youngster.' Haverdale took off his cap and wiped sweat from his bald head. 'There's no glory in war: just blood and hardship and sordid death.' He glanced at Jack. 'You were in Burma, Windrush; you know something of the reality.'

Jack looked at the tens of thousands of allied infantry forming up and the formidable Russian positions on the far side of the River Alma. 'Nothing like this, sir. I was at the attack on Rangoon and the siege of Pegu, but the numbers were penny-packets compared to this.'

Haverdale grunted. 'Nobody outside the Indian Army has seen numbers like this since Waterloo,' he said. 'We're witnessing history; God help us. Three major powers, four if you include the Turks, all battling it out over some tom-fool dispute that nobody cares a damn about except the politicians.'

'Something's happening!' Jack tried to keep the excitement from his voice as the allied generals gave orders and gallopers set off along the massed armies. Jack watched enviously as the horsemen moved from regiment to regiment and the British Army began to reform into long lines. The Light Division was on the left, the Second Division on the right, with the First and Third Division in support. The Fourth Division, including the 113th, was at the rear. Despite their recent harrowing experiences of cholera, despite the weakness of many of the men and the disorganisation of the landing, despite their disheartening wait before the campaign began, the scarlet-coated men moved and looked like soldiers. They wanted to fight.

Jack felt a surge of pride. He wished he was there, poised to advance against a brave and stubborn enemy. He had waited all his life for this kind of battle.

'When do we get our orders?' Jack looked down at the 113th. They sprawled in an untidy heap in the rear of the British lines, some flat on their backs with exhaustion, others grouped, talking and smoking. The Bishop was reading his book, Logan, Riley and Hitchins were playing cards, Coleman stared into space while Ogden slept in a crumpled heap. Even further back, behind the Fourth Division, the wives and women of the army were making a din. Presumably, Charlotte Riley was there with the others, plotting her revenge on Snodgrass, or tending to her day-to-day chores.

'When do we join the battle?' Jack looked at the officers; Murphy was slumped against the back of an araba, round-shouldered and old. Snodgrass was erect, concealing a silver flask behind his hand as he gave himself Scotch courage. Fleming looked terrified, and the ensigns were just terribly young, schoolboys out of their depth in this place that would soon be a scene of carnage.

Despite his memories of the battles in Burma, despite the horrors he knew would be unleashed in a few moments, Jack still wanted to be in the attack on the Russian positions. He looked down on the 113th and his own thirty men and wanted to lead them forward, knowing some would die, some would be horribly maimed, but he was a British soldier. He belonged here as he belonged nowhere else. This place, for all its ugly, sordid monstrosity, was home.

'Look at that.' Haverdale pointed to a new-built structure in the rear of the Russian positions. 'Can you see that?'

'I see it,' Jack borrowed the telescope again. 'What is it?'

'That is an observation platform,' Haverdale said. 'So the officer's wives and the high officials from Sebastopol can watch the Russian artillery decimate us.' He lowered his voice. 'It's free entertainment for the civilians.'

Jack nodded. 'I see.' He focussed the telescope on the platform. 'I have never seen a full-scale battle,' he said, 'but what I saw in Burma was gruesome. I would not wish to expose a woman to such sights. Women don't belong in wars.'

Haverdale's laugh was as bitter as anything Jack had ever heard. 'Oh, there speaks a man with no experience of women! They can be every bit as callous as men, young Windrush, and more calculating. If it were in their interests, they would watch the butchery of ten thousand men without turning a hair.' He took the telescope back. 'Just look at them, laughing and joking together and positively drooling at the prospect of seeing our men diced, sliced and slaughtered. What an evil set of she-devils to be sure! Look at that one with the sunbonnet on, quaffing champagne no doubt! Go on, look!' He handed over the telescope.

Jack examined the Russian lines; the Russian left flank was closest to the sea so would be vulnerable to the guns of the Royal Navy if the Admiral deployed them properly. The bulk of the Russians were in the centre, behind a redoubt of some dozen or fourteen cannons, and on the right. Also in the centre ran the road to Sebastopol, which marked the boundary between the British and French armies.

'Can you see her?' Haverdale insisted.

'I was looking at the armies, sir,' Jack said.

'Oh forget the armies; let the generals worry about the armies.' Haverdale pointed to the stand that held the civilians. 'Look at the women and that one in the hat in particular. See? She is beside that fellow with the eye patch.'

'What?' Jack's attention shifted from the formations to the spectators. Ignoring the women, he searched for the man with the eye-patch. 'Dear God; there he is again!' The man was quite distinct, half a head taller than his companions and carrying his telescope. As Jack watched the eye-patch man altered the direction of his gaze, so he looked directly at Jack. They examined each other: English-speaking civilian and British officer across the field when thousands of men were about to face each other in unimaginable slaughter.

'You see her?' Haverdale sounded quite excited.

'I see her,' Jack confirmed. 'Sir, I must speak to the colonel.'

'There is no time, Windrush. Can you not hear the bugle? We're moving!'

'Oh, sweet Lord.' Handing back the telescope, Jack ran down to join his command. The man with the eye-patch would have to wait. He had more important things to do than chase after a one-eyed civilian.

'We have our orders,' Murphy's voice was faint as he sat on his horse. 'We are to move in support of the left flank of the Light Division.' He looked over his men. 'This is our opportunity to prove ourselves, men. Let's make the 113th a regiment that all others aspire to!'

'That man lives in a different world,' Haverdale said. 'We're behind the Highland Brigade with orders not to move forward unless required. Does Colonel Murphy think the Sawnies need our help? They'll massacre anything that moves and then take the bayonet to whatever is left.'

'Right men, form up!' Ignoring Haverdale's cynicism, Jack tried to control his emotions, with excitement and apprehension struggling with fear. Compared to some of these men he was a stripling; compared to others, he was a veteran.

Still in the rear of the army, the 113th marched forward, rank after rank of misfits and hopeless cases. These were men who should be in jail and men who the jail would reject; the scum of the British Army, the maladjusted outcasts of society clad in bright scarlet and sent to face the Queen's enemies.

'Look at them; bought for a shilling a day and Her Majesty should get tenpence change.' Haverdale shook his head. 'God, I hate the thought of this rubbish marching behind me, and we allow them muskets, too.'

Jack looked to his right as they marched, noting the topography of the Heights of Alma, with a sheer cliff near the sea, then a series of ravines allowing access to the hills. Even before the army reached the Heights, they had to descend a slope and cross the river that swept broad and blue and deceptively innocent between them. And all the time under the fire of massed Russian musketry and well-sited Russian artillery.

'I've never seen anything so formidable as that.' Haverdale gave his opinion in a low voice. 'I was through the Peninsula with the 52nd as a young ensign, even younger than you are now, Windrush, and I don't think that Wellington would try a frontal assault on that. Raglan, however, does not have the Duke's perspicacity.'

Jack saw the spurts of white smoke from the Russian batteries a second before he heard the rumble of the cannon.

'They've opened fire!' he said.

Haverdale fumbled for his watch. 'The battle begins at half-past one,' he said. 'May God help us all.'

'We're not spectators here,' Snodgrass shouted. 'Keep marching! You're not watching some blasted theatre show!'

Again, Jack felt the collective change in the 113th as they marched, with officers and NCOs urging the men on and the boots thudding across the rough grass and newly-cropped fields. Jack glanced over his men. The Bishop was staring stolidly ahead, expressionless; Coleman was chewing something, probably tobacco. Logan wore his habitual pugnacious scowl as if he hated the world and all in it; Hitchins looked nervous, as did the muscular Ogden. Thorpe was humming something he recognised. It was one of the songs they had sung in Burma, two years and a lifetime ago… These were his men, his responsibility, and his care.

'They're all lying down!' Thorpe stated the obvious as the Light, and First Division of the British Army took to the ground.

'New tactics,' Haverdale murmured. 'If we all lie down the Russians might copy us, and then we will rise suddenly and take them by surprise.'

'Is that right, sir?' Thorpe said, until the hurtful laughter of Coleman caused him to look away.

Out of range of the Russian cannon, the 113th had an excellent view of the battlefield.

'Make way for the guns!' The shout was loud and clear as a battery of British nine-pounders clattered forward and unlimbered on the left flank of the Light Division. Some men of the 113th cheered as they opened fire, with their lighter calibre guns adding higher pitched cracks to the deeper grumbles of the Russian artillery.

'Look to the right!' Snodgrass shouted and every available telescope trained on the seaward side of the Heights. The French had swarmed up to the Russian left flank but had halted there to wait for artillery, and the Russians had taken the opportunity to move batteries of their guns to counteract the threat.

'We're moving!' Elliot sounded very excited. 'Our lines are advancing!'

Jack watched as the men of the Light and Second divisions rose to their feet and, as the Russian artillery increased their rate of fire, carefully dressed in line, with the officers, on foot or horseback, walking along the ranks as if on parade.

'Look at them go!' Elliot said. 'Oh, how I wish I were with them!'

'Don't we all,' Jack said softly.

Two miles wide and preceded by the green uniforms of the Rifle Brigade, the British Army moved forward in its first European battle since Waterloo. There was a dip to get to the River Alma, and Jack watched as the Rifles plunged down, heedless of the Russian fire. He felt the hesitation in the 113th as men and officers watched the battle unfold. The entire Light Division was now swarming down the slopes, plunging into the vineyards around the village of Bourliouk.

'We'll have that village in a few minutes.' Fleming managed to sound gloomy.

'Look!' Haverdale shook his head. 'What devilry are the Russians up to now?'

Flames were bursting from the houses of Bourliouk as the Russians put torches to the thatch. They must have stuffed each house with straw first, to judge by the speed with which the flames took, and a dense cloud of smoke drifted across the lower slopes.

'It's a smoke screen,' Jack said. 'The Russians have made a smoke screen!'

Hitchins grunted. 'Bloody fools; the wind's about to change. The smoke will blow back in their faces in a minute.'

The British pushed on to the Alma River, the green uniforms of the Rifles ahead of the massed red ranks and already both were taking casualties. Men fell in ones and twos and small groups, their bodies crumpled and sad.

Cannonballs raised tall fountains of water, and musket bullets fell like hail; redcoats and green coated men fell, to float downstream as greasy blood swirled on the surface of the water. A tall officer was first to reach the far bank, and then the Rifles were on the lower slopes of the Heights, climbing the hill known as Kourgane, with the massive defences of the Great Redoubt in front now partially masked by thick powder-smoke.

'Look at the dog!' Coleman pointed ahead, where a greyhound pranced through the open formation of the Rifle Brigade, its sharp barking distinct above the deeper boom of the cannon.

'The silly bugger is chasing the cannon balls!' Elliot had a telescope focussed. 'It thinks it's a game.'

'It will be some blasted game if it gets its fool head blown off,' Haverdale said.

As the artillery blasted at them, the leading men were clambering up the hill and advancing on the Russian positions in a series of scarlet snakes that wrapped around the lower slopes of the Alma Heights.

Then they stopped.

'What the devil?' Elliot asked.

'God only knows,' Jack said.

'At the double!' Murphy's voice sounded, hoarse but determined. 'Now the army is waiting; it is our chance to catch up. Forward the 113th!'

'We're going the wrong way,' Thorpe's voice was quite distinct. 'The Ruskies are over the river, and we're going along it.'

'We're going behind the First division,' Coleman told him. 'So we're out of the way and have a clear field behind us when we run.'

'Oh,' Jack was aware of the pause. 'Are we going to run then?'

'The officers think so.' Riley didn't keep the bitterness out of his voice.

'They're firing! The Rifles are firing!' Elliot's voice rose to a high-pitched squeal as he pointed at what everybody could already see. The Rifles were pushing upward with minuscule puffs of smoke marking where the individual men fired. In front of them the darker-clad Russians withdrew, muskets busy as they retired.

The British artillery was firing in support of the advance as the Light and Second Division strode up behind the Rifles. Jack saw the Russian artillery bowl over man after man; saw great holes torn in the ranks, only for the redcoats to close up as neatly as if they were on parade. Stricken by cholera, weak, tired, hungry and exhausted, the British infantry marched on to a position as well-defended as any they had faced in the Peninsula or India.

'What the deuce…' Haverdale shook his head again as one regiment formed square as if to repel a cavalry attack, then reformed into line and continued the advance. Others halted in the vineyard as the Russian artillery, supported by sharpshooters, made deadly practice of the now-confused British. Regiments merged, some men losing their courage as they sheltered behind the stone walls of the vineyard, others eager to rush forward and close with the Russians.

'They're just a blasted mob,' Haverdale didn't hide his bitterness, 'and they castigate our regiment! Look at them: where is the leadership?'

'The First Division is moving!' Major Snodgrass' sudden shout diverted attention from the battle as both the First and Third divisions also formed into a long double line and began an immaculate march down to the river.

They crossed without breaking formation, with the guardsmen who made up the right flank of the First Division halting as they reached the vineyards.

In front, the massed mob of the Second and Light Division charged out of the smoke and on to the Great Redoubt. The Russian artillery fired, tearing great holes in the ranks, bowling men and files of men over, and then suddenly ceased fire as the British infantry entered the redoubt, colours proudly displayed and with the sun prickling reflections from the tips of bayonets.

'They're running!' Elliot yelled. 'The Russians are running! We've captured the Great Redoubt!'

'We've won,' Snodgrass sounded incredulous.

'Aye,' Haverdale said, 'and the 113th just sat and watched.'

'At least we did not run,' Riley's voice floated from the ranks.

'It's not finished yet, boys!' Colonel Murphy's telescope had never wavered from the battle since the first shot had been fired. 'The Russians are counter-attacking.'

Two ponderous columns of infantry were moving downhill, slowly approaching the disorganised Light Division.

'They're not Russian,' Fleming said. 'They're French. If it were an attack, they would move faster.'

'They're Russian,' Murphy said.

Faced with this massive new force, the Light Division began to withdraw. A sudden lull in the firing brought the shrill bugle call of 'Retire' across the Alma to the 113th, as their cheers abruptly stilled and they watched through rents in the smoke as triumph turned to disaster.

The Scots Fusilier Guards were in the van as a runner reached General Bentinck, begging his support for the retreating Light Division. The Scots Guards surged forward, lost their formation as they scrambled over the vineyards but continued onward while their two sister Guard regiments halted to dress their ranks. As the Scots Guards advanced unsupported, the 23rd Fusiliers in front of them broke and scrambled downhill. Somebody ordered that the 'Fusiliers should retire' and the Scots Fusilier Guards obeyed the order, so there was a confused mass of Guardsmen and Fusiliers withdrawing before the Russian advance.

'What a blasted shambles!' Haverdale said.

On the left flank of the First Division, Sir Colin Campbell's Highland Brigade was moving forward, kilts swishing above the ground and Minié rifles held ready. Campbell rode in front, his cocked hat distinctive above the feather bonnets of his Highlanders.

'I hope we are to follow the Sawnies!' Murphy said.

'Was there a galloper?' Fleming asked. 'Were there any orders?'

'Who needs orders? We're British soldiers: there is the enemy; what should we do but advance toward them?' Snodgrass seemed to have forgotten his contempt for his own regiment.

Murphy looked around. 'Windrush! Ride ahead and inform General Campbell that the 113th is waiting to support the Highlanders.'

Jack started. 'My men—

'Your men have other officers and their NCOs. Give the general my compliments and my message.'

'Yes, sir!' Jack had one last glance at his men. 'Look after them, Elliot,' he shouted, mounted his horse and spurred toward the Highlanders.

Chapter Six

**Alma River
20 September 1854**

Jack had often heard of the Highland regiments; most people reckoned them amongst the best of the British Army, and in his mind, he considered them as nearly equal to the Guards or the Royal Malvens. Today was the first time he'd seen them close up. Expecting mature, bearded warriors of herculean stature as in the novels of Walter Scott, he was surprised to see that save for their exotic uniforms they appeared little different from men in other regiments. The men of the 93rd, the Sutherland Highlanders, looked even younger, if anything, with only a few mature men scattered through the youthful ranks.

General Sir Colin Campbell was the opposite; a man of vast military experience, he had a lined, wrinkled face and the shrewdest eyes Jack had ever seen.

'We're moving forward, Windrush. You'd best stay with us for now, and I will use you as a runner if we need the 113th.'

'Yes, sir.' Jack glanced behind him, where the 113th was forming up.

'Loose cartridges!' Campbell gave the order and the Highland Brigade obeyed. Jack watched as the kilted regiments prepared for war. Then more orders cracked across the brigade.

'With ball cartridge, load!'

The sounds were curiously loud, blotting out the more distant rumble of battle; the rattle of equipment, the soft clicking of the elongated bullets dropping down the barrels of the new Minié rifles and the subdued mutter of conversation. The Highlanders were preparing for their first battle against European opposition since Waterloo, nearly forty years before.

'We are going into battle, men,' Campbell said, 'for most of you it is the first time. Pay no attention to your wounded comrades; let them lie until the bandsmen and stretcher parties come for them. Don't be in any hurry to fire; wait for orders and then aim low. Keep steady and keep silent.' He rode along the front of the men with his wrinkled face concerned. 'The army will be watching you. Make me proud of the Highland Brigade.'

As a psalm arose from the Highlander's ranks, Campbell gave the order to advance. They marched three regiments abreast until they reached the river at a spot where it altered course to the north-east.

'Cross in echelon,' Campbell ordered at once, and Jack watched as the regiments reformed and forded the river one after the other.

'That's the result of months of training, young Windrush,' Campbell said; he looked up as a staff officer galloped up to him. 'Here's the Duke himself.'

Jack watched as Campbell spoke to the Duke of Cambridge about the stalled advance of the Guards. He heard the Duke say, 'There will be a disaster unless the First Division is withdrawn, Sir Colin.'

'No, Your Grace. A disaster is certain if there is a withdrawal.'

When the Duke rode away, Campbell raised his voice. 'It were better that every man of Her Majesty's Guards should lie dead upon the field of battle than that they should turn their backs upon the enemy.' He looked across the battlefield. 'While the Guards recapture the Great Redoubt, Windrush, we will advance in echelon up the east shoulder of Kourgane, take that smaller Russian battery of the Lesser Redoubt and hit the enemy in the flank. Remain at my side in case we need your 113th.'

'Yes, sir.' Jack was unsure whether to feel flattered by the attention or nervous as Campbell pushed his horse in front of the 42nd Foot, the most advanced of the Highland regiments, faced the Russian lines and said calmly and simply, 'Forward, 42nd.'

Jack swallowed hard. This deliberate advance against entrenched European infantry and artillery was unlike anything he had experienced in Burma. He had heard that Campbell had a reputation for methodical, even ponderous movement but there was nothing slow about this advance as he led the Highland Brigade up the flank of Kourgane. They passed the 77th Foot, standing in line, and the 88th Foot, the Connaught Rangers, known as the Devil's Own, a regiment whose reputation for wildness was surpassed only by their fighting ability.

The Rangers had formed square and yelled insults as the Highlanders marched past.

'Let the Scotchmen go on! They'll do the work!'

The Highlanders replied in kind, shaking fists and roaring their high-spirited insults in Gaelic and Lowland Scots. God help the Russians if Campbell unleashed this lot among them. Jack glanced behind him. The Highland regiments remained in echelon, one after the other and except for their response to the Connaught Rangers; they saved their breath for the advance. Jack flinched as the cannon in the Little Redoubt fired, jetting out orange flame and white smoke.

Campbell noticed Jack's reaction. 'Never mind the shine, Windrush. Never let the men see you flinch. You are a British officer; better to die than waver.'

Once beyond the 88th, Campbell sent forward Captain Montgomery with a cloud of skirmishers to clear the ground of any light Russian sharpshooters. 'You stay with me, Windrush. I may yet need the 113th to guard my rear.'

'Yes, sir.' Jack tried not to duck as the Russian battery fired again. Campbell barely spared the Little Redoubt a glance.

'We'll have the beggars out of there in a trice.' Campbell frowned. 'The Guards are in the Great Redoubt: ride ahead, Windrush and remind Montgomery that he has carte blanche to fire at will.'

With one glance behind him, Jack saw the entire Highland Brigade streaming up the slope. Across the river and far in the rear of the fighting, the 113th stood as a solid block of red. 'Yes, sir.' He kicked in his heels and bounded forward to find Montgomery.

'General Campbell's compliments sir, and you are free to fire at will.'

'I know that, dammit.' Montgomery was a long-faced man who looked perfectly at home in the forefront of battle. 'There are the Russians now.'

As the reformed Guards Brigade pushed into the Great Redoubt, the Russians split, with most retreating at speed and a few hundred attaching themselves to a vast Russian column which marched south to counter the Highland Brigade.

'That's the Kazan regiment, I believe.' Montgomery raised his voice. 'Right my lads, there's your target. Shoot them flat!'

'Wait!' A staff officer in finery and panic, rode across the front of the skirmishers. 'Don't fire! They're French!'

'The devil they are!' Montgomery said.

'Na, there's nae mistaking thon devils.' A private of the 42nd raised his Minié without a qualm and fired into the advancing mass of Russians.

'They're French!' the staff officer nearly wailed, but as the other skirmishers opened fire on them, Campbell arrived with the main body of the 42nd.

Jack took a deep breath. After their rapid ascent of the hill, the 42nd were panting; the Russians far outnumbered them, and their supporting regiments were still climbing in the rear. Jack wondered what the 42nd would do. *What would the 113th do? They would either charge, if they had the breath, or halt, form a line and fire a volley. Neither choice was perfect; a charge may not be effective with the men blown by the climb, and after firing, the men would have to reload their rifles, which would allow the Russians time to close.*

Montgomery had no doubt. 'Watch and learn,' he said.

The 42nd neither halted nor charged. With the red hackles bright in their bonnets and bare knees twinkling beneath the dark green of their kilts, they continued to march, presented their rifles and fired without halting. Their cheers rose high, an exultant challenge to the Gods of War, the Czar and anybody else who ever doubted the skill and courage of British infantry in general and the 42nd in particular.

Shocked by such unexpected tactics, the Kazan Regiment flinched. As the Russians were marching in column, only the first few ranks could reply to the murderous fire of the 42nd, and they turned around and retreated.

Jack stared. 'I've never seen troops march and fire at the same time,' he said.

'Neither has anybody else,' Montgomery didn't attempt to hide the pride in his voice, 'but we are the forty-twa, the Black Watch.'

For a moment Jack wished he could instill such confidence and discipline into the 113th, but he knew his men lacked the cohesiveness and the fine officers of the Black Watch.

'Watch your flank, 42nd!' Campbell's voice cut through the jubilation. Jack saw another body of Russian troops emerge from behind a spur of the hill at the side of the Highlanders. If they hit the 42nd like that, they could roll up the regiment and destroy them.

As the left flank company of the 42nd wheeled to face this new danger, the second Highland regiment, the 93rd, came up the hill behind and to the left of the 42nd. Rather than catch the 42nd in the flank, the Russians were themselves caught by the 93rd. Once more, hundreds of Highland bullets ripped into the Russians. This regiment, the Sousdal, fought back. Still outnumbering the

British, they returned fire, so clouds of white powder smoke rolled across the hill and men on both sides fell.

'Stubborn buggers, these Russians,' Montgomery said. 'Keep firing my lads!'

Jack saw the movement first. Dim through the smoke; he saw a further mass of Russians appear beyond the extreme left flank of the 93rd, with cavalry supporting the infantry.

'If that lot take us…' Jack trotted back to Campbell. 'Sir! Shall I bring up the 113th?' He measured the distance his regiment would have to cover. 'We can catch the Russians unaware, sir.'

'Devil take it, man,' Campbell was as calm as if he was walking the streets of his native Glasgow, 'you want to share the glory do you?' He gave a sour grin. 'There will be plenty of fighting for your boys, Windrush, don't you fret. In the meantime, let my Highlanders win their battle.'

The third of the Highland battalions, the 79th Camerons, crested the rise with a cheer and a volley that tore considerable gaps in the Russians. They marched on, alternately cheering and firing, pressing the Russians before them.

'Now there is something you won't see every day,' Montgomery approved.

The sudden rattle of horse equipment caught Jack's attention. Two batteries of horse artillery had forded the Alma and ridden right up the hill. With the horses panting and heaving, the gunners unlimbered and fired straight into the Russians. It was a situation for which the God of battles had created artillery; supporting infantry in the field and with a perfect target of the massed enemy over open sights. Grapeshot and solid balls lambasted the Russians, who were driven back into the shelter of a dip.

'The Russians are running!' The words ran the length of the British line.

For a moment Jack saw the stand in which the Russian civilians had sat. He saw the panic as they realised the Allies had defeated their army and were pushing forward all along the line. The woman who had so captivated Haverdale was on her feet, gathering her parasol and baggage, and only two men remained. One was a broad-shouldered man with a shock of fair hair, the other the tall civilian with the eye-patch. Jack looked at them for a second and then gunsmoke drifted across the field, and he lost sight of them.

'Windrush,' Campbell's voice was rough in his ear. 'My compliments to Colonel Murphy and I will not require the services of the 113th Foot this day.'

Looking around the field, with the dead Russians either lying in heaps or in full retreat and the Highlanders reloading and laughing among themselves, Jack wondered if Raglan would ever require his regiment in this campaign.

Chapter Seven

**Crimea
September 1854**

'You're a lucky beggar,' Elliot said, 'you were involved in the battle while we had to sit here and watch.'

'I never drew my sword or fired a shot,' Jack replied.

'But you were there!' Elliot insisted. 'You were at the most famous victory since Waterloo!'

Jack looked around him. They stood on the Heights of Alma with the debris of battle all around them. To the right, the French were carefully shifting their wounded to covered ambulances that took them quickly to the shore. Less organised, the British carried their injured bodily. Although Colonel Murphy had graciously permitted his three arabas to be used for that purpose, most British casualties jolted on litters.

As night fell the 113th camped on the battlefield, through darkness punctured by the hideous sounds of the wounded groaning in pain and begging for water and the worse sounds that emanated from the men screaming under the surgeon's saw.

'Another day survived,' Coleman sounded satisfied. He moved a Russian corpse to use as a pillow.

'God bless the old 113th,' Thorpe said. 'The army doesn't trust us, so we avoid the battles. We're the safest regiment in the army.'

Jack closed his eyes. That was the last accolade he wished to hear. Battles were hellish things, but he had to try and forge a career, and only the blood sacrifice of brave men would do that. Suddenly he hated this profession he'd chosen, and that his family had chosen for generations. What evil creature had ever devised this terrible game called war?

'A famous victory,' Jack repeated his words of the previous day. He saw one Fusilier, minus an arm and a leg, being rolled carelessly onto a litter. 'Be careful with that man, damn you!' he yelled.

'No point in shouting at them,' Haverdale said. 'They're untrained in that sort of thing. Treat them like beasts, and they will act like beasts.'

'You men of the 113th,' the Duke of Cambridge rode up, 'I want you to dig graves for the dead. Bury them.'

'Yes, Your Grace,' Murphy said. His face was unreadable as the Duke wheeled his horse and rode away.

'There we go now,' Snodgrass said, 'we have a new name. We are no longer the Baby Butchers. Now we are the Gravediggers.'

The allies were two days working on their casualties before they could pay attention to the Russians. After that length of time, lying unattended in the open, many of the wounded had died.

'Best thing for them,' Thorpe said. He nodded to one staring-eyed Russian. He lay in a grotesque squat with his back to a stone wall and his intestines in front of him, now furred with flies. 'I mean, how could that lad have lived without his guts? What could the doctors have done for him except stuff them back inside and stitch him up?'

'Their officers don't care a bugger for them.' Logan pushed at the corpse with his foot. 'He's stiff as a board, this one.'

The Allies dug mass graves for the dead; twenty-four huge pits into which they placed the smashed and mutilated bodies that had once been soldiers.

'You look after the burial detail, Windrush,' Snodgrass said. 'I'm sure your men can handle that.'

'I'm sure they can sir,' Jack agreed. 'They tend to handle whatever jobs the army throws at them.'

Snodgrass grunted. 'Get it done Windrush.'

'Strange,' Riley paused to look at a long row of Russian corpses. 'Just a few days ago these were men like us. They ate and slept and joked and had hopes for the future.'

'Aye; hopes to kill the British and get out of the Army,' Logan said. 'These bastards would have slaughtered us without thinking about it.'

'As we would them,' Riley murmured. 'We're not that different.'

'Bloody right we are,' Logan dropped his spade and glowered up at the taller man. 'We're bloody British, and they're bloody Russian. Kill the lot of them and send them to hell.'

'Quite.' Riley withdrew a pace. 'As you say; we are very different from them.'

'Aye; and don't forget it, Riley.' Logan stepped closer and pushed his forehead against the bridge of Riley's nose. 'Bloody Russian lover, you.'

'Right men; enough of that!' Jack nodded to O'Neill, who pushed them apart. 'We've got a job to do here and bickering amongst ourselves won't make it easier.'

'Sir?' Coleman looked up from the depths of the grave. 'How are we not attacking Sebastopol yet? I mean, we beat the Russians and sent them running so how come we aren't attacking Sebastopol? I mean, that's why we're here, isn't it?'

'We'll attack when the generals believe it's right,' Jack said. 'We don't have to worry about that sort of thing.'

Jack could feel the disgust as the men lifted the broken bodies, some with arms or legs missing, some with faces smashed into unrecognisable pulp, some with their internal organs spilling out, some looking peaceful, as if asleep, but all covered in a black fur of flies. Flies that rose in an angry cloud, to alight on the lips and eyes of Jack's men as they worked, so they swatted and cursed and spat out insects that minutes before had been burrowing inside the rotting corpses of Russian soldiers.

'I think that's the lot,' Jack waved a hand in a futile attempt to ward off the flies that clouded around him. 'I can't see any others.'

'You're covered in blood, sir,' O'Neill pointed out, less than tactfully. 'And other things.'

Jack looked down at himself. Blood was the least of his worries.

'Sir!' The Bishop called out. 'Here's another one, sir.'

'Leave the bastard to rot,' Thorpe said.

'They are Christians like us and deserve a Christian burial,' the Bishop said.

'I'm not a Christian,' Coleman said. 'What's Christ ever done for me? I've never met him coming down the street.'

'Maybe if you had, you would be a better person.' The Bishop ignored the hoots of the others as he hauled the body of the Russian from a shell hole. 'There's not much left of this poor fellow. Just his top half; both his legs are shot away.'

'Roll him in a blanket, and we'll take him to his friends,' Jack said.

'He's an officer,' Coleman said. 'Should we not bury him separately, sir?'

'We're all the same in the eyes of the Lord,' the Bishop told him. 'We're all God's children.'

The Russian officer stared up at them through wide blue eyes. He was about forty, Jack estimated, but with the uniform torn by battle, he couldn't even guess at the rank. They brought him to the last of the graves and added his body. Somehow that final man made more impression on Jack than all the others. He had looked utterly forlorn, a man who must have hoped for help as he lay after the battle with his legs smashed and his army defeated.

'He looked very lonely there,' Jack said quietly.

'Death is a lonely place,' Riley spoke softly. 'But life can be lonely as well.'

Jack glanced at him. 'Especially when one does not quite fit in,' he said.

'That is so,' Riley said, then looked away. 'Sorry, sir.'

'No need for apologies, Riley.' Jack stepped away. 'Right men, get those shovels working and cover these poor lads up. Move it – we've got a war to win.'

With the earth piled over the eighteen hundred Russian corpses, Jack looked over his men. 'You're filthy,' he said.

'So are you, sir,' O'Neill reminded.

'Bathing parade,' Jack decided. 'Down to the beach and we'll get this stuff washed off us.' He nodded to O'Neill. 'The men are unhappy, corporal.'

They stood in a hunched group, round-shouldered and tired, smeared with blood and worse than blood.

'Heads up!' O'Neill roared. 'You are British soldiers.'

'We're bloody gravediggers,' Coleman said.

'Somebody had to do it; the job fell to us, and that's all there is to it,' O'Neill said. 'Now heads up and march!'

'Sing!' Jack shouted. 'Sing out loud!'

They were silent, stubborn as they marched, until Riley began, with words unfamiliar to Jack:

As a fair one of England was musing by the rolling sea,
There came a wayworn traveller and landed by her side,
That goddess of the British throne, whose robes was rich and costly,
Which struck the stranger with amaze, and thus to her he cried—

One by one the others joined in, picking up the words that they knew and humming the rest.

'O lady fair, why wander here, haste your country to cheer,
Your enemies with evil eyes their threats of war declare,
So man your ships with hardy tars, they will
Boldly gain your cause,
Arouse up little England, and stop the Russian bear.'

'Little England be buggered,' Logan spat. 'There's more Paddies and Sawnies here than anything else.'

The others cat-called his words and in a few moments they were happily exchanging national insults, Scots against English, Irish against Welsh, pushing and jostling together like old friends or soldiers in any regiment in the British Army.

Avoiding the acres of wounded who lay on the beach waiting for transport to Scutari; Jack led his men to a nearly secluded cove where the sea broke silver on a strip of shining shingle. There were no bodies in the surf, no sick men or discarded military equipment to mar the illusion of tranquillity. It seemed very peaceful, with a seabird screaming and the water pristine and clear.

'Right men: strip, wash the filth off your clothes and bathe. We are soldiers, not Resurrection men.'

'I'm not sure about that,' Coleman said, 'I've burked a few gulls in my time.'

Jack pretended not to hear. For a second, he wondered if it was bad for discipline for the men to see an officer undress, decided that they would see a lot worse on campaign and ripped off his uniform. The kiss of clean air on his bare skin was refreshing, and he stepped into the sea.

'In you come, men!'

Some of the men were shy about stripping, others blasé while most turned their backs until they got into the water. Within a few moments they were larking and splashing around, so Jack had a mental image of his school days when life was good, he believed he was rich, and he had joined his schoolfellows in the river. The accents were different, the men a few years older, but the spirit was the same.

He shook his head; those days were long gone now.

It was quite a domestic scene, a score of naked men engaged in washing their uniforms, exchanging crude banter and raucous laughter under the sky of an enemy country. It was hard to imagine they were only three miles from a scene of slaughter and agony, and even now there were hundreds of sick and wounded only quarter of a mile along the coast.

Jack noticed Coleman and Thorpe, with Ogden and Logan in a muttering huddle just above the tide. Coleman looked up when he saw Jack and gave a greasy smile.

'What's happening, men?' Jack waded through the surf. 'You're all very intent there.'

'Nothing, sir.' Coleman put both hands behind his back as the others scattered along the beach.

'Come back here!' Jack felt more like a schoolmaster than a pupil as he called his errant men together. They came reluctantly, with guilty grins or even more tell-tale, a total lack of expression.

'Hand it over, Coleman!' Jack put out his hand.

'What, sir?'

'Whatever it is you're concealing behind your back. Come on now: hand it over.'

'It's nothing, sir.' Coleman produced both hands but was unable to stop the small sound of something landing on the shingle.

'Step away, man!' Jack ordered.

O'Neill pushed Coleman aside. A rough handkerchief lay on the shingle, wrapped around something. Jack picked it up and unfastened the bow on top. There were a few copper coins inside.

'These are Russian,' Jack said. 'You've been looting.'

Coleman nodded. 'Everybody does it,' he said, defensively. 'Officers as well as the men.'

Jack remembered the two golden statues he'd removed from the Burmese temple. He felt the other men crowd around him and knew they waited to see what he would do. Officially, looting was probably frowned on. He could put Coleman on a charge and Snodgrass would probably have him flogged. But that would be grossly unfair if others were equally guilty and considering that he'd done the same thing in Burma.

'Where did this come from?' He already knew the answer.

'The Russian bodies,' Coleman muttered. 'We never stole from the wounded,' he said, 'only the dead and they don't need it. Besides, it would have only got buried with them so where's the harm?'

Where indeed? Soldiers had always looted; it was one of the traditions of war, one of the very few perquisites they had for risking life and limb for the glory of Empire and the profit of industrialists and company shareholders who took none of the risks and pocketed all the profits. Profits, Jack told himself, which were ten thousand, no, a hundred thousand times more than this small collection of copper coins. Profits that men such as Coleman would never see in their lifetime and could probably not comprehend. And what was the difference between taking a few coins from a dead enemy and stealing carts from live Allies?

'The Duke of Wellington used to hang looters,' he said.

Coleman shifted uncomfortably. Shorn of his brave uniform he looked scrawny, a battered child of the slums with a concave belly and gaunt face. The other men were in little better physical shape, thin, some with ribs showing through their skin, while Ogden was brawny, with a bare patch on his hairy chest. Jack frowned, seeing the mark of a brand there: BC – bad character. He had been in the army before he came to the 113th. That was worth knowing.

Jack realised that he'd been staring at Coleman for a full minute while the thoughts ran through his head. The poor man looked terrified. He raised his voice. 'Bring me all that you have stolen!'

One by one the men shuffled forward and put their takings on the ground at his feet. They were all roughly the same; a few copper coins or a single silver coin; a leather pocket-book; a battered silver watch; a silk handkerchief that must have come from an officer and a small notepad.

'Did you divide this all fairly?' Jack asked.

'Yes, sir,' Thorpe replied.

'Who was in charge?'

'I was, sir,' O'Neill said.

Jack took a deep breath. He could hear the hushing of the sea above the nervous breathing of the men. 'I thought as much.' He lifted the notepad and ruffled through the pages. 'Where did this come from?'

'That Russian officer that the Bishop found, sir,' Thorpe said and added generously, 'you can have it if you like.'

'Thank you.' Jack did not hide the sarcasm although it was probably wasted on these men. He looked around at the apprehensive faces; he was their officer, responsible for their mental and moral well-being as much as for their physical behaviour. 'You all know that looting is not allowed—'

'Oh! Look at all the naked men!'

The female voice had a startling effect on the 113th. Soldiers who had faced all the horrors of the Burmese jungle and were ready to face Russian bayonets and artillery started covering themselves and turned away from the two women who slowly rode past.

Jack had a brief glimpse of a strikingly handsome dark-haired girl and her older, frowning companion, and then he reached for his uniform trousers and began to haul them on. Still wet from the sea, they clung to his legs, so he staggered, reached out for support, realised he'd grabbed hold of the rump of the older woman's horse, let go and fell full on his face on the shingle. He rolled over on his back, still fighting to pull up his tight trousers.

'Oh, don't get dressed on our behalf,' the dark-haired beauty ran her gaze over him.

The older woman kicked in her spurs, so the horse jerked forward. 'Come along Helen. There is nothing for us here. We have no desire to witness a rabble of undressed men.'

'On the contrary...' Helen's eyes darted from man to man before returning to Jack as he struggled with his half-mast trousers.

'Come along.' Taking hold of the reins of Helen's horse, the older woman guided her away. Helen looked over her shoulder, caught Jack's eye and smiled. He pulled up his trousers, too late to protect his modesty and unable to restrain the flush of utter embarrassment that crossed his face.

'Well, sir?'

Jack realised that the men had recovered from their panic at the sight of the women and had reassembled around him.

'Get your clothes on,' he said, 'in case some other women come cavorting past. We're meant to be fighting the Russians, not providing free entertainment to every blasted female in the Crimea.'

'Sir,' Coleman said, 'about the looting, sir.'

Jack looked along the beach. The horsewomen were a good thirty yards away. Dark-haired Helen turned again and waved.

'Looting?' He dropped the notebook. 'If you find anything that might be of military value let me know. Otherwise, make sure I don't catch you again.'

Somehow, he knew that had been the correct decision. It may not have been the decision that officers in other regiments would have made, and certainly, his father would not have condoned such actions in the Royal Malverns, or Colin Campbell with the Black Watch, but for these men of the 113th, it was right. And that dark-haired girl, Helen, possessed the most charming of smiles.

Chapter Eight

**Crimea
23 September 1854**

'Have you heard what's happening, Windy?' Elliot made himself as comfortable as he could by sitting on the side of a grave mound.

Jack looked over the Allied camp, where the French had their neat row of dog-tents, and the British belatedly had erected their own larger tents. 'I know our big-wigs, and the French commanders have been talking.'

Elliot produced a pewter hip flask, took a swallow and passed it over to Jack. It was brandy, rough, powerful and probably distilled somewhere in the French camp. *Trust the French to have all the comforts of home.* 'We've been here for days now,' he said, 'with the men falling like flies from cholera and dysentery and Raglan and the Froggies disagreeing what to do next.'

'I know that much,' Jack returned the flask and refused a second sip.

'Well,' Elliot tipped the flask down his throat, 'the original idea was for a quick assault on Sebastopol, as you know, teach the Ruskies a lesson and get out before winter comes in.'

'I know that much too,' Jack said. 'Is there anything new to add? I've been busy burying bodies and taking the wounded and sick to the beach.'

Elliot shrugged. 'Well, our Lord Raglan wanted to go straight over the north side of the wall and right into Sebastopol, but Saint what's-his-name thought that was too difficult for his men. And that was after we took the Russians prized defensive position at the Alma too. The Froggies think it would be much trouble, so they say we would have a flank march right around the city and launch a surprise attack from the south.'

'So we give the Ruskies time to prepare their defences, before we take them by surprise,' Jack said.

'That's the ticket!' Elliot said. 'Sound strategy, what?'

'Could not be better,' Jack said. 'Who needs enemies when we have Allies like that?' This time he accepted the brandy.

'On your feet.' Fleming was as gloomy as ever. 'We're moving in an hour. Get your men ready.'

'Where are we going, Flem?' Elliot asked.

'That's sir to you, and we're going wherever we are ordered.'

There was a seven-mile march that 23rd September, as the allied army dragged itself from the bloodied banks of the Alma to the River Katcha. They marched in the same formation as before, but with fewer men and less enthusiasm, despite their recent victory.

'Look at them,' Elliot pointed to the French. 'They had quarter of the fighting we had and a tenth the casualties, and they look like they suffered a defeat rather than they won a triumph.'

'Blasted French,' Preston said, 'always arse over tip. They probably think Waterloo was a victory and Bonaparte is waiting over the next rise for them.'

As the army marched, their booted feet flattened the grass and scuffed aside the helmets, muskets and various items of equipment the retreating Russians had abandoned.

'The Ruskies know they were beaten anyway,' Jack said. He raised his voice, 'Logan! Put that down!'

The small man glowered back, with the Russian coat draped across his arm. 'It might come in handy, sir.'

'It's burning hot, dammit man, and you've collected sufficient Russian accoutrements to set up a market stall!'

'It gets cold at night, sir…' Logan looked up as O'Neill grabbed the coat, threw it to the ground and emphasised Jack's order with a hefty kick to Logan's backside.

The Allies halted at the River Katcha, with the men throwing themselves into the stream to cool down so by the time the 113th got there with the 4th Division, the water was nothing more than a churned muddy morass.

'Drink and fill your water bottles,' Snodgrass ordered. 'Don't mind the mud.'

Jack glanced at O'Neill and frowned. 'The men are thirsty, corporal, but I think they can wait another twenty minutes.'

'The longer we wait, the worse the condition of the water, sir,' O'Neill's voice was hoarse.

Jack took a deep breath. He remembered the cool springs of the Malvern Hills; they were a long way from Herefordshire here. 'I don't like my men drinking filthy water, O'Neill.'

'They're used to it, sir,' O'Neill's eyes darted to the water, with the river slow and fouled between shallow banks. Vultures circled in the brassy sky above, aware that where the army marched, corpses would invariably follow.

'Sir,' Jack threw a salute to Snodgrass. 'I think I saw a couple of Cossacks on the flank.'

Snodgrass grunted and looked inland. 'I can't see anything.'

'No, sir; they could have moved on.' Jack waited a moment. 'Should I send out a few men to see?'

'You can't trust the men, Windrush. You'd best go and take a look yourself. God knows our cavalry are hard pressed enough.'

'Yes, sir.'

Borrowing Elliot's telescope and gathering his men, Jack led them upstream, above the mess created by the allied army to where the water was clear and bright. 'Right lads. Drink, fill your bottles and wash, in that order.'

'You mentioned Cossacks, sir?' O'Neill reminded.

'So I did,' Jack agreed. 'I'll take Coleman and Thorpe and have a look while you take care of the men.'

O'Neill nodded. 'There were no Cossacks, were there? You're a devious devil, sir. A devious devil.'

'Thank you, Corporal.'

The banks were higher and steeper upstream, with the scent of wild thyme replacing the foul stinks from the army, so Jack found a small rise, extended the telescope and studied the landscape all around. It was similar to Salisbury Plain, he thought, with rolling downland and few signs of human habitation. Only the odd stunted tree or small bush broke the flower-dotted swathes of grass.

'Fine country for sheep,' he said to himself and looked for signs of the enemy.

There were none. The entire Russian army in all its pomp and glory, gun, baggage, hard-riding Cossacks and grey-coated infantry, had vanished. On a whim, he shifted around to study the British Army; looking at regiment after regiment. Jack's gaze shifted from Campbell's kilted Highlanders with their feather bonnets and the bagpipes whose drone and wail he could hear above the buzz of orders and voices, to the scarlet jackets of the line infantry and the gorgeous array of the cavalry.

The girl seemed to leap into focus in the centre of his lens; dark-haired, tall and astride that light horse, she and the older woman were laughing at something. What was her name again? Helen – that was it. He had never seen a woman so beautiful, but what on earth was such a peach doing with the army? He saw her dismount with a single graceful swing and land with a swish of her skirt that he nearly heard, and then she placed her hand on the arm of an officer.

Who was that? Jack tried to see, but Helen's horse blocked his view. 'Move aside, damn you,' he muttered.

'Sir,' O'Neill's voice broke his reverie. 'The men are ready.'

'Right, Corporal,' Jack said. He glanced at his watch, realised that he'd been staring at Helen for about ten minutes and rose to his feet. 'I saw no Russians here.'

'No, Sir, nor did I,' O'Neill said. Only when they were on their way back did O'Neill say, 'She was a looker, sir.'

Chapter Nine

**Crimea
24 September 1854**

'The blasted Russians have scuppered us!' Elliot sounded angry. 'They've placed a whole line of battleships across Sebastopol harbour! Our ships can't get past them or the shore batteries to bombard the town!'

Jack nodded. 'I'm sure Admiral Dundas can cope with the Russians.'

'There's more.' To judge by the numbers of officers who clustered around him, Elliot seemed to have access to information that others did not. 'They've built a whole new battery of great massive cannon at the mouth of the Belbek.'

'And?' Jack asked. 'We're nowhere near the blasted Belbek.'

'You've got a lot to learn yet, Windrush,' Haverdale said. 'If there is a battery there, that means we can't land supplies. We'll have to find a harbour soon; we can't live off the land here.'

'It's the Froggies that are panicking,' Elliot enjoyed holding court. 'You know how they're scared of wet water anyway. They want to leave the coast and march inland.'

'Away from the cover of the Navy?' Jack shook his head. 'That would be plain stupidity.'

'It's what I heard,' Elliot sounded stubborn.

'And how the devil did you hear that?' Jack asked. 'Have you got Lord Raglan's private ear?'

'Something like that,' Elliot said, evasively. 'You'll see if I'm right.'

Later that day the 113th got their orders in line with the rest of the army. Leaving the coast, they marched inland, precisely as Elliot had predicted.

'What for are we going this way, sir?' Logan asked as they marched away from the coast. 'We're leaving the ships behind.'

'I know that Logan,' Jack said, 'Lord Raglan knows what he's doing.' He pretended not to hear Coleman's low comment or Thorpe's shout of derision.

They marched across the plain with men falling from the heat, cholera or exhaustion and the allied army adding abandoned equipment to that left behind by the retreating Russians.

'Sir!' Riley said as they crested a ridge above the sullen River Belbek. 'Over there – it's Sebastopol.'

Jack was only one of many men who ran to the ridge and peered across. There, a short four miles away, the north wall of Sebastopol loomed up. Jack stared across the open ground toward the city. 'It's very impressive,' he said. *And soon we will be smashing that with artillery and our men will be running through the streets, looting and destroying.*

Some of the serene buildings reminded him of Bath. 'They'll be the barracks,' Elliot told everybody who cared to listen. 'And these are churches,' he pointed out the apparently religious buildings.

'And these lovely private houses,' Jack said innocently, 'will people live in them?'

'Yes they will,' Elliot said.

'And will people worship in the churches?' Jack asked.

Realising that Jack was teasing him, Elliot closed his mouth. Jack continued to survey the city as the sun gleamed on white stone walls and green roofs, while ships displayed the proud Russian ensign as they floated on water that sparkled silver and blue. The walls looked low, the defences unfinished although hundreds of Russian soldiers and sailors scurried around strengthening them as they watched.

'We could walk in and take it,.' Coleman looked at Jack. 'It's easier than Rangoon sir, or Pegu.' He raised his voice to educate his colleagues. 'In Burma lads, the Burmese had great big stockades to guard their cities; the Ruskies only have walls and incomplete bastions.'

'The Russians will have garrisoned it well, you mark my words,' Jack said. *But why the devil don't we just attack now, before they make the defences stronger? It's only a few miles away, and there's no Russian army in sight.*

'We licked their army,' Logan echoed Jack's thoughts. 'They're beat and running. We can take the bloody place and get back home.'

'How about it, sir?' Thorpe asked. 'How about doing what you and me did in Burma and lead the regiment across? The other regiments would follow us, and we could win the war right now, sir.'

For a moment Jack was tempted. To break orders and lead a successful attack that won the war. What a way to make his name! There would be inevitable promotion, honour, fame even. And then he thought of the alternative. If nobody followed and he and his small handful of the 113th charged alone, they would be massacred or worse, forced to turn tail. There would be failure, scandal and dishonour.

'Sorry, Thorpe, it wouldn't work. We have to follow orders.'

'Bugger orders,' somebody grunted until a shocked sergeant roared him into silence.

The Allies moved again, away from the sea and their supplies, marching around Sebastopol and with every hour allowing the Russians time to build up the defences and repair the broken morale of their men.

The terrain altered from a bald plain to dense brushwood where the leading regiments had to hack their way through scrub and the Rifles, out in front, had to feel for paths and hope the Russians had not prepared an ambush. Only the artillery was permitted to use the road, so the infantry sweated in the heat, held their muskets above their head to escape the tangled undergrowth and swore as thorns snarled in their clothes and impeded their progress. Jack grunted as the supple bough of a branch, released by the man in front, swung back and knocked his shako off, and he heard Coleman release a whole volley of curses as thorns ripped into his uniform and they struggled on, angry, hot and frustrated.

'We're lucky it's only the Russians and not the Burmese,' Coleman gave his opinion, 'they would have a hundred ambushes to stop us.'

Panting and sweating in the rear of the army, Jack could only agree. If the Allies had missed a trick by not attacking at once, the Russian command was proving equally inept by not trying to stem the Allies advance. A few successful ambushes could cause considerable casualties among the Allies and raise Russian morale.

As if to prove his point, there was a sudden burst of musketry from ahead, followed by some sporadic cheering. Cannon boomed, deep and menacing, and then silence.

'What was that?' somebody asked.

'How the devil should I know?' Jack said irritably. About to say that if he was in a decent regiment and not the blasted 113th he might find out, he bit off the words before he spoke them. There was no sense in saying what everybody already knew to be the truth.

'The Russians made a stand,' the words came down the line, 'and we shoved them aside.'

Not surprisingly it was Elliot who found out that the advance guard of the British had come across a lone Russian regiment backed by some artillery. The Russian infantry had fired a single volley and then run, leaving a great deal of booty behind.

The 113th kept moving, slightly more warily. The undergrowth closed in on them, claustrophobic, containing the struggling men within a close green horizon, vicious with thorns. Without warning, the brushwood ended at a clearing of around five acres, with two pot-holed roads intersecting at a smouldering building which looked more like a barracks than a farm. Smoke rose from the interior.

'That's McKenzie's farm.' Elliot seemed to know everything. 'This is where the Russians tried to fight.'

'That'll be wee Willie McKenzie,' Logan muttered. 'He was ayeways moving house.'

Thorpe looked at him, evidently unsure if he was telling the truth or not. Jack checked his men; they were all still there, staggering, sweating, suffering and complaining but still marching, still carrying their muskets, still soldiering on. For a regiment rumoured to be the worst in the army, the 113th was holding out remarkably well.

'We've lost twelve men to heat and disease so far,' Major Snodgrass said, 'and without hearing a shot fired.'

'At this rate,' Fleming said, 'all the Russians have to do is allow Lord Raglan to march the men around the walls of Sebastopol and they will have won. We won't have any army left to fight with.'

They halted on the Mackenzie Heights, with the men throwing themselves on the ground in heat-induced exhaustion until the officers and NCOs forced them to eat and prepare the camp. Some slept where they lay. When three more men of the 113th died during the night, only their close colleagues grieved; the army was growing accustomed to death. The march resumed next day with the men toiling on their circuitous route around the city they had come so far to attack. They left the ridge, forded the Tchernaya River or crossed by the Traktir Bridge and marched on, seemingly forever, bleeding men as heat or disease thinned the ranks. Eventually, and to Jack's surprise, they came in sight of the sea again, and halted for a rest above a small port whose very name seemed to chill him with a portent of disaster.

'Balaklava,' Elliot said. 'And there it is; our first major conquest since we arrived in Russia.'

The conquest was not entirely without powder as the Russians occupied an ancient Genoese fort that sat on a mound outside the town and contested the British advance with artillery. HMS Agamemnon responded with broadsides while the Rifles attacked from the landward side. The fort surrendered within the hour, and Balaklava fell.

'The war progresses satisfactorily,' Snodgrass said.

'Yes, sir,' Jack agreed. 'If only our regiment could take part.'

'Perhaps it is for the best that we do not,' Haverdale said.

Jack looked down on Balaklava. Set beside a small oval inlet about half a mile long and quarter of a mile wide, the village would not have been out of place in Cornwall with its white-walled, green-tiled villas and carefully tended gardens all sparkling and serene under the Crimean sun. There were clematis and roses, honeysuckle and vines decorating the garden walls, while the glittering waters of the pool-like harbour held reflections of the heights and slopes all around. Surrounding the village and stretching upward on the heights were carefully regulated vegetable patches, not unlike the cottage gardens of the labourers in Herefordshire.

'I had no idea that Russia could be so beautiful,' Jack said. 'It's a lovely harbour. Raglan was right all along. It will be far better bringing in stores here than landing on the open beach.'

'Your faith in our august commander is touching, my young friend,' Haverdale said. 'This is only your second campaign, I think. Now listen, all the supplies for our army, food, water, clothing, boots, tents, fodder for the horses, ammunition, cannon, wagons, and replacements have to come in here, and the sick, wounded and prisoners have to be taken out.' He nodded down to the port. 'Suddenly it has gotten a lot smaller, don't you think?'

Jack nodded. He couldn't dispute the facts, but at that moment he was much more concerned with the two figures who were riding into the village. He took a deep breath as he watched Helen and her older companion walk their horses as casually as if they were entering a settlement in peaceful England.

Haverdale caught the direction of his glance. 'Oh, don't you worry about these two,' he said. 'Mrs. Colonel Maxwell is an old hand at campaigning. She goes everywhere her husband goes and often places he is feared to tread.'

'Is that Colonel Maxwell's wife?' Jack asked.

'Wife and daughter,' Haverdale dismissed them casually. 'Now there's something worth looking at!' He pointed as a large ship slowly steamed to the harbour entrance. 'There is HMS Agamemnon; the largest ship in the fleet!'

As the ship slid into harbour with her bulk dwarfing the pretty little houses, Jack saw Helen and Mrs. Maxwell standing to watch, and then the ship moved on, and his view of Helen and Balaklava vanished. 'Beauty and the Beast,' he said softly.

'Quite,' Haverdale said, although Jack doubted he had any idea of the images that were running through his mind.

'Of course, the 113th will not be in Balaklava,' Haverdale said. 'Campbell and the 93rd Highlanders are to be its defence and garrison.'

'Where are we going, sir?' Jack stared down at Balaklava but Helen had vanished and the magic moment had passed. His gaze lingered for a moment.

'Up there,' Haverdale pointed to the heights that overlooked the village.

Then I can look down on Balaklava; I may see her from time to time.

Colonel Murphy looked very old as he addressed the officers. 'The British Army is losing around a hundred men a day to cholera and general sickness. Because of these high losses, General Raglan has at last decided to put the 113th in with the fighting regiments. Apart from a handful of men who saw action in Burma, this is our first chance since the disaster in the Punjab to claim our place as a fighting regiment. Make me proud of the 113th.'

'We will, sir,' Snodgrass said.

'I want the 113th to be known as a regiment of fighting gentlemen,' Murphy said. 'We want nothing underhand, nothing that will be in any way detrimental to the good name of the 113th. Remember that my lads, we are a regiment of fighting gentlemen.'

'Quite right, sir!' Snodgrass shouted. Only Jack heard his sotto-voice mutter, 'or filthy scoundrels.'

At last, I have my chance! We are to be a fighting regiment!

'They're still arguing about it,' Elliot reported. 'Our general, Sir George Cathcart, is all hot for an immediate assault on Sebastopol, but the Frenchies are for holding back and having a formal siege. Our Sir George said that we could walk into Sebastopol without losing a man, but the Frenchies don't agree. They say that their morale is low and if the first attack fails, they may not have the heart to make another.'

'How do you know these things, Elliot?' Jack asked. 'Do you have a personal carrier pigeon inside the general's tent or something?'

He was surprised that Elliot didn't immediately come back with some quip. Instead, he was quiet for a few moments.

'Come now Elliot; I was merely complimenting you on your knowledge. I don't honestly believe that you have a personal carrier pigeon.'

The 113th spent that night digging trenches along the ridge that overlooked Sebastopol. Much to Jack's disappointment, even if he stretched his neck to the utmost, he couldn't see anything of Balaklava, some eight or nine miles along a steep track.

'The Russians could send out patrols,' Jack said, 'so make sure the trenches are deep enough to grant us protection.' Although he was there to supervise operations, Jack quickly realised that Private Ogden knew much more about digging than he ever would.

'You were a navigator weren't you, Ogden?'

'Yes, sir,' Ogden backed away a pace as if it had been a crime to work as a railway labourer.

'All right then – you spent half your life working with a spade; you show the lads what to do.'

'Yes, sir.' Ogden's ordinarily surly face lightened a fraction. He straightened his shoulders with this new responsibility.

From their position on the ridge overlooking Sebastopol, the 113th could see the Russians steadily improving the defences, while the Allies prepared for a bombardment and a siege.

'General Cathcart was convinced that Sebastopol would have fallen to a determined assault as soon as the Allies arrived,' Elliot said.

'Even I heard that one,' Jack said. 'Without the benefit of your carrier pigeon.'

'I don't have such a pigeon,' Elliot insisted.

Colonel Murphy called the officers together. 'Every regiment has to provide working parties to build defences and bring artillery from the ships. The 113th, as the regiment least affected by disease, will provide twice as many. Elliot, you and Windrush help bring up the guns. Fleming, you, Haverdale and Preston dig up here. Major Snodgrass, I need you to liaise with the other regiments.'

Jack had no objections to taking a working party to Balaklava to help unload artillery. He hoped that he might chance upon Helen somewhere near the harbour, so he was quite light-hearted when he led his men down from the ridge.

'Dear God, what's happened?' He stopped dead when he saw Balaklava. Where only a few days back this had been a neat, pretty little village of pristine villas and colourful gardens, now there was a wrecked shambles with walls pulled down, gardens dug up, and flowers trampled.

'We happened,' Elliot said. 'The British Army happened.' He looked around. 'About thirty thousand men with dysentery or cholera, lacking firewood or shelter marching through an enemy village; what do you expect?'

Jack nodded. Of all the houses that fronted the sea by the harbour, only one had retained its original character. Two stories high, the green tiled roof reflected the sunlight, while colourful flowers still decorated the outside wall. He knew instinctively that Mrs. Colonel Maxwell had commandeered that house. No Russian would stand against her and not even the most desperate of British private soldiers would wish to cross that formidable woman.

'You there, Lieutenant!' The voice was lofty, imperious even, and Jack halted. Mrs. Colonel Maxwell stared at him from the gate of the house. 'Come here.'

Jack obeyed, giving a small bow.

'Who are you, sir?' Mrs. Maxwell frowned. 'I seem to recognise you.'

'Lieutenant Jack Windrush of the 113th, Ma'am, at your service.' Jack noticed a movement at the small window immediately beside the door.

Mrs. Maxwell gave the tiniest incline of her head. 'No, I don't know the name, unless you are related to the late General Windrush. No,' she said again, dismissing the idea. 'General Windrush's boy is in the Royal Malverns. Well, Lieutenant Windrush, I want you to take a message to my husband. He is Colonel Maxwell of the 118th.'

Jack nodded. 'Yes, of course, Ma'am.'

'Wait here,' Mrs. Maxwell ordered. As soon as she disappeared, the small window opened, and Helen thrust her head outside. 'We've undoubtedly met before, Jack Windrush,' she said at once.

Jack felt the colour flush to his cheeks. 'Yes, we have,' he said.

Helen's smile was pure mischief. She scanned him, up and down and back up again. 'You look quite dashing in your uniform,' she said and vanished as her mother returned to the door.

'Take this, Lieutenant,' Mrs. Maxwell said sharply, 'and tell Colonel Maxwell I send my compliments.'

'Yes, Ma'am,' Jack said. 'I do have my duty to complete first…'

'I realise that, Lieutenant! Of course, you must do your duty first. Now be off with you, you have cannon to unload.'

Immediately Mrs. Maxwell shut the door, the small window opened, and Helen appeared again and continued as if she had not been interrupted. 'You look quite dashing in uniform, but I preferred you without.'

Jack opened his mouth, but no words came.

'But you don't look the slightest bit dashing when you stand there catching flies,' Helen said. 'Can you speak, Lieutenant Jack Windrush?'

'Of course, I can speak, Miss Helen,' Jack said.

'Oh now?' Her eyes widened. 'I see you know my name! For shame sir, sneaking around learning about a lady behind her back.'

'There was no need to sneak, Miss Helen.' Jack decided that the best way to deal with this lady was to treat her as he used to treat the village girls in Malvern. 'Your name and reputation go before you. You, after all, are the young woman who spies on men when they are bathing.'

Her face coloured, but with delight and not embarrassment. 'And you, sir, are the man who parades himself unclad in front of two most respectable ladies!' She closed the shutters before he could find the words to retaliate. Only as he turned to stalk away in dignified silence did she open them again. 'And a most delicious sight it was too, if I may make so bold.'

'Oh you are the bold one, without mistake,' Jack said, realised that Mrs. Maxwell was opening an upstairs window and marched away quickly. Helen's smile remained with him even after the burning flush on his face died away.

Chapter Ten

**Siege of Sebastopol
October 1854**

'Well Jack, I fear we have missed the boat.' Elliot raised the flask. Alcohol had flushed his face and slurred his voice. 'The Russians have strengthened all their bastions, they have over three hundred heavy guns to defend Sebastopol, they've built a pontoon bridge across the south bay of the harbour, and they've brought in thousands of veterans.'

Jack nodded. 'I knew all that,' he said. Rumours and stories spread around the trenches nearly as quickly as cholera. 'Your pigeon was late with that news.'

'Ah,' Elliot said, 'but did you hear the latest? The Russians have been sending out raiding parties to capture prisoners.'

'I did hear that, too,' Jack said. He stood up to survey his men. Wagons sprinkled the road to Balaklava; most were empty as they returned to the ships in the harbour. There were some Crimean bullock wagons; a few camel-powered carts carried from Varna, a dozen Maltese mule-carts that had carried vegetables or what fruit or bread they could get. Beside them, threading to the tented camp in a steady stream were the heavier artillery wagons, laden with fascines to protect the batteries his men had helped to dig, or shot and shell and powder for the guns themselves.

Jack ducked as a cannon from Sebastopol opened fire. He saw the jet of smoke an instant before he heard the flat report of the gun. The smoke lingered around the bastion for a second and then there was a whizz and a loud bang away to his left. He straightened up. Elliot had lowered his flask.

'Blasted Russians: when are we going to fire back? We've plenty guns, damn them.'

Jack nodded. 'I don't know; we've been here for days, digging for the guns as the Russians watch us and shoot whenever they have a fancy for it.'

Elliot stood up and waved a small fist. 'Your time is coming, Russians. We'll get you!'

At first sight, the Allied trench system looked impressive with its lines of parallels – trenches that lay parallel to the walls of Sebastopol, connected by saps or communication trenches. Each successive parallel was closer to the city, so lessening the distance any attacking force had to cover, yet even the closest was hundreds of yards away. Advancing that distance under fire from Russian cannon and musketry would be suicidal unless the Allied artillery succeeded in blowing a breach in the defences.

Each sap was dug in a zig-zag to ensure the Russians could not fire a charge of grapeshot down the length, killing or maiming a large number of men. It was a procedure that besieging armies had employed for centuries: tried, tested and slow. Too slow in Jack's opinion, for the British Army had to end this siege quick and withdraw, or the cruel Russian winter would claim hundreds of lives. He remembered what had happened to Bonaparte's troops in their invasion and shivered. *God help us if we have to endure a winter here.*

'We're getting closer.' Jack did not reveal his thoughts.

'We are,' Elliot agreed. 'When Raglan thinks we have a parallel close enough to the walls, he will blast a breach with the artillery and in we charge.' He smacked his fist on the hard ground. 'Smack! And that's it over. Once our boys get in there with the bayonet, the city is ours.'

Jack nodded. 'I know the theory' he said and continued his examination of the allied lines. They looked well enough until he remembered that as well as the Russians within Sebastopol there was a Russian army under General Menshikov waiting inland to attack the Allies from the rear and squeeze them between two forces.

'I wish we knew the strength of Menshikov's army,' Jack said.

'He is somewhere along the Tchernaya River,' Elliot waved a vague hand. 'There's nothing to worry about. After the Alma, they'll be wary of us. He won't try an open battle again.'

'I heard where he's said to be.' Jack shifted his attention back to the British lines. The trenches faced the walls of Sebastopol, with gun batteries at irregular intervals, yet even to his inexperienced eyes, it was evident that the lines were not complete. There were gaps between the trenches.

'Rocky ground,' Haverdale had said with a shrug. 'Our lads can't dig through rocks.'

'Yes they can, sir,' Ogden, greatly daring, had said. 'We hack through a lot worse than that when we build the railways. Gunpowder can blast through the hardest of rock.'

An officious sergeant had roared Ogden to silence for daring to speak to an officer without permission, and the gaps in the British lines remained. Not that it mattered much, Jack reasoned, for the trenches did not entirely circumnavigate Sebastopol anyway.

The higher he moved, the better the view Jack had of the Allied lines. The focus of the siege was the harbour of Sebastopol, for the British were primarily a sea power with the army seen as a supporting arm. The harbours were formed into the rough shape of the letter T, with the larger of the two, the Man of War Harbour, as the upright. Sebastopol had grown around the seaport, with the main population centre as well as the barracks that Elliot had previously noticed, the dockyard and all the naval headquarters based around this Man of War harbour.

The cross-bar of the T was known as the Main Harbour, around which the Russians under Todtleben had been frantically and successfully building formidable defences in the time the Allies had allowed them. Jack shook his head; if only they had attacked immediately. He grunted: *nobody has ever won a war with 'if onlys'.* Todtleben's defences were mainly earthworks in a U shape, manned by regular soldiers and sailors as well as the robust, skilled dock workers.

After centuries of use, earthworks, as Jack had learned from his studies of military science, were formidable to breach. They had low silhouettes that did not invite attack, sides that were angled to deflect cannon balls and were made of thick, packed earth that merely absorbed the impact of shot. The outer Russian defences, now manned by over thirty thousand men, were equally formidable. Tall walls of earth, fortified by stone, were loop-holed for riflemen, with artillery platforms, known as bastions, to provide focal points.

'These bastions are the keys to Sebastopol,' Haverdale said soberly. 'If we can take these, then the city will fall. If we can't, then the Russians can thumb their noses at us from now until Judgment Day.'

'All of them?' Jack had not noticed Haverdale join him. 'Do you think we have to capture all the bastions?'

'Only two matter,' Haverdale pointed them out. 'There is the Malakoff. Our engineers reckon that is twenty-eight feet high, and as you can see it is stone built and semi-circular. The engineers estimate that the walls are about five feet thick, thirty feet or so in diameter and we know it holds five great heavy guns.'

'Only five?' Jack wasn't impressed. 'We captured larger fortifications at the Alma.'

'Not like that one.' Haverdale sounded sombre. 'Not advancing over open ground under intense rifle and artillery fire to take a position so high up. Then there is the Great Redan.'

Jack looked to the south where the Great Redan, a vee-shaped monstrosity, was close to a position known as the Barrack Battery.

'The bastions are mutually supportive,' Haverdale said, 'so if we attack one, we run into fire from the others. Hit in front and on both flanks, we'll incur heavy losses and,' he jerked a thumb backward, 'we've already lost hundreds of men to cholera, and we're losing more every day.' He pulled a cheroot from his pocket lit it and puffed out a plume of blue smoke. 'This will not be an easy war to win.'

Surrounding the city was the Upland, a rough, windswept or sun-baked, shelterless plateau which rose to three thousand feet. It was here that the bulk of the Allied army had camped and from here the trenches probed toward the city. The French occupied the left with one flank protected by the sea and their right resting on the British lines. On the right, the British right flank was exposed to possible attack by any Russian force in the interior. It sat on the Inkerman Heights, an area of broken ground riddled with ravines and covered in thick scrub forestry.

In the interior, in a Crimean peninsula that was virtually unknown to the British, Jack knew that Prince Menshikov was mustering a Russian army, hoping for weakness in the British lines that he could exploit. Unless cholera and dysentery burnt itself out, all Menshikov had to do was keep his army intact and wait. With the current losses, there would be no British Army remaining within a few months.

'But we've got artillery too, sir,' Jack said, 'these new 68-pounder Lancaster guns are the best in the world.'

'Eight-inch beauties,' Elliot enthused, 'the first rifled artillery produced; they'll show the Ruskies.'

'We'll see,' Haverdale said. 'Until we do, you two would be best getting to know the trenches. Don't get caught out at night. The Russians have been sending out patrols to harass us.'

Jack nodded. 'So Elliot told me, sir.'

'That man knows too much for a new lieutenant,' Haverdale said. 'Too clever by half, him. Now, our weakness is these ravines, and in particular, that one.' He pointed to the largest, where the Woronzov Road ran through the centre of the British lines on its way to Sebastopol. 'As you know the Woronzov Road divides our lines into the left and right attacks. If the Russians push there, they have a direct highway to the city, from where they can launch a sally, and they will split us in half.'

'They don't need to get into the city this way, sir,' Jack said. 'They have access across the harbour to the north, or through Karabelnaya in the very north.'

Haverdale nodded grimly. 'I am as aware of that as you are, Windrush. So as you can see, things are not all according to plan. They very seldom are in war, of course.' He stood up and watched as the Russians fired another salvo of cannon. One shot landed in a sap – a small trench – a hundred yards away, scattering a group of infantry who were digging under the instructions of a young engineer officer. The smoke cleared, a party carried away a writhing man and the work continued – one minor incident in a war that had already claimed thousands of lives.

'This war will not be over by Christmas, mark my words.' Haverdale finished his cheroot and flicked away the stump. 'The Russian is a bonny fighter when well led, and his lads are tough as teak.'

Night brought autumnal chill, and the 113th huddled into their trenches, cuddling their Brown Bess muskets and facing the distant walls of Sebastopol.

'Rations,' Jack said softly, passing around what there was to his men. 'Black bread, a small onion and a sip of rum-and-water.' He ducked as a Russian gun directly opposite fired, with the flare of the shot bright orange through the dark. He didn't see where the shot landed.

'It's past time we were firing back,' Elliot grumbled. 'When we do, we'll tumble their blessed walls into the dirt, I can tell you.'

Jack nodded, unable to share Elliot's enthusiasm. He looked at his section of the line. The 113th had taken over from the 1st Foot, the Royal Scots, and were responsible for the trenches beside the Woronzov Road, with their left resting on a battery named Chapman's after its commander.

'Listen,' O'Neill whispered. 'Somebody's out there!'

'Silence, lads,' Jack passed the word along. There was another grumble of gunfire from the Russians, more shot pounding into the British positions, more flashes from the walls of Sebastopol and the acrid drift of powder smoke in the night. Somewhere, ludicrously, a dog barked, the sound homely but somehow depressing.

'This is like bloody Burma,' Coleman said, 'waiting for the dacoits to murder the sentries.'

'Stand to your arms,' Jack said, and added, 'fix bayonets!' He heard the sinister slither of steel and the significant click as the men fitted the long bayonets in place. If the Russians sent a raiding party against the 113th, they would find themselves facing some of the toughest street fighters in the British Army, and that meant the toughest in the world.

He crawled along his section of the line; Ogden was humming quietly and gave him a fleeting smile. O'Neill looked pensive; Logan was repeating some Scottish slogan *C'mon then ya bastards* again and again. Hitchins looked nervous, so Jack patted his shoulder; Thorpe gave a small smile, 'just like Pegu, eh?'. Riley was staring ahead into the black, and the Bishop sighed as he passed.

'God bless us all, sir.'

'All right Bishop? How do you feel about fighting, with you being a devout Methodist?'

The Bishop thought for a moment before he replied. 'Even Christ threw the money changers out of the Temple, sir.'

'So he did,' Jack agreed, 'so he did.'

'Listen!' Hitchins hissed, 'over there!'

There was the sound of a scuffle over to the left beyond the battery, a long, drawn-out hopeless cry, cut off, and an outburst of firing, with the muzzle flashes of muskets vivid through the night.

'Ready lads!' Jack unholstered his revolver and tried to peer into the dark.

'Hold your fire,' Snodgrass ordered urgently, 'you might shoot our own men.'

They listened as the firing died away to a few sporadic shots, then nothing. There was the sound of a man sobbing, then silence.

'What was all that about?' Elliot sounded shaken.

'We won't know until morning,' Jack said. 'Just watch your front; the Russians are up to all the tricks.'

'Should I go forward and have a look, sir?' It was not like Hitchins to volunteer.

Jack touched him on the shoulder. 'Thank you, Hitchins, but not this time. We don't know who or what is out there.' He checked the chamber of his revolver, counted the cartridges and closed it with a snap that made Riley start. Another Russian cannon fired and then silence. The dog howled.

'They're using dishonourable methods,' Colonel Murphy said after they filed wearily out of the trenches. 'They're creeping up to our positions at night and grabbing our men, then bayonetting them.'

'The dirty blackguards,' Elliot said. 'We should complain to their general. That's not war; that's murder.'

Jack agreed, although he wondered where one could draw the line between a single killing that became illegal murder, and vast numbers of deaths that became a glorious victory.

'Warn your men,' Murphy said. 'We will have to think of a way to counter this foul method of fighting. It is not the work of gentlemen at all.'

'I thought it was something like that,' O'Neill said with a shrug. 'I'll pass the word on to the lads before we go back into the trenches.' He looked up as a wagon creaked to a halt, and a group of women clambered out. 'Here's trouble!'

'Trouble yourself, Corporal O'Neill.' Charlotte Riley tossed her mane of blonde hair. 'Where's that useless man of mine?'

'He's over there,' O'Neill gestured with a stubby thumb. 'About forty paces past the lieutenant in the second tent.'

Charlotte gave a brief, half mocking curtsey to Jack. 'Good day to you, Lieutenant Windrush. I'm here to see Jethro.'

Jack hid his smile. He had never thought of Riley having a first name and certainly never thought of him being Jethro. 'He'll be tired, Mrs. Riley' he said.

'I'll soon cure him of that.' Charlotte strode away, shouting. 'Jethro! I'm here!'

Jack saw Logan and Thorpe scurry out of the tent, look back in and drag out Coleman to leave Charlotte alone with her husband. 'We don't need the British Army here, Corporal, we can just send out Charlotte Riley. The Czar would pack his crown and run to the peace table, pleading for mercy.'

O'Neill grinned. 'The Czar has nothing to worry about, sir. Charlotte has no argument with him. It's Major Snodgrass I'm concerned about.'

'Major Snodgrass? Because he had Riley flogged?'

'Yes, sir. Charlotte is not a forgiving kind of woman.' O'Neill wasn't smiling. 'If I were Major Snodgrass, I'd avoid being alone with him on a dark night.'

Jack nodded. His knowledge of women was limited. While other youths in his school had expended time and energy in rolling kitchen maids and the daughters of farm servants in the hay, he had concentrated on reading military tactics and drill techniques. There had been his longing for Myat in Burma, but that had been a hopeless pursuit. There were many occasions when he wished he had a broader experience of life. 'I hope she has sufficient sense not to overstep herself and land Riley in more trouble. Officially she doesn't even exist.'

'We're aware of that, sir.' O'Neill looked away. 'That's why I told you.'

'Thank you, O'Neill.' Jack suddenly realised that he'd been allowed a glimpse into the world of the other ranks. Officers and men served in the same regiments and faced the same dangers of battle and disease, but their lives were parallel, with only occasional areas where they merged. The men knew each other's lives intimately, the good and bad, even the details of their marriages and sweethearts. Living in such close confinement as a barrack block where married couples inhabited the same room as the single men with only a hung blanket as a screen, they could hardly be otherwise.

Although he was tired, Jack couldn't sleep. Instead, he walked along the road toward Balaklava, stopping at the gap that overlooked the town. He stared downward, hoping that by some miracle Helen would appear. He'd never felt this way about any woman before and found the sensation troubling. Thinking about her interfered with his single-minded determination to rise in the army and regain his proper position in the world.

Ever since that unfortunate meeting on the beach, she had intruded on his thoughts and unknowingly interfered in his decisions. It was like an itch that he couldn't scratch – except that he had no desire to lose it. Jack sighed. He knew nothing about love and romance. He had no sisters, he had hardly known his mother, or more accurately, his step-mother, except as a force of authority and a figure to fear, and his hopeless yearning after Myat in Burma had not been a success. Each had been different, but none had been as significant as Helen was. In a crisis, he could only turn to his stock of military maxims for help.

What would the old Masters of war have said about such a situation? Was Bonaparte correct when he said that 'women are nothing but machines for producing children'? Bonaparte had little time for them, yet his love affair with Josephine was famed throughout the world. He was certainly correct when he said that 'nothing is more difficult, and therefore more precious than to be able to decide.'

Jack stood on the ridge, looking down on Balaklava and knowing that he must make a decision soon, or his mind would be racked with uncertainty for the foreseeable future and that was not a good thing during a campaign.

Clausewitz would have agreed with that. 'It is even better to act quickly and err than to hesitate until the time of action is past' according to Clausewitz. He had backed that by saying that 'no military leader has ever become great without audacity.' Would Clausewitz have considered it audacious to pursue that forward, bright-eyed and entirely enchanting woman?

Jack looked backwards, where camp-fires illuminated the lines of British tents; that way lay duty and honour, and then downward to the confusion of Balaklava. In this direction lay something indefinable, something he could not understand. *Why am I so taken with Helen?*

I'm scared. The words came from nowhere. *I'm scared to approach that woman in case she ridicules me. Well dammit, what did Bonaparte and Clausewitz have to say about fear? I don't know; I only know what the greatest general of them all said about it. 'The only thing I am afraid of is fear;' well if Wellington himself thought that, then that is the best advice to follow. After all, Wellington defeated Napoleon and had a string of mistresses.*

Jack found himself grinning. He didn't want a string of mistresses. He wanted only one woman, and she was down there behind her shutters.

He'd made the decision.

'Riley!' Jack shouted as they readied themselves for the trenches.

Riley marched to him, slammed to attention and threw a smart salute. 'Sir!'

'Is Mrs. Riley still in camp?'

Riley's eyes swivelled to the side and back. 'She is about to leave, sir.'

'I would be obliged if you could ask her to perform an act of kindness for me.' *God that sounded stilted. Damn it: I don't care. I'm on new territory here.*

'Sir?' Riley looked confused, as well he might.

'Would you ask her to deliver this note for me,' Jack handed over a folded and sealed square of paper.

'Yes, sir.' Riley took the note as if it was more delicate than the most precious of jewels. He glanced at the address, looked at Jack and wisely said no more.

'That is all, Riley. Dismissed.'

Jack knew he was taking a significant gamble in using one of his men in such a manner. He knew it was probably bad for discipline and most likely contrary to the Queen's Regulations. *And I do not care a damn.*

* * *

They stood on the ridge on the right of the British lines, with a pale moon above them highlighting the scene. The sounds of camp and town drifted dimly to them, while somewhere traffic rumbled on the road.

'That will be the Russians.' Jack spoke awkwardly. 'They bring supplies into Sebastopol at night.'

'Oh, do they?' Helen said. 'I was most surprised to receive your note,' she sounded suddenly more enthusiastic. 'How clever it was of you to give it to the servant to hand to me rather than through Mother.'

'I was not sure if your mother would approve of me meeting you like this.'

'Oh, she would not.' Helen laughed. 'Mother would not approve of me meeting any young man. She has kept me in close confinement these past one-and-twenty years. I have hardly been able to turn without her being there with a warm shawl or a stout pair of boots to protect me from the weather, or a veil to keep the sun from damaging my complexion! And all the time boys of much fewer years were serving in the ranks or donning the uniform of the Queen!'

'She was doing her best to look after you,' Jack said. 'It must have been hard for her bringing you up safely while surrounded by soldiers and natives.' He felt her shiver and adjusted the shawl around her shoulders.

'I used to plead with her to send me to school in England,' Helen pulled the shawl further up her neck. 'So I would have some measure of freedom.'

Remembering the confinement and rigid discipline of his school days, and the stiff faces of the crocodiles of school girls that he'd seen under the strict control of acid-faced schoolmistresses, Jack wasn't sure if Helen's life would have been any freer under those regimes. He decided it was better not to disagree with her on such short acquaintance. There would be plenty time for arguments later.

Later? What am I thinking here?

They stood side by side without touching, cold under the northerly wind yet neither moving away. Now that Jack had Helen all to himself, he found that the power of speech had deserted him. He had nothing to say except a discussion of military tactics, a conversation about the war or anecdotes of Burma and did not think that any of these subjects would interest her. *What is wrong with me?*

'How do you like Balaklava?' It was a terrible question. Luckily Helen either hadn't heard it, or she brushed it aside as unimportant.

'Isn't this exciting!' Helen seemed to realise that Jack's conversational topics were limited. 'With all our brave men just waiting to storm the city and the Russians, stubborn in defence, doomed but unable to admit it.'

'It certainly is something,' Jack was glad to talk about something he understood. His initial enthusiasm died as he guessed she was talking to please him. 'I hope I'm not causing you trouble with your mother by meeting you like this. Without a chaperone, I mean.' He knew it was clumsy. Convention dictated that gentlemen did not take out young ladies until they had the permission of the father.

'Oh, never mind her.' Helen dismissed her formidable mother as if she didn't matter. 'I don't intend to live my life wrapped in cotton wool. I intend to wear out my life, not rust it out sewing samplers and drawing pictures of pretty flowers. I have had sufficient restriction. I want to be free!' She spread her arms, nearly rapping his nose with her fingers. 'Oh, Lieutenant Windrush! I do apologise!'

'It's perfectly all right,' Jack stepped further away. This evening wasn't going as he'd planned. He stood in silence for a few more minutes with Helen at his side. She shivered.

'It's getting cold,' she looked at him with wide grey eyes.

'Yes,' Jack agreed. 'Perhaps you would be warmer back inside the house.' He knew she was disappointed, but he didn't know what else to say or do. They walked back to her house side by side, not touching, not speaking, both frustrated. When they reached the harbour and saw her house lights burning, Jack was tempted to shake her hand.

'Well, goodbye,' he said, 'and thank you.'

'You have nothing to thank me for,' she said, turning away. 'Nor I you.'

Jack knew she was crying. He felt sick.

Chapter Eleven

Siege of Sebastopol
October 1854

The trenches were as cold as before, but Jack's men filed in to replace others of the regiment with a new feeling of determination. It was three days since their first experience in the lines, and each night the Russians had crept forward to capture and kill British soldiers in some sections along the front.

'Right men,' Jack said. 'Tonight the 113th will help create a new sap and a new line of trenches. It's digging duties for all and for God's sake, listen for the Russians!'

'It's our turn tonight, boys,' Logan said with a grin that would have done credit to a fighting dog. He stamped his boots on the ground. 'Are you ready for them?'

'They've taken men from all the best regiments,' one grey-haired sergeant said, 'what makes you think it'll be any different with us?'

Jack was about to reply when Thorpe spoke. 'We're the 113th,' he said.

'The Baby Butchers,' the sergeant said. 'The men who ran at Chillianwala.'

'Maybe you lot bloody ran,' Thorpe said, 'We're the lads of Pegu and Rangoon, when you were sitting in quarters swatting mozzies we were fighting the Burmese, and they were harder men than a few bloody Ruskies.'

'But not as hard as us,' Coleman said, and Jack couldn't stop his swell of pride. It was a small beginning but a lot better than nothing. His small section of the 113th was beginning to believe in itself. The hardships and sacrifices of Burma had not been in vain.

The men exchanged banter with the departing company as they took their places in the trenches, grumbling at the cold, the weather, the dark, the sergeants and the officers.

'They seem happy enough,' Jack said.

'Oh, the lads are always happy when they're complaining,' O'Neill said. 'It's when they stop grousing and start praying that you have to worry.'

Jack nodded. It was another piece of military lore to add to his store. He counted his men. 'I should have twenty-four,' he said. 'I see twenty-five. I've heard of men avoiding front-line duty; never men coming up for extra duty.' He sighed. 'It's not Mrs. Riley come to join us again, is it?

'Oh, it's all right, sir,' Riley said. 'It's not Charlotte. It's something that Logan and I came up with.'

'Logan and you?' Jack looked at the well-spoken soldier, always tidy and well presented, and the disreputable, bitter-eyed Logan who even his colleagues avoided.

'And Mrs. Riley, sir,' Riley said. 'She helped, so in a manner of speaking she is here in spirit if not in body.'

'I think your lady wife is always with you in spirit.' Jack kept the envy from his voice. 'She helped what, exactly, Riley?'

'We call him Arthur sir. Mrs. Riley thought up the name; it's after the Duke of Wellington.' Riley spoke without emotion, while Logan stood at his side with a wicked grin on his face.

'Show me,' Jack ordered.

'Here he is, sir,' Logan grabbed hold of the nearest man and dragged him for Jack's attention. 'It's a dummy sir, made with sandbags and bits of wood and with a uniform on top.'

'That's the uniform of the 118th,' Jack said. 'How did you get that? No, don't tell me. I don't think I want to know.'

'They're a bit careless sir,' Logan said. 'They leave things lying around...'

'I said I don't want to know,' Jack repeated. He examined the dummy. 'It's very lifelike,' he said. 'Who made the face?'

'That was Charlotte... Mrs. Riley, sir,' Riley said. 'She's a wonder with the needle and thread. She used to work in a theatre you see...' He stopped, no doubt wondering if he had overstepped the line of familiarity between a man from the ranks and an officer.

'That would explain her ability to pose as a soldier,' Jack murmured. 'So what's your plan?'

'We don't have a plan, sir,' Riley admitted. 'We don't know how the Russians operate. All we know is that they grab our men from the trenches and murder them. Well then, they can grab Arthur and murder him if they like.'

'Except our Arthur has a nice wee surprise for him, sir' Logan said.

'What sort of surprise, Logan? No, maybe it's best that I don't know,' Jack said. 'Just ensure that none of our men is hurt.'

He moved on, checking the men had loaded their muskets, and the locks were clean, that the bayonets were lightly greased so they would slide easily from scabbards, that the sandbags gave adequate protection, and everybody had their meagre rations. He posted three men to keep watch on the dark distance between the trench and Sebastopol and ensured there was a rota, so the sentries were relieved at regular intervals.

'And now we wait,' he said, checking his revolver was loaded. 'And we dig.'

Every night was darker and colder than the preceding, with a wind that cut like the lash of a nagaika, the Cossack whip, but also concealed the noise of pick and shovel as the lines inched closer, spadeful of dirt by spadeful of rocky soil. Jack led the first of the working parties, carrying gabions, the cylindrical wickerwork baskets that the men filled with earth and positioned in front of them to provide cover from Russian shot as they dug.

'I hope we take this Sebastopol place soon.' Elliot sounded nervous as he led forward the second working party. He looked up. 'Who's that man?'

Jack glanced along the line of trenches. His men were either digging or huddled against the gabions, presenting as little a target as possible for any Russian shot, except for one whose head and shoulders thrust above the others. 'Oh, that's our latest recruit,' he said. 'Arthur Wellington.' He grinned at the expression on Elliot's face. 'Don't you worry about him. He's in good hands.'

'The Russians will get him...' Even as Elliot spoke, the dummy lifted into the air and slithered headfirst toward the distant walls of Sebastopol. Elliot's voice rose an octave. 'God help him!'

Jack put a steadying hand on Elliot's shoulder. 'Wait, Elliot.'

'We must help him!' Elliot shook off Jack's hand, drew his revolver and fired three quick shots into the dark.

'Wait!' Jack's words were unavailing as nervous soldiers followed Elliot's example and musketry broke out along the British front, with the muzzle flares giving surreal images of levelled muskets, gaunt-faced British soldiers, and the line of trenches stretching as far as the gun battery.

'Cease fire!' Jack shouted. 'Cease fire!'

The explosion took them all by surprise. Jack reeled back as something blew up with an immense noise and an eye-scorching flash less than twenty yards in front of the trench. He had a momentary vision of a man flying in the air, heard somebody scream and then there was silence and the stink of burned gunpowder.

'What the devil?'

'I told you our Arthur had a wee surprise, sir,' Logan said. 'He had fifty pounds of gunpowder stuffed in his breeks. We had planned on waiting till the Ruskies had gathered him in before blowing him up so we would get all of them, but somebody started to shoot early, sir.'

'It was a good plan,' Jack approved.

'Permission to go over the trench sir and see what's happened?' Riley had no expression on his face.

'I'm coming too, Riley, and Logan, you and Hitchins come with me.'

Jack rolled over the lip of the trench, keeping low and quiet, remembering similar expeditions outside Pegu in Burma. The same mixture of excitement and sickness returned, and the same desire to excel, to gain promotion and return to a position of respect that was hard to obtain within the lowly 113th.

The acrid stench of powder smoke drifted past, augmented by a soft, low moaning. Jack moved toward the noise, jinking slightly in case some sharp-eyed Russian rifleman was searching for a target. He came to the first body in a matter of minutes, a slender man in a dark grey coat, missing the head and one arm. The second corpse was a few yards beyond, shredded nearly beyond recognition.

'Arthur done his stuff then,' Logan regarded the bodies with neither repugnance nor regret. 'These boys won't be back to murder our lads.'

'Sir.' Riley lifted something from the ground. 'This is interesting. This may be how the Russians captured our soldiers.'

Jack stepped across to him. Riley held a long pole with a thin flexible loop of whalebone at the end.

'See, sir?' Riley held the loop open. 'This is large enough to slip over a man's head. The Russians must have crept up to the trenches, found a man, dropped this loop over his head and pulled him from the trench to bayonet him.'

'Murdering bastards.' Logan stepped over another Russian body.

'Sir,' Hitchins said. 'There's somebody alive here.'

The man lay on his back with his uniform blackened and torn and both hands covering his face. 'He's a Russian, sir,' Riley said. 'Burned by the explosion.'

'Bring him back,' Jack said. 'Our medical people might be able to patch him together.'

'Here's another Ruski, sir,' Logan said. There was the sound of a kick. 'Up you get, you!' He pushed a tall man over on his side. 'You're no' deid; you can stand.'

'This one's an officer, sir, or he's wearing an officer's uniform anyway.' Riley said. 'Not sure about the rank.'

The officer's uniform was torn, and his face marked by gunpowder and smoke. Broad and erect, he looked haughtily down at Logan through eyes made paler by comparison to his smoke-blackened face. 'Who are you?'

'Lieutenant Jack Windrush, 113th Foot,' Jack said.

The Russian gave a little start as he looked at Jack and then averted his eyes and said nothing. Logan lifted his bayonet hopefully as the officer staggered. Jack shook his head and pushed the blade down.

'Best hurry sir,' Hitchins said, 'lest the Russians send out a search party to find their men.'

Jack nodded. He had a wounded Russian infantryman and a dazed Russian officer. One had to be cared for, and the other handed over for interrogation.

Logan grunted, 'We could wait for the Ruskies, sir. Get some of our own back after them firing at us for days and days.' He tapped the lock of his musket hopefully.

'No,' Jack decided. 'I appreciate your enthusiasm, Logan, but there'll be other opportunities. We'll get these prisoners back.'

Riley and Hitchins helped support the wounded Russian, with Jack leading them back to the trenches and Logan pushing the officer before him, glancing over his shoulder and apparently hopeful of meeting a Russian patrol.

'What do you have there?' Snodgrass asked.

'A couple of Russian prisoners, sir,' Jack said.

Snodgrass raised his eyebrows. 'I don't think some stray Russians will be any good to us.'

'One is an officer,' Jack said, 'I'm not sure what rank.'

'Oh, a gentleman.' Snodgrass' attitude changed when he saw the officer. 'We'll clean him up and keep him.' He glanced at the wounded man without interest. 'Bring the officer to the rear and let's have a look at him.' He hesitated. 'Just put the other one back over the trench and let his men come for him if they will.'

'He's wounded, sir.' A moment earlier, Logan had been willing to bayonet any Russian in sight; now he stood up to Major Snodgrass, a man far above him in rank and social standing. 'If we put him back, he'll just die, and that's not right.'

Logan typified the British soldier, Jack thought – one never knew how they were going to react. They merged utter callousness in battle with a soft heart possibly based on their harsh childhood. They could empathise with the enemy when they were not busily devising the best ways of slaughtering them.

Snodgrass stared at Logan for a second, as if looking at something unpleasant he had inadvertently stepped in. 'What's your name?' His voice was deceptively gentle.

'Logan.' The small man did not lower his glare. For one horrible second, Jack thought he was going to ask *what's yours?*

'I'll have you flogged for impudence,' Snodgrass said, just as the Russian artillery fired again.

The first ball passed overhead with a sound similar to ripping canvas. The second struck the back of the trench wall three yards from where Snodgrass stood, with the impact knocking sandbags from the parapet facing the enemy and the *parados* at the rear, which was intended to afford some protection from shells landing behind them. Snodgrass sprawled in the mud at the bottom of the trench with his hat falling into a puddle.

Jack helped Snodgrass to his feet as Logan remained at attention and watched, expressionless.

'The Russian officer may have important information.' Snodgrass tried to dust himself down and succeeded only in spreading Crimean mud over his tunic. 'We'll get him behind the lines so we can interrogate him.'

'You can take them both, sir,' Jack said, but Snodgrass was already hurrying toward the sap. 'Sir, I can't leave my men here without me.'

'I'll look after them, sir.' Elliot said.

Jack hesitated until Haverdale appeared. 'The Major ordered you to accompany him, Windrush. You'd better go.'

'My men...'

'We'll be fine, sir,' O'Neill said.

'Elliot and I will look after them for the few minutes you will be away.' Haverdale pointed to the sap down which Snodgrass had disappeared. 'Go.'

Perhaps because of the loss of their patrol, the Russian gunners began a fusillade, firing shot after shot toward the British lines, concentrating on the section held by the 113th. The men crouched behind the sandbags, held their hats close on to their heads and swore their hatred of the Russian gunners, the Crimea, their officers and anything else that came to mind.

'Bastards know exactly where we are,' Logan said. He turned around and gestured in the direction of Sebastopol. 'Just you wait! We'll get you!'

'Come on, Logie!' Riley pulled him away. 'They'll keep.'

'Halloa!' The surgeon was fat and cheerful, despite the row of bodies outside his tent. 'What's to do?' He held up a lantern. 'What's this?'

'A Russian soldier,' Snodgrass said. 'We captured him prowling outside our lines.'

'You werenae there to capture him!' Logan said, until Riley nudged him hard in the ribs.

'Prowling was he now?' The surgeon had a long look at the Russian. 'He must have prowled into an explosion.' When he looked up his eyes were shrewd. 'And as we are not firing at them, that poses an interesting question…'

'That doesn't matter,' Snodgrass said. 'I want him patched up, so he's fit to answer questions.'

'He knows nothing,' the Russian officer said shortly. 'He is a moujik.'

'He may well be only a peasant, sir, but you are not,' Snodgrass said. 'May we have your name and rank?'

The officer gave an abrupt bow. As he straightened up, light from the surgeon's lantern highlighted his face, so Jack saw him properly for the first time. Mud and powder smoke smeared the broad face, while the moustache was a lot less neat than the last time he'd seen it, but there was no mistaking the face with those light, bright eyes.

Stevensen. This is the Swedish diplomat whose house I broke into in Malta.

Jack opened his mouth to speak and closed it hurriedly as the Russian straightened up. 'I am Grigory Kutuzov, Major, Plastun Cossacks.'

'I am Major Snodgrass of the 113th Foot.'

'And this?' Kutuzov motioned to Jack.

'Jack Windrush, sir, Lieutenant, 113th Foot,' Jack answered automatically. He held Kutuzov's gaze, knowing the Cossack had recognised him.

'Have any of you been wounded?' The surgeon asked. 'If so, I will attend to you as soon as I have fixed up this poor chap. If not, please leave me in peace.'

Jack heard Colonel Murphy's cough before he arrived. 'What's all this?' Murphy looked at them through bloodshot eyes. 'Why are two of my officers standing here when they should be in the trenches with the men?'

'We brought back two prisoners, sir,' Snodgrass said. 'This gentleman is Major Kutuzov.'

'Does it need two officers and two men to escort two prisoners?' Murphy coughed again, spitting up blood. 'Snodgrass, make your report, Windrush; take these two men back to the trenches where they belong. I won't have anybody saying the 113th is deficient in their duty.'

Kutuzov grunted. 'My men will say that the 113th are not gentlemen. My officers will report your dishonourable conduct to General Raglan.'

Jack saw an expression of dismay cross Murphy's face. 'My regiment is as honourable as any in the British Army.' He glanced at Jack, 'I ordered you back to your post, Windrush!'

'Yes, sir,' Jack said and ushered Logan and Riley before him. He wanted to hear what was being said but an order was an order.

'That cut-your-throat Ruski was a bit of a blackguard, sir,' Riley said. 'I did not much care for him.'

'Nor he for us, Riley,' Jack said. He ducked as a Russian shot hit the ground twenty yards away, sending shards of rock as deadly as shrapnel all around. 'You'd think we were enemies or something.'

'There was more than that, sir,' Riley said softly. 'He was the fellow from Dar-il-Sliem in Malta, and he knew us right away.'

'I am aware of that, Riley,' Jack said as all his hopes of putting his dishonourable spying activities behind him vanished.

Chapter Twelve

**Siege of Sebastopol
October 1854**

The bombardment began on the morning of the 17th October. After days of preparation, days of taking Russian artillery fire without retaliating, the Allies were at last hitting back. The Russians, seemingly supplied with endless ammunition, greeted the cold dawn with desultory shelling, aiming at the so-far silent Allied artillery.

'There they go,' Coleman grumbled, as he huddled into his greatcoat and hugged the nearest gabion. 'If it's not bloody sharpshooters, its bloody artillery firing at us. You'd think they had nothing better to do than blast away at the bloody 113th, these Ruskies.'

'Aye,' Riley said, 'you'd think there was a war on or something.'

'About time we fired back.' Logan lifted his musket. 'But we haven't even got a decent musket between us.' He turned to Jack. 'Hey. Sir, when are we getting these new Minié rifles? These old Brown Bess things are nae good at all. Wellington rejected this one before Waterloo.'

Most of the British regiments had taken possession of the new Minié Rifle, which was far superior to the smooth bore Brown Bess musket that the British soldier had carried since the days of Marlborough.

'It will fire, and it will kill,' Jack knew it would be bad for discipline if he agreed with Logan. 'It was good enough to defeat the French, and it will be good enough to defeat the Russians.'

Logan looked as if he was going to continue his complaint, just as the British guns opened up. 'Jesus,' he said, 'we're firing at the buggers!'

'So we are,' Jack said.

At half past six that morning a solitary signal gun sounded from the Allied camp and the artillery began their long-awaited bombardment of Sebastopol. Seventy-three British and fifty-three French guns opened fire, backed by the broadsides of the Royal Navy and the French fleet. After their exertions in the trenches, the 113th was not expected to take part in any infantry assault if the bombardment was successful and breached the outer Russian defences. Instead, they stood up behind their frail barricades and watched the results.

'What a show!' Elliot said. 'They say it's the biggest artillery duel in history.'

Jack nodded. He could hardly hear Elliot's words through the incessant pounding of the cannonade.

With the allied lines around 1300 yards from Sebastopol, the tremendous conical shot from the 68- pounder Lancasters and 32- pounder naval guns and from every other piece of artillery the Allies possessed hammered away at the batteries and walls of Sebastopol, as the Russian artillery replied shot for shot and shell for shell.

'They say that the walls will collapse this morning.' Elliot nearly bounced with excitement. 'And then the Russians will capitulate.' He scanned what he could see of the walls through the drifting smoke, as if searching for a white flag.

'Two days,' Fleming said. 'At the least, two days. The Russians are a stubborn breed. They will hold out until we have flattened all their defences and our men have stormed their fortress.'

'This is hotter than the attack on Rangoon,' Jack said, 'and I thought that was hotter than hell.'

'That was only a skirmish,' said Elliot, who hadn't been there. 'This is war! They say over two thousand guns are firing!'

'Who says?' Jack asked mildly.

Elliot looked at him and shrugged. 'Somebody,' he said vaguely.

The Russians had as many guns as the Allies, positioned behind solid stone and secure earthworks and were fighting in their own country. Using Haverdale's telescope, Jack could watch the Russian artillerymen as they laboured at their guns, every bit as feverishly as the British worked theirs. He could hear the whizz and howl of shot passing over his head in both directions and feel the shudder as shot ploughed into the earth or against the sandbags along the line of his trench.

'For the love of God!' That was Thorpe, cursing and struggling as a Russian shot smashed down the sandbag wall behind which he'd been sheltering. Jack reached him as he sprawled face up in the bottom of the trench with legs kicking and a burst sandbag rapidly emptying its hundredweight of soil on top of him.

'Am I hit, sir? Am I dead?'

'Not yet, Thorpe!' Jack shoved the bag aside, ducked as another shot screamed above his head and helped Thorpe up. 'You're still alive.' Thorpe was shaking. 'Take a deep breath man and return to duty.'

'Yes, sir.'

Elliot cheered. 'Oh, good shot, sir!'

A British shell had landed on the barrel of a Russian cannon directly opposite the 113th, upending the gun and scattering its crew. More followed as the British gunners exploited their success. Someone on the Russian side was screaming, the terrible sound reaching across to the British lines. Nobody commented on that. They had heard too many British wounded yelling in agony, to celebrate or commiserate; the untried army was learning the rules.

About three hours into the artillery battle there was a tremendous explosion from the French lines, with a massive cloud of white powder smoke rising high and then spreading across the front.

'What the devil…' Fleming ducked to the bottom of the trench.

'Elliot,' Haverdale ordered, 'off you go and find out what happened.'

Elliot was back within half an hour; white-faced except where powder smoke had smeared him. 'The Ruskies hit a French powder magazine,' he said. 'There's dead men and wounded men everywhere. It's awful.'

Within the hour there was another explosion from the French side, and their fire slackened and stopped.

'We're on our own now,' Snodgrass said. 'That's best. We don't need the blasted Froggies anyway; they're a liability.'

'They're a damned sight better organised than we are, sir,' Haverdale said, just as a British shell exploded within the Great Redan, blasting it wide open and tumbling down the walls. The Russian guns fell momentarily silent. Jack saw a body sprawled among the shattered stones, blood pumping from a severed limb.

'Now!' Haverdale shouted, 'now's the time.' He stood up. 'The Russians are reeling; put the infantry in now!'

Nothing happened. There was no order to attack, no frantic bugle call prompting the British infantry to swarm across the rough ground to take the Great Redan while the Russians were at their most vulnerable. The British artillery continued to pound away as the Russians rectified the damage.

Jack had another idea of leading the 113th in a wild charge to capture Sebastopol, end the war and bring glory to the regiment and himself. He glanced around, knowing his men would follow, but a dozen British soldiers could not capture Sebastopol on their own. It wasn't a viable proposition. He watched as the Russians remounted a gun and had it back in action; then a second and the third. The chance had gone; the siege must continue.

Jack was aware of the flash an instant before he heard the sound, followed by a period of utter confusion. He was aware of being thrown into the air with a terrible roaring in his ears and a sensation of floating; when nothing much mattered except his overwhelming but transient desire to laugh. He landed on something soft, and lay there, unable to breathe as some mighty weight crushed down on him. He gasped for air, seeing only darkness; he had no cohesive thought.

I am dead. I am dead without having kissed a girl yet alone had a woman. What a waste of a life. I wish I had spoken longer to Helen.

'Sir?' The voice came from far away, disembodied, distant, something detached from this reality of black solidity. It had nothing to do with him. It was only a voice.

'Sir?' It came again, small, insignificant.

Jack shifted slightly, opened his eyes and closed them quickly as a searing light blinded him. 'What? Leave me alone.' He heard the echo of his own words, like a shadow of somebody he had once been.

Rough hands around him, somebody pulling him upright, something hard thrust into his mouth, clearing away the soil and mud. More fingers in his ears and eyes, scooping out the dirt. He blinked, closed his eyes in pain. 'Here, drink this.' Riley's voice, and then he was aware of something damp spread across his face. 'It's not his blood.'

'What?' Jack asked, instinctively swallowed and gagged at the harsh burn in his throat.

'It's whisky, sir,' Logan's voice, harsh, guttural and concerned. 'I got it frae a lad in the Royals.'

'What happened?' Jack looked around. The entire section of the trench where he'd been standing had vanished, flattened beyond recognition, with gabions upended and sandbags tossed this way and that. On the space where the trench floor had been was a black hole, three feet in diameter, with a sticky reddish paste that he knew had once been a man.

'That was Ogden sir,' Riley said. 'He took the full force.'

'Ogden?' *That muscular, capable ex-navigator, dead – killed in an instant before he had ever had a chance to retaliate against the Russians.*

'He was a good man.' Jack felt the harshness of dirt in his throat. He swallowed more of Logan's whisky, burning away the Crimea. 'Anybody else killed, Riley?'

'Jackson sir, from Lieutenant Fleming's men.'

Jack nodded. Jackson was a quiet man to whom he'd never spoken. 'Anybody wounded?'

'O'Keefe sir, and maybe yourself.'

Jack felt himself. 'Nothing's broken, Riley. Thank you for digging me out. How long was I down for?'

Riley shook his head. 'About fifteen minutes, sir.'

'Thank you. It seemed like eternity.' Jack shook away his confusion. 'Get the trench dug again, men. We need cover. Sandbags and spades…'

By nightfall, it was evident that the massive bombardment had not been effective. The British buried their dead and carried the few wounded to the gentle ministrations of the surgeon and the 113th sat at the bottom of their trench.

'Now what?' Coleman asked. 'We fired all bloody day, and the walls are still there.'

'We may as well go home,' Thorpe buried his head in his hands, 'for all the good we're doing here.'

'The generals know what they're doing,' Hitchins said. 'Wait and see.'

'Buck up lads.' Jack shared their disappointment. 'That was only one day's bombardment. Here comes the quartermaster with the ration rum.' As expected, the prospect of something alcoholic helped salve the frustrations of the siege. Jack looked toward Sebastopol, where the walls seemed as secure as ever, and powder smoke drifted from the muzzles of the Russian artillery.

'Post the pickets, Windrush.' Haverdale's eyes narrowed. 'Are you up to it? You look a bit rough.'

'I'm all right, sir,' Jack said.

'If you say so. Get the pickets out then, and eat something. We're being relieved at three in the morning. Get some sleep until then.'

No longer as keen as he had been, Elliot took charge of the pickets as Jack and his men ate rations of pork and onions, a hard biscuit, a mouthful of rum and half a bottle of muddy water to wash away the taste of powder smoke. Jack lay down on the foot of the muddy trench. He knew that he'd done nothing to further the reputation of the 113th or himself, but he had done his duty; a soldier could do no more. Tomorrow was always another day. *How many more tomorrows like this can I take?*

When he closed his eyes, he was back under that pile of dirt, suffocating.

Chapter Thirteen

**Siege of Sebastopol
October 1854**

Colonel Murphy leaned back in his chair as the canvas of his tent rustled above his head. 'You are well aware that we're attempting to raise the reputation of the 113th, Windrush.'

Jack nodded, 'Yes, sir.'

'That means that we must not only be the best of regiments in the field, but also be known as gentlemen.'

'Yes, sir.' Jack stood at attention, as tense as any private soldier called before a duty officer. Major Snodgrass stood at the entrance of the tent, while Murphy's desk was a litter of papers and maps, with his holstered revolver acting as a paperweight and his sword hanging across the back of his chair. There were two glass-fronted cases behind Murphy's desk, one for the Queen's Colour and one for the Regimental Colour. While the Queen's Colour remained in place, the case holding the Regimental Colour was empty.

'You see correctly, Windrush,' Murphy said. 'Somebody has stolen the Regimental Colour.' He shook his head. 'To lose one of the colours in action is a disgrace. To lose a colour from one's tent…' He shook his head. 'There is nothing worse.'

'Was it the Zouaves sir?' Jack asked. 'Our men have sometimes borrowed supplies from them, and they may have wished to retaliate.'

'I do not know, damn it!' Murphy said. He glowered at Jack. 'I expect my officers to find the culprit, Windrush. The regiment is disgraced by the loss, and doubly disgraced when Major Kutuzov informed me about your conduct in the line.'

'My conduct, sir¿Jack stiffened to attention, his eyes still on the empty display case. 'I'm afraid I don't understand.'

Colonel Murphy stood up, coughed and sat back down again. 'If what Major Kutuzov tells me is correct, Windrush, then you set a trap for him.'

'The Russians were not acting according to any rules of gentlemanly conduct I have ever heard of, sir.' Jack was surprised that Murphy allowed him to explain. 'They were creeping up to our trenches at night and looping a wire over the heads of our sentries, dragging them out of the trenches and slitting their throats, sir. It's the sort of behaviour one would expect from Burmese dacoits rather than European soldiers.'

'Indeed,' Murphy said. 'I don't disagree with you, Windrush, but we are British soldiers. We fight fair and according to the rules. That is what sets us above all the other nations; that is what makes us better. We are honourable and must be seen to be beyond approach. Do you understand that?'

'Yes, sir.' Jack could only agree.

'It doesn't matter what tricks the enemy employs; we cannot stoop to their level. What would Her Majesty say if she heard that soldiers who hold her commission were resorting to tricks such as explosive dummies to defeat the foe?'

'I see, sir.' Jack had an image of Queen Victoria reading a letter sent from Lord Raglan directly to her, informing her of the reprehensible behaviour of one Lieutenant Jack Windrush of the 113th Foot. The Queen would immediately collapse in a fit and Prince Albert would revive her with smelling-salts before she retired to bed with a warm cloth over her forehead and a brace of servants dancing attendance on her. He wondered if he should tell the colonel that Kutuzov had also acted as a spy. He decided it would be impossible without admitting his behaviour in Malta. The old fellow was sick enough and knowing that one of his officers had stooped to such depths may give him an attack of apoplexy. Jack realised that Colonel Murphy was speaking again.

'So, considering that Windrush, I had no option but to release the prisoners you took. Major Kutuzov will be returned to Sebastopol. That is all; dismissed.'

'Yes, sir.' Jack saluted. When he was summoned to see the colonel, Jack had expected something much worse than to merely be informed that his prisoner was being sent back. Ensign Elliot had already informed him of the theft of the Regimental Colour.

'Oh, and Jack…'

'Sir?' That was the first time Murphy had called him by his first name.

'I'm afraid I shall have to make my displeasure at this incident known. I want you to take charge of the pickets for the rest of the week.'

'Yes, sir.'

'No more explosive dummies, Jack; all right?'

'No more, sir.'

The lines had advanced another few yards closer to Sebastopol, making the distance for any attack less, and thereby decreasing the time that the attackers would be under fire. As before, the 113th was directly opposite the Great Redan, with their forward saps probing into the ravaged dangers of no-man's land.

'Right lads.' Jack looked over his picket. They were his men, Logan, Riley, Thorpe and Coleman with O'Neill, now a sergeant, as his NCO. 'We are the closest men to the Russians so keep quiet and keep your heads down. Their sharpshooters fire at anything that moves.'

'They like to target officers, sir,' Riley said helpfully. 'That's what I heard. They'll miss the chance to shoot a private if they think it gives them a better shot at an officer.'

'Thank you, Riley; that is very reassuring.' Jack paused for a second. 'Did you all hear about the theft of the Colours?'

'We heard, sir,' Riley answered for them all. 'We blame the Zouaves. We got some of their brandy, you see.'

'Well Riley, it is a matter of regimental honour that we get it back.' Jack guessed that his men knew more than they were saying. 'If you hear anything, you let me know.'

'Yes, sir,' Logan's response was too quick and correct to be genuine.

'I will get extra rum for the man or men who get it back,' Jack promised.

'Thank you, sir,' Riley said. 'I will make sure your message is passed on.'

'Rum will make a wee change from the whisky and brandy,' Logan said with that greasy grin that Jack had learned meant he was gloating over some secret.

The sap zig-zagged forward, bolstered by sandbags and gabions until it ended in a sandbagged enclosure. 'Here we are,' Jack whispered. 'You know the drill; listen for enemy movement and watch for Russian patrols.'

'What if a patrol comes, sir?' Coleman asked.

'We kill the bastards,' Logan said.

'Quite,' Jack agreed. 'And we try and not get killed ourselves.'

That same northwesterly wind cut into them as if they wore no uniforms at all, causing them to crouch under the sandbagged parapets, hug their rags to them and wish for dawn.

'If this is Russia, then they can keep it,' Coleman said. 'I wish I was back in Burma.'

'All you did there was complain about the heat and the insects,' Thorpe reminded. 'Here it's the cold and the wind. Make up your mind, man!'

'I hate them all,' Coleman replied, 'but not as much as I hate you, Thorpey!'

'Keep the noise down,' Jack whispered. 'We may as well fly a flag that tells the Russians where we are.'

'They probably know anyway,' Logan said. 'They send out their spies from Sebastopol.'

Jack grunted: that was truer than Logan realised.

They lay against the parapet, facing all around; fingers on the cold triggers of their muskets, hoping the dirt and damp would not prevent the weapons from firing, breathing softly as the Russians fired the occasional cannon to keep the British awake. Far above, fast clouds whisked across the remains of the moon.

'This is your last night on picket duty sir,' O'Neill broke a long silence.

'It is,' Jack agreed quietly. It had been a long week.

They both heard the sound at the same time. It was only a soft chunk that would have been unnoticed in any other situation, but both men had been on picket duty in Burma as well as in the Crimea and knew what it meant.

'That was somebody kicking a stone,' O'Neill nudged Riley and Logan to ensure they were alert.

'There's somebody out there.' Although Jack whispered, his words sounded like a shout in a small room.

'Over there,' Coleman lifted his musket. Already cocked, he had only to squeeze the trigger. 'I hear them.'

As Jack focussed on the patch of blackness Coleman had indicated, he also saw men emerge one by one into his vision. 'Eight, ten, twelve men,' he said. 'Maybe more.' They moved slowly, one behind the other in a long line, spaced out and with their muskets carried in both hands, muzzles parallel to the ground.

Jack pondered. He had six men, including himself. He could give them a volley and hope to kill or injure enough, so the remainder fled, or he could allow them to pass and then report their presence to Major Snodgrass. If he fired and they attacked, he would be outnumbered, perhaps as much as two to one. On the other hand, he was a British officer and his duty was to defeat the enemy. He raised his revolver.

'Sir!' O'Neill hissed, 'they're ours! They're British soldiers, sir!'

'What the devil…' Jack started. 'Are you sure, O'Neill?'

'Yes, sir.'

'Stand down!' Jack passed the word in an urgent whisper. He saw the relief on Coleman's face, and the near disappointment as Logan uncocked his musket and relaxed as much as he ever could.

Jack watched the patrol pass; he now counted fifteen men led by a slender officer with a forage cap on his head. They moved slowly across the front of the British lines and disappeared into the night.

'I wonder what that was all about?' O'Neill whispered.

'I wonder why nobody warned us.' Jack didn't try and conceal his anger. 'We could have shot our own men.'

The rain started half an hour later, carried by the northerly wind. It sliced at the faces of the watching men, slid under their tunics and wet them to the skin after only a few moments. 'Wish I was back in Burma.' Coleman glowered at Thorpe. 'At least the rain was warm there.' He looked up suddenly. 'Somebody's out there, sir.'

'Christ it's like Sauchiehall Street on a Saturday night,' Logan cocked his musket.

'Are you sure?'

'I smell them, sir,' Coleman said, 'Garlic or something.'

'Watch out for that wire loop, lads,' O'Neill warned.

At that moment the Russian artillery in the Great Redan fired a salvo, with the muzzle flares allowing a glimpse of the ground between the trenches and the city.

'Jesus!' Coleman blasphemed.

After an instant of brightness, darkness returned, but there had been sufficient time for Jack to see a group of Russian infantry, directly in front of their position.

'How many?' he asked quickly.

'At least ten.' The sound of Coleman cocking his musket was very loud.

'More than that,' O'Neill added.

'Are we sure they're not ours?' Jack lifted his revolver and pointed it into the dark.

'Russians.' O'Neill sounded definite.

'Can we fire on these buggers then?' Logan evidently resented missing the opportunity to shoot at the earlier British patrol.

'Yes.' Jack showed the way by loosing off two quick shots.

Logan yelled some incomprehensible slogan and fired; with the others following suit, so muzzle flares lit the front of the sap in a succession of light and darkness. There was a single long yell from in front.

'Fire at will, boys,' Jack said. 'Thorpe – get you back to Major Snodgrass, give him my compliments and inform him that we are engaging a strong Russian patrol.'

Thorpe hesitated for only a second before he returned down the sap. Jack waited until his men had all loosed a round before he fired again, trying to fill in the gaps between the men firing and re-loading their ponderous muskets. There were shouts from the darkness and the blaze and blast of Russian musketry and the hoarse voice of an officer giving orders.

'I can't see a thing!' Coleman complained as he thumbed back the hammer of his musket and fired in the direction of the Russian voice.

'Neither can they!' Jack said. 'Keep firing!'

There was a frantic yell, and somebody jumped over the sandbagged lip of the sap to land among them. Jack saw the Russian lift his bayoneted musket to strike, realise that there was little space to wield the clumsy weapon in the sap and then Logan unfastened his bayonet and jumped on the Russian's back. Before Jack could turn, there was a flash of steel, and the Russian collapsed in a welter of spurting blood.

'That's one for Oggy,' Logan said as he calmly clicked his bayonet into place.

'They've pulled back,' O'Neill said. 'I wonder how many we got?'

'Anybody hurt?' Jack asked.

'No, sir,' O'Neill replied.

'Reload and keep watch.' It was quiet out there and with the moon now down, too dark to make out anything. A Russian cannon boomed out opposite the French position with the sound echoing and fading.

'I can slip over and have a look,' O'Neill said quietly.

'No; they'll expect that. Sit tight.'

There was a minute's silence that stretched to two minutes, then five, then ten. Half an hour passed without movement from the front, and Jack was beginning to relax when the guns of the Great Redan fired again. No sooner had the volley screeched overhead when there was a loud yell in front, and a dozen muskets fired in unison.

'Here they come again!' O'Neill roared.

'C'mon, you bastards!' Logan fired at once and rose up as if to leave the sap and charge into the Russians.

'Get back down, you crazy Scottish bastard!' Riley hauled at his tunic. 'There's hundreds of them!'

Once again Jack fired into the dark, hoping that at least some of his shots found their mark.

'It's time that Thorpey was back with reinforcements,' O'Neill said. 'He's been gone a good forty minutes now.'

Fire and fire again. Jack swore when his revolver jammed, banged it against his knee to clear it, heard the cartridge rattle to the ground, thrust in another with a shaking hand and fired a third time. Every muzzle flash revealed a minuscule vignette of the situation, so he had images of grey-coated Russians advancing, of men with wide staring eyes, of gleaming bayonets and open mouths, of men falling as musket balls smashed into them, and of a tall officer at the back, giving orders. And then, as abruptly as the images were there, they were gone, plunged into darkness made more intense by the brightness of only a second before.

Then there were the sounds; the abrupt crack of the muskets, the hoarse, scared yells of charging men, Logan's wild slogans and O'Neill's Gaelic curses, Riley's oaths that would fit better into Eton rather than Russia and Coleman's non-stop swearing.

And then silence, save for the low moaning of two men somewhere in front of them. Powder smoke drifted briefly, to be shredded by the wind and vanish. Jack fumbled for cartridges in the dark.

'Anybody hurt?'

'No, sir, but I'm running low on ammunition.' Coleman said. 'I'm firing them like it was a full-scale battle.'

'Me too, sir,' Riley said.

Jack nodded. 'We're due to be relieved at three,' he glanced at his watch. *Half past one; where the devil is Thorpe with the reinforcements?*

'Maybe we should pull back to the line, sir,' O'Neill suggested. 'We've done enough here.'

Jack shook his head. 'No, Sergeant; we stay.' In any other regiment, he would have withdrawn the picket back to the main line, but he knew that the 113th was constantly under observation and always looked on with suspicion. If any of the 113th withdrew so much as a yard, military fingers would be pointing, and military tongues would be crying accusations such as 'cowardice' and 'failure'. He had to hold on for the sake of the regiment. If the reputation of the 113th was redeemed, then he might be able to hold up his head again in decent society.

'As you wish, sir,' O'Neill said. 'All the same, I'll be happier when Thorpey brings the reinforcements.'

Jack allowed himself a quiet nod. 'So will I, O'Neill. So will I.'

'There's something not right here, sir,' O'Neill said. 'These Russian lads know exactly where we are and by now, they'll how there are only a few of us. Why don't they just toss in a couple of bombs? They could destroy us in seconds that way. Or all of them come at once, even?'

'Maybe they don't have any,' Coleman said.

'Maybe they want to see how good we are,' Riley said.

'Bloody better than they'll ever be,' Logan said. 'Bloody Russian barbarians.'

A cannon fired from the Malakoff, signalling another desultory cannonade that lasted fifteen minutes. None of the shots came near the sap. The firing ended abruptly in a silence so complete it was painful. A dog barked somewhere in the British lines. White smoke drifted, tingling sensitive nostrils, to be blown away by the chilling wind. A nervous picket in the French lines fired a musket; others followed, then silence again. The darkness closed in, cold, brittle, frightening.

'Lieutenant Jack Windrush of the 113th Foot!' the shout came from their front. 'Are you Lieutenant Windrush of the 113th Foot!'

'Who is that?' Jack called out.

'I am Major Grigory Kutuzov of the Plastun Cossacks. Are you Lieutenant Windrush of the 113th Foot?'

The name brought a shiver to Jack's spine. 'I am Windrush.'

'I have your Colonel Maxwell.'

Jack flinched. Colonel Maxwell? That must be Helen's father. 'What has that to do with me?'

'Unless you surrender, I will execute him,' Kutuzov said.

'Tell the Russian to...' Logan's suggestion was crude and to the point.

'They won't shoot him,' O'Neill said. 'The Russian officers are gentlemen. They won't act like brute beasts.'

'The army officers won't' Jack said, 'I'm not sure about the Cossacks. They have their own laws. They were the cutting edge of the Russian advance into Asia, the wild free horsemen of the steppe. The Plastun Cossacks are their infantry; they like night attacks and the knife.' His military reading had not all been in vain.

'How do they know your name, sir?' O'Neill asked.

'That's the man we took prisoner a few days ago,' Jack said. 'Colonel Murphy had him released.

'I see, sir,' O'Neill said.

'Two minutes,' Kutuzov said. 'And then we hang him like a dog, with a thin wire around his neck. There are five of you there. I want all five men to stand up.'

There was another voice, lower and hoarse as if in pain. 'For God's sake, Windrush, don't let them execute me! Help me, for pity's sake.'

'Sir,' Logan spoke quietly. 'We could charge them and free the colonel.'

Jack nodded. 'I had thought of that.' One quick bayonet charge would create mayhem among the Russians, but he had no idea where the Russians were or how many there were. If they succeeded, he would be a hero. If he failed, he would be probably condemning his men to death, as well as Colonel Maxwell.

'One minute remaining, Lieutenant Windrush.'

'Windrush; for God's own sake!' Colonel Maxwell sounded as if he was in agony.

'Will you treat my men decently?' Jack shouted.

'Of course, I will. Your men will be cared for, and you will be placed with our other British officers. And Colonel Maxwell will be treated as my honoured guest – or hanged slowly to choke in his own blood. It all depends on you, Lieutenant.'

There was no choice. Jack knew he could withdraw and leave a British officer to be hanged, charge forward and perhaps get all his men killed, or surrender and hopefully save everybody's life.

Jack swore; he gave a mouthful of oaths that impressed even Logan as he made the decision that was inevitable from the beginning. He knew that he could never condemn Helen's father to such a terrible death.

'We surrender,' he said. 'We're coming out.'

'I never thought I'd hear you say that sir,' O'Neill sounded disapproving.

'I never imagined saying it,' Jack felt sick. After all his dreams and hopes, after wishing that the 113th would be sent on campaign, here he was tamely surrendering without a wound or a casualty. 'Come on lads and let's hope these Russians keep their word.' *What will Helen think?*

Chapter Fourteen

Sebastopol
October 1854

Major Kutuzov was waiting with a smile on his face and Colonel Maxwell at his side. The Colonel, bare-headed and dark-haired, stood erect with his hands tied behind his back and a gag over his mouth. As soon as Windrush led his men forward, a score of Cossack infantry, rough-haired men with dark grey uniforms, took away their muskets and unfastened their cross belts.

'Hey, you!' Logan refused to let go his musket until Jack snapped at him.

'Let it go, Logan. We're their prisoners now.'

Growling, Logan threw his musket hard on the ground and glared at the Cossack who picked it up. 'We'll meet later,' he promised.

'Our positions are reversed this time, Lieutenant Windrush.' With his uniform not mangled and his face not blackened by powder, Kutuzov looked every inch the debonair Cossack officer or the intense Swedish merchant. Above middle height and broad, he gave a little bow. 'Thank you for being sensible, Lieutenant Windrush. It would not have been an easy decision to make, but I am afraid I left you little choice.' He pointed to Maxwell. 'You will see that I had to bind and gag the unfortunate Colonel to ensure he didn't spoil my plan.'

'You said you would treat my men well,' Jack reminded.

'We will grant them every courtesy,' Kutuzov said, 'and so will you and the so-determined Colonel Maxwell who was so very gallant as he led his raid against Sebastopol earlier tonight and so unfortunate as to get caught.'

That explained Maxwell's capture. 'Untie him,' Jack ordered. 'He is a prisoner of war and a British officer.'

'But of course, Lieutenant Windrush.' Kutuzov bowed, clicking his heels. 'I shall permit you to do so, and to remove that most inconvenient gag that prevented our brave colonel from ordering you to fight on.'

'What do you mean?'

Kutuzov smiled again. 'Colonel Maxwell would never have pleaded for his life. I had to prevent him from causing even more bloodshed.' He looked away for a second and then spoke again in a drawl so affected it could have come from the officer's mess of the Grenadier Guards. 'Oh, come now, Lieutenant Windrush, did you believe that a British officer would act in such a manner? I am surprised at you.'

'That was a low, underhand sort of trick.' Jack untied Maxwell's hands and gently removed the gag.

'No more so than filling a dummy soldier with gunpowder,' Kutuzov's smile vanished.

Maxwell wiped a hand across his mouth. 'Would you have hanged me, you scoundrel?'

'Perhaps,' Kutuzov said. 'If I had to. I learned all manner of blackguard tricks in my schooling days.'

'Some school you went to,' Jack said.

'It was.' Kutuzov began to sing:

>'Con ci na mus;
>O so da les;
>Quid si le mus?'

'What?' Maxwell stared at him, 'I know that song!'

'So you should; you sang it often enough at Winchester.' Kutuzov bowed again. 'You were a senior when I was a fag. Come on; my men will escort you back to Sebastopol.'

'You are a cad, sir,' Maxwell said calmly.

'Perhaps so, colonel,' Kutuzov said, 'but a victorious cad.'

The house was large, with similar green roof tiles to those Jack had admired in Balaklava and steps up to double wooden doors. Kutuzov had three Cossack infantry escort them into a large room with tall, multi-paned windows and ornate French furniture, all brilliantly lit by a crystal chandelier. Between the windows, gold-framed mirrors reflected the light into a room filled with elegant French furniture.

'You will forgive me if I keep you two gentlemen apart,' Kutuzov said. 'I do so like it when my guests stay a while, and somehow I suspect that leaving you together might tempt you to try and escape. I assure you that I have guards all around the house and they have orders to shoot on sight. I think of my guests as family and an unnecessary death in the family is always unpleasant, don't you agree?'

'Oh assuredly,' Maxwell gave a little bow. 'You are quite correct of course, Major Kutuzov. We will try to escape as soon as we can.'

Kutuzov gave another of his little heel-clicking bows. 'As you should, of course, Colonel. I will warn my guards to be especially vigilant. They will kill you if they catch you.'

'Well then,' Maxwell said, 'they had better not catch us.'

'There is a very simple solution,' Kutuzov said. 'You can give me your parole, either for twenty-four hours at a time or the duration of your visit to Sebastopol. That way you will have the freedom to wander in the city.'

Jack glanced at Maxwell, seeing him properly for the first time. He was about five foot ten inches in height, with mobile, humorous eyes and a new bruise above his left eye.

'I would never have ordered you to surrender to save my life,' Maxwell said.

'I could not continue, and have you murdered,' Jack told him.

Maxwell nodded. 'This is not the place to discuss such things.'

'Do I have your parole, gentlemen?' Kutuzov's smile did not falter.

'Certainly not,' Maxwell said at once. 'You have my men in captivity, and you shall also have me.'

'As you wish, Colonel. And you, Lieutenant Windrush?' Kutuzov asked.

'I am with Colonel Maxwell,' Jack said.

'You may change your minds later,' Kutuzov said. 'If so, you may ask your guards to notify me. Are you both certain that is your choice?'

'Certain, sir,' Jack said.

'I have said as much.' Maxwell gave Kutuzov a look that may have been disgust that his word could ever be doubted.

'Then I shall have you both escorted to your new quarters.' Kutuzov gave another bow and snapped something to the Cossack guards, who came at the double, bayonets fixed and eyes wary.

With a Cossack at each elbow and one at his back, Jack was quickly separated from Maxwell and hustled out of the house. It was nearly dawn, and the streets of large, clean buildings were busy with men in military and naval uniforms. He saw no woman as the Cossacks hurried him through a doorway flanked by two flaming torches into a sizeable factory-style building, where there were more uniforms and more Cossacks; then a flight of stairs descending to a solid door guarded by two hefty-looking guards.

After a short conversation with the Cossacks, the guards opened the door, and Jack was hustled through and down another flight of steps to a broad, vaulted stone corridor that stretched into the gloomy distance and off which were half a dozen iron-studded wooden doors.

'This isn't as nice as that last house,' Jack tried to make light of his situation although he was beginning to wonder if he'd made the correct choice. The Cossacks didn't reply but lifted a bunch of medieval-looking keys from a hook on the wall, unlocked one of the doors and pushed him inside.

He sprawled on a stone-flagged floor and heard the door clang shut behind him. The sound seemed to resonate inside his head for a long time.

Darkness. Only darkness. For an instant, Jack was back in the trench buried under a pile of dirt after the shell had exploded. He fought the panic, took a deep breath of the stuffy air and pushed himself to his feet. The darkness already looked less intense, and he realised he was in a bare stone chamber with a vaulted ceiling, lit by two tiny arched windows. He became aware that he was not alone; simple wooden bunks lined the walls, each one occupied by a man.

'Morning sir. So you decided to join us then?' Sergeant O'Neill raised his voice. 'Right lads, officer in the room. Stand to attention!'

'Thank you, men,' Jack said as he acknowledged O'Neill's salute. 'Relax now; this is no place for parade ground drill.' There were a dozen men present, all British soldiers. Logan was there, with Coleman and men from other regiments. 'Where's Riley?'

'Not with us, sir.'

'I see that, O'Neill. Do you know where he is?'

'They asked our names, sir and that Cossack major looked at us right close and then hustled him away. I don't know where they took him.'

Jack nodded. That didn't sound good. Why would the Russians single out Riley? The only possible reason was for the burglary at Dar-il-Sliem.

'Thank you, O'Neill. Major Kutuzov appears to be a gentleman. He gave his word that we would be well treated, so I have no reason to think otherwise.'

'Do you know where we are sir?' O'Neill asked. 'We were hurried here so quickly, I didn't have a chance to look.'

'In a large building in central Sebastopol,' Jack told him. 'That is all I saw. The Russians took me to a short interview with Major Kutuzov and then brought me here.'

'What do we do now, sir?' O'Neill asked.

'Nothing.' Coleman slipped onto one of the bunks, lay on his back and folded his hands behind his head. 'We sit tight as a bug until the war ends and we're exchanged and sent home. No more digging trenches; no more cookhouse duties, no more getting killed by Russian cannonballs.'

Logan lifted a stray boot from the bunk beside him and threw it at Coleman. 'Maybe you like being in jail, you bugger, but I dinnae.'

'Does it bring back too many memories then?' One of the other soldiers asked and swore when Logan threw another boot at him and jumped off the bed to finish things.

'Enough!' Jack was glad that O'Neill was present to separate the two. 'Let's see if there is any way out of here. Like Logan, I don't fancy being in a Russian jail until they decide to exchange prisoners.'

'Why bother? We're safe and dry, and the rations won't be any worse than when we were in the army.' Coleman said.

'You're still in the army,' Jack said.

'You made us surrender,' Coleman said, 'and now you want us to get out.'

'That's enough from you,' O'Neill said, 'any more and I'll have you on a charge.'

The other men in the room, privates from the 118th Foot and wounded men from other regiments looked on with interest.

'What regiment are you lot from?' The Rifleman had both legs swathed in bandages.

'113th Foot,' Logan said defiantly. 'How?'

The Rifleman groaned. 'The bloody Baby Butchers. Stop grousing and leave real soldiers in peace for God's sake.'

'How do you mean, real soldiers!' Logan reacted predictably until O'Neill pulled him back.

'Let it rest, Logan. He doesn't know us yet.'

'Coleman,' Jack said, 'poke at the walls and see if there are any weaknesses. O'Neill, try the door. They locked us in, but the locks may be weak. Logan; you're the smallest here, see if you might fit through the window.'

'And how am I going to get up there?' Even at full stretch, Logan was three feet short of the window.

'Get on my shoulders,' one of the 118th got out of bed. 'Come on Sawnie.' He knelt on the bed immediately below the window and allowed Logan to mount his shoulders.

'The window is too wee,' Logan said, 'and it's barred as well.' He tugged at the bars. 'Firmly set in the stone as well. Bloody Russians.'

'How about the door, O'Neill?'

'Solid oak sir and the lock is huge. The hinges are set in stone as well.'

'The walls?' Jack felt his hopes slide away.

'Stone, sir. I can't see anything but stone.' Despite his earlier complaints, Coleman was pushing at the walls.

'We'll have to think of another way, then,' Jack said. 'Anybody have any ideas?'

Most of the soldiers stared blankly at him. Officers in the British Army didn't ask their men's opinion of anything, let alone ask for original thought. Infantry soldiers were there to follow orders and kill or die on demand. Nothing else. Only his men of the 113th responded.

'We could wait till they feed us, kill the guard and break out,' Logan said.

'Or try and break the lock at night-time,' O'Neill was slightly more practical.

'Even then, we're in the basement of some huge building with Russian guards everywhere,' Jack pointed out.

The Russians had taken his watch, so he had no method of judging the time. He began to pace the floor, walking up and down between the rows of bunks as he tried to think of a solution. After a while he realised he was only tiring himself out and irritating the patient soldiers, so he found a vacant bunk and lay down, hands behind his head.

He was in that position when the door opened, and half a dozen Russian soldiers entered. True to his nature, Logan threw himself at them, to be banged over the head with a musket butt and kicked as he lay on the floor. Two of the Russians grabbed Jack and hauled him outside, slamming the door behind him.

'You are the officer?' A man Jack took to be in charge asked. 'You are Windrush?'

'I am Lieutenant Windrush,' Jack agreed and they pushed him across the broad corridor and down another flight of stairs to a small room. They opened the door and shoved him inside.

'What the devil?'

Four men stood there. One was as broad as he was tall, with a flat, ugly face and forearms like a blacksmith. The second was Major Kutuzov, smiling as he watched Jack stare at him in confusion. The third was the tall man with the eye-patch, and the fourth was slender, elegant and thoroughly sinister.

'Lieutenant Windrush,' Kutuzov was still smiling. 'I am sure you know why you're here.'

Jack looked around the room. It held a wooden chair and a flat, bare table with ominous-looking straps across it. In one corner was a vast sink brimming with water, in another there was a brazier.

'I know I am a prisoner of war,' he heard the nervousness in his voice. 'And as such am entitled to decent treatment. You gave your word for that.'

'I did.' Kutuzov said, 'and I will keep my word. All British or French army officers or men who fall into my hands by the fortunes of war will be treated correctly.'

Jack looked around. 'So what is this place?'

'This is an interrogation room,' Kutuzov said. 'This is where we find out truths that the owner may sometimes be…' he exchanged a smile with the man with the eye-patch, 'reluctant to share.'

'It's a torture chamber,' Jack said.

Kutuzov shrugged. 'Some may call it that.'

'I am a British officer,' Jack said, 'and I demand to be treated as such.'

'You are also a spy,' Kutuzov said, 'and could be treated as a spy.'

'I'm no spy!' Jack protested as the squat man wrapped those powerful arms around him, lifted him bodily and dumped him on top of the table. The elegant man was waiting there and with moves so swift they must have been practised a score of times, the pair of them spread-eagled Jack face up and strapped him securely.

Kutuzov smiled down on him. 'You do not look very comfortable there, Lieutenant Windrush. I saw you at in Malta as you fled the scene of your theft, and never thought to see you again until I heard that you were at that encounter at the Alma.' He gestured to the man with the eye-patch. 'My compatriot here witnessed you hiding behind the savages in skirts.'

Jack hoped that his glare conveyed at least some of his dislike while hiding the fear that gnawed at him.

'And then you played that dirty trick on me with the explosive dummy.' Kutuzov shook his head. 'That gave me both your name and your regiment. The infamous 113th Foot, the Baby Butchers. Your commander, the sickly Colonel Murphy is every inch the English gentleman and would not dream of further sullying the name of his regiment by allowing an officer to be captured using such dishonourable methods. How fortunate for us all.'

Kutuzov shook his head. 'Except you, of course, my dear young spy.' He lit a long cheroot and inhaled slowly. 'I had to wait until you were on picket duty and then lose some of my Cossacks to capture you. The gallant Colonel Maxwell was a fortunate happenchance.' He drew on his cheroot until the end glowed red and touched it to Jack's forehead.

Jack flinched and pulled away as best he could.

'Now my young spy. I do not think that you would go to Dar-il-Sliem in Malta without orders. All you have to tell me is who sent you and what your orders were, and then there will be no more unpleasantness.'

Jack looked around. There was no point in yelling for help, and he was prepared to guess that Kutuzov already knew more about Bulloch than he did. All the same, honour dictated that he should say nothing. 'I do not know,' he said.

'Then we shall have to help you know,' Kutuzov said. 'My two companions here are very experienced in making people remember what they do not know.'

'I'm sure that they are,' Jack tried to hide his fear.

Kutuzov stepped back. 'We will leave you to think about what may happen, Lieutenant Windrush. When we return, I hope to find you in a more amenable frame of mind. We will leave a lantern on in case the dark scares you.'

The four men left, with only the aroma of Kutuzov's cheroot and the horrors of Jack's imagination to remind that they had been there. He tugged at the straps, becoming ever more frustrated as he realised he was unable to do anything other than lie there and wait for whatever nightmare Kutuzov and his colleagues had in mind. He swore softly and desperately to himself, repeating the mantra, 'I am not a spy, I am not a spy,' while hating the knowledge that he had acted as one and had been caught out.

'If I had joined the Royal Malverns, I would never have been asked to act the spy.'

By leaving the lantern burning, Kutuzov had allowed him to view the other objects in the room, which fed his imagination, as was probably intended. He wondered to what use the sink could be put, or the brazier, and the hooks he now saw in the ceiling.

'This is like something out of the Spanish Inquisition,' he said. 'Damn it to hell, I'm a British officer, and this is 1854, not 1554.' He tore at the straps again, pointlessly. He hadn't expected life as an army officer to include this sort of experience.

He heard the faint click of the door and tensed himself for the torture to come. 'Good evening Sir. If you hold on a moment, I'll soon have you out of these things.'

'Riley!' Jack looked up. 'How did you get free?' He couldn't express his relief.

Riley began to unfasten the straps. 'Their locks are ancient, sir. It was easy to open the cell door.'

'How did you know I was in here?'

'Just a guess sir,' Riley had his arms unfastened and began work on his legs. 'They had me in here, you see, so it wasn't hard to work out that you would be next.'

Jack sat up, rubbing the places where the straps had bitten into his flesh. 'I am happy to see you, Riley.' That was an understatement.

'Glad to see you too, sir.' Riley sounded unemotional, as all public-school boys should be.

'What sort of questions were they asking you?' When Jack slid off the table his legs were shaking so much, he nearly fell.

'Careful there, sir; you're all a tremble.' Riley supported him with strong hands. 'Take a minute now, or you'll be on the ground.'

'Thank you, Riley.' Jack took a deep breath and stepped free. 'I came over a bit dizzy there.'

'Yes, sir. They were asking who sent us to Dar-il-Sliem and what we were looking for, sir.' Riley kept his hands stretched out.

'Did you tell them anything?'

'No, sir. It was not hard to convince them that I was only a simple private soldier and I knew nothing.' His smile reminded Jack of a sixth form schoolboy. 'Their private soldiers are only peasants, sir. They would not have the ability to crack a crib or the imagination to know what to do even if they did.'

'Some officers think that about our men.' *I wish I hadn't said that.*

'I'm sure there are sir, just as there are some of the men who would not believe the officers know what day it is.' Riley stepped back. 'Begging your pardon sir.'

Jack didn't hide his smile. 'I think you and I know better. There are many very good men in the ranks, and fine men among the officers.'

'Yes, sir. This way if you please,' Riley opened the door a crack, peered outside, gave a brief nod and slipped out. Jack joined him, feeling a mixture of relief at having left the torture chamber and apprehension at the thought of being caught again.

'This way again sir, if you please.' Rather than heading up the stairs Riley pushed open the door to steps that led downward. 'Watch your head, sir; it's rather low and dark here.'

'How did you find this?' Jack winced as he banged his head.

'People are predictable, sir. Escapees would run to the nearest exit; so it's better to head in the opposite direction, the place the Russians won't look.' Riley stopped at a small door halfway down the stairs. 'The door's locked, sir, so give me a second.' There was a gentle click. 'There we go: may I go first, sir?'

'Yes, lead on, MacDuff.'

The door led to complete darkness until Riley lit a lamp and Jack saw they were in a long stone chamber. 'I've no idea what this room is, sir, but it's out of the way and empty so it will do us just now.'

Jack nodded. 'Let's hope nobody comes here while we decide what's best to do.' Somehow it seemed correct to use the inclusive 'we' rather than 'I' as an officer should. 'Now can we get out of this blasted building, Riley?'

'We can try sir.' Riley hesitated a moment. 'I don't like leaving the men behind sir.'

'No more do I, Riley,' Jack said.

'I mean sir, I would prefer to take Logie and the rest along with us, or at least try to.'

Jack considered the idea. 'Is that practical, Riley? Two of us may slip out of the building somehow but half a dozen men, or more if the other prisoners join us, will be hard to keep quiet.'

'We can try, sir.' Riley didn't withdraw, and Jack was struck with the loyalty that the men in the ranks displayed for each other. He had been brought up to believe that only gentlemen had such qualities as faithfulness, while the rankers were little better than beasts or children, and infinitely less important than horses. That, he had learned, was patently untrue and time and again he had witnessed scenes of amazing devotion and selflessness from the men.

'The Russians will treat them fairly.' Jack had no doubts about that. He knew that the British or the French would do their best for prisoners of war, while spies were brave but seen as dishonourable and treated as criminals by all sides. That was just the way things were.

'Yes, sir,' Riley said.

Jack sighed. He was their officer; he had led them into captivity out of honest concern for the life of an officer. He could not honourably leave them to rot, while he escaped. 'Damn it, man, of course, we'll try and get them out.'

'Thank you, sir,' Riley said. 'I knew you would agree.'

Military life seemed to be composed of long periods of waiting for something to happen and then very intense sessions of wishing it hadn't. Sitting on a stone shelf, hoping that no Russian would enter, Jack was aware of an occasional tremble underfoot.

'Can you feel that, sir?' Riley asked.

'That's the artillery firing,' Jack said. 'Either theirs firing at us or ours at them; I don't know which.'

'Do you think the siege will last much longer, sir?'

Jack shook his head. 'I really couldn't say. The Navy took a pounding the other day when they tried to bombard the walls, so it may be longer than we expect.'

They were quiet, listening to the rumble of the guns. Jack broke the tension with a direct question. 'You were a public-school man, were you not, Riley?'

There was a moment's hesitation before Riley replied. 'Yes, I was, sir.' He hesitated as faint voices floated to them, the words obscure but Russian. 'I think they've discovered that we've gone, sir.'

'Let's hope they don't come here.' Jack scanned the room for weapons. There were none; the place was stark. 'What made a man from your background take the Queen's Shilling?' He had no real desire to probe into Riley's private life, but he was curious as to his motive for joining the ranks.

Riley leaned back against the wall and closed his eyes. 'Adventure, sir. I was always a bit wild and liked to test myself out. After I left Eton, I followed quite a few careers including cracksman and in the theatre; that was where I met Charlotte.' He shrugged. 'Eventually, it was a toss-up between joining the Army or John Company, but Charlotte had a bad feeling about India, so I chose the army instead.'

'It's a hard life for a woman.' Jack knew that there was a great deal left unsaid.

'So is the theatre, sir.'

Jack nodded. 'I can imagine,' he said. He felt the trembling as Sebastopol's artillery fired again and he stood up. 'It's been quiet for over an hour now, Riley. I think we should try something.'

'Yes, sir.'

They left the room silently, with Riley closing the door behind them, and moved back up the stairs, one careful step at a time. The higher up the stairs he climbed, the more apprehensive Jack felt until he had to stop and take deep breaths. *What would Helen think of you? Scared of your own shadow.*

'Are you all right, sir?' Riley asked.

'I am perfectly all right,' Jack tried to sound like an irritable officer rather than a nervous man.

The door to the torture chamber was shut. Jack didn't look in as he passed and moved upward and upward to the corridor in which lay the cells.

'Sir,' Riley put a hand on his arm. 'Voices.'

Jack glanced around for somewhere to hide. 'Back down the stairs,' he said.

'In here, sir,' Riley slipped something into the lock of the nearest door and pushed it open. They moved into a long shady room with a table and six chairs overlooked by a single round-headed window. There were six glasses on the table and three decanters of clear liquid, presumably vodka, with two large ash-trays in the middle. Two maps hung on the wall; one of the world, the other of the Crimean peninsula, while six lamps hung from hooks on the wall. A small door in the far wall indicated a cupboard.

'It's some kind of office,' Jack said.

'Yes, sir,' Riley agreed. 'Listen!'

The voices grew louder and stopped just outside their door. 'They're coming in here,' Jack looked around quickly. Hiding under the table wasn't possible. 'Through that door!'

It was a store cupboard, as Jack had thought, a small room with a foot-square window and long wooden shelves on the wall, filled with papers, bottles of ink and a tray of pens. Jack eyed the half dozen bottles of vodka and hoped Riley wasn't a drinking man. 'There's no way out.' Riley sounded surprisingly calm.

'So we stay here and hope they don't come in.' Jack looked around for a weapon. Once again there was nothing. He heard people enter the office next door. There was the sound of footsteps, the scuffing of chairs on the wooden floor, a cough, a laugh and the low murmur of voices.

Riley was on his knees, probing at the lock. 'I've jammed the door, sir,' he whispered. 'They'll need a skilled locksmith to open that.'

'How do we get out?' Jack asked.

'Oh, I can get us out again,' Riley said.

'Good man. Now we keep quiet and hope they leave soon.'

Another hour passed, with the voices next door rising and falling, punctuated by the occasional laugh. Tobacco smoke drifted under the door into the room, aromatic at first and then thickening to become stuffy and unpleasant.

'Privateers.'

The single English word within the guttural Russian caught Jack's attention. He looked up – privateers, he knew, were private ships converted to carry guns and licensed by a government to attack an enemy's merchant shipping. It was a method of nautical warfare that maritime states had used for centuries, and during the wars with France and the USA in the eighteenth and early nineteenth century, had made some serious inroads into British merchant shipping. Did Russia possess any privateers? The Royal Navy had pinned the Russian navy into harbours, and if they emerged, they would be engaged and defeated.

'The United States would make hay with the British shipping.'

The words and the accent startled Jack. It was the man with the eye-patch he had seen in Dar-il-Sliem in Malta and at the battle of the Alma. Jack had thought he might be from Australia or some other colony. Now the words indicated that he was from the United States. What on earth was an American doing talking with Russians in a besieged town in the Crimea?

As the conversation switched from Russian to English, Jack made out an occasional phrase, none of which made much sense to him. He heard the words 'Alaska' and 'whaling fleet' as well as other mentions of privateers. He listened without understanding and hoped that nobody discovered them in their small room. There was a sudden outburst of laughter, the sound of chair-legs scraping on the floor and the noise level rose and then fell. Jack heard the door close. Silence descended.

'I think they've gone,' he began until Riley shook his head violently and put a finger to his mouth.

There was a faint shuffling, and somebody tried the door to their room. Jack stood back, ready to attack anybody who came in. The door shook and held. The handle turned again, and somebody made a sound of impatience. The outer door banged impatiently.

'That would have been a servant clearing away,' Riley said. 'He's gone to look for a key for this door.' Bending to the lock, he opened it in seconds. 'We'd better leave quickly.'

The stairs were empty as they hurried to the level where the Russians held the 113th prisoners. The corridor was as broad as before, with lamps casting pools of yellow light over the rough stonework. There was an empty vodka bottle on the floor. Jack's mind was busy; he would like to try and analyse the conversation he'd partially overheard, but that would have to wait. At present he needed all his attention to survive. Pushing the words to the back of his mind, he concentrated on trying to escape from this labyrinth of a place.

Two guards were on patrol, both sturdy looking men in the uniform of Cossacks, complete with musket, long *khanjali* knife and a whip. They paced back and forward, dark uniformed, grim-faced, with the distinctive *shasqua* sword with its lack of guard loose at their waists and an old-fashioned musket in their right hands. They looked fierce and eminently capable of disposing of a single, tired British officer and an old-Etonian cracksman private soldier.

Jack took a deep breath. If Logan or O'Neill were here, he had no doubt they could deal with these Cossacks, but he lacked Logan's aggression or O'Neill's muscles. He knew Riley was skilful in opening locks; he had no idea how he was in the nitty-gritty boots-and-bayonets reality of soldiering.

'Sir; if I may,' Riley said. 'We'd be better to watch the guards and see if they have a system, a routine before we do anything. They might have regular patrols like policemen on their beat.'

About to comment on Riley's personal knowledge of such things, Jack nodded instead. 'Good thinking, Riley.'

Standing in the deep recess of a doorway, Jack watched the guards pacing the length of the corridor and back, with their boots ringing on the floor. Big men with fierce moustaches, they moved slowly and slightly erratically; one kicked the empty vodka bottle and watched it skittle across the floor. *Riley is correct; they have a fixed routine, crossing the path of each other every three minutes; they've also been drinking, which could help us.*

'We take them one at a time,' Jack said. 'And when both are out, we'll let our men out.'

'We've no weapons.' Riley sounded more anxious than Jack liked. 'I wish Logie was with us.'

'He'll be here in a few minutes if this goes well.' *And if it goes ill, we'll either be back in a dungeon or dead.*

The nearest Cossack looked every bit as bored as any British sentry would in similar circumstances. He glanced vaguely at the door behind which the 113th prisoners were held and moved on.

Jack removed his tunic, took a last look at Riley, waited until the Cossack had taken two steps past him and launched himself forward. The Cossack turned, mouth open to shout a warning until Jack threw his tunic over his head to muffle any sound. Riley pulled the Cossack into the doorway and tried to draw the man's *sashqua*, gasping with effort. The Cossack was strong, determined to win and very dangerous. He twisted in Jack's grasp, lashing out with fists and feet in his attempt to escape until Riley finally wrestled the *sashqua* free and thrust it into his body. Wickedly sharp, it entered easily, spurting blood.

Although Jack stuffed the left arm of his tunic hard into the Cossack's mouth to stifle his roar of pain, sufficient noise escaped to alert the second guard, who dropped his musket, drew his *sashqua* and charged forward with what Jack took to be a war-cry.

Riley stared at him, holding the first Cossack's *sashqua* but apparently unsure what to do. Jack swore, grabbed at the fallen musket, missed, scrabbled on the ground and lifted it just as the Cossack made a viciously angry slash at Riley.

Jack saw Riley close his eyes and parry by pure luck. As the Cossack recovered to thrust forward, Jack swung the musket butt, swore when he missed and nearly overbalanced. The Cossack returned quickly and cut underhand, only to land the blade with a juddering thud in the stock of the musket.

Riley saw his chance, lifted the *sashqua* and plunged it into the Cossack's side. The man stiffened, turned around and grabbed for the *khanjali* at his waist.

'You blaggard!' Riley tried to withdraw his blade, failed as it stuck within the Cossack, let go the hilt and jumped back as the *khanjali* stabbed underhand at his groin. Jack swung the barrel of the musket across the Cossack's head, heard the satisfying crack of contact and saw the man stagger.

'Sir!' Riley kept out of the way of the Cossack's blade as Jack swung the musket again and again until the man at last fell.

Jack felt himself panting. 'Thank God for that,' he said.

'Sorry sir, I was not much use there.'

'You pinked them both,' Jack said. 'Now hurry and open the cell door. All that noise will have alerted the rest.' He looked around. 'How the devil will we get out of here?'

'You'll think of something, sir.' Riley lifted the bunch of keys from its hook on the wall. His hand shook so much that they rattled. 'Which key?'

'Try them all one by one.' Jack lifted the Cossack's *sashqua*; it was light and beautifully balanced. He moved to the door that led upstairs. 'The Russians will be here in a second.'

'Yes, sir.'

Jack could hear the nervousness in Riley's voice. The cracksman who was so calm when robbing a house was obviously less happy killing people.

There were voices from above, the bark of orders and feet on the stairs. 'Here they come!'

There was a clatter, and a curse as Riley dropped the keys, the scuff of metal as he picked them back up and then Jack had other things to worry about as half a dozen Cossacks roared down the stairs toward him.

Jack knew he was outnumbered by fresh, fit and angry men while he was nearing exhaustion after a night without sleep and a nerve-stretching day. But as the Russians bunched at the foot of the stairs, he realised that they were too angry to fight with their customary skill. Their very numbers on a narrow staircase would hamper their movements, while the high wall on their right would make it harder for them to wield their swords. They were also born and bred to the steppes, out of their depth in these confined spaces.

'Hurry with that door, for God's sake!'

Pushed from behind, the first Cossack stumbled on the bottom stair, and Jack sliced at him, opening the back of his head. The man yelled and fell in front of his colleagues, blocking their path, so they had to lift their feet to step over his body. That gave Jack the opportunity of a vicious upward swing that sliced open the man's thigh and had him fall back among his colleagues, shouting in pain. Jack followed through with a serious of lunges that thrust his sword into at least one more man, and then he had to defend frantically as the Cossacks pushed past their wounded colleagues to get at him.

'Riley!'

'I'm going as fast as I can! I can't find the right key!'

'Pick the blasted lock then!'

As Jack fought one Cossack, others struggled past, so three were in the corridor, slashing at him but still getting in each other's way in their eagerness to kill.

'Riley!' Jack heard his voice rise high as two Cossacks came around him, their sashquas probing for an opening.

At last, the door opened, and a press of redcoats burst out. They had not wasted their time in captivity and O'Neill, and Logan carried bludgeons fashioned from bed frames. Without any hesitation they jumped on the Cossacks, dodging the swords as they launched their furious counter-attack. The noise was appalling as Logan jumped into the air to swing his chair leg while O'Neill lifted a discarded *sashqua*. He was no swordsman, but the blade was so well balanced it needed little skill.

Taken by surprise, even such expert fighting men as the Cossacks were overpowered by the sheer aggression of the British soldiers. One by one they fell, with the last trying to run until Logan grabbed him by the leg and dragged him back down to O'Neill, who thrust downward between his shoulder blades.

Jack looked at his men as they stood, panting with exertion.

'Right lads; there are eight of us here. There may be more British held in these cells; Riley, open the doors. I don't know how we'll get away, but let's try it.'

'Here, Riley, how come you got out?' Logan was examining one of the Cossack *sashquas*.

'Leave him; he's busy,' Jack said.

Most of the cells were empty. Two held civilian prisoners who cowered away as soon as the doors opened. One man, heavily bearded and naked, was chained to the wall.

'There's been the devil's work here,' a soldier of the 118th said.

'How do we get out, sir?' Coleman lifted a Cossack musket, checked the lock and tested the balance. 'Poor stuff this,' he said, 'and I thought our muskets were bad.'

'Windrush! Is that you?' Colonel Maxwell burst out of his cell. 'Good man!' He looked around. 'Now let's get out of this hellish place. How many men?'

'Eight British sir, plus you and me, and sundry Russians.'

'Forget the Russian prisoners, man. They are criminals, looters and murders.' Maxwell nodded to the man from the 118th. 'Ah, Black, it's a pleasure to see you.'

'Thank you, sir.' Black threw a sharp salute.

'Now then,' Maxwell seemed quite calm. 'How best to proceed, eh? Do you have any idea where we are, Windrush?'

'I only know we're in a building in Sebastopol, sir,' Windrush said. 'I don't know any more than that.'

'Nor do I,' Maxwell said. 'Perhaps one of these Russian fellows could be of assistance after all.' Moving to the nearest of the prisoners, he lifted him by the hair and spoke in rapid Russian.

The man cringed and replied. After a few moments, Maxwell let him fall back to the ground. 'He thinks there is a way out over here,' he said. 'Tell you what, put on these Russian uniforms, eh? That could be interesting. You and me and some of the men. Choose the least bloody of the Cossack uniforms and the least British looking of the men.' He laughed. 'That red-headed sergeant of yours looks as much like a Cossack as I look like a Chinaman.'

Jack slipped on one of the Cossack coats and watched as Riley and Coleman did the same. Riley looked like an actor in a coat while Coleman's saturnine, now unshaven face fitted the uniform exactly.

'We'll have to grow quick moustaches,' Logan's small body looked swamped in the Cossack coat.

'It won't do, I'm afraid Logan,' Jack said. 'You will have to continue as a prisoner.'

'Aye, sir.' Logan threw the coat on the floor. 'This thing's crawling with lice anyway.'

'Don't worry about the itch,' Maxwell said cheerfully, 'lice come with the territory. Come along, Windrush. Bring your men with you.'

Surprised that there was no second wave of attackers, Jack followed Maxwell to the far side of the corridor, where another flight of stairs led upward.

'If we meet anybody,' Maxwell said. 'You let me do the talking. We are Cossack guards taking the wicked British prisoners to another place to interrogate them, damn their hides.'

'Yes, sir,' Jack agreed.

They moved quickly, with Jack warning his men not to speak as they ran upwards on flights of stone steps that seemed to go on forever. Eventually, they came to what Jack took to be a side door guarded by a single Cossack sentry.

'What now?' Jack reached for the sashqua at his belt.

'Leave it to me,' Maxwell said and spoke sharply in Russian.

The sentry immediately slammed to attention. When Maxwell spoke again, the man saluted and drew the bolts on the door. Maxwell stepped outside the door, Jack ushered his men outside, checking he had not left anybody behind. He was encouraging the last man when the sentry looked directly at him. The Cossack's face was badly burned, with fresh bandages covering the entire left side, Jack and the Cossack recognised each other at the same time. This was the man he'd taken prisoner after the dummy had exploded.

The Cossack reached for his sword just as Logan turned back to see what was happening. Both men hesitated; Logan stepped forward, and the Cossack released the hilt of his sword and stepped back, jerking his head toward the street outside.

'Here,' Logan thundered, 'you're the Russian fellow that Snoddie was going to leave.' He held out his hand, as to an old friend. 'Glad you got back safely.'

Jack watched in bewilderment as the Cossack shook Logan's hand. He waited for an instant to hustle the last of his men outside and banged shut the door in case the Russian changed his mind.

'You're a lucky man, Logan,' he said. *Will I ever understand these men of the 113th?*

Logan nodded down to his right sleeve. 'It's all right, sir. I knew what I was doing.' He flicked his wrist, and a *khanjali* dropped into his hand. 'I got that off one of them Cossack fellows, sir. If he had been unfriendly...'

'Well done, Logan.' *No, I never will understand these men. Maybe that's a good thing.*

Maxwell stopped them immediately outside the building, and Jack looked around. They were in a broad street jostling with people, grey-coated soldiers marching past in columns, groups of black-clad sailors with their distinctive swaying gait, and bodies of horsemen, Cossack or hussars, as well as slow moving carts, piled with barrels of gunpowder or cannonballs. As they watched, a long line of horses pulled green field artillery pieces with one gunner casually puffing at his pipe as he sat on a wagon of ammunition. Next came five officious-looking men who may have been low-level staff officers and finally a droshky, the heavy four-wheeled Russian carriage, which was forced to stop as a slow-moving column of infantry blocked the road.

Watching everything was a scattering of civilians, *moujik's* selling hot drinks, colourfully dressed women offering rolls and milk to the passing infantrymen and some younger girls cheering the marching troops and being soundly kissed in return as the Russian officers ignored such indiscipline.

'They don't look all that different from us,' Riley observed.

'Maybe not from you, Riley,' Coleman said, 'I always thought you were half foreign anyway.'

'Mind your bloody mouth,' Logan snarled. 'You look more like a bloody Cossacks than the Cossacks do in that coat.'

'And you?' Coleman gave a brief laugh. 'You're a Sawney bastard; more foreign than all these Ruskies, you bloody savage.'

Ignoring the by-play as the habitual banter of British soldiers, Jack noticed that Maxwell was watching everything with intense interest.

'Something's happening,' Maxwell said. 'This is not just normal troop movement. These men are moving far too purposefully for that. Look at their faces; they're grim, not merely men moving from one barrack to another.'

'Maybe we've broken in, sir?' Jack asked hopefully.

'I can't hear gunfire,' Maxwell said. 'Except for the usual desultory stuff. If there were a battle that would be all we would hear. No, there's something else. I think these boys are marching to a battle that hasn't started yet.'

'Do you think they're going to sortie against us?' Jack asked. 'If the garrison came out and these Russian generals out there in the interior, Menshikov and Liprandi, attack at the same time we would be caught between two fires.'

'We would be in a position of serious difficulty,' Maxwell glanced at him. 'That is possible. In the meantime, our duty is to get out. By the way, I never got the chance to thank you for rescuing me, Windrush.'

'It was just my duty, sir.'

Maxwell looked away with a small smile on his face. 'Oh, was that what it was. Now, here's our opportunity to get out of here, if your nerve holds, Windrush.' He nodded. 'The general has left his droshky.'

For a second Jack was perplexed, and then he realised that the general had left his carriage to try and force his way through the column of infantry.

'It's open sir; they'll see that most of us are wearing British uniforms.'

'There's nothing like a bit of bluff and rank pulling to make people do as you wish,' Maxwell seemed to be enjoying the situation. He shouted in Russian and ushered everybody into the droshky, where they had to squeeze together in a great huddle. 'Act like a guard!' Maxwell hissed so Jack looked as menacing as he could.

As the British clambered on board, the driver looked around in surprise. Maxwell shouted at him, grabbed him by the lapels of his coat and threw him off the driving seat. Grabbing hold of the reins himself, he guided the droshky in a half circle past the strangely apathetic crowd, so it was heading in the opposite direction.

'If we did that in Britain the people would be clamouring to find out what was happening,' Jack said, wonderingly.

'This is Russia,' Maxwell said. 'They are different to us. They're used to obeying authority without question. Now sit tight,' Maxwell flicked the reins, giving the horse a hearty crack that set him trotting down the street. Soldiers and civilians scattered before him as he raced along with Jack trying to look important.

'Stop grinning, Riley, and the rest of you, look like dejected prisoners, not mill-workers on a trip!' Jack snatched at the side of the droshky as they swayed alarmingly.

The guns started again. Jack heard the rumble like distant thunder, and then the individual barks of cannon and rolling volleys of infantry fire.

'The boys are fighting,' Logan said.

'Here we go,' Maxwell spoke over his shoulder. All at once Jack realised that the happy-go-lucky attitude was only a pose. Maxwell's eyes were as level and hard as any he had ever seen. Rather than some man acting out his boyhood, Maxwell was living on a very precarious edge between life and death. He was no mere regimental officer captured by chance and escaping with luck, but somebody far more dangerous.

Who and what the devil are you, Colonel Maxwell?

Jack didn't know where they were; he only knew that they were passing through an area of Sebastopol that had been under bombardment. There were damaged gun caissons, the barrel of a cannon that had split under fire, a thin trail of wounded men limping past, troops of haggard-looking horsemen and a waggon packed with bodies trailing an ominous thread of blood.

'Duck down,' Jack ordered his men. 'We won't be popular with all these wounded Russians.' He heard Maxwell shouting in Russian and saw the droshky swerve to avoid another waggon, and then they were squeezing through a deep gateway where guards jumped to attention, and passing earthworks crowded with soldiers. Jack had time to see bearded and moustached artillerymen peering outward and piles of cannonballs waiting to be fired at the

British lines. Except for the uniforms, they looked the mirror image of their compatriots on the Allied side.

Sentries stared or saluted, officers stepped aside, and a body of cavalry split smartly into two lines so the droshky could pass through. Maxwell acknowledged their salutes with all the arrogance of a senior officer, cracked the reins on the rump of the horse and powered on, through the Russian lines and into a bank of smoke. There was the sound of gunfire ahead and a block of stolidly marching Russian infantry. The cheering from ahead was undoubtedly Russian.

'Oh, dear God,' Maxwell hauled on the reins. 'What the deuce is happening here?'

Chapter Fifteen

**Balaklava
25th October 1854**

The ear-battering batter of a volley of cannon shook the air around them, followed by another, and then another. The infantry marched on, grey coats seemingly constricting, eyes fixed ahead.

'We're entering a battle,' Jack shouted above the noise. 'From the Russian side.'

Maxwell flicked the reins again, pulled the droshky aside and headed for the meagre shelter of a dip beside the road. The vehicle creaked and jolted over the rough ground, with the horse straining with the extra weight it had to pull.

'This beast won't last much longer,' Maxwell said. When he looked at Jack, even his ready smile appeared forced. 'I had hoped to race across the space between Sebastopol and our lines and hope for luck to protect us, but it appears that the Russians have mounted an attack. Do you know where we are?'

'No, sir,' Jack said. 'I'm not sure at all.'

'We're about a quarter of a mile behind the Russian front line.' Maxwell explained. 'Over to our right is the escarpment of Sapoune Ridge.' He pointed. 'That holds three roads including that which passes our port of Balaklava. You'll know it as the Woronzov Road, and it's called that because the estates of Count Woronzov lie across it – not that you care a two-penny damn about that. What is more important, and as you are aware, it dips and then rises to the Causeway Heights, with the North Valley on one side and the South Valley on the other.'

'Yes, sir,' Jack nodded.

'As you know, we have gun emplacements along the Causeway Heights as part of the outer defences of Balaklava.' Maxwell said. 'And Balaklava is vital to our army as all our supplies land there. It appears that the Russians are trying to capture or cut our supply line. If Balaklava falls, we cannot remain here; the Russians have won.'

'Yes, sir,' Jack realised that Maxwell's attitude had altered entirely; he was deadly serious. The contrast emphasised how much danger they were in.

'Beyond the Causeway Heights and to the north of Balaklava is the village of Kadikoi,' Maxwell continued, 'you will have passed through it as you travelled from the port to the siege lines around Sebastopol.'

Jack nodded. *The last time I passed that way I was coming back from meeting Helen and what a fudge that turned out.* 'It is a nothing sort of place sir,' he said.

'It is a nothing place yet it is also the key to the defence of Balaklava, and so the lynchpin of this whole war.' Although Maxwell was calm, the tension in his voice was evident.

Jack nodded, trying to build up a map of the area in his head. As a junior officer, his day-to-day world didn't extend to such things. He was aware of the position of his men, and how to get them fed, he worried about their health and any casualties, and he was mindful of any Russians in his immediate vicinity. The larger picture he left to men of far higher rank than he had, although he'd spent many hours trying to study military theory when his duties permitted.

'Have you got that?' Maxwell asked.

'Yes, sir,' Jack said.

'Good, now this ridge,' Maxwell indicated the bleak, bare undulating area on which they stood, 'is known as the Fedioukine Hills. As you see, the Russians have occupied them. Over there,' he pointed to the Causeway Heights and the Woronzov Road, 'is our front line. That's where we have our artillery positions, manned by the Turks, and that is where I'd hoped to go.'

'I see sir,' Jack said.

'Aye,' Maxwell took a deep breath. 'Unfortunately, it seems that the Russians have got there first. They have found the weakest point in our positions, which are strong nowhere, and it looks as if they're probing hard. I doubt the Turks will hold for long; they may already have broken.' He looked over his shoulder. 'You men – is there a telescope in the carriage? A senior officer may have one.'

'Come on lads! Give it over!' Jack knew his men too well; they would have lifted everything of value within seconds of entering the droshky.

Grinning without shame, Coleman produced a leather-bound case from beneath his tunic.

'Thank you,' Maxwell said dryly. 'We can't see much from here, Windrush. Follow me, and we'll see what progress General Liprandi is making.' Leaving the men in shelter and with orders to keep well out of sight, Maxwell took Jack to a small knoll where, still wearing their Cossack uniforms, they watched Liprandi's march to capture Balaklava.

Jack swallowed as he saw the Russian army uncoiling on its advance toward the terribly thin British defences. 'How many men do they have, sir?'

'As far as our intelligence reckons,' Maxwell said, 'they have around 22,000 infantry, 3,400 cavalry and 78 guns.' He handed over the telescope. 'Of course, Lord Raglan doesn't believe in intelligence. He does not agree with using such ungentlemanly methods of warfare as spies so we must blunder in the dark, while the Russians read the Times and have their agents reporting all our movements. Look,' Maxwell pointed to the Causeway Heights. 'As I thought, the Russians have already taken our gun positions on the Heights. That would be the firing we heard, and the cause of the wounded we saw. The Turks must have put up a fight; good for Johnny Turk!'

Jack scanned the area, noting the drifting smoke and watching the Russians moving seemingly lazily over the gun positions that were intended to defend Balaklava. He had a sudden image of Kutuzov and his Cossacks galloping into Balaklava, booting down the door of Helen's house, bursting in— *oh dear God! Helen!*

'Sir!' Jack spoke with new urgency. 'They are moving against Balaklava! Where are our men? I hope Lord Raglan knows what he's doing.'

Maxwell's look wasn't pleasant. 'Lord Raglan is a fool to his gentlemanly nature,' he said. 'He has divided the command to ensure that nobody's feelings are hurt.' He closed his mouth with a snap. 'I only hope that Campbell can rectify the situation.'

Jack decided it was best to say no more, despite the racing of his heart. He remembered Campbell as the craggy-faced Scotsman who had commanded the Highland Brigade with such skill at the Alma. *If anybody can stop the Russians, Campbell can.*

'Sir!' Jack pointed. Faint in the distance, he saw a mass of Russian cavalry head toward Balaklava. The Russians had already destroyed the outer line of

British defences. If they captured Kadikoi, they would hold the lynchpin of the entire British Army and could take the port of Balaklava.

'What happens now will decide who wins this battle,' Maxwell said, 'and perhaps who wins this war.'

'Oh God!' Jack felt sick. 'I wish I was there to help!'

'Calm yourself, Windrush,' Maxwell said sternly. 'There is nothing we can do save watch.' He lowered his head and his voice. 'And perhaps pray, if you will. My wife is in Balaklava; and my daughter.'

That was a new side to the devil-may-care Colonel Maxwell. 'I know that sir.' Jack had seldom been more aware of anything in his life.

At first, there seemed nothing to stop the Russian advance. Campbell had withdrawn the single British defending regiment, the 93rd Sutherland Highlanders, and the Turks were broken. The Russian cavalry powered on, squadron after squadron of mounted men, the vanguard of tens of thousands of men intent on driving these invaders out of their sacred homeland.

'Have a look youngster,' Maxwell handed over the telescope. 'You are witnessing history in the making.'

'Thank you, sir.' With his heart heavy with the knowledge of impending defeat, Jack took the telescope and focussed on the Russians. All at once they leapt into his vision, tall men, blue or black-clad on large horses riding in perfect formation, side-by-side in great blocks and nothing before them except the bare slope. Once they took Kadikoi, they would debouch through the cutting and clatter through the streets of Balaklava, butchering everyone who stood in their path. *Helen...*

'Dear God!' Even as Jack looked, a miracle occurred. A long double line of red-coated infantry appeared on the crest of the slight ridge in front of Kadikoi, flanked by a body of Turks on either side. 'It's the 93rd!' For a moment Jack saw the entire scene, the thin scarlet line of Scottish infantry, the shifting mass of Turks and the hundreds of Russian cavalry cantering toward them.

'There's Campbell now.' Maxwell sounded calm, as if he had expected no less.

And then the situation altered. The Turks on either flank fired a single ragged volley and scattered to the rear, leaving the 93rd Highlanders isolated and unsupported against the advancing Russians. Jack knew that according to all the axioms of warfare, infantry not supported by artillery and with exposed flanks would be overrun by cavalry, but neither Campbell nor the 93rd Highlanders seemed to let that fact bother them.

'They're going to die where they stand.' Maxwell must have had extraordinary eyesight to watch the encounter from this distance, but Jack was so engrossed with the unfolding drama that he had no intention of relinquishing control of the telescope. He saw the spurts of smoke merging into a cloud of powder-smoke a second before he heard the high cracking of the Highlanders' volley. The Russian cavalry continued to advance.

The 93rd fired a second volley, this time backed by some British artillery that Jack heard but couldn't see. Rather than advance straight toward the thin red line, the Russians faltered, and the squadrons of cavalry veered smartly to the left.

'They're trying to turn Campbell's right flank,' Maxwell said. 'They would as well try and rake moonshine from a pond.'

Jack flinched as a shiver ran through the ranks of the 93rd, as if they wished to charge the Russian cavalry but Campbell had them in hand. He ordered his grenadier company on the right to turn to meet this new perceived threat, and again the Highlanders fired a volley which took decisive effect on the Russian ranks. Jack saw cavalrymen reel in the saddle, with one man falling backwards across the rump of his horse. The horsemen immediately wheeled around and retreated over the causeway.

'Well done, Campbell,' Maxwell said quietly. 'We may have been witness to one of the decisive moments of the entire war. Three volleys that turned everything around.'

Jack nodded. His studies of military history and tactics had not included any encounter where infantry had fought off large numbers of cavalry without forming a defensive square.

'Now, more importantly,' Maxwell said, 'how are we going to get ourselves through the Russian lines and back to our men?' Taking back the telescope, he scanned the ground. 'I think the best way is to go westward around the Russian flank and try to get to the Sapoune Ridge; our cavalry still seems to be there, the Lights and Heavies. With Lord Raglan in charge anything could happen, so we had better move quickly. Are you game?'

Jack nodded. Two nights without sleep added to the strain of skirmishes with the Russians and watching a battle were taking their toll. 'I am game, sir.'

'Get the men together. We'll have to go on foot. That Russian carriage will be too conspicuous in the middle of an army.'

It was nerve-wracking moving over that bare countryside, seeking what cover there was while formations of Russian troops marched or rode past them. There was the occasional sputter of gunfire, followed by periods of eerie silence when all they heard was gruff orders carried by the wind, the jingle of horses' bits or the rattle of equipment as a gun battery altered its position. As they moved over the undulating ground, they had brief views of troop movements, and then they descended into hollows where they could see nothing at all.

'Wait!' Maxwell said. 'Listen!' From the bottom of a shallow valley, they heard the shrill notes of a British trumpet sounding the charge, echoing in the terrible silence. The sound raised the small hairs on the back of Jack's head. 'Get to higher ground,' Maxwell ordered, 'we must see what's happening.'

'Follow me, men,' Jack ordered. 'Get up to the crest there.'

There was a single spur of the Fedioukine Hills protruding southward, a hundred yards from where they stood. They scrambled up, swearing as they heard the trumpet sound again and again and the distinct drum-beat of hundreds of horses' hooves on the ground.

'There! Look, oh God, look!' Riley pointed.

The angle of the hills gave them only a partial view, sufficient to see the British Heavy Brigade charging uphill from the South Valley at some unseen enemy. Distinct on the air they heard a curious high moaning, like a million swarming bees.

'That's the Scots Greys,' Maxwell said. 'Only they make that noise.'

A few seconds later there came a wild cheer, followed by a scattering of carbine shots and silence broken only by the pounding of hooves and a low mutter, the roar of combat subdued by distance. Jack looked at Maxwell, who shook his head. 'I can't see a thing through that blasted hill,' he said.

'Look!' Riley pointed further to the west, where further squadrons of the Heavy Brigade were charging into the fray. 'The Inniskilling Dragoons, the 5th Dragoons, the 4th Dragoons… the entire Heavy Brigade is in action!'

'Look! Oh look, look!' Coleman and Logan spoke together, staring toward the South Valley as in ones and twos, and then in great groups, Russian cavalry appeared, fleeing in the opposite direction to the charge of the Heavies. 'They're running; they're beaten!'

'Good man, General Scarlett,' Maxwell said as the Russian cavalry streamed up to the Causeway Heights, toward the shelter of the recently captured Turkish guns. As soon as the fleeing Russians were clear of the Heavies, British artillery opened fire on them, sending roundshot bouncing among the scattered horsemen. 'The Lights should have attacked when the Russians were in such disorder.' Maxwell shook his head. 'This is the strangest of battles I ever did see.'

'If the Russians have been repulsed,' Jack said, 'perhaps we can re-join our army in peace?'

Maxwell smiled. 'I fear there may be very many angry and frustrated Russians between us and home.' He raised his voice in a sharp order. 'Take off your tunics, men; red coats show up a long way. We will move slowly and with caution.'

There was little cover on the bare slopes, so they dodged from rock to rock, hoping that the Russians were too occupied in fighting their battle to worry about a stray handful of escaped prisoners.

'Sir!' Coleman hissed. 'Russians ahead!'

Maxwell signalled for them to stop as a regiment of Russian infantry halted nearby. The Russians spread out, some lying, some sitting as a man moved around with a keg, doling out great spoonfuls of vodka.

'Behind that rock,' Maxwell ordered.

There was barely room to move behind the boulder, with the Russians a bare fifty yards away and the occasional grumble of gunfire from the south hinting at the occasional encounter between British and Russians. The Russians took their time, lying on their backs and talking in low voices, drinking the vodka, sharing the occasional joke. The wind rose, whispering through the rough grass.

'How long have we been here for?' Coleman asked.

'About an hour and a half,' Riley answered.

'Maybe we'll be here all night,' Coleman said.

'We can leave you behind if you like,' Logan said. 'You're a lazy bastard anyway.'

'They're on the move!' Jack whispered.

A Russian officer barked a command, and the Russians rose into their ranks, brushing crumbs of black bread from their fronts and adjusting their uniforms in the same manner as British infantry in the same position. Or, Jack reasoned, any infantry in the world from the days of the Roman legions onward. Soldiers shared universal similarities, whatever their nationality or allegiance.

'Now it gets interesting,' Maxwell said. 'We have to pass across the Woronzov Road with no cover. The Russians will have it under close observation and so will our boys.'

'The Ruskies are undoubtedly retreating now,' Jack said. 'They're taking our guns away. They probably think they've won the day.'

They watched as Russian working parties arrived at the redoubts they had captured from the Turks earlier that day. *I wish I could lead a company of the 113th to retake these guns.*

'Our Lord Raglan won't like that one bit,' Maxwell said quietly. 'Wellington never lost a gun, you know.'

'So I heard,' Jack murmured.

'The cavalry is doing something,' Coleman said.

'Which cavalry?' Riley asked. 'Ours of theirs?'

'Ours,' Coleman replied. 'Look!'

Once again Jack was in the frustrating position of observing an action while not being able to take part. He felt torn between exultation and anxiety as he watched the entire British Light Brigade begin to advance along the North Valley, between the Fedioukine Hills and the Causeway Heights. They moved toward a vast Russian force of cavalry and infantry that stood behind strong batteries of heavy artillery at the eastern end of the valley.

'And what do they intend to do?' Riley asked.

'It looks like they're going to try and retake the guns,' Jack said. 'In a minute they'll wheel right and get up the Causeway Heights.'

'Good lads, the Lights,' Coleman said. 'Look at them; riding in perfect formation.'

Jack nodded. The Light Brigade trotted forward along the bottom of the valley in two lines, soon altering to three, with the 13th Light Dragons and the 17th Lancers in front, followed by the 11th Hussars and then the 8th Hussars and 4th Light Dragoons. With the valley around a mile in width, the cavalry occupied only the centre and as they advanced, the second and third lines became detached, so there were large spaces between the various units.

'What the devil are they doing?' Maxwell asked angrily as the cavalry remained in the centre of the valley, riding straight at the Russian gun batteries. 'Go for the Heights man; recapture the British guns!'

Instead of wheeling to the Heights, the Light Brigade cantered forward toward the heavy Russian batteries. With Russian artillery on the Fedioukine Hills to their left and more on the Causeway Heights to their right, they moved through a gauntlet of fire, made all the hotter by the Russian batteries in front.

Oh, dear God in heaven; they're charging the entire Russian army!

Earlier that day Jack had seen unsupported British infantry defeat an attack by Russian cavalry. Now he was watching unsupported British cavalry advance against Russian artillery. Surrounded on three sides, the Light Brigade didn't hesitate. They rode on, keeping formation as the Russians destroyed them with artillery augmented by musketry from battalions of Russian infantry. Men and horses fell as the Russian artillery thundered at them, so the ground was a litter of broken men and wounded horses, but the ranks closed and continued, closed and continued. Jack saw the lances lowered and the sabres drawn and ready, the thin slivers of steel somehow puny against the might of the cannon.

Riding in front on his chestnut charger, Ronald, Lord Cardigan was a splendid figure and apparently in complete command. He had given orders that his men were not to break formation and charge until they were sufficiently close to the enemy for such a move to be effective. At last – as the watchers on the Heights were shocked into silent horror at the sight of the pointless destruction of so many hundreds of brave men – the Light Brigade charged.

Jack didn't hear the thrilling sound of the trumpet; above all the screams and gunshot he doubted he would have, but when the remnants of the leading line of the brigade were about a hundred yards from the Russian battery the men surged forward in a mad charge, with Cardigan in their midst. And then the twelve Russian cannon in their front fired a final volley.

When the smoke cleared Jack saw the Russian gunners flying in retreat and a tangle of broken men and horses piled in front of the Russian cannon. Then he saw the smoke-stained survivors of the Light Brigade take their revenge on the Russians. They had ridden through hell, they had seen half their friends killed or hideously maimed by these gunners, and now they were on them, sabre or lance in hand and revenge the only thing on their mind.

It was the Russians turn to die as the British cavalry sliced and hacked at them in a furious bloodlust that Jack had never seen before. His experiences in Burma, he realised, had been small scale and gentlemanly compared to this slaughter at the guns. Jack saw the 13th Light Dragoons on the right dispose of all the gunners they could find, then charge a larger formation of Russian cavalry that was behind the artillery, pushing them back in panic and pursuing them for quarter of a mile before a regiment of Russian lancers cut the dragoons off.

Hacking their way through the lancers, Jack watched in silence as the few survivors of the 13th Light Dragoon began the long withdrawal to the British lines. On the left the 17th Lancers did the same, pushing Russian cavalry back until they were cut off, then withdrawing through the Russians and returning along the North Valley as the Russian guns on either side continued to fire.

'I've never seen anything like it,' Jack said softly.

'Neither has anybody else,' Maxwell said. 'Nobody's ever done it before, and I doubt anybody will ever do it again. What was Lord Cardigan thinking of?'

In the centre, another handful of the 17th Lancers also charged and pursued a large body of Russian cavalry before returning. Jack watched small bodies of British cavalry regiments chase and scatter Russian forces ten and twenty times their strength before withdrawing, leaving panicked Russian horsemen and dead gunners around the Russian artillery.

'That was murder.' Jack indicated the floor of the valley, sprinkled with the bodies of dead men, while the wounded lay screaming or tried to crawl back with shattered limbs and perforated bodies.

'It saved us though.' Maxwell sounded strained. 'Look.'

Coming toward them on magnificent white horses, a squadron of the French *Chasseurs d'Afrique* charged toward the Russian guns on the Fedioukine Hills. 'Best throw off that Russian uniform,' Maxwell advised. 'I doubt these French lads will have the time to ask our nationality before they spit us.'

'Vive la France,' Riley said quietly.

As the French cavalry approached, all Jack could think was that there had been another battle and the 113th had once more not been involved. They remained a regiment without a battle honour, and he was still an undistinguished lieutenant without hope of promotion or recognition. All his experiences had been pointless; he had achieved nothing. *There is one good thing. Helen is safe.*

Chapter Sixteen

**British Lines
October 1854**

The northerly wind whistled around the tent, pulling the stiff canvas against the poles and pushing a draught through the flap.

Colonel Murphy sighed and tapped his fingers on the simple deal desk that Jack thought he must have purchased in Balaklava. 'So let me get this straight, Windrush. You had your men surrender to try and save the life of a British officer and then you broke out of a Russian jail by picking the locks and pretending to be Russian soldiers.'

'Yes sir,' Jack said. He could feel Colonel Maxwell's approval as he sat a few feet away.

'Is there any more, Windrush?'

'Well yes, sir there is.' Jack wasn't sure how his colonel would react to the next few moments.

'Well?' Murphy looked up, coughed and looked away again.

'I have a request, sir.'

'And what is that, pray?' Murphy narrowed his eyes.

'I would like to pass a message on to a Mr. Bulloch, sir. I do not know where I may find him, but I know he was with General Reading in Malta.'

'Bulloch, you say?' Murphy looked puzzled. 'Now Windrush, your personal affairs are nothing to do with me, and I am not a post office for your letters.'

'Excuse me, if I may intrude here?' Maxwell frowned and held up a hand. 'I know of Joseph Bulloch. May I ask in what capacity you knew him, Lieutenant?'

'I'd rather not say, sir.' *I wish I had never mentioned the name.*

'The devil you won't!' Murphy's sudden agitation brought a spurt of blood to his mouth. He stopped to wipe it away as Jack tactfully averted his eyes. 'This is not some boyhood game, Windrush. You are an officer of some three years standing now, and you should know how the army operates. I damn well order you to tell me who this Bulloch is and what he has to do with the 113th.'

'If you would permit me to interrupt?' Maxwell said smoothly. 'Joseph Bulloch is a government man, Colonel Murphy.'

'Do you mean he is a blasted politician?' Murphy's tone, as much as his words, indicated his low opinion of politicians.

'No Colonel. He works for the foreign office, dealing with rather delicate matters of foreign diplomacy.' Maxwell spoke without expression.

'What?' Murphy may have been a crusty old soldier, but he wasn't stupid. 'You mean he's a spy?'

'He is a bit more than that, Colonel Murphy,' Maxwell said. 'He manages political agents, as he calls them.'

Murphy leaned back, shaking his head. 'A spymaster.' His glower at Jack was poisonous. 'How do you know such a man, Windrush?'

'I worked for him sir.' Jack admitted.

Murphy's expression froze somewhere between horror and disgust. 'You are a British officer, sir.'

'I am, sir,' Jack said.

'And yet you are a *spy*.' Murphy said the word as if it was a curse. He shook his head. 'My regiment, my poor, poor regiment. First the massacre of the innocents, then the debacle at Chillianwala, then the disgrace of losing our regimental colours and now this! An officer who is a spy!'

Jack said nothing. The wind increased, rattling the guy-ropes of the tent and causing the canvas above Murphy's head to rustle and bulge.

'I have another question for you, Windrush, since you do not care to answer my last comment.' Murphy alternated between anger and sorrow. 'Is the information you intend to transmit to Mr. Bulloch connected to your spying activities?'

Jack opened his mouth and closed it again.

'I order you to answer, Windrush.'

Unable to deny his spying activities, Jack could only say, 'Yes, sir.'

'In that case, Windrush, I will have nothing to do with it.' Murphy said. 'I will add to that, Windrush; the 113th Foot will have nothing more to do with you.'

'Sir?' Jack felt as if somebody had punched him in the stomach.

'You know that I'm attempting to improve the reputation of the 113th, Windrush.' Murphy's tone was slightly friendlier. 'To do so, I must eradicate any hint of irregular conduct among the men, or ungentlemanly behaviour from the officers. British officers do not act as spies. Although I think you have the makings of a reasonably efficient lieutenant, Windrush, your espionage activities can do only harm to what remains of the reputation of the 113th.'

Jack took an involuntary step backwards. 'Sir, I have no intention of resigning my commission. I do not think you have the authority to make me.'

'I could convene a court-martial, Windrush, although that would make you look even worse. You can resign your commission and seek another regiment—'

'Which I cannot afford!' The words slipped out before Jack realised it. While acting as a spy was ungentlemanly, so was discussing his financial situation. *A true gentleman does not mention such matters.*

He stood at attention in the ensuing brittle silence, waiting for further disaster.

'There is a simple solution,' Maxwell said quietly. 'You may transfer to the 118th. My regiment.'

Jack felt the colour surge to his face. The temptation to leave the 113th with its reputation for cowardice and crime was overwhelming. It was a chance that he'd been hoping for since he had received his commission. Yet something prevented him from immediately accepting.

'Thank you, sir, but the 113th is my regiment. I would prefer to remain at home.'

Murphy gave an audible grunt. 'This is no longer your home, Windrush,' Murphy said. 'I do not wish you in the 113th.'

'I think that clears things up, Windrush,' Maxwell said. 'Welcome to the 118th. We have things to discuss.' He looked across to Murphy. 'Will you also be getting rid of Lieutenant Windrush's partners in crime?'

Murphy started. 'And who would that be? Not young Elliot, surely?'

'Not Lieutenant Elliot. I mean his gang of blackguards: Riley and Logan, Coleman and Thorpe, Hitchins and Ogden.' Maxwell glanced at Jack. 'You should be aware, Colonel Murphy, that Riley was a professional thief while Hitchins was a poacher. A magistrate gave him the choice of joining the army or going to jail. He made the wrong choice.'

'Ogden's dead,' Jack said. 'He was a good man.' He looked at Maxwell, aware that he was manipulating the situation but unsure why.

'Take them all,' Murphy waved an irritable hand. 'I do not need men tainted with such dishonour.'

'Thank you, Colonel,' Maxwell gave a small bow. 'Come on Windrush; you are mine now.'

No sooner had they left the tent than Maxwell pulled Jack aside. 'You didn't tell me you were working for Joe Bulloch!' A new urgency had replaced his erstwhile urbane manner.

'It did not come into the conversation,' Jack said. 'We had other things to bother about.'

'What message do you have for him?' Maxwell was insistent. 'Come on, man!'

Jack frowned. 'How well do you know him, sir?'

'A devil of a lot better than you do, Windrush.' Maxwell took his arm and guided him through the ranked tents. 'In here.' His tent was similar to that of Murphy's, except more tidy and with a map of the siege opened on the pile of packing crates that passed for a desk. 'Now tell me everything.'

'It's not much,' Jack said, 'but Riley and I were hiding when we heard some people talking.'

'Go on.' Maxwell listened as Jack explained his previous actions in Malta and everything he had overheard. 'This American. Do you think he was the same man as you saw in Malta?'

'I'm certain, sir.'

Maxwell nodded grimly. 'John Anderson.'

'You know him, sir?' Jack said. Apparently, Colonel Maxwell was more than a regimental officer.

'We've crossed paths before,' Maxwell said. He looked up with something like his old smile. 'You stumbled upon the very man I was trying to get into Sebastopol to find.'

'You were going into Sebastopol?'

Maxwell nodded. 'The patrol I led was to drop me off near the city. Things didn't work out quite as planned. However, your arrival altered the situation.' His eyes narrowed. 'Are you certain he was the same man as you saw in Malta?'

'Yes,' Jack said.

'Then that is bad.'

'I told you the words I heard,' Jack said. 'They mean nothing to me.'

'They mean a lot to me.' Maxwell sounded as sober as Jack had heard him. 'Maybe Bulloch would be better explaining this to you, Windrush but as you are already involved, I'll give you a brief outline.' He poured them both a drink from a dark bottle. 'French brandy,' he said, 'from my Zouave friends.'

'Thank you.'

'Now, you know that we, the French and the Turks are facing Russia in this war. You may also know that Austria is hovering in the wings, not quite sure which way to jump, and Sardinia is also considering joining in to show the Powers how important they are.'

Jack sipped at the brandy. 'No, sir. I wasn't aware that Austria and Sardinia might take part.'

'Well, they may. That is a fact, and the grim reality is that we need all the help we can get. Oh, when it comes to an open battle our troops are as brave as they come; you saw that at the Alma, and they will carry on without complaint whatever the conditions. You see that every day in the trenches.'

'They are good soldiers, sir.' Jack thought about Coleman and Thorpe. They complained about everything but still got the job done.

'Other armies may have mutinies and panic retreats; not ours.' Maxwell said. 'That is the good side. The bad side is the lack of experience in the higher command.' He leaned closer to Jack. 'I trust you to keep anything between us confidential, Lieutenant. You may think I am croaking by saying all this, but you know it's correct. Our commanders dislike each other, and although we have vast experience in fighting in India, many of our higher commanders don't like so-called Indian soldiers. They don't think that experience fighting Afghans and Sikhs, or even Burmese, is relevant when it comes to fighting Europeans.'

'I had heard that sir.' Jack had noticed the tension between officers who had experience of the wars in India and those who had not. He'd put it down to pure jealousy. Perhaps that old British failing of class consciousness and snobbery had more to do with it.

'Add to that our poor administration and lack of numbers,' Maxwell said. 'Look at our men; we're losing about fifty to a hundred a day through sickness and disease and maybe two or three to Russian fire.' He stopped and shook his head. 'I don't know what the situation was like in Burma,' he said.

'About the same, sir. We lost far more to disease than to the enemy.'

'We can't continue like this,' Maxwell said. 'Apart from the suffering to our poor fellows, our army is diminishing at a frightening rate. That's why we need the Austrians and Sardinians as Allies. We're not like France and Prussia, or even Russia. We don't have conscription to build up our army.'

'No, sir,' Jack said.

'And that is where your American friend, John Anderson comes in,' Maxwell said. 'Mr. Bulloch will have told you a little about this Stevensen fellow in Malta. I never saw the fellow, but he was Russian of course, a Russian agent taking notes on British shipping in Valetta to see what ships and what regiments are sailing to the Crimea.'

'I had guessed as much, sir,' Jack said. 'There is another thing that you should know and may wish to pass on to Mr. Bulloch, sir.'

'What may that be, Windrush?' Maxwell had the glass to his lips.

'That fellow Stevensen, sir; he and Major Kutuzov are one and the same.'

The glass halted with the contents untouched. 'Now that I didn't know, young Windrush.' Maxwell placed the glass carefully on his desk. 'That would explain why he held me and came looking for you. Thank you, Lieutenant. That will go in my report to Mr. Bulloch.' Maxwell held up his hand. He was wasting his time spying on us; however successful he was with other matters. *The Thunderer* is giving out as much information about our troop movements as any Russian could desire. It's Russia's best ally in this war.'

Jack nodded. 'I have heard that.'

'And so on to your American fellow. John Anderson, as I said, originally came from Maryland but he marched west with the American army.' Maxwell sloshed more brandy into his glass, offered the bottle to Jack and smiled when he declined. 'All the more for me then.'

'Why are the Americans interested in this war?' Jack asked. 'They have nothing to do with the Crimea.'

'No, they don't. You are right,' Maxwell said. 'But they have no love for us, you know. We have already fought two wars with America: their independence war back in the 1770s and that stupid little debacle in 1812 when they tried to snatch Canada, and we burned their capital.'

'And lost at New Orleans,' Jack murmured.

'Quite,' Maxwell agreed. 'The United States is expanding rapidly; they seem set to fill up half that continent. As you are also aware, they recently fought a war with Mexico and grabbed California and other areas on the west, giving them a Pacific coastline.'

Jack nodded. 'Yes sir, but the Pacific is a long way from the Crimea.'

'But not so far away from the Russian possessions in Alaska.' Maxwell searched through the papers on his desk and unfolded a map of the world. He pointed to the west coast of North America. 'Here is California,' he said, 'and up here is Alaska, where the Russians are. And in between are our North American possessions.'

'I see, sir,' Jack said.

'Now, I have it on good authority that Russia is not particularly interested in retaining Alaska. They are moving southward in Asia toward Bokhara and Samarkand, which will put their southern frontier dangerously near our possessions in India.'

'Hence our Afghan war,' Jack said and was surprised by Maxwell's nod of approval.

'You have been doing your prep, haven't you? That's unusual in a junior officer. But you're right; that was why we moved into that God-forsaken country.' Maxwell poured himself a third glass of brandy, again offered the bottle to Jack and sat back down. 'Now, more important for the current situation, the United States is already giving some clandestine aid to the Russians. They allow Russian ships to sail under the American flag, and supply their North Pacific bases, while American companies have a monopoly to sell the Russian American company's goods, things like that.'

'Would the USA join in a war with Russia against us?' Jack asked.

'They would be foolish to do so in the long run,' Maxwell said. 'Although short term the results would be unpleasant. The United States has a huge number of merchant ships that could be armed and used as privateers, which could do untold damage to our shipping in the early stages, but this is 1854, not 1814. Naval technology has progressed apace, and no armed merchant vessel could stand against a modern warship, so after a year or so the Royal Navy would sweep them off the seas.' He drew the bottle closer. 'However, that first year would be crucial and may be sufficient to tip the balance in Russia's favour, and would certainly divert British attention from this land war to the sea. You will not have heard of the Cottman Mission?'

'I have not,' Jack agreed.

'It is fairly secretive. All we know is that an American named Thomas Cottman was in St Petersburg early this year and spoke to various Russian big-wigs about the USA buying Alaska. That's all.'

'Does that concern us?'

Maxwell shrugged. 'The USA owning Alaska is neither here nor there. It is far more important that the USA could float privateers to attack our merchant shipping while we're in a European War. That information you found tends to confirm our suspicions.'

'Yes, sir.' Still numbed by his hasty dismissal from the 113th, Jack found this deluge of new information bewildering.

'Of course, Windrush,' Maxwell said, 'I do not expect you to involve yourself any more in such things. I have had you transferred to my 118th, and you will do your duty like any other regimental officer.' His smile was kindlier than Jack had expected. 'I suggest that you put all this political work behind you now and concentrate on your real job.' Maxwell stood up. 'Now, you have given me much to think about, while you should forget all about Anderson and his like. You leave them to me and take your men to the 118th; then go and get some sleep. I want you on duty in the trenches tomorrow.'

Jack nodded. *It has been an eventful day.*

Chapter Seventeen

**British Lines
October 1854**

'Bloody 118th bloody Foot; bloody army; bloody weather and bloody Russians!' Coleman was doing his best to disprove Colonel Maxwell's words that the British soldier accepted all discomforts without complaint.

'That's the spirit, Coleman!' Jack encouraged him. 'We're in the 118th now; part of the Second Division so let them see how the old 113th view the war.'

'Bugger the 113th,' Coleman spoke with feeling. 'They can't even take care of their Colours.'

Jack looked around at his new surroundings. He knew he should feel in disgrace at being removed from the 113th, but instead, he felt fresh enthusiasm at being part of a regiment that was young in the British Army but much more accepted. The 118th carried no regimental stigma such as the Baby Butcher tag of the 113th; they had not run in terror at Chillianwala and were not composed of the men the other units of the British Army had rejected. He was part of a respectable British regiment in the second division, a fighting unit of which he could be proud.

'Welcome to the 118th,' Captain Dearden had said with a tired smile. 'You transferred from the 113th, I heard.'

'Yes, sir,' Jack waited for the habitual abuse, but Dearden only nodded.

'Sound move, Lieutenant;' he said. 'And I heard you were in Burma and escaped from Sebastopol.'

'I did, sir,' Jack agreed.

'The Colonel told us about you.' Dearden held out his hand. 'Veterans are doubly welcome.' He had glanced over Jack's men. 'They seem a handy bunch as well. With the number of men we're losing now we're grateful for a soldier of any quality, yet alone men who have tasted powder-smoke and fought the Russians.' He nodded his approval.

'Thank you, sir,' Jack said.

'Nothing to thank me for.' Dearden must have been around thirty-five, Jack guessed, but strain and fatigue had added at least ten years to his face. 'Now get settled in and get to know the men.' He had called Jack back and lowered his voice. 'Best not get too close to them, Jack. It's harder when they die if you knew them well.'

Jack nodded. That was good, if belated advice from an experienced officer.

The men were a decent bunch, Jack decided, mainly countrymen from southern England with a sprinkling of Scots and the ubiquitous Irishmen. Two were Welsh, saturnine, dark-haired men with sardonic humour and wiry bodies. He tried to learn some names as they rested in camp preparatory to another day in the trenches. There was Corporal O'Hara, who seemed surprisingly popular with his men, and Aitken, a Border Scot with curly blonde hair he had trouble keeping under control. Behind them were Fletcher from Hampshire with his big slow smile and equally large slow body. Then there was Williams from South Wales and Smith, a man with a shock of red hair and a vacant look about him.

'Have your men ever used the new Minié Rifle?' Dearden asked.

'No, sir.' Jack admitted. 'We had the old Brown Bess, India pattern that we brought with us from Burma.'

'Ah.' Dearden had a smug look on his face. 'Then they're in for a treat, Windrush. It's a sound weapon. I'll have Corporal O'Hara teach them the basics. You attend too, eh? Best to know what the men are doing in case you have to fire the thing yourself.'

'Yes, sir,' Jack agreed.

'No time like the present eh?' Dearden said. 'We don't waste time in the 118th, you see. Follow Nelson's advice – waste not a minute! Come along, then.'

Despite his Irish name, O'Hara had a broad Liverpool accent, a red face and a cheerful demeanour that won Jack's liking and the respect of the men in minutes. He ushered them to a natural amphitheatre, quarter of a mile behind the tented camp of the Second Division and handed out a Minié to each of the men from the 113th, plus one to Jack.

'Here we are then, lads, and you, Sir. This rifle is the Minié, the best thing to come out of France since Bonaparte. Except for brandy of course; and women.' He allowed the men to laugh. 'As you see, it is over ten pounds in weight and, if you stick the muzzle against your eye…' he demonstrated, 'it has three greasy grooves in the barrel, so it is a rifle, rather than a musket.'

Jack watched the men hold the muzzle against their eye. 'Make sure that thing's not loaded, Coleman!' He acknowledged the laughter of Thorpe and Logan. 'Sorry to interrupt, Corporal O'Hara.'

O'Hara held a small oval bullet high between finger and thumb. 'This is the bullet. It is conical, not round as you have used until now, and it's a bit smaller, with a little hollow in its arse.' Once again, he accepted the small ripple of laughter. 'You will all note the grooves that fit the rifling in the barrel. Don't we, Coleman?'

'Oh yes, Corporal,' Coleman said.

O'Hara grinned. 'Good; you can explain it all to me later. When you have a big bad Russian in your sights and press the trigger, expanding gas smacks the arse of the bullet, and it shoots into the rifling, which spins it like a child's top. That makes it more accurate, see? And it goes further too, so we can destroy them before they can get at us.'

'Corporal,' O'Neill asked, 'how far do they carry?'

O'Hara pursed his lips. 'They are said to be accurate up to six hundred yards,' he said. 'I've never fired one that far, although I heard that the Sawnies slaughtered the Russian cavalry at long range at Balaklava.'

Riley looked at Jack, who shook his head and allowed O'Hara to continue.

'This beauty,' he held up the Minié, 'can fire a bullet through four inches of pine at half a mile, so if the Ruskies are in column, you shoot the leading man and kill the fellow behind him as well. I have heard that one bullet can kill fifteen men in a row, but I doubt that. Now, pay attention lads, and you too Sir, if you will. With the old Brown Bess, you had to ram the bullet down the barrel, which took time. With this one, you merely drop it in, so you load quicker, fire faster and hit longer.' O'Hara looked around. 'Any questions? No? So why are you sitting around looking at me? Get these bloody things cleaned, you idle buggers.'

Jack wondered if the corporal had forgotten that there was an officer in the audience. *Better not remind him.*

The camp was busy with men and officers, a few supply wagons coming up the atrocious track from Balaklava and the surgeon inspecting the sick.

'Where are your boots, soldier?' The female voice was unexpected, and the sight of two horsewomen was so surprising that Jack had to look twice to confirm he was correct.

The private stood to attention. 'I lost them, ma'am. The mud in the trenches sucked them right off my feet.'

'That won't do,' Mrs. Colonel Maxwell said sternly. 'You will get frostbite with no boots on.'

'That's the colonel's lady and their daughter,' Dearden said. 'The wife is a decent soul; she's accompanied Colonel Maxwell all over the globe.'

'We have met before, briefly,' Jack said.

Helen rode straight-backed through the camp. Although she must have been aware that every male eye would be fixed hungrily on her, she appeared quite relaxed, even taking the time to smile to the men who spoke to her and laughing at the sallies of O'Hara.

'Did you meet young Helen as well?' Dearden asked.

'Very briefly,' Jack gave a guarded reply. The memory of his attempted dalliance still embarrassed him.

'She is a wild young thing,' Dearden shook his head. 'It doesn't pay to allow children too much freedom, and she was brought up in and around army camps and barracks all around the globe. Children should be sent away to school as early as possible if they are to be respectable. That girl will be trouble; mark my words.'

'I can believe that,' Jack said. It was common knowledge that all young boys should be sent away to school to be educated as soon as they reached the age of seven, if not earlier. He had not thought about girls; presumably, the same rules would apply.

'Dearden...' Colonel Maxwell appeared at the entrance of his tent, 'No – Windrush, you'll do. I want you to get down to Balaklava and see about getting us a pair of soldier's boots.' Mrs. Maxwell's voice sounded again, and Maxwell withdrew inside the tent for a few seconds. When he emerged, he was slightly flushed. 'No, Windrush, I think many of the men may have lost their boots. You had better get a couple of dozen pairs.' He looked over his shoulder and then out again. 'Take my daughter's horse to carry them.'

'Yes, sir,' Jack said.

Helen smiled down at him from the back of the horse. 'I've just come from Balaklava' she said, 'and now I have an escort to take me back.'

'I don't think the Colonel intended you to come along as well.' Jack couldn't meet her smile.

'Father said to take my horse,' Helen pointed out. 'He must know that Maida does not react well to others riding him. Therefore, I must come along too.' She smiled down at him. 'Or are you going to drag me off and leave me here among all these men, alone?'

'I wasn't going to do that,' Jack said. 'I rather hoped you would dismount of your own accord.'

'Well, I rather think that I won't,' Helen said.

Jack sighed. Dearden was correct; this girl was trouble. 'Do you ever do as you're told?'

'No,' Helen's smile was every bit as engaging as her father's. 'Shall we repair to Balaklava before you get into trouble from your colonel?'

Swallowing his pride, Jack steeled himself for what he knew would be a very harrowing journey. He decided to keep quiet and allow Helen to do the talking. From what he'd seen of the girl, that should be easy enough for her. *Why am I acting in this manner? I like her; I like her so much that I cannot get her out of my head. Why can't I talk to her as easily as I spoke to Myat in Burma?*

When Jack had first viewed Balaklava, it had been a picturesque seaside resort with lovely little villas and colourful gardens. Now, as the only port for the British Army, the character had altered entirely. Shipping packed the harbor, while a thousand different types of stores filled the wharves. High ranking British staff officers had taken over many of the best houses. Bluejackets and redcoats swarmed everywhere, talking and joking with the Crimean women in their colourful costumes who seemed to accept the occupation phlegmatically, or tried to sell food and luxury items to the British at ten times their proper value.

The stores were piled haphazardly as if the seamen had merely unloaded them from the ships and left them, uncaring if they reached their destination or not. Cases and kegs, barrels and boxes were side by side at the dockside with cannon-balls, waggon wheels and rotting vegetables.

'I see you met her then?' At first, Jack didn't recognise the woman who spoke to him. Charlotte Riley wore a Tatar fez on her head with a bash maram, a long gauze scarf that covered the back of her head and descended to her shoulders.

Jack glanced at Helen, who had hardly uttered a word on their journey from the camp. 'We met,' he said briefly.

Charlotte was carrying a large jug of water. She looked from Helen to Jack and back. 'Not with any great friendship, I see.'

Helen's smile was as broad as ever. 'He is the most awkward man, Mrs. Riley,' she said brightly. 'He sent you with a note to my servant to arrange an assignation, and then stood as tongue-tied as a mule.'

'All men are awkward, Miss Helen,' Charlotte said. 'My Riley was as bad. It comes from these all-boys schools, you see. They are fine at their boy's games of war and sport but when it comes to anything important…' She rolled her eyes. 'They can be frightfully threadbare. We have to lead them by the nose all the time.'

'Excuse me, ladies,' Jack felt himself flushing with embarrassment at being the subject of their conversation.

'Oh, you are excused, Lieutenant Windrush.' Charlotte gave a bright smile. 'Don't mind our women-chatter. You go about your duty.'

'He can't,' Helen said, 'he needs Maida, my horse, for that.'

'If he was not a gentleman,' Charlotte said gently, 'he would take it from you.'

'I'd like to see him try,' Helen said hotly.

Charlotte smiled and unfastened a triangular amulet from around her neck. 'You would like no such thing,' she said. 'However, you may like this, Miss Maxwell. It is a local Tatar amulet that fends off the evil eye. In your case, the eye is in you both.' She shook her head. 'You two are your own worst enemies.'

'What do you mean, Mrs. Riley?' Helen asked.

Charlotte straightened up. 'I have a word for the private ears of you two. Lieutenant Jack, Miss Helen, is shy around women, especially you, and you are too stubborn to help him.' She faced Jack. 'And Miss Maxwell is not shy at all but does not know how to break your reserve, Lieutenant Windrush.' Charlotte threw the amulet to Jack, who caught it with his left hand. 'Give it to her when you can talk.' She gave a small curtsey. 'And you, Miss Maxwell, are devilish self-willed. Accept the amulet when you can listen where there are no words.'

'How is that possible?' Helen looked puzzled.

'You will learn, or you will never hold a man.' Charlotte lifted her chin. 'Have the Russians killed that Major Speck yet, Lieutenant?'

'We don't have a Major Speck.'

'Snodgrass.'

'He's still alive,' Jack said. *Why call him Major Speck?*

'For the time being,' Charlotte walked away, her hips swinging.

'Speck means a bad thing,' Helen said quietly. 'I believe that Charlotte means some mischief to your Major Snodgrass.'

Jack nodded. 'I am aware of that. It is fortunate that I cannot think of any situation where she will be in a position to do that,' he said.

They were silent; both occupied with their thoughts as Jack searched through the accumulation on the wharves, found the military stores and signed for twenty pairs of soldiers' boots. He tried to avoid any contact with Helen as he silently draped them across the back of Maida.

'I can hold them in place,' Helen said, 'if you don't mind me interfering in your duty.'

'Thank you,' Jack said. *I can't think of anything else to say.*

They began the silent walk back. With every step, Jack dragged his mind for some method of breaking this impasse, some phrase that could ease the tension between them. *We're nearly there, and we haven't spoken! What can I say? All I can think of was Wellington's quote: the only thing I am afraid of is fear. Jack stopped short. That is entirely relevant. I am scared, not of Helen, but of looking foolish, and what is more foolish than allowing this opportunity to talk to her to slip through my fingers?*

'Miss Maxwell,' he said formally, as she looked down at him. 'I have no words to express my feelings.'

'I am aware you have no words, Lieutenant Windrush.' She said no more. They stood on the outskirts of the camp with the light fading and the night-picket filing past.

'I have taken an extraordinary liking to you, Miss Maxwell.' Although they were true, he had to force the words out.

'Thank you, Lieutenant Windrush.' She bowed from the saddle, meeting his gaze, not smiling.

'I think this would be a suitable time to hand over this.' Jack passed the amulet up to her. 'I will try to talk now.'

She caught it, fumbled and held it tight. 'I have been listening to your silence for the past five miles.' Releasing the reins, she reached down toward him. 'Jack…'

'Windrush!' Colonel Maxwell appeared from behind the tents. 'Is my daughter safe?'

'Of course, sir,' Jack said.

'Good, then get you to the front. One of my other lieutenants has gone sick, and I need an officer to replace him.'

'Yes, sir.' Jack caught Helen's eye. 'I have to go; duty calls.'

'It always will,' she said, with infinite sadness in her voice.

'As you can see,' Dearden kept his voice low, as befitted the perilous position of being in the front line, 'the Second Division maintains a chain of outposts to guard the flank of the army.'

'Yes, sir.' Jack looked out on the bleak uplands of the Crimea, compared the landscape to the lush lands of Burma and wished he was back at Pegu or Rangoon. With Helen at his side.

'There was a bit of a battle fought here the other day when you were recovering from the affair at Balaklava. We gave the Russians the right-about-turn and chased them back.'

'I heard of that, sir.' For an instant, Jack cursed that once again the 113th had not been involved, and then he remembered that the affairs of the 113th were no longer vital to him. He was Lieutenant Windrush of the 118th now and all the evil times of the past were behind him.

'The Russians seem to have no name for this upland area,' Rearden said, 'so we call it Mount Inkerman or the Inkerman Heights, and that is the name by which the world will know it henceforth and forever.' He gave a small smile. 'Or until somebody higher up than me decides to change it.'

Inkerman Heights was a rough area of ravines and ridges, with the Tchernaya Valley below. Unlike the grassy plain over which the Allies had marched only six weeks before, the Heights were green with tangled scrubby bushes and low oak trees with spreading branches.

'Take notice of these two prominent heights.' Dearden indicated two higher points in the undulating landscape. 'The smaller one is known as Shell Hill, although some call it Cossack Hill and others Funk Point. Why Funk Point, you may wonder?'

'I did wonder, sir.'

'It is Funk Point because that is the most forward of our positions; beyond that are the Russians.'

Jack nodded. 'I see, sir. The men are in a bit of a funk when they're there.'

'More apprehensive than afraid.' Dearden qualified his meaning of the term 'funk'.

'Yes, sir.'

'The even higher one slightly to the south is Home Ridge.' Dearden waited until Jack nodded to ensure he had identified the hills. 'Now,' Dearden continued, 'this whole flank is dangerous because the Russians can approach us from the city or the great spaces beyond. The Heights themselves, as you see, are cut up by a brace of ravines called the Careenage Ravine and the Quarry Ravine. The latter holds the Post Road into Sebastopol.'

'I see sir.' Jack scanned the rough ground. 'So the Russians can come at us from the city or through these ravines.'

'That's correct,' Dearden said, 'so pray there is no mist or fog to hide them, although with winter coming on…' He left the rest unsaid.

'As you see, the Second Division holds Home Ridge; it is our temporary home until we capture Sebastopol. We have forward pickets out there.' Dearden nodded to the wind-swept, bush laden uplands. 'If the Russians attack, the pickets will hold until they ascertain their strength. If they can deal with them, then that is what they will do. If not, then they will fall back on our main position here.' Dearden indicated the line of shallow trenches, periodically supported by cannon in sandbagged breastworks.

'It does not seem very well fortified sir, given the importance of the position.'

Dearden nodded. 'I am aware of that. What we do have is an earthen bank in the Quarry Ravine where the Post Road meets a smaller road. We call the earthwork the Barrier, although any half-determined rush by a company or two could take it. We also have the two-gun Sandbag Battery on that hill spur over there, the Kitspur. The guns are no longer there, but the redoubt is handy to shelter the men on a wet night.'

'Is that it, sir?'

'Not quite,' Dearden said. 'There is one sandbagged redoubt on that hill there.' He handed Jack the telescope. 'See it? It is between both the ravines and to the flank of the Barrier. If the Russians took that, they could position a battery there that would catch our men at the Barrier in the flank and make them untenable.'

'Does it have a name, sir?'

'Indeed. We call that the Fatal Redoubt.' Dearden smiled. 'The name speaks for itself.'

'Can't we dig more emplacements, sir and strengthen the defences?'

'Who would dig them?' Rearden looked around. 'The regiment lost scores to cholera even before we got here, took casualties at the Alma and are losing men to disease and the weather every day. Unless General Raglan can send us a couple of hundred Turks to act as labourers, we just don't have the manpower. We barely have enough troops to man the trenches without expending their energy in digging. We are down to less than five hundred men, Windrush.' Dearden sighed. 'But complaining never won a war.'

'No, sir.'

Dearden looked at him levelly. 'We can always fight a battle, Windrush, and win it by God, but we are poor at sieges and taking cities. Let us hope this war is over soon, or there won't be a British Army to fight anybody.'

'You said that we beat them last time they tried here, sir.'

'That was only a sortie, Windrush. And I happen to know that the Russians are being reinforced. Two divisions of General Dannenburg's 4th Corps are marching in from Bessarabia; that will give the Russians a considerable advantage in men over us.' Dearden's hand was steady as he lit a cheroot. 'Keep the men on their toes, Windrush.'

'Yes, sir.' Jack looked over the terrain and shivered. This Crimea seemed to be hard and unyielding, and the Russian soldiers were brave and skilful soldiers. They would have to take Sebastopol soon, or the winter would be upon them. This campaign was not going as he hoped it would.

Chapter Eighteen

Balaklava
3rd November 1854

'There's something about to happen.' Helen stood at Jack's side, nearly but not quite touching and with her bonnet tied down tightly against the wind. She pulled her coat around her, adjusted her amulet and shivered. 'I hate this place.' She looked over the harbour of Balaklava with its crowded shipping and the constant bustle. 'I have lived in half the world, and I have never hated a place like I hate this one. I don't like the climate or the people or the place itself.'

'It's only geography,' Jack said. 'I'm sure you've been in worse places.'

'India, South Africa, Ireland, Lower Canada, Malta and here.' Helen listed her father's postings and her life. 'India was hot and spicy, South Africa crisp and beautiful, Ireland wet and misty and Malta hot and friendly. Canada was huge and here is cold and bleak and sinister.'

'And England?' Jack had a sudden longing for the Malvern Hills and the soft mists of Herefordshire.

'I've never been to England,' Helen said.

'Never?' Jack looked at her in astonishment. 'So where do you call home? Where are you from?'

Helen shrugged. 'Here, there and nowhere. Wherever I am; wherever father is stationed. I don't know – does it matter?'

'Yes, it matters a great deal.' Jack tried to explain. 'You need an anchor, somewhere to hang your hat when things are bad, an escape inside your mind when the dacoits are coming through the jungle for you, and you wonder why you are there and the reason you are fighting. It's a spiritual thing, somewhere to give a meaning to life.'

Helen shook her head. 'I've never had that. I've spent my life living in military cantonments and such like establishments.' Jack thought she looked most appealing when she wrinkled her nose. 'Probably the regiment is my home, if anywhere is.'

'I have to show you the Malvern Hills.' Jack couldn't hide his enthusiasm. 'I'll take you there someday. We will climb to the top of the Beacon at night and watch the dawn rise over Worcestershire, with the mist low across the fields and the sun burning it off field by field. We will see the church spires protruding from the greyness, and then the tops of the trees and then, inch-by-inch and field-by-field the countryside will reveal itself. The little villages and farmhouses will appear, and the roads and tracks. You'll watch as the entire sweep of the second most beautiful county in the most perfect country on earth.'

'Second most beautiful? Why not the most beautiful?' Helen looked puzzled.

'You will see that in the evening.' Jack had been ready for the question. He found talking to her much easier now; perhaps the amulet helped. 'The sun dips over Herefordshire then, toward the blue hills of the Welsh Marches.'

'If it is so perfect,' Helen asked sweetly, 'why did you leave?'

'A man has to do his duty,' Jack said.

She smiled. 'You sound like my father.'

'He is a good man,' Jack said.

Helen frowned, 'He is one of the jolliest fellows under the sun, but a good man? She shrugged. 'I cannot judge.' She shivered as the wind blasted icy from the heights to the north. 'It's cold.'

'It is,' Jack agreed.

She gave a small smile and shivered. 'You may be a very brave soldier Jack Windrush, but even although you have learned how to talk, you still don't know much about women do you?'

'I haven't had the chance.' Jack had learned enough to know that honesty was the best policy with Helen.

Helen's smile widened. 'Well, Mr. Lieutenant Jack, here is some more free advice for you:

The lady's waist is 22 inches round
A gentleman's arm is 22 inches long
How admirable are thy ways O nature.'

'Poetry?' Jack was bemused. He shook his head. 'I don't know much poetry – I know Homer…'

Helen shook her head. 'That was an invitation, you oaf!' She edged slightly closer. 'Now let's try again. I'm cold.'

'What?'

When Jack stared at her, she took hold of his arm and wrapped it around her. 'You men! Do you have to be shown everything?'

Jack was aware of the warmth of her body under his hand. She was firm yet yielding and infinitely alluring.

'There – isn't that better?' She smiled up at his face. 'For a while there I thought you were proof against my allurements!'

'Proof against…' Jack smiled and tentatively squeezed her closer. It felt good. 'No, Helen, hardly that.'

They were silent for a few moments, yet happy. The erstwhile awkwardness was diminishing, if not yet entirely gone. Helen broke the spell with a necessary question.

'When are you going back to the trenches?'

'I am back tonight,' Jack said quietly.

'Be careful,' Helen said. 'Something is going to happen.'

'You sound so very solemn.' Jack tried to lighten the mood, although he remembered Dearden's warnings about the Russian armies in the interior.

'No, Jack.' When she twisted within his embrace her eyes were wide and very grey. 'I can feel it. A soldier's daughter gets a feeling for such things. I am certain that there is trouble imminent.'

Jack nodded. 'Thank you. I will keep alert and make sure my men don't fall asleep.'

'These Russians are different from us,' Helen said. 'They think differently and feel differently. I know you love England, and all it stands for, but the Russians have an even deeper attachment. To them, they are part of Russia. It is holy, deep in their soul.' She looked up. 'They will not give up their city easily, Jack.'

'Then we will have to take it from them' Jack experienced a wave of stubbornness.

She looked up with her mouth slightly parted and sighed. 'Jack, I think you should kiss me now.'

For one instant Jack had the ridiculous notion of telling her that he had never kissed a girl in his life. Instead, he bent his head closer and allowed her to take the initiative. Her lips were softer than he expected. *She is nothing like Myat. Why not?*

'You were reluctant there,' she said, 'but you cannot stand against what I want. Don't you know the truth?'

'No,' Jack said. *I'm utterly confused. I want to be with this girl who twists me inside out.*

Helen smiled again and said, 'I hope you like poetry: I am an in a poetical mood and

> *A man's a fool who tries by force or skill*
> *To stay the torrent of a woman's will.*
> *For when she will, she will, you may depend on't*
> *And when she won't, she won't, so there's an end on't'*

Do you like poetry, Jack?'

Her eyes held him, so he did not want to withdraw. 'I find your poetry intriguing,' he said. 'It is nothing like Homer.'

Helen laughed. 'That's because Homer is long dead and I am very much alive.' She looked away and spoke quietly, so he had to strain to hear her. 'Please try to forgive me, Mama, for what I am about to do again, and say thereafter.'

Without another word, she kissed him, long and soundly, and then pulled away. 'Do you know what my mother would say about this?'

'No.' Jack touched his mouth. 'Tell me. What would your mother say?'

'It is something she read somewhere. She would say,' Helen lowered her voice an octave to mimic her mother's deeper tones. 'All the world loves a lover, Helen, but that does not keep that same world from watching their every movement and criticising severely any breach of good manners. Any public display of affection anywhere at any time is grossly unrefined. Love is sacred, and it should not be thrown open to the rude comments of strangers.'

'I see,' Jack said. *What would my mother have said? Or my step-mother, rather?*

'So that is why I had to ask for mother's forgiveness in advance for I am about to give another public display of affection.'

'You are…' Jack's conversation stopped when Helen cupped his face in her hands and kissed him longer and with more passion than he had ever been kissed before. 'There now, Jack Windrush. If that does not tell you something of my feelings for you, then I don't know what will.'

Jack stared at her, touching his lips with his right hand. 'I think you have made your feelings very plain.' He dropped his hand. 'Now all that remains is for me to reciprocate.' His kiss took her by surprise and afterwards both were very quiet as they looked over the harbour.

'It is getting dark,' Helen said at last.

'It is,' Jack agreed.

'I had better be getting back to mother.'

'You had,' Jack said. *Please don't go yet. There is so much I wish to say.*

Helen made no move to leave. Jack did not encourage her.

'Jack,' she said at length. 'You will be careful, won't you?'

'Of course, I will,' he said.

'I don't want to lose you so soon after I have found you.'

Jack could think of nothing to say. He touched her lightly on the arm, and then they walked down to the village, passing a score of red-coated soldiers and blue-jacketed seamen. He returned their salutes automatically.

'Good-bye, Jack.' They stood on the threshold of her house.

He could think of nothing to say that would help. 'Good-bye Helen.'

As he turned, she followed him, crushing him in a suddenly fierce embrace. 'Oh, I wish you did not have to go!'

He allowed her a few moments before freeing himself. He kissed her lightly on the forehead. 'But you know I must. It is a soldier's duty, and I am a soldier.'

Helen reached out. 'I know,' she said, walked into the house and closed the door.

Chapter Nineteen

**Inverman Heights
5th November 1854**

Mist rolled in during the night, accompanied by a drizzling rain that soaked through the men's coats and penetrated every layer of clothing that they had. Jack huddled at the bottom of the trench, cursing the weather. He checked his men. The old Burma hands of the 113th had placed a sock or a piece of rag over the muzzles and locks of their Minié rifles to keep out the rain and had waterproofed their ammunition pouches as best they could. The men of the 118th, young soldiers straight out from England, had taken no such precautions and had their rifles stacked, muzzle up to the rain. Jack moved among them, telling them what he wanted to be done and showing them how to do it, man by man. He knew it was too important a task to leave to the sergeants, for a soldier whose rifle could not fire had only his bayonet and one main advantage the British had was the quality and stopping power of the Minié rifle.

'Everything all right, Windrush?' Dearden asked. He hunched into his great coat, turned his back to the wind and lit a cheroot. The tiny pin-prick of light was the only warmth in their section of the trench.

'All right, sir,' Jack said. He was cold, wet and afraid but cold and wet was a soldier's lot, and he would never admit to his fear. He wondered if any of the other soldiers out on Inkerman Ridge were afraid or if it was only him. He glanced around. Logan would never know this knotting of the stomach every time he heard a Russian cannon; Coleman may be afraid, but he would merely grouse about it and move on to something else. Riley was as cool-headed a man as he had ever known; he would rationalise his fear and put it in some compartment within his head and forget it.

'Some of the men look a bit apprehensive.' Dearden nearly echoed Jack's thoughts. 'We all are of course, but we can't let it show.' He pulled at his cheroot. 'You don't indulge do you, Windrush?'

For a moment Jack thought Dearden was asking if he was afraid. 'Cheroots? Oh, no sir. I don't smoke.'

'Very wise. It's a filthy habit although it does help to settle the nerves.' He gave a brief grin. 'Well, keep alert, Windrush and make sure the picket at Fatal Redoubt is changed regularly. I don't want the men to be out there for more than three hours at a time. Now that would be bad for the nerves, what?'

'Yes, sir,' Jack agreed. He looked up; the weather was deteriorating. After a full day of rain there had been a temporary lull when mist and drizzle took its place, but now the rain returned, battering down in a chilling downpour that turned the ground to a slippery quagmire and lowered the morale of the men.

'We've got the position of honour here,' Dearden said. 'We are one of the furthest forward of all the British regiments. If the Russians were to break through us, they could roll up the entire line.'

'Yes, sir,' Jack said. He peered forward. 'I can't even see Fatal Redoubt, sir, in this muck.'

'Nor can I, Windrush.' When Dearden tossed away his cheroot, the lit end made a red arc through the air until it landed in a puddle, sizzled for a few seconds and was extinguished by the water. 'Maybe it would be an idea to take a few men forward and ensure the lads there are still all right?'

That was the most casual order Jack had ever heard given. 'Yes, sir.'

'I haven't heard any firing, but it would do the men good to know we have not forgotten them.' Dearden lit another cheroot. 'I hear that the pickets on Shell Hill have already been withdrawn. We only have a dozen men there at Fatal, but I don't think they should withdraw; indeed, I think we should reinforce them. If I were a Russian, I would choose tonight to send forward a party to probe our defences.' He paused to draw life into his cheroot. 'The word for tonight is Rule, and the answer is Britannia.' He nodded. 'Best take some extra rations with you too, Windrush; we don't know what may happen.'

Jack nodded. It was evident that Dearden also had a feeling of foreboding, much as Helen had voiced. 'Thank you, sir.' He watched Dearden slip further along the line of entrenchments.

'O'Neill, bring Coleman, Thorpe and the Bishop,' Jack said. 'No, bring all our old 113th lads. We're going to have a look at Fatal Redoubt.'

'Why us?' Coleman asked. 'Why always us? Do these 118th buggers not know how to soldier?'

'Those men of the 118th have been in Fatal Redoubt for hours,' Jack said, 'while you've been lying comfortably in a nice warm trench. Besides, Coleman, you are one of the 118th now – remember?'

Coleman's retort was too low for Jack to make out although he did hear some oaths. He hid his smile – if Coleman ever stopped complaining, then it would undoubtedly be time to get worried. He looked up; after one last savage downpour, the rain abruptly ended. Now they only had to contend with the mist.

Jack checked the men's equipment and looked out into the sodden dark. He remembered Helen's ominous warnings that something was going to happen and shrugged them off. She was a little upset, nothing more. They had defeated the Russians in every encounter so far and they would do so again, and again and again if need be.

'Ready lads? Keep close and don't get lost out there. I don't want any of us to wander around in this muck all day.'

'Oh, how amiable is our officer; he cares for us,' Thorpe said.

'Does he buggery,' Coleman said. 'He just doesn't want the Ruskies to get these new Minié rifles.'

'They're good.' Logan said quietly. 'I cannae wait to shoot a few Russians.'

'I heard you have a good Russian friend in Sebastopol.' The Bishop gave one of his rare contributions to any conversation. 'You saved his life, and he saved yours.'

Logan glowered at the Bishop as Riley smiled and glanced away before Logan noticed.

'You watch your mouth, Bishop!' Logan said.

'Enough talking,' O'Neill snarled. 'Keep your voices down. The Russians may have pickets out as well.'

Jack felt that familiar tension building up as he cleared the lip of the trench and led them forward through the scrubby oak trees. In the mist, he could hardly see twenty yards in any direction and felt as if he was swimming through a grey, clinging blanket. When he spoke to the men, his voice was distorted, while every footstep seemed to echo again and again, with the scrape of studs on the men's boots as loud as cannon and the soft slither of their uniforms screaming their presence to the Russians.

'Listen!' O'Neill stopped and held up a hand. 'Listen.'

There was definite sound in the mist. Jack heard the pad of horses' hooves, the jingle of harnesses, and the regular tramp of marching men.

'I hear it,' Thorpe said. 'Bloody Russians!'

'Aye, but where are they? In this muck, it's impossible to tell.' Jack listened, aware that his decision may be crucial to all their lives. 'That may just be the normal Russian troop movements along the Post Road. Keep moving to the redoubt men – but be careful.'

With possible Russians on the prowl, they moved slower, testing each step, checking that each bush was what it seemed and was not a Russian soldier waiting for them. Each stunted oak tree was eminently capable of sheltering a Russian sharpshooter and had to be watched and scouted.

'Listen!' That was Coleman. 'Church bells!'

Jack heard them, carried by some freak twist of the fog from Sebastopol. 'Carillons, calling the faithful to worship.'

'I haven't heard that before at this time of night,' O'Neill said.

The sound of bells drifted away as a thicker pocket of mist enveloped them. Thorpe flapped his hand in front of his face. 'I can't see a bloody thing here,' he said and cursed as he tripped over the trailing root of a tree.

'Can we not just shout out and order the picket back?' Coleman asked.

'Not with these bells battering away as if the Pope was visiting,' O'Neill grumbled.

'The Russians don't have a Pope,' the Bishop said quietly. 'They're Orthodox.'

'Stand to your arms!' The voice floated to them from somewhere in the mist, and then there was silence.

'Who said that?' O'Neill asked.

'Not me,' Jack said. 'Keep moving; let's get to the redoubt.'

The musketry was sudden and definite, an outbreak of firing too intense to be merely the reaction of a nervous man.

'Where did that come from?' O'Neil knelt behind the twisted wreck of a tree and cocked his rifle. 'Can anybody tell?'

'Halt now until we can work it out.' Jack pulled the revolver from his holster.

'Shell Hill,' Coleman said. 'That came from Shell Hill.'

Dearden said we had withdrawn our pickets from Shell Hill. Have they been sent out again? What the devil is happening?

'It's stopped now,' Thorpe said.

'Or perhaps we can't hear it anymore like we can't hear the church bells.' Jack said. 'Move on, but keep quiet for God's sake.'

The mist was shifting in a fluky wind, one moment dense, the next sufficiently thin to see twenty yards.

'There it is again,' Riley said. 'That's artillery as well.'

This time it was quite distinctive, volleys of musketry one after the other, too close together to be only one side firing, and then the more substantial boom of cannon.

'That's the Russians,' O'Neill said flatly. 'We don't have any artillery out here.'

'Nor do they,' Jack said, 'or rather, they didn't.'

'Well, somebody has now,' Riley said.

'Pick up the pace,' Jack ordered. 'Get forward to the Fatal Redoubt and see if they know more than we do. Keep together.'

No longer concerned about making a noise, Jack led them at the double, ignoring the shrubs whose trailing branches ripped at their clothing and the gnarled trees that loomed through the gloom. The sound of firing intensified and then drifted away.

'Halt!' The sound of a British voice was welcome. 'What's the word?'

For a second Jack's mind blanked, and then he called out: 'Rule!'

'Britannia,' the word came back. 'Pass friend.'

Fatal Redoubt was little more than a gun emplacement hacked out of the rock and reinforced with sandbags. There was no artillery in place, nothing except a breast-high U of sandbags with the ground scraped away behind them and a view of tangled trees disappearing into the mist. The garrison was taut-faced, with rifles held in white-knuckled hands.

'Who's in charge here?' Jack asked.

'Me, sir.' Despite the situation, the corporal sounded cheerful as he saluted. 'Corporal O'Hara sir.'

'Ah, the Minié expert. Is there no officer here?' Jack looked around. There were about a dozen men, none of any higher rank than the corporal.

'Not any longer, sir. Ensign Thatcher took a party of men to find out what the firing was all about.'

'When was that?'

The corporal screwed up his face with the extra strain of calculating time. 'About half an hour since, sir.'

Jack peered forward into the mist. 'Has anything happened here, Corporal?'

'Nary a thing, sir. We're just sitting tight waiting for Russians or orders.' O'Hara touched the lock of his Minié. 'Are you our relief, sir?'

'We're your reinforcements, O'Hara. Captain Dearden wants us to keep this redoubt secure.'

'Yes, sir.' O'Hara accepted the order without question.

'What are your names, men?' Jack looked at the privates of the 118th. They were lean, like all British soldiers in the Crimea, haggard, bitter-eyed and swaying from fatigue.

'Brodie, sir.' A tall man with a Highland Scottish accent.

'Fraser, sir.' Quiet-voiced, older than his peers and with eyes that slid away.

'Raeburn, sir.' Northern English and still a boy, holding Jack's gaze with defiance and self-respect.

'Aitken, sir.' Pug-nosed and freckled, he looked even younger than Raeburn.

'How old are you, Aitken?' Jack remembered him; a Borderer from Selkirk.

'Eighteen, sir,' his voice broke as he spoke. Jack deducted at least two years from his stated age.

'Fletcher, sir.' He looked ill, with a yellow tinge in his face that was noticeable even in the grey light of dawn.

'When we get back, Fletcher, I want you to visit the surgeon. You are not well,' Jack said.

'I'm all right, sir,' Fletcher said indignantly, stiffening to attention.

The names continued, a roll call from all quarters of the British Isles from Donegal to Cornwall, Caithness to Pembroke. They were homely names, ordinary faces, names with the lilt of the Hebrides or the music of Wales, broad Yorkshire or the thin whine of Essex. These men were his responsibility now in this foreign land, fighting for a cause few would understand. They had joined the army out of poverty or a desire for adventure, to impress a girl or because they lacked the skills or the luck to find employment elsewhere. They had no malice toward the Russians or anybody else; they were here because the Army had sent them here and that was all that mattered.

'The breastworks could be higher, corporal,' Jack pointed to the breast-high barricade of sandbags in front of the shallow scrape of trench.

'Aye sir,' O'Hara replied, 'but if we made it so, we could not get over it to attack the Russians, could we sir?'

It was a typical reply from a British soldier. Jack gave a little smile. 'That is so, corporal. When did you men last eat?'

'Dunno, sir,' O'Hara said.

'We've brought some black bread and dried pork,' Jack said. 'It's not much, but better than grass and mud.'

'Thank you, sir,' O'Hara said.

'Is there any rum, sir?' Fletcher asked. 'It helps keep the cold out.' He coughed harshly, doubling up in obvious pain.

'No, Fletcher…' Jack began until Riley intervened.

'Begging your pardon, sir, but I think Logie… sorry sir, Logan, has something that may suit.'

Logan edged past them. 'Whisky sir. It's not the best sir, but these lads of the 42nd haven't all the equipment, sir.'

Jack was no longer surprised at the ability of British soldiers to find something alcoholic in even the worst of circumstances. Nor was he surprised that the Highland troops of the 42nd would somehow build a still to create whisky out of whatever they could find.

'That's good stuff, Logie,' Fletcher approved.

Leaving them to it, Jack peered over the breastwork. The firing had died down again, or the mist had blanketed the sound.

'Sir!' Hitchins lifted a hand, like a schoolboy hoping to catch the attention of his master. 'I hear something.'

Jack listened, straining into the eerie hush. 'So do I,' he said.

'Something is coming out of the mist,' Hitchins said.

'Bloody Russians,' Logan agreed.

'Stand to your arms!' Jack heard the bite in his voice.

Chapter Twenty

Inkerman Ridge
5th November 1854

Now Jack had a decision to make. Should he stand and meet whatever came against them, or withdraw his handful of men to the slightly more secure lines of the 118th, quarter of a mile to the rear? He looked around him. He knew the mettle of his Burma veterans and guessed that Logan and Hitchins would fight. He wasn't sure about the Bishop with his religious affiliations while Riley was calm in some situation and nervous in others. The men of the 118th seemed to be typical British infantry; they would fight and die if ordered. That was what British soldiers did.

'Here they come, sir!' O'Neill said quietly. 'Shall I order the men to fire?'

'Not yet, Sergeant.' Jack remembered Colonel Maxwell's patrol; he had no desire to shoot into British soldiers.

He peered forward. The mist swirled around, distorting vision, making a mockery of distance, altering perceptions of sound and space. There might be ten thousand Russians out there, or there might be ten. He drew a deep breath to try and control the racing of his heart.

'Can anybody see anything?' he asked quietly.

'I can see bloody mist,' Coleman said.

'Nothing, sir,' O'Hara said.

The noises increased, the sound of feet scuffing on the ground, the rustle of men passing through the tangle of oak trees, the rattle of equipment, a subdued murmur as of a thousand men talking quietly among themselves. Jack heard the confident bark of an order, and then a stronger gust of wind blew a clearing in the mist.

'Sweet Mary Mother of God!' O'Hara said, 'it's the whole Russian Army!'

The mist had hidden their advance until they were within two hundred yards of the Fatal Redoubt. Led by proud officers and with colours displayed in front, they marched slowly, hampered by the rough terrain and the small trees, but they moved with purpose and determination.

Unlike the helmet-wearing infantry of the Alma, these grey-clad men had flat, muffin-style caps on their head. They came forward remorselessly in two dense columns, rank after rank after rank with each step bringing them closer to the Fatal Redoubt. As Jack watched, the colours flopped in the mist and then wavered as a gust of wind caught them, opening the brave flags out.

'Present.' Jack heard the nervousness in his voice. He cleared his throat. 'Present!' He knew he didn't need to give such precise orders: his men knew what to do. Their duty was plain: they were here to defeat the Russian Army, and here it was, marching toward them in all its panoply and glory.

'Wait,' Jack said. He knew that the Minié had a longer range and greater accuracy than the old Brown Bess, but he wanted to ensure that the first volley would make an impact. 'O'Neill and O'Hara, aim for the officers. All the rest of you, shoot into the brown.'

He judged the distance – one hundred and eighty yards; one hundred and seventy. The Russians were close enough for him to make out facial features now; they were no longer a mass of uniforms but men most remarkably like these he commanded here.

'Fire,' he said quietly, and then louder, 'Fire!'

The first volley of the Miniés ripped into the massive column. Men fell; one of the officers in front staggered, recovered and bravely carried on, gesturing to his men. With the unseen musketry taking them by surprise, the head of both Russian columns wavered.

'Fire!' Jack said again. He had twenty men to stand against a Russian force of what seemed many thousand; this would be a very short encounter. As the British rifles fired, a cloud of Russian skirmishers broke into a run toward them. Moving faster than the columns, they were making good progress when a second British force appeared through the mist and took them on the flank. A volley ran out, smashing into skirmishers and the left-hand column alike.

'Who was that?' O'Neill asked as the skirmishers hesitated.

'I have no idea. Fire at will!' Jack allowed his men latitude. That way the faster would not be hampered by the slower or less experienced. He saw the skirmishers turn back as the Minié bullets took savage effect, ripping through men, flattening with contact with bone to spread and cause hideous wounds, tearing great holes in skulls or blowing off arms and legs. With every moment the Russian columns came closer, but correspondingly they became more vulnerable to the British fire so that the powerful Minié bullets were passing through the leading man to kill or injure the man behind him.

'We're slaughtering them,' Logan said and unleashed one of his incomprehensible Glaswegian slogans.

'They're getting very close.' Thorpe glanced behind him as if measuring the distance back to the main British lines.

That second British party rose from cover and unleashed rolling volleys on the Russian skirmishers, sending the survivors scurrying back to the columns. There were about thirty of them, tall Guardsmen in uniforms that seemed immaculate despite the conditions.

'You don't mind if we join you, do you, Lieutenant?' The captain in charge was debonair and very calm. 'Goodlake, Coldstream Guards.'

'Join us by all means, sir,' Jack said. 'Jack Windrush, late of the 113th, now of the 118th.'

'Good man, Windrush.' Goodlake indicated his men. 'We've been roving all over these Inkerman Heights doing whatever damage we can.' He raised his voice. 'Keep firing, Guards!'

Still vastly outnumbered, the reinforced British of the Fatal Redoubt increased their fire, watching the leading ranks of the Russians tumble down, and others take their place in a never-ending procession of grey uniforms that advanced through the mist. They appeared like giants stepping over their dead and wounded to get at this minuscule pocket of British resistance.

'There's plenty of them,' Jack said. He had emptied his revolver without realising it and now reloaded, fumbling the fat brass cartridges with a shaking hand.

'More than you realise, Windrush, I think. I would say that the Russians have sent Soimonoff and Pauloff's armies against us, one army on either side of the Quarry Ravine. Of course, it's too early to tell yet for sure.' Goodlake reloaded his revolver. 'You're not falling back, I see?'

'No sir,' Jack said. 'I have orders to hold on here.'

'Good man. Death or glory, eh?' Goodlake fired at the Russians, now only forty yards away. 'It shouldn't be long now before it's the former. I'd get my men to fix bayonets if I were you – except that pugnacious little fellow there; he seems ready to take on the whole of Russia himself.'

Logan was kneeling on the lip of the breastwork, bayonet already in place, shouting obscenities as he fired and reloaded with an enthusiasm Jack had never seen before.

'Logie!' That was Riley, looking after his friend. 'Get back down, you stupid bugger!'

'He will soon have to,' Jack said. He glanced along the breastwork. His 113th and 118th were firing steadily, while the Guards were acting like Guardsmen always acted; disciplined, unemotional, exact, unhurried. Perfect soldiers. Compared to the approaching masses their numbers were nothing; the Russians should roll over them without thought. Indeed, they didn't even break formation but marched on, absorbing their losses with apparent impunity.

'Here they come,' Goodlake murmured. Transferring his revolver to his left hand, he drew his sword. 'It has been an honour to fight alongside you, Windrush.'

Thousands strong, the Russians marched like some steam-powered machine, stepping over their dead with the colours hanging limply above them and the men chanting something— No, Jack realised, they were singing something. A hymn! They were singing a hymn as they marched to kill and be killed.

'Bayonets, lads! Over the parapet and at them.'

Jack knew it was hopeless; there were too few British, too many Russians. He would die here at Fatal Redoubt, never having achieved success, never having regained his reputation or position back, never having known love except for these few kisses from Helen.

He heard the click as practised hands pressed bayonets into place, and then there were more men, another order from a familiar voice: 'Stand fast 118th! Keep your heads down lads!' Immediately after came the ear-splitting thunder of a volley from a regiment of British infantry.

The entire front three rows of the Russian column were thrown back by the fusillade of bullets, and some men behind them staggered and fell. Others turned away or held hands up to their face as if to deflect the bullets.

'Fire!' Jack roared. 'Fire away men!'

'Open fire the Guards!' Goodlake echoed.

'Fire!' That was Maxwell's voice, distinct above the rattle of musketry. The Russians had stopped singing now, and only the yells and groans of the wounded sounded.

The British rifles sounded again; more Russians fell. The column began to splinter as men turned away, unwilling or unable to face that storm of shot.

'Fire!' Jack ordered as the Russians wavered.

He watched as the column disintegrated, with the men, so brave only seconds before, finally losing their nerve as they saw so many of their colleagues falling around them.

'Fire!' Goodlake and Maxwell shouted together. Guardsmen and soldiers of the line fired into the retreating mass, bringing down more men, killing and wounding sons, brothers, husbands, brave Russian soldiers defending their Holy soil. White powder smoke merged with the clammy greyness of the mist, reducing visibility once again. Unable to face the fire of an unknown number of men, the Russians broke and fled; only the dead and wounded remained.

Jack sat on the far side of the trench, shaking with reaction.

'That was a smart little action.' Goodlake sounded as calm as if he was calling for a cab in Oxford Street. 'I'll take my merry little band and be on my way now. We have a roving commission you see, lending support where it is needed and moving off when it is not.' He flipped a finger to his hat by way of salute. 'My respects to you, Colonel.'

'And mine to you, Captain,' Maxwell returned the salute with one just as perfunctory.

'You came at a good time, sir,' Jack said.

'Thank the general.' Maxwell sounded cheerful. 'General De Lacy Evans is lying injured on a ship in Balaklava harbour, as you may know.'

Jack nodded. 'So I heard, sir.'

'We have that crazy Irishman, Pennefather in charge now. Do you know of him, Windrush?'

'Not much, sir.'

'Not much, sir,' Maxwell repeated. 'Well, Windrush, he has one maxim in war: whenever you see a head, hit it.'

'I see, sir.' Jack controlled his trembling sufficiently to smile. 'That seems apt, sir.'

'De Lacy would have the pickets withdrawn to a line of defence at Home Ridge.' Maxwell looked around him as he spoke, gauging his men, watching for any movement by the enemy. 'Pennefather has other ideas. He has ordered us to sit tight here, at our most advanced post, and hold the Russians. We are to shoot as soon as we see them and he will send us reinforcements if they become available.'

'If, sir?'

'If, Windrush.' There was no expression on Maxwell's face.

'And if they do not become available?'

'Then we hold on anyway.' Maxwell raised his eyebrows. 'Any questions?'

'No, sir.'

'Good man.' Maxwell moved along the redoubt, giving orders, positioning the men where they would do the most good, encouraging the shaken, congratulating the young. 'Keep your muzzles downward,' Maxwell said, 'and don't waste ammunition; there is little more where that came from.' He had them adding rocks to the breastwork and using bayonets to deepen the shallow trench, bringing in dead wood as cover and clearing as much of the scrub and brushwood in front of the redoubt as they could.

'We need to deny them cover,' he explained, 'and create a killing area where we can see them clearly and shoot them flat.'

Jack saw the ranks of the 118th extend in either direction, like a line of blood-coloured ants. They moved with as much purpose as the Russian column had done as they strengthened the defences. In the centre of the Fatal Redoubt, Maxwell ordered that the Regimental Colour be raised, with the Union Flag in the corner and the fly buff and clean, with the number 118 and the battle honours prominent.

'Here we are then,' Maxwell said, 'and here we stay.' He jerked a thumb to the rear, 'and we have friends.'

Jack looked over his shoulder, squinting into the fog. He had been too occupied with his own affairs to notice that two nine-pounders of the Royal Artillery had taken up position there, complete with limbers, horses and their crews of stalwart looking gunners. One man sat astride the barrel of the left-hand gun, calmly smoking a clay pipe.

'Pity help the Russians,' the Bishop said, 'we have nearly five hundred rifles now and half the artillery. We'll massacre them.'

'Five hundred rifles and two guns,' Coleman said, 'and they only have forty thousand men and a hundred guns.' He whistled. 'The poor Ruskies have not got a chance.' He laughed. 'Anyway Bishop, I thought you were on their side!

When they came up singing their hymns, I thought you were going to go up and join them.'

The noise of battle had drowned the tolling of the church bells inside Sebastopol, but now a drift of wind brought the sound to them, adding to the surreal atmosphere of a battle fought in shifting mist.

'You don't understand, Coley,' the Bishop said quietly. 'The Russians call this land Holy Russia. They are calling on the land, their Holy Land, as well as the Lord to help them.'

'How can the land help them?' Coleman jabbed his toe against the side of the trench. 'It's just mud and rocks!'

'The same way the Russian winter helped them defeat Napoleon,' the Bishop said. 'Now we're not just facing guns and bayonets but something else.'

Jack heard the words, remembered what Helen had said about the Russians attachment to their country and shivered. It was with some relief that he heard Colonel Maxwell talking.

'Off to our right,' Maxwell said, 'is the Sandbag battery, where we hold. To our left is the Barrier, which we also hold. In between is a space called The Gap and the 118th are smack in the middle. If we know this is the weakest point, then so do the Russians, and you can guarantee that they will come at us again and again with everything they have.' He looked up at the Regimental Colour hanging from its pole. 'We stay, and we fight for the Colours.'

Stepping in front of the Fatal Redoubt, Maxwell waited until all his men could see him. The talking and banter stopped. Sergeants called the men to attention and officers doused their cheroots.

'All right men, stand easy,' Maxwell said. 'Now you know I am not a man for ceremony, and I am not much given to prosing, but on this occasion, I think I should address you for a few moments while we are peaceful.' He closed his mouth as a battery opened up somewhere with an ear-shattering crash. 'Or nearly peaceful, anyway. It seems that our friends the enemy do not wish me to speak, which is all the more reason to do so.'

The men laughed at that, a good sound in the middle of a contested field.

'We are in the position of honour. You have heard of the exploits of the Guards and the Highlanders at the Alma, of the cavalry and the 93rd at Balaklava. Now it is our turn. We are the 118th,' Maxwell pointed to the regimental colour in the centre of the line. 'That is the heart and soul of the regiment. I have planted that as a sign and warning to the Russians. Our Colours say: "you cannot go further." If we lose the Colours, the Regiment loses its honour, and we all die in disgrace. I know I can count on you all to ensure that does not happen.'

There was a moment's silence as the men tried to digest the information and then one man shouted.

'Three cheers for the colonel!'

The men cheered, with the sound resounding across the Heights of Inkerman.

'And three more for the regiment!' Captain Dearden added, and then 'and now a tiger!'

No sooner had the echoes of the last cheer died away than they heard singing from behind the ridge in front.

'That's the Russians coming back,' Logan said.

'Stand to your arms!' Maxwell ordered. 'Here they come lads, hot as hell and thick as thieves. Make Great Britain proud of the 118th!'

Jack cheered with the rest. He could see behind the Colonel's stirring words to the other side of the coin. The 118th may well be at the post of honour, but that also meant that the Russians had to pass them to get through and roll up the British flank. The more stubborn the 118th was, the more they would suffer, and as no man in the regiment would wish to see the colours captured, they would die where they stood.

God help us all, but it is the Russians who have the church bells and who are singing the hymns.

After a temporary lull, the mist had thickened again, just as the Russians returned to the attack. The sombre hymns announced their advance and Maxwell didn't wait for them to get close.

'Fire at the sounds, lads,' he said. 'Our rifles outrange their muskets, and we are in line while they are in column. We may stall them or even stop them before they even get close!'

Not waiting for a second invitation, the 118th opened up, firing volleys at the command of their company commanders.

'All together now,' Dearden said. 'Don't waste bullets and aim at the shine; at the count of three... straighten that rifle Fletcher; you're not after wild duck... fire!'

Volley after volley sounded, with the recoil banging back into shoulders already tender and the gun-smoke acrid in their nostrils, and then the Russian skirmishers emerged from the smoke.

'Grenadier company, target the skirmishers with individual fire! The rest, continue to fire at the columns!'

The first shot of the artillery made Jack start; he had forgotten they were there. They opened with roundshot over the heads of the skirmishers toward the columns as they appeared from the mist, and two rounds later changed to case-shot, which scattered at close quarters, dangerously close to the 118th as the hundreds of small projectiles fanned across the ground in front and bowled over the skirmishers.

'We're massacring them,' Thorpe said.

'Here comes the reply.' Coleman didn't share Thorpe's optimism as unseen Russian cannon opened in support of their men. The first salvo was well over. The next ploughed up the ground in front of the Redoubt and the third smashed into the newly constructed stone breastwork a few yards to the side, killing two of the 118th outright and severely wounding a third.

'They must have an observer out.' Dearden sounded quite calm. 'They are using the Colours as their marker.'

'Maybe we should take them down,' a nervous young ensign suggested. Jack didn't reply to him. To haul down the colours was tantamount to surrender, or an admission of defeat.

'You've got a lot to learn, lad,' Dearden said. He glanced over his shoulder at the British artillery. 'I hope these boys have the Russians range.'

As he spoke, the British guns elevated their barrels and fired in what Jack hoped was the direction of the Russian artillery. The reply came a few moments later, half a dozen cannon balls that hammered onto the space between the Fatal Redoubt and the artillery.

'That's much heavier stuff than ours,' Dearden said. 'They're eighteen pounders at least.'

The two British guns fired back, hopelessly outnumbered by more powerful artillery.

'Here they come again!' O'Neill yelled. 'Take it steady boys; mark your target and shoot low.'

As the skirmishers melted away the Russians advanced in two columns, singing again, long coats flicking against their ankles and with the flags brave above their heads.

'Did these lads not learn last time?' Hitchins said. 'They can't beat us this way.' As he spoke, he fired and loaded, sending shot after shot into the column, as his colleagues all along the line were doing.

'How many are we killing?' Thorpe asked.

'All of them,' Logan said. 'Come on, you Russians!'

Jack heard the noise of the oncoming ball an instant before it landed. He looked up in horror and saw as if in slow motion, the ugly black sphere coming towards him. It hit the ground twenty yards short of the parapet, bounced and rolled forward, ploughing up the ground in a deep furrow. It threw the stones of the parapet aside as if they were made of cotton wool and took both legs off a soldier who had been staring at it hurtling toward him.

Jack looked away as the man reached for his legs as if to replace them before the pain hit him and he began to scream. More cannon balls descended, some falling short to plunge into the earth, others landing near the British artillery that still tried to return fire in a contest that was obviously uneven.

'They've got our range now,' Dearden said. 'Our guns are only attracting fire.'

While one of the British guns continued to fire at the Russian battery, the other returned to its original target and fired a charge of case shot that sliced into the left-hand Russian column. Jack saw men falling as though a giant scythe had whittled them down, and then the column closed up and marched on into the fire of the 118th Foot.

'They're very stubborn men, these Russians.' Dearden raised his voice. 'Fire away boys; knock them flat!'

Colonel Maxwell marched the length of the 118th position, shouting encouragement, giving advice, refusing to duck for the Russian cannonballs or the Russian musketry that crackled from the head of both columns.

'As long as they remain in column, we muster more firepower than them,' Dearden said. 'We can start to worry if their commanders deploy into line because then they'll be able to outflank us on both sides.' He paused to correct the aim of Fletcher. 'Aim low, Fletcher! Their weakness will be the moment they alter formation. The Colonel will see that.'

The Russian artillery had found its mark, with shots landing among the 118th with terrible regularity, smashing the sandbags and rocks of the breastwork, flattening the trenches, tearing off arms and legs, smashing men into unrecognisable lumps of bone and blood and brains and intestines.

'Get down! Lie down,' Maxwell ordered. 'You're just getting slaughtered there.' He stood erect to ensure the 118th obeyed his orders, taking to ground to lessen the target they made for the Russian gunners.

The cannonballs continued to pound the lines as Maxwell slowly walked along the British positions. Taking a deep breath, Jack stood up. The regimental colours still stood, now smoke stained, ripped by shot and sodden with rain and mist. For a moment Jack saw Colonel Maxwell in silhouette with the flag behind him, looking like an image straight from a newspaper report on some heroic British victory that did not mention the screaming wounded and the rows of twisted corpses.

'Here they come!'

Rather than deploy into line, the Russians charged forward in columns, relying on sheer weight to break through the thin British line. However, they had only covered fifty yards when they blocked the line of fire of their own artillery.

'Up, 118th! Up on your feet!'

The men jumped up, perhaps surprising the advancing Russians who may have thought they had withdrawn.

'Volley fire!' Maxwell's voice was calm. 'Fire!'

The closer the Russians came, the more efficient the Minié as the bullets tore through two or three men at one time. The Russians faltered after the first volley and stopped completely after the second. After that, the attack began to disintegrate until a handful of surviving officers roared out orders.

'Fire!' Maxwell shouted again.

The 118th blasted out another volley. Maxwell checked the ammunition pouch of the man at his side and shouted.

'Now, 118th, at them with the bayonet!'

It was the first time Jack had seen a fully-fledged bayonet charge, and it was like nothing he had expected. It was exhilarating, yet terrifying, as nearly five hundred British soldiers swarmed over the lip of the breastwork to launch themselves, yelling and shouting, at the shaken Russian column.

Shattered by repeated volleys of rifle fire and with the nine-pounder having ripped into them with blasts of canister, the men of the left-hand Russian column refused to face this new threat of a long line of gleaming bayonets emerging from behind the battered breastwork. They scattered and fled. Seeing they were alone, the right-hand column shredded as well, despite the efforts of the officers.

'Follow them, boys!' Fletcher yelled, 'chase them all the way back to St Petersburg!'

Jumping over the bodies of the Russian dead, Jack ran forward with the rest. He saw Logan duck under the thrust of a terrified Russian soldier and impale the man with his bayonet, twist and withdraw as the army had taught him. He saw Hitchins and Thorpe chasing a dozen men, roaring in excited triumph; he saw Fraser and Raeburn hammering at a giant Russian with the butts of their Miniés, and then the mist closed in again, and everybody vanished in the clinging grey.

'Back to the redoubt!' Maxwell shouted. 'Back to the redoubt! God only knows how many Russians are out here!'

Jack echoed the command, hearing his voice distorted and lost in the mist. A trumpeter sounded the recall, again and again, the sound tinny at times, intense at others as the grey blanket swirled and closed and shifted again. In ones and twos and dozens, the men of the 118th began to drift back, some reluctant to relinquish their victory, others glad to seek the shelter of the Fatal Redoubt.

As the British pulled back, the Russian artillery began to fire, its efforts redoubled after the rest and its targets exposed. Now it was the British turn to take casualties as men fell under the pitiless iron balls and the vicious hail of canister.

'Back men, get back!' Maxwell ran forward into the mist, waving his sword and shouting as he urged his men back to shelter. Jack joined him, hunting for stragglers, looking in particular for the men who had transferred from the 113th, feeling the vulnerability of a man on a plateau swept by a dozen large pieces of artillery.

'Here we are, sir!' Logan was slouching back, rifle slung across his back and with Riley at his side. 'All safe and well.'

'Get to the redoubt.' Jack ducked as a roundshot screamed overhead. 'The Russians will be back soon.'

'That's all right, sir,' Logan unslung his rifle and wiped greasy blood from the bayonet. 'Then we'll kill more of the bastards.'

'Come on, Logie.' Riley took him by the arm and pulled him toward the redoubt. He flinched as a roundshot landed a few yards away, to roll across the ground. 'We'll get killed ourselves here.'

Turning around, Logan made an obscene gesture toward the Russians. 'Come on then you bastards! Try and kill wee Donnie Logan!'

'I'll kill you if you don't get to the redoubt!' Jack promised. 'We need your rifle and bayonet, Logan and you're no good to the Queen if your brains are splattered all over the ground.'

'There's no problem about that sir,' Coleman said. 'He doesn't have any brains to get spattered!'

'I'll do for you, Coley!' Logan made a lunge at Coleman until O'Neill and Riley held him back.

'Only in the 113th would I be stopping two of my own men fight in the middle of a battle!' O'Neill shouted. 'Come on you two!'

'We're not in the 113th now,' Jack reminded, 'we're in the 118th!'

'Bugger the 118th,' Logan said, and Coleman nodded.

'You're right there, Logie, bugger the 118th.'

They withdrew together, with Coleman and Riley jinking in an attempt to avoid the Russian fire and Logan walking slowly, defying any Russian to shoot him. 'I'm not bobbing for they bastards!'

'Roll call!' Colonel Maxwell shouted. 'Come on lads! Answer to your names.'

The men took their positions, ducking as the Russian artillery continued its now desultory bombardment. The roll call began, with too many gaps and a few comments added:

'A cannon ball took his head right off, sir.'

'Pounded to smash, sir.'

'I haven't seen him, sir.'

And then the Russian artillery fire increased, hammering at the 118th and the two British guns that continued their outmatched duel with the Russians. There was a concerted wail from the 118th when a salvo from the Russians found its target and landed square on the British nine pounders. Jack shuddered as he saw the wheels shot away from both guns and the ammunition waggon shattered; he saw two brave gunners trying to drag the vehicle further away as flames licked around it. Both men fell as what remained of the wagon collapsed in a burning frenzy.

'Get your heads down!' Jack roared. 'It's going to explode!'

The men nearest to him, the men of the 113th, glanced at the tower of smoke from the waggon and threw themselves to the ground as Dearden repeated Jack's order as loudly as he could. Some of the 118th heard others did not, so a few stood up to stare at the carnage. The flames reached the gunpowder.

The explosion sounded like the end of the world. Jack felt the force of the blast lift him and then drop him back to the ground, half blinded and deaf. He lay there, stunned as the world around him moved in slow motion and entirely without sound.

Somebody was shaking him by the shoulder. Jack looked up; saw O'Neill standing over him with his mouth moving but no sound coming. He shifted, counted his arms and legs – all were there and all attached to his body. He tried to sit up, took hold of O'Neill's hand for support and knew his legs had answered although he could not feel the ground beneath his feet. He slid back down, holding handfuls of rocky dirt for support.

'What happened?' Jack knew that he spoke, although he couldn't hear his own words. He saw O'Neill's mouth open and shut but heard nothing.

'Never mind.' Jack pulled himself to a sitting position and looked around. The explosion had caused devastation. Both guns were destroyed, their barrels pointing skyward, their wheels detached and their crews lying in lifeless, smouldering bundles at the edge of a black crater. There were casualties among the 118th as well, men lying in crumpled heaps, others as blackened horrors, writhing and screaming as their clothes and skin burned.

Jack stood up, staggered and ducked. The Russian artillery – encouraged by the success of their attack on the British guns – was now concentrating on the Fatal Redoubt. He saw a ball smash into the breastwork, sending sandbags flying and a man sprawling. Other men lay in the bottom of the shallow trench, groaning or fighting their agony. Despite the barrage, the Regimental Colours were still in place, brave above the carnage.

Jack realised that a buzzing had replaced his deafness, an insistent sound that was irritating amidst this battle. He shook his head to clear it, swore as a cannonball smeared overhead and ducked as it landed on the back of the trench, spreading savage splinters of stone. A man fell, clutching at his throat; blood spurted.

Maxwell was gesturing, waving his hand and shouting. Jack couldn't make out the words but saw the men leaving the trench to move forward, out of the direct line of Russian fire. The dead and wounded remained; and the flag, now limp, proclaiming that the 118th held this line.

Dearden grabbed Jack's arm and said something, then repeated it, obviously louder. Jack shook his head and pointed to his ears. That buzzing continued, now loud, now lower. Dearden gestured backwards, presumably ordering Jack to retreat out of the fighting. Jack shook his head vigorously and pushed on; looking at Maxwell to see what he wished them to do. He couldn't retire; he must fight and be seen fighting; he must regain his position in the world. That was more important than death.

And Helen?

About a hundred yards forward of the breastworks, Maxwell ordered them to lie prone and face their front. Jack followed his lead, lying on the damp ground among the splintered oak trees and underneath the arc of Russian shot. That buzzing in his ears was fading now as the effects of the explosion wore off and he could hear intermittent sounds. There was musketry all around, either in distinct volleys or non-stop crackling, as well as the heavier boom of artillery. It was evident that they were only one part of a major battle but with the drifting mist and the problematic, broken terrain, he could never see more than a hundred yards and sometimes less than ten.

'Sir!' That was O'Neill. Jack looked up, delighted that he had regained at least some of his hearing. O'Neill spoke loudly and slowly. 'Colonel Maxwell's compliments, sir and could you take some men forward and see what is happening?' O'Neill handed over a telescope. 'Colonel Maxwell says you may borrow this sir.'

Jack nodded. 'You'd best come too, O'Neill. Bring Coleman, Raeburn, Kelly and Fletcher.' Coleman would complain, but he was steady under fire, while the other three seemed good men. It would not do for him to be seen favouring the men from the 113th all the time.

The mist seemed thicker the further forward he advanced, while the ground was littered with the dead and wounded from the previous two Russian attacks. Some of the oaks were utterly shattered by artillery, most scarred by musketry.

'Vahda,' one young, handsome young Russian pleaded, 'vahda.' He lay on his side with a smashed thigh and an open wound in his chest.

'The poor bugger wants water.' Kelly was a hard-faced man from Lancashire. 'Here, son.' He knelt at the Russian's side and tipped his water bottle into the man's mouth. 'Your stretcher men will be here for you soon.'

The Russian lay back with water trickling out of his mouth.

'Come on Kelly,' Jack said. 'We can't care for all of them.'

Kelly replaced his water bottle. 'Yes, sir. This young lad looks a lot like my brother.'

They had not gone ten steps when a shot rang out. Kelly yelled and slid to the ground with a wound in his back. The young Russian he'd helped was sitting up, holding his musket; smoke drifted from the barrel.

'You bastard!' Coleman stared for a second and then ran back, stabbing the Russian with his bayonet, 'you dirty murdering bastard!'

'Kelly!' Fletcher held him. 'He's dead sir.' He looked up. 'Why? He was trying to help the man!'

Jack shook his head. 'I don't know why Fletcher. I don't know. Kelly was a good soldier and a good man.'

Coleman stood up, his face taut and bayonet bloody. 'Why did he do that? Kelly was helping him!'

'I don't know, Coleman,' Jack repeated. 'I only know it is a warning for us to be even more vigilant. Move on lads.'

Fletcher dragged Kelly to the lee of a tree and removed some items from his pocket. 'It's a letter to his mother, sir,' he explained, 'and his watch. I'm not going to keep them sir; I was going to send them back to his mother.'

'I know that Fletcher,' Jack said. Although he would not trust any of the 113th as far as he could reach, the men of the 118th, in common with most British soldiers, would do anything for their colleagues. Thieving from a fellow soldier in the same regiment, or a dead or wounded man, was beyond their pale. They had their own code and stuck to it.

They moved on. Nobody suggested taking Kelly's body with them or even burying it. Already by this stage of the war practicalities had overtaken the British soldier's habitual sentimentality.

About quarter of a mile ahead of the Fatal Redoubt the ground dropped in another of the many ravines that seamed the Inkerman Ridge. Jack stopped at the edge and peered over.

'Oh, good God in heaven.'

All he could see were Russian troops, thousands of grey-coated soldiers with flat caps and long muskets, with a body of men moving through them wearing the uniform of Cossacks.

'Cossacks,' O'Neill said quietly. 'That can only be trouble.'

'Yes indeed.' Jack rolled out Maxwell's telescope. He scanned the infantry, watching their mouths move as they sang, and the swing and thrust of their shoulders. Despite their recent reverses, these men had high morale; they would not be easily defeated. Swinging the telescope around, he focussed on the group of officers who led the Cossacks. In front, riding a small, sturdy pony, was Major Kutuzov. 'I think we'd better get back,' he said. 'That's Kutuzov, the Russian who captured us a few weeks ago.'

'What's he doing here?' O'Neill wondered.

Jack thought of the regimental flag in its prominent position and wondered if that had lured Kutuzov out of Sebastopol. The major would undoubtedly know that Colonel Maxwell commanded the 118th, and he would probably be aware that he had worked for Joseph Bulloch. 'I'm not sure,' he said, 'we'd best report that to the Colonel.'

They didn't stop on the return journey, closing their ears and minds to any thoughts of sympathy for the wounded men. The Russian guns were still busy when they returned.

'Sir,' Jack handed over the telescope. 'There is a deep ravine about quarter of a mile ahead, with thousands of Russians mustering in it. Most are ordinary line infantry as best as I could judge. Others are Cossacks.'

'Mounted?'

'No sir; on foot. They are led by Major Kutuzov.' He saw Maxwell's head jerk up at the name.

'Kutuzov! Then we must ensure the good major gets a suitable reception. Thank you, Windrush. Now get you back to your position and prepare your men. I think this war is set to get very interesting indeed.'

Chapter Twenty-One

Inkerman Ridge
5th November 1854

They came forty minutes later, dense columns of Russian infantry emerging from the mist, preceded by a host of skirmishers and with the Cossacks in the centre. The infantry was singing, a low rhythmic growl that stirred something deep within Jack.

'They are still advancing in column,' Dearden said. 'Don't these Russians learn anything?'

'I'd expect more from Kutuzov,' Jack said. 'I thought he was cleverer than that.'

'Kutuzov is only a major,' Colonel Maxwell reminded. 'Soimonoff or Dannenberg will have given the tactical orders.'

'Steady men,' Jack said, 'don't waste ammunition; we don't know when we will get more.'

'Fire as soon as they are in range,' Maxwell ordered, 'and don't allow them to get too close.' Lifting a rifle from the hands of a dead man, he gave an example, aiming and firing at anybody that showed through gaps in the mist. 'Use the advantage the Minié gives us.'

Jack followed his example. The Minié rifle had an abrupt kick, but felt good against his shoulder.

The skirmishers were more cautious than before, remaining in cover to fire and dashing forward to the next tree or outcrop of rock. Their muzzle flashes sparked through the mist, and their firing was accurate, so the 118th soon began to take casualties, man after man falling backwards.

'They're getting good,' Dearden said.

'Too good.' Jack flinched as a bullet hissed past him.

The singing stopped. Jack peered into the mist. 'I can't see a blessed thing,' he said.

The artillery took him by surprise. In their previous assault, the Russian infantry had blocked their guns. Now the guns opened up again, looping over their infantry in a maelstrom of shot fiercer and harder than before that landed on the diminishing 118th.

'Get to ground!' Maxwell ordered.

The Russians knew exactly where the British positions were and pounded away for fifteen hard minutes, levelling much of the breastwork, throwing the sandbags down, killing and maiming the defenders.

'They're set to pulverise us out of existence,' Jack said.

Lying beside him at the bottom of the trench with both hands keeping his shako in place, Dearden shook his head. 'Not so! They're softening us up.'

'Kutuzov will have the Russians lying down too,' Maxwell said. 'They are under the arc of their artillery, but closer to us than on the previous attack.'

Jack nodded. That made sense. When the artillery stopped, the Russians would have less distance to cover as they charged. The British would be diminished in number, shocked by the bombardment and would have less time in which to create a defence. Whatever orders Soimonoff or Dannenberg may have given, he was prepared to wager that Kutuzov had worked this particular move out.

The artillery ended in a stunning silence. There was no singing. There was no firing by the skirmishers. Jack looked up, dazed by the cessation of the cannonade and then the Russians were on them. Thousands of men in grey uniforms advancing at the run, silent save for the shush of feet over damp ground and the rattle of equipment. In the centre were the Cossacks with Kutuzov at their head, shasqua in hand.

'Here they come, boys!' Jack fired the Minié, pulled out his revolver and fired round after round until it was empty. He didn't wait to see if he had hit anybody but loaded quickly as the 118th sprang to life, men firing and loading so the front rank of Russians fell in droves. He saw Aitken clap a hand to his face and slide to the bottom of the trench, and then Maxwell was rallying his men, calling on the trumpeter to blow for his life, firing his Minié, dropping it to draw his revolver.

Jack had heard it said that bayonet charges worked by psychology; that no troops ever stood against a bayonet charge and there were no bayonet-to-bayonet battles in modern warfare. He was not alone in witnessing the falseness of that fable. At Inkerman, British and Russian soldiers both stood against the bayonet charge of the other.

Now the 118th rose from their shattered trench to face the Russians. Only two men turned to run; Jack didn't see who they were. Once they came close, the Russians let out a howl that raised the hair on the back of Jack's neck and charged. He saw his men lunge forward in what became the most vicious face to face battle he'd ever seen. Men from age sixteen to fifty, private soldiers and officers from all the corners of the British Isles thrust long bayonets into men from St Petersburg and Ukraine, the Steppes and the bitter north, Crimea and Livonia. The Russians came on in style like the brave soldiers they were, buoyed up by their numbers and the knowledge that they were fighting for their own Holy soil. The British met them with tenacious dogged savagery, knowing that if the Russians broke through here, they could sweep up the flank of the entire British and Allied army, relieve the siege of Sebastopol and perhaps win the war.

There was no thought of retreat and no concept of surrender from either side.

'They're after the Colours!' Corporal O'Hara shouted. 'Rally around the Colours, boys!'

Jack spared time for a single glance at the Redoubt, off to his right; the Colours still flew, proud and defiant with the number 118 hidden in the folds of damp cloth, but still there. As long as the Colours stood, the regiment existed, and the British held this section of Inkerman Heights.

He fired the last round in his revolver, saw a Russian infantryman crumple, ducked under the clumsy swing of a musket butt and kicked out with his boot. Brodie was down, roaring his hate; Jack lifted his discarded rifle, aimed and squeezed the trigger, cursed when he realised it was empty and instead fought with the bayonet.

They kept coming in an endless mass; brave Russian soldiers packed so tightly together that they were unable to properly wield their bayonets until they jumped or clambered over the breastwork, and in those few seconds when the attackers rose above the defenders they were exposed to a bayonet in the thigh, belly or groin. That was how many died, crumpled in screaming agony with their intestines slashed open or a blade thrust through their privates. Even so, there were too many Russians, Jack saw; the 118th could not kill them all.

First one, then two, then half a dozen leapt the breastwork unopposed and landed in the trench to fight on more equal terms.

It was a battle of bravery and butchery. The Russians hadn't expected to survive the fire of a regiment of British infantry. Nor had they expected the British to stand and fight if they reached them in such high numbers. Neither side was prepared to yield.

Men fought, struggled and fell, cursing, men lost their rifles and fought with the bayonet and butt, and when they bent or broke, they fought with boots and fists, head-butting their opponents, gouging out eyes and biting at throats. Jack saw Riley on the ground with a Russian poised with his bayonet until Logan jumped on the back of the Russian, grabbed his hair and pulled his head back. There was the flash of steel, and the Russian fell, with Logan snarling on top of him with a khanjali in his hand.

A wounded British soldier lay on his face, with every Russian that passed plunging a bayonet into his back. The man groaned and writhed with each wound, yet continued to live.

Jack looked around. The ground in front of the redoubt was a shifting carpet of dead and wounded Russian soldiers. The trench and breastworks were packed with fighting men, wounded men and the staring dead of both sides.

The battle was in the balance. The 118th was all but done, exhausted, outnumbered, dying by inches, but ordered to stay put until reinforced, they stood and killed and died.

There was a general surge toward the centre as the Russians tried to capture the Colours and the British to defend it. Through the shredding mist, Jack saw Kutuzov lead a substantial body of his Cossacks toward the flag and knew that was where the battle would be decided, win or lose.

'With me O'Neill!' Hacking down a lone Russian with hardly a thought, Jack pushed toward Kutuzov. He didn't have to look to know that O'Neill was at his back.

Maxwell was exactly where he should be, standing beside the flag with his sword in one hand and pistol in the other, the very epitome of a gallant commander. *Except that gallant British commanders do not also act the spy. Nothing is quite as it seemed; life and war and politics and international relations were not as clear-cut or straightforward as the history books make them.*

Kutuzov's Cossacks charged straight at Maxwell, with Kutuzov at the rear, directing their movements. The Cossacks sliced down two British soldiers and grabbed at Maxwell, who swung his sabre, neatly transfixing the closest man. The second closed on him, with others following, hauling him down to the ground, prodding bayonets into his arms and legs to disable but not kill him.

'They're trying to capture the colonel,' O'Neill said. 'They must want an officer as a prisoner! The Russians get a reward for every British officer they capture!'

Jack felt nothing as Thorpe thrust his bayonet into a Russian and Coleman smashed the man's skull with the butt of his rifle. He remembered that torture chamber in Sebastopol and knew that Kutuzov was particular in the officers he wanted to capture.

Jack paused; he had to decide now. He couldn't allow Kutuzov to capture and torture Maxwell to find out whatever information he had about Bulloch and his organisation. He couldn't see Helen's father dragged away in front of his eyes. But neither could he leave his men to fight alone.

The Cossacks dragged Maxwell fifty yards in front of the redoubt and dumped him, standing over him as if he was some treasure, which in a way he was, Jack reasoned.

'They've got the colonel!' Dearden yelled. 'The Russians have got the colonel!'

'I'll get him back, sir!' Jack jumped over the breastwork, with O'Neill and Coleman at his side. Logan and Riley were not far behind, and then Thorpe at the rear.

Taken by surprise by this unexpected counter-attack, the Cossacks staggered, until Kutuzov, still ten yards behind his men, pointed to Jack and roared a string of orders.

'Thorpe, Coleman!' Jack shouted. 'Guard our backs!'

The Cossack guards moved to meet them, lunging with their bayonets. Jack parried the first, sidestepped the second and felt utter relief when Logan and O'Neill thrust in with bayonet and rifle butt. Leaving them to deal with the Cossacks, Jack knelt over Maxwell. 'Here we are again, sir.'

The colonel looked up through dazed eyes. 'Hello, Windrush. Did they capture you too?'

'No, sir,' Jack shouted above the noise; 'we've come to rescue you!' He looked up as his men arrived.

'I'll get him, sir.' Although Coleman was slender, he was as wiry and tough as any man in the army. Ignoring Maxwell's cry of pain, he hoisted him on his back and headed back to the Redoubt, with the colonel, wounded in a dozen places by Russian bayonets, leaking blood.

'Back to the line, men!' Jack yelled.

'They're running, sir.' Riley said, and Jack saw that he was correct. Kutuzov's last push to secure Maxwell had been the high tide of the Russian attack. Now the grey waves were ebbing, bayonetting the British wounded as they retreated and leaving scores of their comrades on the ground.

'Shall we go after them, sir?' Logan asked eagerly.

'No; let them go,' Jack said. He was bone-weary and knew his men must be every bit as exhausted. It was all they could do to hold the line in defence, yet alone expend vital energy in chasing a still far more numerous foe.

'Hitchins, you're a strong man; take the Colonel back to our lines. Thorpe will help you; find a surgeon.' He knew it was wrong to give an individual priority because of his rank; he also knew that if the Russians came again with such force or determination, they would break through and capture Maxwell, putting him to whatever devilish tortures that Kutuzov's mind could devise. *Better a death by Russian bayonets than the slow agony of torture.*

Jack looked around to see what remained of the Fatal Redoubt and nearly wished that he hadn't.

Dear God; what a mess!

Chapter Twenty-Two

Inkerman Ridge
5th November 1854

Captain Dearden was dead; his mouth open in a soundless scream to protest at the agony of the Russian bayonet that protruded obscenely from his belly. Corporal O'Hara lay across his body, writhing as he stared at the gaping holes in his chest and the blood that pumped from the ragged stump of his left arm. Beside him, Aitken crouched, choking on the blood that filled his mouth and ran in dark rivulets down his chin and chest. Half a score Russian infantrymen lay among them, shot or bayoneted, unheeded in death as the world had neglected them in life.

'Get the bodies,' Jack ordered. 'Pile them up into the breastwork.'

The men stared at him. Their eyes were dazed, their mouths slack with shock, but they did as he ordered, adding the corpses of friends and enemies to the low barricade of sandbags that was their only protection against the dropping musket balls and murderous round shot.

'Here they come again!' Coleman gripped the blood-sticky stock of his Minié rifle and staggered to his feet. The once-proud scarlet of his tunic was torn and shredded; his face was powder stained, gaunt and unshaven; blood congealed on the ragged hole in his trousers just above the left knee.

'Hot as hell and thick as thieves.' Thorpe spat blood on his hands and ran a grimy thumb over the length of his bayonet. 'Just listen to them.'

Jack peered through the shredded mist and rain. Across the ridge, the Russians were not yet visible, but they were vocal enough, chanting that same deep throated battle hymn with which they'd advanced so often before. Was it three times or four? It might even be five; he could not be sure, but he knew that each time they recoiled they left the small detachment of British weaker and fewer in numbers.

'Ammunition? Has anybody got any spare ammunition?'

Jack already knew the answer. They had used up all their own in repelling the Russian attacks and had robbed their dead comrades of what they had. He checked the ammunition pouch he'd lifted from the dead body of Brodie. 'I have three balls left.'

Thorpe spat again. 'That's one more than any man needs.'

There was no response to the attempted humour. Coleman poked his head beyond the breastwork and shuddered. 'Jesus, there's still thousands of them.'

Jack joined him. Coleman was right. A chance slant of wind blew a gap in the mist, revealing the full strength of the Russians. They seemed to stretch right across the ridge, an unbroken wall of flapping grey coats and wickedly long bayonets advancing slowly and steadily through the stunted, tangled oak trees of the Inkerman Ridge.

'I thought somebody said the Russians could never face British bayonets.' Logan curled disproportionately large hands around the stock of his Minié.

'Aye, but nobody told them that.' Thorpe tilted the barrel of his rifle, looked down the fouled bore and dropped in his last bullet. Once that was fired, he had only his bayonet and as much courage as remained after the long, long day of horror and death.

'Are we so important?' Raeburn raised his voice. 'Are we so important that they must throw the entire Russian army at us?' He looked around; his eyes red-rimmed with fatigue and wide with fear. 'There's only a few of us left!' At that moment he looked all of his seventeen years, a boy in a man's world, a child near to the brink of tears.

'It's not us that's important,' Jack told him. 'It's the position. If they take this redoubt and the battery, they have the lynchpin of the whole British line. We must hold.'

'Listen to him!' Thorpe mocked. 'If they take this redoubt! There's not even a gun left in the bloody thing! And who do you think you are, anyway? Bloody Wellington? Not Lord Raglan anyway – you haven't the stupidity!'

'I'm your officer!' Jack reminded. But he knew that hardly mattered just now. They were about to die beneath a torrent of Russian bayonets. He was the only surviving officer within this company of malcontents, an interloper in a closed society of men who had been fighting merely to exist since the day the world had cursed them with birth. He no more belonged here than he belonged anywhere else, but now it seemed that he would die beside these hard-faced, bitter-eyed men that he would have despised in another place, another world.

The singing increased, accompanied by the rhythmic drumbeat of boots on the ground and the sinister swishing of the long grey coats.

'Up we go men!'

There was a weary sigh, a long drawn out curse and the half-hidden sound of somebody praying, but the red-coated soldiers rose from the slight sanctuary of their corpse-and-sandbag barricade and looked outward toward the advancing enemy.

The Russians were closer so that Jack could make out details of their flat, expressionless faces as they marched forward. They had advanced before, and the company had sent them reeling back, as the tangled bodies on the ground proved, but this time there were many more of them and correspondingly fewer of the regiment to fight. He looked around the thinned ranks. They had started with nearly five hundred men, but now there were less than thirty fit to fight. They had probably a hundred rounds in total, and there must be two thousand Russians closing on them.

'They're brave men.' The Bishop gave a calm opinion. He sighted along the barrel of his rifle. 'Thank God for the grace of the Minié though. These beauties can kill two or three men at once.'

'When God granted us that, I would have liked him to grant us another thousand men as well. We're the 113th, the worst regiment in the British Army. A regimental disgrace, that's what we are.' Thorpe gave a twisted grin.

'So why fight for that?' Coleman jerked a stubby thumb at the flag that drooped from its staff.

Jack looked over his shoulder. He had nearly forgotten than Colonel Maxwell had thrust in the flagpole a few hours and a lifetime before, but now it was there, flapping above them with the multi-crossed flag of Union, the symbol of British pride and fortitude and hope in the canton with that alien number embroidered in black across the buff field.

'If we're such a bloody disgrace, why fight for that regimental flag?'

'Drag the bloody thing down!' Logan agreed. 'It's nothing to do with us anyway!'

'What?' Jack stared as his youthful ideas of honour and patriotism surfaced once more. 'It's got the British flag on it!'

'The British flag!' Riley mocked. 'Would that be the same Britain that rejected you and me?'

Fletcher leaned against the sandbags and said nothing. He had no education, but he was as sharp and perceptive as any university-trained solicitor. His deep eyes switched from Jack to Riley and back.

'Yes. Take the flag down boys!'

Jack reached for the flap of his holster, remembered his revolver was empty and raised his voice. 'We will not surrender; the Russians are coming!'

The bayonet was cold against his throat as he stared into the slum-bitter eyes of Logan and heard that harsh gutter voice grate in his ear.

'You keep your neb out of this, Lieutenant. That's not our flag, and we're not fighting for it.' Logan's grin was entirely without humour or mercy as the ragged privates lowered the flag. Jack heard the roar of triumph from the advancing Russians and felt despair chill him. Major Snodgrass had been correct all along. The 113th didn't have the stomach for a fight; when things got tough, they ran or surrendered. Now the Russians would take the centre of the British line and roll up both flanks. His weakness had lost the battle.

Jack glanced from the Russians to Logan and stepped forward. He felt, rather than saw, Coleman and Thorpe lower their bayonets.

'What the devil are you men doing?'

'Taking the flag down, sir' Riley answered calmly.

'I never signed on for the 118th,' Logan said. He folded the Regimental Colour up with surprising neatness, 'I signed on for the 113th.'

'We are in the 118th now,' Jack stared at him.

'No, sir. We are the 113th,' Logan said stubbornly.

There it was. There was that indefinable difference that was the essence of the British soldier; in that simple sentence resided the soul of the British Army. Other nations fought for the Emperor or national glory, for the Holy Soil as seemed to be the Russian way, or for the Motherland. The British soldiers did not. Oh, some might have notions of honour and glory, as the officers did, but most were pragmatic, tough-minded men who lived with a different code. First was friendship to their colleagues and second to their regiment. Among themselves, they would bicker and fight, argue and grouse, as was common in every family, but as soon as an outsider criticised the regiment all would rise in aggressive support. It was the regimental tradition that made the British Army the force it was, not some ephemeral invocation to a higher cause. God help the politician who ever tried to remove the regimental formations from the British Army: nothing would ever be the same again.

As Jack watched, Riley reached inside his tunic and produced another rectangle of silk. The buff colours of the 113th came into view.

'I heard that the Zouaves stole that,' Jack said dryly. 'Our Colonel Murphy and General Raglan himself both sent formal complaints to the French.'

'No, it wasnae the French. It was our boy Riley here.' Logan sounded quite proud that his colleague was a skilled thief. 'He broke into the case while the colonel was sleeping.'

'Well, our boy Riley there had better keep that to himself,' Jack said, 'because if it ever got around he would be in serious trouble.'

Logan snorted. 'We'll all be deid in a few minutes,' he said, 'so he winnae be in any trouble at all.'

Jack looked across the Inkerman Ridge. For the first time that day the mist had cleared, and he had a view as far as the ravine. The Russians were in line rather than column, row after row of them filling his vision. The long grey coats flapped around marching legs, with flat caps on top of white, determined faces and the glint of thousands of wickedly sharp bayonets coming toward them. What did he have to stop them? Jack looked around the remnants of his position. The breastwork was flattened, with the rents blocked with British and Russian dead, the Fatal Redoubt nothing more than a name and a charnel house. He was the only officer left alive and unwounded. He had lost the day, and he was bickering with his men over a colourful square of cloth.

'Here we go then; the last stand of the 118th.' He looked up at the Colours and felt his mouth twist into a smile. 'Or the first stand of the 113th.'

As a child, he had dreamed of gaining military glory in situations such as this, where he stood beside the flag facing the enemy hordes. However, in his boyhood fantasies, the colours had been those of the Royal Malverns, and he had been a hero. There was no heroism in reality; only sordid agony, contorted death and the battered, sweat-and-smoke streaked faces of frightened yet savagely determined men. His men; men he was proud to fight beside and die beside.

'Here they are, sir.' O'Neill sounded resigned to the inevitability of death. He hefted his rifle.

'Let's send them back then,' Jack said. 'Take your positions, 113th.'

Silently the men filed back to the breastwork in and around the remains of the Fatal Redoubt, with the flag of the 113th sullen above and the sound of Russian singing as a sombre backdrop.

'Wait until they are at five hundred paces,' Jack said. 'We don't have much ammunition left.'

He took a deep breath of mixed powder smoke and the shredded remnants of mist. Within ten minutes the Russians would have over-run this position, and there was nothing to stop them rolling up the British flank.

Jack didn't see who fired first; he only knew that the others followed the example in a ragged volley that dropped half a dozen Russians. 'Good shooting, men,' he approved quietly.

Four hundred yards. The Russians increased their pace. He saw Kutuzov surrounded by his guard of Cossacks in the centre of the line and deliberately aimed at him.

Whatever else happens, Kutuzov, or Stevensen, or whatever you choose to call yourself, you will die here. He pressed the trigger.

Fouled by a day of near constant use, the Minié rifle had a tremendous kick which bruised his shoulder. One of the Cossacks beside Kutuzov staggered.

'Missed by God!'

Reaching into his pocket, Jack fumbled for cartridges, counted only two and removed one. He loaded slowly, trying to ignore the Russian infantry who were now only three hundred yards from the breastwork, and aimed again.

Kutuzov looked directly at him, the moustached face unsmiling, and the pale blue eyes unemotional as Jack lined up the muzzle of his Minié square between them. Taking a deep breath, he pressed the trigger, rode the kick and cursed as the powder smoke drifted into his eyes. The Russians continued to march with Kutuzov, unharmed, among them.

'I have one bullet remaining,' Jack said. He was aware of the soldiers firing on either side of him, of their swearing and grunting, of the sweat and powder and fear, yet none of that mattered. This battle on Inkerman Ridge, this entire war, had contracted to a personal duel between him and Kutuzov. One of them, perhaps both of them, would die before the day ended.

One hundred yards away, the first Russian line halted.

'What are they doing?' Coleman asked.

The Russians stood erect, before, in an impressive display of discipline, they crashed their musket butts to their shoulders. All at once, hundreds of Russian muskets aimed at the few remaining British within the Fatal Redoubt.

'Get down!' Jack roared, pushing Logan and Riley beneath the battered breastwork. He heard the Russian volley crash out and saw splinters of stone scattering from the rocks, puffs of sand from the sandbags and half a dozen corpses in the breastwork twitching as musket ball smashed into them.

'Anybody hurt?' No reply. 'Back up boys; here they come.'

Immediately they fired the volley, the foremost Russian line had charged. Jack lifted his rifle and looked for Kutuzov, failed to see him and aimed at the nearest Russian. Seventy yards; fifty, thirty; there were perhaps four hundred Russians in the charge, and less than fifty defenders fit to fight. It would all be over in a few moments. Russian bayonets loomed up at the breastwork.

Goodbye Helen.

The volley came from the left flank, tearing into the Russians, scything scores of men to the ground. The Russian attack faltered, and Jack shouted. 'Stand fast!' He looked to the left as a second volley rang out; more Russians fell, and a familiar voice sounded.

'Hold the barricade, 113th!'

Major Snodgrass jumped down beside Jack. 'Good to see that you're still alive, Windrush. Colonel Maxwell told us you would need support.'

Jack nodded, too dazed to understand. 'It's good to see you too, sir. And the 113th.'

'We're the last regiment into the fight,' Snodgrass sounded remarkably calm. 'Pennefather trusts us no more than Raglan or anybody else does.' He glanced around, checking the line, working out what was happening in this section of the battle. The 113th volleys had shattered the foremost Russian line, which was now in retreat, colliding with the second in a confusion of grey-coated infantrymen. Snodgrass didn't hide his grin.

'There's your target 113th! Fire!' The volley smashed into the milling Russians. 'And keep firing!' Snodgrass began a slow walk along the ranks.

'Here, private,' Jack turned to the nearest man, 'pass me a handful of cartridges if you please.' He held out his hand.

'Sorry sir, you've got a rifle, and we've still got the old Brown Bess.'

Jack started as he recognised the soldier. The man was small, with blonde hair and wide eyes. Jack lowered his voice. 'What the devil are you doing here?'

Charlotte Riley met his gaze, unflinching. 'I came to make sure my husband is all right!'

'He would be more all right knowing that you're safe!' Jack said. 'Now get out of the firing line and keep out of trouble.'

'They're coming again!' That was O'Neill's voice.

The Russians had reorganised, and the survivors of the first wave joined the second in attacking the redoubt. There were perhaps five hundred bayonets, five hundred men determined to fight for their Holy Soil.

'This fight is not won yet,' O'Neill said.

'It will be.' Snodgrass had returned.

'That's Major Kutuzov in the middle of the Cossacks,' Jack tried to point him out as the 113th settled in to fire at the now-advancing Russians.

'The fellow we captured and released,' Snodgrass said. 'Perhaps being gentlemen is not always the best idea.' He looked at his men. 'Our blackguards seem to behaving themselves so far.'

'Chillianwala was a long time ago,' Jack reminded. 'The regiment has changed a lot since then.'

'We will see if it has learned how to fight,' Snodgrass said grimly.

Jack noted that Riley was beside his wife, and then the Russians closed, the firing grew intense, and he had no time for anything except the situation directly in front of him.

Jack noticed at once that the firing of the newly-arrived 113th was not as fast, as accurate or as effective as that of the 118th had been. The Brown Bess muskets lacked the range and power of the Minié rifles. With no ammunition, Jack could only watch and encourage.

'Meet them, 113th!' Snodgrass shouted. 'Remember these are the men who bayonetted and murdered our wounded! Make Colonel Murphy proud of you!'

As the Russians came within ten yards of the breastwork, most of the 113th rose out of the trenches with the bayonet. Jack estimated that half a dozen men cowered away; the nerve of one man broke, and he turned and fled. Jack saw Charlotte Riley mount the parapet with the rest until Riley took hold of her arm and pushed her back.

'Keep out of danger, you silly muffin!'

Should I help? No, this is between Riley and Charlotte; I have my duty to do.

After so many years of being ostracised and treated like third class citizens, even by the other regiments in the army, the 113th, at last, had the opportunity to prove themselves. They unleashed their pent-up frustration on the advancing Russians, although the oaths they shouted were directed at their previous humiliation as much as at the Russians.

With his Cossacks surrounding him, Kutuzov was in the centre of the Russian line. Perhaps sensing that the British had thrown in the last of their reserves, he came fast with a shasqua in one hand and a pistol in the other. Jack saw a pair of British soldiers lower their bayonets and rush toward him, only for the Cossacks to cut both down before they got near Kutuzov.

With no ammunition and his sword lost, Jack hefted his bayonetted Minié, climbed over the parapet and walked toward Kutuzov. He ignored the odd musket-ball that still whizzed around; he knew that this was between him and the Russian Major. Fate had decided that. He watched as four Cossacks closed defensively around Kutuzov.

'Fight me, Kutuzov,' Jack shouted calmly, 'fight me fair, you cowardly Russian blackguard!'

Shasquas drawn, the Cossacks closed on him, until Riley and Logan leapt to block them, with others of the 113th close behind. Only two of the Cossacks remained to rush at Jack as Kutuzov watched.

'Call them off and fight me fair!' Jack parried the first slash of the shasqua, shaken by the force of the blade as it crashed against the barrel of his rifle.

'Leave him to me, Windrush.' Snodgrass stepped forward, drawing his sword. 'It has been years since I last participated in an action.'

Hard pressed by the Cossacks, Jack didn't reply. It was all he could do to defend himself, yet alone attack. The Cossacks were skilled and brave, fighting to protect their officer as Jack lunged and parried with the bayonetted rifle. As one stumbled, Jack slashed at him, saw the quick flow of blood from the man's neck and spared a second to see Kutuzov face Snodgrass, saw their blades cross, and then both Cossacks launched a concerted attack on him. Jack was forced backwards, slashing with his bayonet in a figure of eight formation in a desperate attempt to defend himself. He glanced aside and saw Riley on his back with a Cossack poised above him, shasqua ready to plunge into his chest. He heard the report of the Brown Bess and saw the Cossack stagger. Riley saw his chance and wriggled free, allowing Logan a brief opening to finish the Cossack off.

An unknown soldier of the 113th came to Jack's aid, thrusting his bayonet into the wounded Cossack, grunting with effort. 'That's done for you, you Russian bastard!'

In the brief respite, Jack glanced backwards at the redoubt. Charlotte stood on the parapet, smoking musket in hand. She waved to her husband and slowly began to reload.

With their own two Cossacks now disposed of, Logan and Riley came to help Jack. They swarmed over his remaining adversary in seconds, hacking him down and thrusting in their bayonets without thought or pity.

Panting, drooping from exhaustion, Jack looked around. All along the line the 113th, the despised, unwanted 113th, were fighting and holding. Only here in the centre were the Russians pushing forward. Led by Kutuzov, they had created a bulge in the British defences and were teetering on the parapet of the Fatal Redoubt. If the Russians broke through, they could still win this battle. Nothing was decided – Snodgrass had said that 113th was the last regiment; there were no reserves. If the 113th didn't hold, there was nothing to stop the Russians.

Jack raised his rifle as another swarm of Cossacks moved toward him. Exhausted, he hardly had the energy to stand yet alone fight. He saw Snodgrass reel before an attack by Kutuzov; the commander of the final British regiment against the man who led the centre of the Russian line. Forget Dannenberg and Pauloff, Soimonoff, Raglan and Pennefather; on Inkerman Ridge; it was the man on the spot who mattered; the fate of the battle and perhaps the war hinged on that duel.

Younger, fitter and skilful, Kutuzov was winning. He pressed back Snodgrass, forced him onto the defensive with a series of vicious cuts that had the British officer retreating. As Jack watched, Kutuzov feinted to Snodgrass's left, altered the angle of his blow and flicked the sword from the hand of the British officer.

Jack saw Snodgrass flinch before the Russian. He saw Snodgrass lift his right hand in supplication as if to plead for his life, and then the single musket shot rang out. Jack distinctly saw the puff of white smoke jet from behind the sandbags. He saw the Russian stagger back and crumple to the ground with an expression of disbelief on his face. He saw Snodgrass recover his composure and glance around, as if to see if anybody had witnessed his moment of fear. For one second Jack saw Snodgrass sneer, then lift his sabre, plunge it into the already prone body of Kutuzov and straddle the corpse, shouting in triumph.

Jack looked over his shoulder; Charlotte held the musket that had fired the fatal shot. He met her eyes, saw her expression of disappointment and knew that she had missed her target. She hadn't been aiming for Kutuzov but for Snodgrass, the man who had mistreated her husband.

And the situation changed.

With the death of their leader, the Cossacks wavered, and the impetus disappeared from the Russian attack. They did not turn and flee; the battle was not over; the killing on both sides continued, but the dynamics altered. The advantage slid over to the men of the 113th. There must have been some unconscious instinct among the men, for all would be too concerned with their individual corners of the fight to be aware of what had happened in the centre, but while the Russians began to flag, the men of the 113th found renewed strength.

'On them, 113th!' Waving his blood-smeared sword, Major Snodgrass pressed them forward. Jack watched, too spent to move as Lieutenant Elliot grabbed the staff that held the colours of the 113th and carried it forward. The 113th surged into the oak-tangled ridge of Inkerman, following the retreating, still fighting Russians.

'Well, sir; the 113th have played their part.' O'Neill was bleeding from a cut to his face.

'They have,' Jack said. He watched as Charlotte ran forward to her husband and he knew that the story was not over yet. He suspected that in the morass of the battle, nobody else had seen that single musket shot or the expression on her face. Charlotte Riley had turned that battle, and nobody would ever thank her for it. When eventually the rewards were handed out, her part and her name would not be mentioned. No history book would laud her contribution; officially she was never there. She was only a woman, the wife of a ranker, less than a pawn in this bloody game of war and diplomacy and politics. Major Snodgrass was a lucky man; Jack thought he would be best advised to watch his back for he doubted that Charlotte Riley would give up after only one attempt.

Chapter Twenty-Three

**Second Division Camp
November 1854**

Heavily bandaged, yet too stubborn to be shipped to the hospital at Scutari, Colonel Maxwell sat at his desk with Jack standing before him. A soldier servant stood at the side, quietly unobtrusive.

'Well Windrush, things have changed. As you know, both the 113th and the 118th suffered grievous losses in the battle on Inkerman Heights.'

'Yes, sir,' Jack agreed.

'General Raglan has decided to merge both units into one, and as the 113th is the senior, we shall retain that number. This is only a temporary measure of course; it will take an Act of Parliament to make such a decision permanent.'

'I see, sir.' Jack glanced at the cased Colours of both regiments that stood in the corner. The 113th Regimental Colour was no longer pristine, with the silk powder-stained and ragged where bullet or ball had ripped the silk. Like the men, it was now a veteran of battle.

'You may know that poor Colonel Murphy was sent home with consumption and has had to send in his papers.'

'I had heard that, sir. He retired knowing that his regiment had gained some respect at Inkerman.' Despite his lingering resentment that Murphy had sent him away from the 113th, Jack had no real ill-will toward the man. 'He will find comfort in that.'

'He was a good soldier with a difficult task,' Maxwell said. 'I am to take over command of the 113th now.'

'Yes, sir.' Jack was not sure what Murphy would have thought of a spy taking command of his beloved regiment. *I'll keep that thought to myself.* 'Congratulations sir, it will be an honour to serve with you.'

'Oh, quite,' Maxwell murmured. He shook his head slowly. 'You will also have heard that since Inkerman, General Raglan has made it quite clear that we must dig in for a long siege. We do not have the numbers for an assault, even though the Russians are dispirited; they have met us in the field on three occasions, and we have bested them each time.'

'I had heard we are here for some time, sir.'

'And what are your thoughts on the subject, Windrush?'

Jack shrugged. 'I don't have any, sir. I would have wished we had assaulted Sebastopol back in September after the Alma, but we didn't, and that is that. If we have to stand a winter siege, then a winter siege it is.'

Maxwell struggled to reach the brandy bottle until the servant came to his help.

Jack glanced at the servant. 'There is that other matter, sir.'

Maxwell understood. 'This man is Smith, Windrush. You may speak freely in front of him.'

'Yes, sir. There is the American fellow.'

'John Anderson.' Maxwell closed his eyes at the bite of brandy. 'As far as I know, he is still within Sebastopol. After the recent defeats of the Russian army, I cannot see the United States backing them in this war. They may give clandestine help, but they will not be invading Canada or floating a thousand privateers to harass our shipping.'

'That is good to hear, sir.'

'Indeed. The sacrifice of the 118th was not in vain.' Maxwell sipped at the brandy. 'Three factors turned that battle. General Pennefather, the bravery of the British soldier and our stand.' He gave a small grin. 'Major Snodgrass is quite the hero; a lion of what we can call society here.'

About to mention Charlotte Riley's part, Jack kept quiet. *It won't help anybody to bring that episode into the open.*

'Will you be remaining within the regiment then, Windrush?'

'Yes, sir.' Jack said. He had nowhere else to go, and with Maxwell as the colonel, he would hopefully see more of Helen.

Maxwell gave a small smile. 'You do not intend to resign your commission then, Lieutenant?'

'No, sir.' Jack shook his head. 'Why should I?'

'Many officers are doing just that, Windrush. They are opting for the comfort of London rather than the hardships of a Crimean winter.'

Jack didn't admit that he couldn't afford to make such a move. If he left the army his grudged allowance from his step-mother would cease, and with no other source of income, he could not exist.

'You may also have heard that Captain Haverdale has resigned his commission?' Maxwell's eyes were intense as his gaze fixed on Jack.

'I am surprised to hear that sir. I considered Captain Haverdale to be a dedicated and efficient officer.'

'He is all of that, and I would wish an equally dedicated and efficient officer to take his place.' Maxwell's gaze didn't falter.

'Yes, sir.' *Well, that's obvious.*

'Haverdale is selling his captaincy for a fraction of the going rate,' Maxwell said. 'Are you aware of the price of a captaincy, Lieutenant?'

'Yes, sir.' In common with most officers in Queen Victoria's Army, Jack kept an eye on the current prices for buying promotion. 'A captaincy costs around two thousand pounds.'

'Then you may be surprised that Haverdale is selling his for nine hundred.'

'I am sir.' Jack forced a smile. 'That is only about one hundred and fifty pounds more than the price for a lieutenant's commission.'

'Are you also aware that for a lieutenant to take the step up, he only has to pay the difference between the price of his rank and that of a captaincy?'

'I was sir, but I don't have the readies…' It was an admission Jack didn't like to make.

'Find the money, Windrush. That's an order. I need good men in my regiment. I expect to find you a captain before the end of the week.' Maxwell leaned back. 'And now to other matters. I am arranging a more cheerful meeting in Balaklava, and I would like you to attend in your new rank of Captain.'

'Thank you, sir,' Jack said. 'I would be delighted.' He wondered if Helen would be there.

'Good man,' Maxwell said. 'It will be quite a family affair, you see. It's my daughter Helen's twenty-first birthday party, and I am inviting as many of my officers as can be spared from regimental duties.' He smiled at Jack over the rim of his brandy glass. 'My Helen is quite taken with you, Windrush.'

'That is good to hear, sir.' Jack tried to hide his delight at the prospect of meeting Helen again.

'I intend to send them both to England as soon after the party as possible,' Maxwell said quietly. 'I don't wish them to endure the rigours of a Crimean winter and it is time that Helen saw home.'

Jack started. 'Yes, sir.' He could think of nothing else to say.

We hope you enjoyed reading *Windrush: Crimea*. If you have a moment, please leave us a review - even if it's a short one. We want to hear from you.
The story continues in *Windrush: Blood Price*.
Want to get notified when one of Creativia's books is free to download? Join our spam-free newsletter at www.creativia.org.

Best regards,
Malcolm Archibald and the Creativia Team

About the Author

Born and raised in Edinburgh, the sternly-romantic capital of Scotland, I grew up with a father and other male relatives imbued with the military, a Jacobite grandmother who collected books and ran her own business and a grandfather from the legend-crammed island of Arran. With such varied geographical and emotional influences, it was natural that I should write.

Edinburgh's Old Town is crammed with stories and legends, ghosts and murders. I spent a great deal of my childhood walking the dark streets and exploring the hidden closes and wynds. In Arran I wandered the shrouded hills where druids, heroes, smugglers and the spirits of ancient warriors abound, mixed with great herds of deer and the rising call of eagles through the mist.

Work followed with many jobs that took me to an intimate knowledge of the Border hill farms to Edinburgh's financial sector and other occupations that are best forgotten. In between I met my wife. Engaged within five weeks we married the following year and that was the best decision of my life, bar none.

At 40 the University of Dundee took me under their friendly wing for four of the best years I have ever experienced. I emerged with a degree in history, and I wrote. Always I wrote.

Malcolm Archibald